THE GOLD

MAGGIE
Cox

A BRIDE FOR THE TAKING

THE GOLD COLLECTION

June 2016

July 2016

August 2016

September 2016

THE GOLD COLLECTION

MAGGIE

Cox

A BRIDE FOR THE TAKING

MILLS &
BOON

First Published in Great Britain 2016
By Mills & Boon, an imprint of HarperCollins*Publishers*
1 London Bridge Street, London, SE1 9GF

A BRIDE FOR THE TAKING © 2016 Harlequin Books S.A.

Distracted by Her Virtue © 2012 Maggie Cox
The Lost Wife © 2011 Maggie Cox
The Brooding Stranger © 2011 Maggie Cox

ISBN: 978-0-263-92215-8

24-0816

Our policy is to use papers that are natural, renewable and recyclable products and made from wood grown in sustainable forests.
The logging and manufacturing processes conform to the legal environmental regulations of the country of origin.

Printed and bound in Spain
by CPI, Barcelona

DISTRACTED BY
HER VIRTUE

*To Lesley who never fails to make me laugh
and see the funny side of things!
You are such a blessing and I'm so glad
that we're friends.*

Maggie Cox is passionate about stories that can uplift and transport people out of their daily worries to a more magical place, be they romance novels or fairytales. What people want most, she believes, is true connection. She feels blessed to be married to a lovely man who never fails to make her laugh, and has two beautiful sons and two much loved grandchildren.

CHAPTER ONE

As JARRETT picked his way carefully down the steep grassy bank that was made potentially treacherous by the odd jagged stone hidden amongst the greenery the chocolate-brown Lab accompanying him passed him with a swift, much more sure-footed tread. He lifted his head to follow the dog's enthusiastic trail, and his gaze was suddenly captured by an unexpected sight. At the foot of the valley just ahead, down by the familiar babbling brook that the dog usually made a beeline for, he spied the unfamiliar figure of a lithe young woman dressed in jeans and a khaki-coloured weatherproof jacket. Her hands held a camera, and as he observed her she dropped to her haunches to photograph something.

At this distance it was hard to see what it was, but it crossed Jarrett's mind that the woman might be one of those horticulturists who occasionally visited the area, cataloguing some rare plant or flower. It was a fine spring day and, having just closed the deal on a prime parcel of land not twenty miles from here, Jarrett was predisposed to be sociable.

'Hello there!' he called out as he drew nearer, and the woman lifted her head and glanced round at him, startled. As he drew nearer, the beauty of her face literally stopped him in his tracks. *Who was she?* Inside his chest his heart thumped hard—as though he'd sprinted down that treacherous hillside. He'd never come across eyes of such a light green hue before…like the softest summer grass. And the silky mantle of chestnut hair that flowed down over her shoulders was the perfect foil to bring out the colour, he thought with pleasure as his lips formed an appreciative smile. 'It's a beautiful day, isn't it?'

'Charlie? Charlie, come over here to me right now!'

He hadn't seen the child, but at the woman's urgent-voiced command, like an arrow expertly released from its bow to fly towards its target, he appeared out of a distant clump of trees and threw himself into her lap, almost knocking her over. *Was she his mother?* Jarrett wondered. She looked almost too young.

Though she might just be a passing stranger, the need to know who she was wouldn't leave him alone. 'I didn't mean to startle you,' he apologised, holding out his hand, 'My name's Jarrett Gaskill. I live on the other side of that rise up there.'

If he'd been expecting her to reciprocate with similar information then he was doomed to disappointment. Glancing at his outstretched hand, the green-eyed beauty made no move to take it. Instead she laid down her camera, sat back on the grass and tenderly patted the small boy on his back, as if to reassure him that everything was all right. The child's riot of dark curls was tucked beneath her chin as if he wanted to hide.

'I know it may not look like it, but I'm not taking pictures purely for my own amusement. I'm actually working.'

The bewitching green eyes flashed, but for a moment Jarrett's attention was more captivated by her voice. There was such resolve and firmness in its husky tones—a *warning* too—that it took him aback. *Did she think he presented some kind of threat to her and the child?*

The thought made him retreat a couple of steps, and he let his hand drop uselessly down by his side. As if to remind him of his presence, the chocolate Lab that he was dog-sitting for his sister Beth nudged his muzzle into his palm and gave him a lick. The creature had done his usual trick of galloping joyfully through the water, and as a result was now sopping wet from head to tail. 'It's all right, boy…we'll be on our way in just a minute.'

'Was there something else?'

The woman appeared almost affronted that he might be contemplating staying for even a second longer when she'd clearly demonstrated that his presence wasn't welcome. Swallowing down the disagreeable sense of rejection that curdled briefly in the pit of his stomach, Jarrett met her unflinching glare with an equally unwavering one of his own. His lip even curled a little mockingly. 'No…I was simply passing the time of day. Nothing more sinister than that.'

'Don't be offended. It's just that when I'm working I have to give my full attention to my subject. If I allow myself to get distracted then the photograph turns out to be useless.'

'In that case I won't distract or disturb you any longer. Enjoy the rest of your day.'

'You too.'

'Come on, Dylan…time for us to go.'

The boy on her lap turned his head to steal a helpless

glance of longing at the dog. Jarrett saw that the child, too, was uncommonly striking. But his bright long-lashed eyes weren't the arresting green of the woman's. They were a dark berry-brown. *Was* she his mother? he wondered again. He'd love to know. More to the point, did she come from one of the nearby villages? Due to the demands of his business, he didn't spend a lot of time at home, but nonetheless he didn't think she was a native of the area. *He was certain he would have heard about her if she was.* Such beauty would not go unnoticed for long.

Despite his curiosity, Jarrett knew that it was time for him to go. As he turned away it felt as if the bright day had suddenly dimmed. Even the memory of the deal he had just closed couldn't diminish the blow to his ego that the green-eyed beauty had dealt him with her indifference and distrust.

'Her name's Sophia Markham. She's moved into High Ridge Hall.'

'What?' The information his sister had so helpfully provided when she'd rung to let him know that she and her husband Paul had returned from their weekend trip to Paris had sent a thunderbolt jack-knifing through Jarrett's heart. He'd been trying to purchase the old manor house for years, but the elderly lady who had lived there until two Christmases ago had doggedly re-fused to sell—even when it became clear that the build-ing was heading for rack and ruin due to her neglect. The place had been standing empty since she'd died, and even though he'd made several enquiries to all the local agencies neither they nor he were any the wiser regarding who owned it or what was going to happen to it now. So now, when Beth so matter-of-factly told him that the girl he'd described down by the stream yesterday had moved into it he was crushed with disappointment.

High Ridge Hall was much more than just a once grand crumbling edifice he yearned to restore to its former glory. Historically, it had always been the seat of one of the richest families in the area. Owning such a place would set the seal on the successes of the past few years during which his 'property empire'—as Beth teasingly called it—had gone from strength to strength. He couldn't help but feel jealous that the green-eyed beauty had moved into the place. She must have some important connections indeed for her to be able to live there—even though it must be falling down round her ears. But then, as he remembered the powerful tug of attraction he'd experienced towards her almost on sight, he was reminded of the lustful heat that had assailed him at just a single glance from her bewitching eyes…

'Local opinion is that she is related to old Miss Wingham,' said Beth. 'How else could she move in? The place wasn't even put up for sale.'

'Damn it all to hell!'

'Mum would turn in her grave if she heard you say that, Jarrett.'

'Thankfully I'm not encumbered by our late mother's religious proclivities—and nor should you be,' he answered irritably.

'Anyway…you say you met her down by the stream in the valley? I hear she has a son. Was he with her?'

'Yes. He was.'

'There's no evidence of a father or husband. Do you

think she's divorced? Or maybe her husband works abroad?'

'You're becoming as nosey as the rest of the village.'

'Don't pretend you're not interested. I hear our Ms Markham is a real looker.'

Jarrett elected not to reply. He was still coming to terms with the idea that purchasing the house—a goal he had set his heart on—was no longer an option. At the other end of the line his sister emitted a long-suffering sigh.

'Couple that with the fact that she's moved into High Ridge Hall, and my guess is that you won't be so eager to fly off on any long-haul business trips any time soon...at least not until you find out how she got the house and who she is.'

'Well, you're wrong about that. As a matter of fact I'm flying out to New York on Friday. I expect to be away for at last a fortnight, if not more.'

'I'm only teasing you, little brother.'

'Don't call me that,' replied Jarrett, who at six foot two could scarcely be described as 'little'.

'To me you'll always be my little brother. And with both our parents gone it's down to me to keep a sisterly eye on you. Changing the subject—have you seen anything of Katie Stewart lately?'

Katie Stewart? The woman he'd taken out on a few dates he hadn't even wanted to go on? She had barely crossed Jarrett's mind. Her company was pleasant enough, but her conversation hardly lit up the world. As attractive as she was, he wouldn't date any woman purely because she was easy on the eye. At the very least she had to be bright and engaging, with a good sense of humour. And of course the most important element of all was that there had to be some fundamental connection between them—an undeniable spark that would keep him interested. At thirty-six he was still single, and it wasn't hard to understand why. The kind of woman his heart secretly yearned for seemed hard to find—at least in *his* world. Beth put it down to pickiness, but Jarrett preferred to consider himself discerning.

'No, I haven't seen Katie Stewart lately. When and *if* I do I'll be sure to give you a report.'

'I just worry about you having no one who really matters to you in your life. All the money and success in the world won't make you happy or keep you warm on those bitter winter nights, Jarrett.'

He grinned into the receiver. 'Now you're sounding like one of those batty psychics that tell you you're going to meet a tall dark stranger if you cross their palm with silver.'

'Is Sophia Markham tall?'

Jarrett's grin immediately turned into a scowl. 'I've no idea. When I saw her she was crouching to take a photograph. Anyway, I've got to get on. I'll bring the dog back to you around lunchtime, shall I?'

'Are you angling for a lunch invitation?'

'Throw a slice of ham between a couple of slices of bread, make me a cup of tea and I won't dash off. I'll stay and have a chat with you.'

'The day I "throw" a slice of ham between two slices of bread and call it lunch, I'll know I've seriously lost the plot!'

Reflecting on some of the wonderful meals his sister had made for him long before she'd gone to catering college and eventually become head chef for one of the high-end restaurants in the west end of London, Jarrett's feelings towards Beth palpably softened. 'You're a true culinary genius, sweetheart, and believe me—both my stomach and my palate are grateful for it. I'll see your around one o'clock, shall I?'

'And don't forget to bring Dylan with you, will you?'

'As if I'd forget… Every time I turn round he's either doing his best to enslave me with those huge seal-pup eyes of his or trip me over!'

As she drew back the ancient tapestry drapes, the rain of dust made Sophia cough violently. She stepped back just in time as the heavy brass curtain rail clattered heavily down onto the dark wooden floor.

'Of all the stupid things to do…' she muttered.

Knowing she'd had a lucky escape, she shook her head, planted her hands on her hips and smiled ruefully. For a while she just stood, watching the dust motes that jumped up from the floor swirl madly in the beam of sunlight that arrowed in through the window. If she'd longed for a project to help quell the misery and despair of the past then she'd found one right enough. It was going to take a good deal of hard toil, sweat and probably tears too to make this house anywhere *near* comfortable enough to enjoy living in. But she hardly had cause for complaint. Not when her eccentric Great-Aunt Mary had bequeathed her such an incredible gift.

Who would have guessed that a woman who had barely even acknowledged her as a child except to frown down at her through her half-moon glasses would turn out to be her guardian angel and fairy god-mother all rolled into one?

'Aunt Mary dislikes most of her family…the adults

at any rate,' Sophia's dad had told her once, even as his merry green eyes twinkled mischievously. 'She doesn't believe that we deserve to count her as a relative. We're a great disappointment to her, I'm sure. When she goes she'll leave this gothic monstrosity of a house to some cat or dog charity…just wait and see!'

Well…her eccentric great-aunt *hadn't* bequeathed High Ridge Hall to an animal charity. *She'd left it to Sophia instead.*

The day before she'd been due to leave the home that she had been forced to sell she'd had a phone call from a solicitor's office in London. They had spent months trying to track her down, to tell her that she was the sole beneficiary in her great-aunt's will. Sophia had been appalled—she hadn't even heard that she'd died. Since her dad had passed away she'd lost touch with practically everyone but her brother David, and she saw him infrequently enough. In a way she was glad. Since her husband's destructive behaviour and alcoholism had grown even worse, she'd become too ashamed to let family or friends see how low she had sunk. To learn that not only had she been left High Ridge Hall but a small amount of money too had been overwhelming.

Dropping down into the one remaining antique chair in the living room that hadn't yet been sold to help meet her deceased husband's mountain of debt, Sophia had cried hard with gratitude and relief at her eleventh-hour reprieve. If her great-aunt hadn't left her beautiful old house to her even contemplating the alternative living arrangements insisted upon by her bullying father-in-law would have been too grim to bear…

Her little son ran in from the kitchen, his dark eyes round as saucers when he saw the dislodged brass rail and the pile of old curtains that half smothered it. 'What happened, Mummy? I heard the loudest bang.'

'The curtain rail fell down. These walls are very old, Charlie. The plaster is crumbling like powder. It's going to take a lot of work to make this room nice again… The whole house is in need of some major attention to make it fit to live in. I'm only grateful that your uncle David was able to take some time off to get a couple of the rooms ready for us before we moved in—otherwise we would have had to camp out in the garden in a tent!'

Charlie was already losing interest in the dramatic incident that had caused him to rush in from the kitchen. Instead he was staring down at the colourful toy he'd carried into the room with him, restlessly turning it over and over between his fingers, as if itching to employ it in some way.

'Can I go out to the garden to play? I want to make a fort. I promise I won't go near the pond.'

'All right, then. As long as you keep in full view of these windows so that I can see you. Promise?'

He grinned, showing a couple of gaps where he'd lost his baby teeth.

Sophia's heart squeezed. 'Give me a hug and a kiss first.'

'You're *always* hugging and kissing me.'

'I know, but I can't help it!' Seizing her young son by the waist, she whirled him round and round until he shrieked with laughter.

'Let me go!' he begged. 'You're making me dizzy!'

When he'd got his bearings again, he threw his mother a disarming grin and rushed out of the house into the wild forest of a garden—the garden that was already keeping Sophia awake at night, as she planned how she was going to make it beautiful again and re-store it to the fairytale garden of her childhood.

As she bent down to retrieve the curtains and the rail, out of the blue an image stole into her mind of the physically arresting man who had stopped to say hello the other day while she'd been taking photographs of wildflowers for her portfolio. His eyes had been elec-trifyingly blue, yet his hair was a thick, curling cap of ebony silk. A small flare of heat imploded inside her. Despite her attraction to him Sophia had been nervous. *What if her father-in-law had sent him to find her... to force her to return to the neighbourhood where she had lived with her late husband?*

God knew the man had the kind of strong, intimi-dating physique that could easily overwhelm her if he tried. She inhaled a long steadying breath. Her worst fears thankfully hadn't come true, but she was still uneasy.

Jarrett Gaskill...what kind of a name was that?

Even if the man had never heard of her illustrious fa-ther-in-law, his name sounded a little too highbrow and pompous for her taste. No doubt he was some ambitious city type who kept a second home here in the coun-try for weekends where he could entertain his London friends and play Lord of the Manor.

The thought brought a briefly cynical smile to her lips, before making her frown. Remembering his mel-lifluous tones, she'd thought he'd sounded sincere enough. Perhaps it was wrong of her to so judge him so quickly. But what did she know of sincere men when she'd been married to the biggest liar and cheat in the country? Tom Abingdon—the man she'd so stupidly rushed headlong into marriage with at eighteen against all advice—had been cruel, possessive, and self-indulgent to excess, as well as vain and self-obsessed, and the signs had been there right from the beginning.

How incredible, how *naive*, that Sophia had once believed she could turn him away from his destructive tendencies and show him that life together could be good. It hadn't taken her long to find out how contemptuous he was of her sincere and innocent impulses. The dark road she'd been travelling with him had grown darker and more twisted day by day, and somehow, because her spirits had sunk so low, she'd been unable to find any means of breaking free.

Towards the end of his life he'd been intent on dragging her and their small son down to even more despicable lows, until one day, in the midst of her growing despair, it had suddenly become clear to her that she had to abandon her youthful dreams of 'happy-ever-after'—she couldn't fix her self-destructive husband's life and she should walk away…right *now*. For Charlie's sake, if not her own.

It was that thought that had rejuvenated hope in her—had spurred her on to make plans to leave him. But fate had had other more finite plans for Tom Abingdon. One night, after a heavy bout of drinking, he'd died in his sleep.

For a few unsteadying moments the sickening hurt and fury at the pain he had caused deluged Sophia's heart and made her suck in her breath. Perhaps it was an apt reminder of the supreme idiocy of her getting involved with anyone ever again. If Tom was anything to go by, it was all too easy to be mesmerised and trapped by a man. Even the liars and cheats of this world could present a normal façade in order to get what they wanted, and it made her vow to be extra careful and much more vigilant.

If she ever saw him again, she promised herself she would give Jarrett Gaskill a wide berth. There was no way she would give *any* man the opportunity to get to know her…to discover the shameful truth of her marriage to a man who had frequently mistreated and degraded her. A new beginning was what she wanted for her and her son. One that didn't include strangers—however friendly—who wanted to pry into her business. Not that she kidded herself for an instant that Jarrett Gaskill would even remember bumping into her and Charlie down by that idyllic little brook.

For the past three weeks Sophia had visited the weekly farmers' market in the town centre. There was nothing like buying fruit and vegetables straight from the source, rather than from a soulless and anodyne supermarket, she thought. It was fresher, smelled better, and the taste far surpassed anything you could buy packaged and wrapped up in plastic.

Drawing her son closer to her side, she accepted the sturdy brown paper bag of apples she'd just bought from a friendly female stallholder and deposited it into her hessian shopping bag, on top of the other fresh produce she'd purchased. Glancing down at the cherubic little face that gazed up at her, she smiled brightly in anticipation of her plans for the afternoon. It was still such a treat to bake pies and cakes without fear of Tom coming home drunk, mocking her efforts and then throwing them against the wall.

'We'll make an apple pie to have with our tea tonight, Charlie,' she promised cheerfully.

'You don't want an extra guest, do you? I'm quite partial to home-made apple pie.'

The arresting male voice was so richly resonant and well-spoken that Sophia glanced up in surprise at the man who had stepped up beside her. Her startled gaze was instantly magnetised by a pair of twinkling blue eyes so rivetingly intense that for a moment she couldn't speak. It was *him*…Jarrett Gaskill. The name that had been warily filed away inside her brain presented itself with worrying ease.

'No…I don't. I've not long moved into my house and it's taking me longer than I expected to get settled. Besides, it's not likely I'd invite someone into my home that I don't even know,' she replied, quickly averting her gaze.

'I told you my name the first time we met, remember?'

Sophia's cheeks burned with heat, because she wasn't able to pretend that she couldn't recall it. 'That's neither here nor there. Knowing a person's name hardly means that you *know* them.'

'True…but an introduction at least creates the opportunity to *get* to know someone.'

'I'm sorry, Mr Gaskill, but I really must get on.'

'You see?' Something akin to delight was mirrored in the azure depths of his compelling glance. 'You *did* remember my name. Perhaps now you'll do me the honour of telling me yours?'

'I don't think so.' Already turning away, Sophia was suddenly eager to leave the busy little market that was set up in the picturesque village square and head for home.

'What a pity. I've got to call you something if we bump into each other again, don't you think?'

'No, you don't. You can simply ignore me.'

His strong brow affected an exaggerated frown. 'I certainly couldn't. That would be the height of bad manners.'

'You really care about things like good manners?'

'Of course. I'd live in dread of my poor deceased mother haunting me if I didn't keep her standards up.'

In spite of her eagerness to extricate herself from this unwanted and surreal conversation, Sophia couldn't suppress a smile. But almost as soon as she'd succumbed to the gesture she firmed her lips into a much more serious line. 'I've really got to go. I've got things to do. Goodbye.'

Firmly tightening her hold on her son's small hand, she was about to walk out into the milling throng exploring the market stalls when the man standing beside her spoke clearly.

'Enjoy that apple pie, Ms Markham...perhaps you'll save me a slice?'

She spun round, her eyes widening in alarm. 'Who told you my name?'

'You've moved into a village...sooner or later everyone learns the name of a newcomer. They also tend to speculate on where they've come from and why they've moved here. Human nature, I guess.'

He shrugged nonchalantly, and Sophia stared. It was hard to ignore the width of those broad, well-defined shoulders beneath his well-worn, expensive-looking leather jacket. The black T-shirt he wore underneath with jeans was stretched across an equally well-defined chest, and he exuded the kind of masculine strength that made her even more wary of him. But more than that she was uncomfortable with the fact that people she didn't even know might be discussing her and her son.

'People should mind their own business! If my name should ever be mentioned in your hearing again, Mr Gaskill, I'd be obliged if you would make it very clear that I want to be left in peace.'

'I don't hold with gossiping about anyone. However, I will endeavour to respect your desire for privacy, Ms Markham.'

Sophia's glance was wary, but she made herself acknowledge his remark just the same. 'Thank you.'

Before Jarrett could engage her further, she took herself and Charlie off into the crowd and didn't once glance back to see if his disturbing blue gaze followed them…even though her heart thudded fit to burst inside her chest at the thought that he might indeed be following her progress…

CHAPTER TWO

CHARLIE was playing in the overgrown front garden as Jarrett drove his Range Rover up to the impressive old house. Glancing out of his window up at the pearlescent sky that threatened rain, he grimaced. Before he talked himself out of it he was on his feet, opening the creaking iron gate that led onto a meandering gravel path sprouting with weeds.

He stopped to talk to the child. 'Hello, there.' Jarrett smiled. 'Your name's Charlie, isn't it?'

'Where's your dog?'

Large dark eyes stared hopefully up at him. He was gratified that the boy seemed to remember him. It was two weeks since they'd last met. He also guessed that he probably didn't have a pet of his own. For some reason, that bothered him.

Dropping down to his haunches, so that he was on the same level as the child, Jarrett frowned with genuine regret. 'I'm afraid that he doesn't belong to me. I was just looking after him for my sister. He's back with her now.'

'Oh.' His young companion was stumped for a moment. Recovering, he fixed his visitor with another interested gaze. 'You called him Dylan.'

'Yes, I did. That's his name.'

'It's a good name. But if I had a dog I'd call him Sam.'

'That's a good name too. Would you like a dog of your own?'

The boy studied him gravely. 'Yes, I would… But Mummy thinks a dog would be too much trouble to take care of—and we've had enough trouble already.'

Jarrett absorbed this very interesting snippet of information, ruffled the boy's unruly dark hair, then rose to his full height again. 'Never mind…perhaps in time she might have a change of heart?'

'No, she won't.' Charlie kicked a nearby pebble with the scuffed toe of his trainer, but not before giving Jarrett a look that said he wished she *could* be persuaded differently. 'Have you come to see her?' he asked.

'Yes, I have. Is she inside?'

'She's painting.'

Did Sophia Markham's creative talent extend beyond photography to painting?

Jarrett was still considering the idea as he strode up to the front door. The faded sandstone of the house reflected the more muted, mellow tones of a bygone age. The whole building was in dire need of some serious maintenance and redecoration, but no one could deny it had tremendous potential and charm. If he owned the place he would know *exactly* which restoration company to hire to help return it to its former glory.

Biting back his disappointment that he would now never have the chance, he made robust use of the heavy brass door-knocker and waited for Sophia to appear. He couldn't deny he was a little apprehensive about seeing the emerald-eyed beauty again. Both times that he'd tried to engage her in conversation she'd been decidedly aloof. He'd already received a warning that all she wanted to do was to be left in peace. And, despite his sister Beth and her friends still speculating on the whereabouts of a man in her life, Jarrett was becoming more and more convinced that, aside from her son, the mysterious Sophia was unattached.

'For goodness' sake, sweetheart, the back door is open. You don't need to—' Sophia bit off the comment that was clearly meant for Charlie and stared up in open-mouthed surprise at Jarrett. *'You!'* She shook her head as if to clear it, and her already loosened ponytail drifted free from its band, so that long silken strands of the glossiest chestnut-brown fell down over her shoulders. A faded pink T-shirt spattered with blue and white paint highlighted the small pert breasts underneath it, and a pair of slim-fitting denims with a large ragged hole in one knee clung to long, slender legs.

Jarrett raised an eyebrow. If she'd appeared in a couture dress from one of the top fashion houses in Paris he couldn't imagine her looking sexier than she did right then. Facing the pair of annoyed and sparkling green eyes that glared back at him, he couldn't deny the powerful surge of sexual heat that tumbled forcefully through him.

'How did you find out where I live?'

'The house has been empty for quite a while. Didn't you think that people would notice when it became occupied again?'

With what looked like a weary effort, she dragged her fingers through her loosened chestnut hair and shrugged. 'I get the feeling that people round here notice a little bit too much.'

'Anyway…my apologies for interrupting what looks like a very industrious Sunday afternoon for you. Your son said you were painting? Does that mean you're a painter as well as a photographer?'

'I'm painting my sitting room…not a canvas.'

'Okay.' He held up his hands, grinning at his mistake. 'At any rate, I dropped by because I have an invitation to give to you—from my sister, Beth.' He produced what was, in his opinion, a ridiculously scented and girly-pink envelope from the inside pocket of his three-quarter-length black leather jacket.

'Have I met your sister?'

Amusement forced one corner of Jarrett's mouth up into his cheek. 'Not yet…but, trust me, she's determined to meet *you*, Ms Markham—or is it Mrs?'

Her expression became even more vexed. She snatched the envelope from him. 'It's Ms. I used to be married, but I'm not any more.'

'So you're divorced?'

He saw her swallow hard. 'No. I'm a widow.'

The news sobered Jarrett's mood. 'I'm sorry.'

'Don't be. I'm *not*. And before you make some specious judgement about that, the topic isn't up for discussion.'

'Fair enough…that's your prerogative.'

The fire in her eyes suddenly died. Gripping the pink envelope he'd handed her as if she'd prefer to rip it to shreds rather than open it, she laid the flat of her free hand against the doorframe, as if needing support. It was as though every ounce of her vitality and strength had leaked away, leaving her visibly weak and shaken.

To be that *angry*...that *aloof*...must take a hell of a lot of energy, Jarrett mused. *What had the woman been through to make her so furious and defensive?* Her remark about not being sorry that she was a widow suggested that her relationship with her husband had not been the stuff of fairytales.

For whatever pain she'd endured in the past, a genuine feeling of compassion arose inside him. 'Ms Markham...Sophia...are you all right?'

'I'm fine.'

With a look of steely resolve she straightened, but he could hardly miss the tears that glistened in her eyes, and the sight made him feel as if he'd just been punched in the gut. He never *had* been able to bear seeing a woman cry...

'How did you know my name was Sophia?' she challenged.

Before Jarrett had the chance to answer, she folded her arms and wryly moved her head from side to side.

'I expect it filtered down to you from the headquarters of the local gossip collective. Am I right?'

'I can't deny it.'

'Do people have such dull and boring lives that they have to pry into the business of a total stranger?' she demanded irritably.

'They most likely *do*. Why do you think they're so addicted to the soaps on TV? The invented drama of a stranger's life is probably far preferable to the reality of their own.'

'I won't have a TV in the house. I'd rather read a book.'

'What about Charlie?' Jarrett ventured, glancing over at the small boy who was once again careening round the giant hollyhocks, mimicking the 'rat-a-tat' sound of machine gun fire.

Sophia winced. 'My son doesn't need to be glued to a television or computer screen to enjoy himself. Besides, a lot of the programmes shown nowadays are so negative and manipulative that he's hardly missing out on anything helpful or essential.'

'So…what kind of books do you like to read?'

'If you're hoping that I'll invite you in to have a cup of tea and discuss my reading habits, then I'm sorry, Mr Gaskill, but I'm going to have to disappoint you. You may keep turning up like the proverbial bad penny, but I'm not going to encourage you.'

'You have something against making friends?'

'I manage just fine without them.'

'What about your son?'

'What *about* him?'

'You might prefer to be reclusive, but what about Charlie? Doesn't he need the companionship of children his own age?'

'He's joining the village primary school in a couple of weeks, so he'll make lots of friends there, I'm sure.'

'My sister Beth's best friend Molly teaches the nursery class. If you come to Beth's little get-together next Saturday you're bound to meet her. Who knows? You might even become friends.'

Sophia huffed out a sigh. 'What *is* it with you? Are you employed to go round the village encouraging fellowship amongst its inhabitants whether they want it or not?'

Jarrett laughed. To be honest, he couldn't remember the last time that a woman's witty repartee had engaged him quite so much—*thrilled* him, even. 'No,

I'm not… Though it seems to me that would be a quite commendable way to spend my time. The downside is I could hardly earn a living doing it.'

Tapping the pink envelope against her thigh, Sophia gave an impatient glance that didn't reflect a similar enjoyment in his company. 'Look…I'm in the middle of decorating the sitting room and I must get on. I'm sorry if I seem a little terse, but I have my work cut out trying to make this place into a home for me and Charlie. Thanks for taking the time and trouble to bring me the invitation. You can tell your sister that I'll think about it and let her know.'

'If you do that much she'll be delighted, I'm sure.' He held out his hand without much hope or expectation that she would take it. He almost stumbled when she slid her cool palm inside his. It was as light and as delicate as a bird.

'Goodbye, Mr Gaskill.' She quickly withdrew it, but not before his skin tingled fiercely from its contact with hers.

'Now that we've introduced ourselves you can call me Jarrett. Goodbye…Sophia.' Before turning away he gave her a deliberately teasing smile, lifted his hand in a wave to Charlie, then strode back down the uneven path and out through the gate to his car…

Reflecting on her most recent encounter with Jarrett Gaskill disturbed Sophia so much that, despite her assertion that she had work to do, the desire to spend the rest of her Sunday afternoon painting the sitting room utterly deserted her. In search of a solution to the hard-to-contain restlessness his visit had left her with, she jumped with Charlie into the small second-hand car she'd recently purchased and drove down to the coast.

The spring day was chilly, but they still ate their fish and chips outside, sitting on a bench overlooking the foaming silver sea, and the gusting wind that blew around them was sufficiently cold to prevent Sophia from dwelling on any of the worries that were usually hovering just below the surface of her conscious thoughts.

When they'd finished eating, she bought her son a crabbing line from a nearby corner shop, along with some bacon to use for bait. Then they walked back down to the seafront, where they enjoyed a pleasantly distracting time fishing about in the murky shallows for baby crabs. After Charlie had diligently counted their catch, they conscientiously dropped them back into the water again.

On the journey home, her exuberant son fell fast asleep in his car seat, worn out by his afternoon's activities. At last Sophia could mull over the man who so persistently seemed to want to get to know her. *She didn't doubt that he had great ability to charm the ladies.* How could he not, with that carved handsome face, those flawless blue eyes and a voice that was mellifluous and compelling?

As she took the road out of the village that led almost straight to High Ridge Hall, she wondered why Jarrett would take the trouble to deliver an invitation to his sister's 'little get-together' by hand? Was it because he wanted to get a chance to look more closely at the house? The idea deflated her and she didn't know why. She knew that High Ridge had always held a fascination not just for local people but also for passing ramblers. The imposing early nineteenth-century edifice demanded more than just a fleeting glance. Her great-aunt had often had to contend with strangers knocking on the door to enquire after its history.

The idea of her elderly relative giving short shrift in response to those enquiries brought an instant smile to Sophia's lips. It also reminded her of the great responsibility of taking care of such a house. With the proceeds from the sale of the house she'd shared with her husband and a not insubstantial part of her inheritance from her aunt already gone to help pay off his debts, it was vital that she was able to revive the photographic career that had promised to take off when she'd left college. The career that when she'd had Charlie she'd foolishly and naively put aside, to be the stay-at-home wife and mother that her husband had demanded she be.

A residence the size and importance of High Ridge demanded that she earn a healthy income to maintain it. What little money that was left from her inheritance after all her outgoings were met wasn't going to last very long. Thankfully she'd kept a note of some of the contacts she'd made after leaving college, and had already been in touch with two very interested parties who liked the sample photos she'd sent them.

Her thoughts gravitated back to Jarrett. The idea of him using his sister's invitation to seize a chance to view the house at close quarters seriously bothered Sophia. She didn't know if that *had* been his motivation for a fact, but still she preferred the notion that it was her company he sought and *not* a closer acquaintance with her home. Warning herself not to forget even for a second that she'd sworn off relationships with men for good after enduring the living nightmare that had been her marriage, she determinedly buried the familiar feelings of failure and loneliness and reaffirmed her vow to put any further thoughts of Jarrett Gaskill aside.

Feeling somewhat calmer at this resolve, she carefully transported her still sleeping son inside the house. Settling him down on the threadbare old couch, she decided to let him doze for a little longer...at least until she'd prepared their dinner.

To please his sister, Jarrett did what she told him he was so naturally adept at and effortlessly mingled and chatted to her and her husband's friends at the little *soirée* she'd arranged—even though he secretly *hated* it. He did enough schmoozing at the corporate functions and meetings relating to his property business without replicating the behaviour in his supposed free time.

It was rare that he had a weekend off, and when he did he much preferred to be left to his own devices. He liked to take long walks in the countryside surrounding his house, listen to opera on his state-of-the-art music centre or catch up on the stack of films he had missed at the cinema because he'd inevitably been working. Yet agreeing to be sociable with his sister's friends and neighbours wasn't the *only* reason that he'd agreed to be present at her house this warm spring Saturday afternoon. All week Jarrett had hardly been able to think about anything but seeing Sophia Markham again. He couldn't forget the sight of her beautiful emerald eyes bathed in tears. It troubled him that she might be sad or lonely, yet if he was honest underneath his compassion he couldn't help wondering if there might be a way to persuade her to sell High Ridge to him. Painting her sitting room by herself didn't suggest that money was exactly plentiful, he mused. And if she agreed to entertain the idea of selling he would pay her a more than fair price.

His hopes lifting, Jarrett looked forward even more to seeing Sophia again. But the get-together had been underway for almost two hours and he was getting bored. There was only so much inconsequential chit-chat he could bear, even for his sister, and there was still no sign of Sophia, although Beth assured him that she'd rung to say she was coming.

He was just debating whether to go up to the house and check to see if anything was amiss when the doorbell's familiar cheery melody chimed through the hallway. As luck would have it he was standing in the vicinity, endeavouring to listen attentively to his brother-in-law Paul's enthusiastic description of the new car he was going to buy. Privately he thought it was a bad choice, and he had just been thinking he would have a quiet word with Beth about it so she could nudge him in the direction of something better when the doorbell had rung. Without a flicker of guilt he moved down the hall to answer it. His body was already tightening warmly in anticipation of seeing High Ridge's lovely new owner again.

'Hi…I'm sorry if we're a little late.'

The statement came out in a breathless rush, and Sophia Markham's apologetic smile as he opened the door rendered him almost speechless because it was so bewitching.

Waiting patiently for his response, she drew Charlie protectively against her side. It wasn't hard to see that the child meant the sun, moon and stars to her.

Staring at her as she stood before him, in faded

jeans, colourful knitted tank-top and long unbuttoned navy blue cardigan, he likened her appearance to a breath of longed-for fresh air that a prisoner might greedily gulp down when he'd been freed from solitary confinement. Today her pretty dark hair hadn't been left loose to flow down over her shoulders—instead she'd fashioned it into two very becoming braids. In contrast, the other women at the small party had seized the opportunity to show off their wardrobes and were dressed up to the nines. Personally, Jarrett thought such a brash display was unnecessary and over the top. He himself had dressed in a casual white shirt and black jeans faded almost to grey—his usual mode of attire when he wasn't at work—and he was very glad to see that Sophia had opted to do the same.

'Don't worry about being late… Beth will kill me for saying it, but you've haven't exactly missed anything. It's good to see you.' After speaking at last, he grinned, then leaned down to squeeze Charlie's shoulder. 'It's good to see you too, Charlie. Why don't you both come inside?'

'Hello, there, I'm Paul Harvey—Beth's husband. How nice to meet you at last, Ms Markham.'

'And you, Mr Harvey.'

'Call me Paul.'

Sophia didn't invite the other man to call her by her first name in return, Jarrett noticed, silently approving. He had no earthly right to feel so possessive towards her, but for reasons he couldn't begin to explain he *did*.

'Let's go and meet everyone,' he suggested, gesturing for her and her son to precede him.

The conversations that littered the air as they walked in abruptly ceased as Jarrett escorted Sophia into the

stylishly furnished living room. Even the softly playing jazz emanating from the music centre seemed to
grow quieter. His sister Beth immediately peeled herself away from the trio of women she'd been deep in
conversation with and presented herself to her new
guest with an enthusiastic handshake, followed by the
characteristic peck on the cheek with which she greeted
all her friends.

'Hi, Sophia, I'm Beth Harvey—Jarrett's sister. I
had no idea you'd be so pretty! I'm so glad you could
come…your son too. Jarrett tells me that his name is
Charlie?'

'That's right.'

Inside that perfectly decorated room, with its carefully chosen, strategically arranged amalgam of modern and antique furniture, surrounded by a bunch of
curious strangers, Sophia looked ill at ease. Her coral
lips were pursed together tightly as she listened to his
sister gush, and Jarrett intuited that she'd rather be anywhere else but here. He was intrigued to know what had
persuaded her to put in an appearance at all. Clearly
she'd wrestled with the decision for some time—why
else had she been so late in arriving? Something else
struck him. He'd always regarded the sister who shared
his own dramatic colouring of ebony hair and blue eyes
as unquestionably pretty. However, next to Sophia's
finely drawn beautiful features and bewitching emerald eyes Beth seemed merely attractive.

Frowning, because he felt such an opinion somehow
betrayed his loyalty to his sibling, he gently touched his
palm to her back in the fitted red dress she was wearing, as if to signal filial support.

'Say hello, Charlie,' Sophia quietly instructed her son.

Bestowing upon Jarrett a gap-toothed grin, the charming small boy with his mop of luxuriant dark curls focused his gaze on him alone. 'Hello, Mr Gaskill. Can I see your sister's dog? Where is he?'

'You've met Dylan before, have you?' Beth dropped down so that she was level with Charlie.

The boy was initially wary, but when she reached for his hand and gently held it for a moment, smiling at him with her great blue eyes, he seemed to relax. 'Yes…we were down by the stream so that my mum could take some photographs for her work. That's when we saw Mr Gaskill and your dog.'

'Well, if you'd like to see him again he's out in the garden, sitting outside his kennel.'

'What's a kennel?'

'It's like a small house for a dog,' Jarrett told him with a teasing wink.

Charlie spun round to gaze up at his mother. 'Can I, Mummy? Can I go out to see Dylan?'

Such an innocent and natural request shouldn't put panic into Sophia's lovely green eyes, but disturbingly Jarrett registered that it did. She even laid a hand possessively on Charlie's shoulder as if to prevent him from leaving.

'Where is the garden?' she immediately quizzed Beth.

'Just out there through the patio doors… Don't worry, it's nowhere near big enough for him to get lost in.'

Biting down on her lip, Sophia was still undoubtedly hesitant. 'I'm sure that's true. There isn't a gate at the back he can get out of?'

'No, there isn't.'

'That's good. Our own garden is a bit like a forest, and I have to keep a close eye on Charlie when he goes out there to play. I suppose I've just got into the habit of making sure he's secure.' She coloured, as if regretting calling attention to her own hardly humble abode. 'It needs a lot of work doing to it, I'm afraid.' she murmured. 'The weeds have gone absolutely rampant in all this rain we've been having, but I'm getting the house into shape before I see to the garden.'

Rising to her full height once again, Beth reassuringly patted the other woman's arm. 'Well, compared to the gardens at High Ridge our garden is fairly modest, I promise you. Charlie can't get lost out there. And there are no ponds or anything like that to worry about either. Besides, he'll have Dylan to play with. Do you want to get his ball and throw it for him, Charlie?'

'Yes, please!' The lad didn't need much inducement.

'His ball is in a box just under the steps,' Beth told him.

As Sophia reluctantly released the light grip on his shoulder, as if intuiting his mother's concern, Charlie turned to throw her a disarming grin. 'I'll be all right, Mummy—promise!' he said, and without further ado he flew out through the open patio doors onto the decking area, where two long tables were laden with platters of what remained of the delicious food Beth had prepared.

The repast still looked appetising in the watery spring sunshine, even though the hungry guests had helped themselves to a fair amount of it already.

Pounding down the wooden steps, fetching the dog's ball and racing out into the neatly mown garden, Charlie called loudly, 'Dylan! Dylan! Do you remember me? I'm Charlie. Come here, boy!'

'I'll introduce you to everyone in a moment—but first let me get you a drink, Sophia.'

Beth cleverly brought the other woman's attention back from her anxious perusal of her disappearing son. Paul had joined them just as Charlie had run out into the garden, and now Jarrett's sister turned to him with one of the dazzling persuasive smiles that her husband had always found so hard to resist.

'Darling? Would you be a love and get Sophia a nice glass of champagne?'

'No!'

The loud, vehement refusal sent a buzz of shock eddying round the other guests—Jarrett included…

CHAPTER THREE

SHE felt like a fool, blurting out her refusal as force-fully as she had. As soon as the impassioned exclamation had left her mouth Sophia had wanted the floor to open up and swallow her. It made her feel like the one jarring note in a symphony that had been harmonious until her arrival. Yet, blunt as her refusal had been, she had good reason to detest alcohol. Living with a violent alcoholic whose behaviour had been coloured by terrifying unpredictable rages was apt to make a woman deeply despise it—*fear* it as well.

'I'm sorry,' she murmured, reddening. 'I just meant to say that I'm teetotal. Do you have some lemonade or cola, perhaps, instead?'

'Sure. No problem.'

Paul Harvey shoved his hands into the pockets of his chinos and Sophia saw that his initially welcoming manner was now tinged with wariness. It made her bitterly regret deciding to attend the party. It was true she'd wrestled with the idea of staying away. *That was why she and Charlie had arrived so late.* As her host turned away to get the promised soft drink, his wife Beth issued her a sympathetic smile. Along with her guests, no doubt she was privately wondering at the reason why the newest member of the village should have reacted to the offer of champagne so violently.

Sophia prayed that the other woman wouldn't take it upon herself to quiz her at any point. The last thing she felt like doing was explaining herself to her perfect-looking hostess with her perfect-looking life, friends and husband. How could such a protected woman even *begin* to understand the pain, degradation and humiliation of the life Sophia had led with her husband? And all the reasons *why* she hated alcohol?

Silently warring with the strongest urge to just turn around and leave, she let her anxious gaze fall into Jarrett's. His strong brow was etched with the faintest frown, yet when his clear blue eyes met hers he somehow transmitted reassurance. She found herself latching onto it like a life raft.

Jarrett didn't yet know what Sophia's issues with alcohol were, but he was determined to find out. He'd genuinely hoped that this party would help her to make some friends, so that she and Charlie wouldn't feel like isolated strangers in the community for long, but already he sensed that her unconventional appearance—not bowing to the dictates of current fashion trends—and her forthright refusal of an alcoholic drink had put the other guests on their guard.

Unfortunately the insular nature of village life didn't exactly nurture a broader view in its inhabitants, he mused. He was thankful that he had seen enough of the world to know that it was the *differences* in people that made them interesting. But he also realised that his desire to help her integrate could turn out to be much more complicated than he'd envisaged. *He* had been the one to encourage her to come to this little get-

together of his sister's and now, without being party to
the reasons why, he saw for himself that what might be
deemed an enjoyable experience by others might actually be *torture* for her. Observing her flushed cheeks
and over-bright eyes, it wasn't hard to guess that what
she'd really like to do was escape as soon as possible.

'Sophia?' He stepped towards the slim brunette, but
not so close that he might overwhelm her. 'Why don't
you and I go and join Charlie and Dylan in the garden?
We'll get your drink on the way, and go sit on the veranda outside the summerhouse.'

Her relief was palpable. Right then, observing her
shining green eyes and schoolgirl plaits, Jarrett thought
her the very personification of beauty and innocence,
and all his protective instincts surged to the fore, making his heart miss a disturbing beat. It was easy to forget about his desire to purchase High Ridge for himself
when he was with her. Yet the thought still occurred
that it might help persuade her to sell if he seriously
started to woo her.

In the large, meticulously mown garden, with its
uniformly neat borders of flowers and shrubs, Jarrett
sat down next to Sophia on the varnished wooden
bench outside the white-painted summerhouse. He silently observed her son throwing the ball to Dylan. The
dog's dark eyes and wagging tail gave the impression
he couldn't believe his luck that somebody wanted to
play with him.

Folding her slim, elegant hands with their short un-
varnished nails round her glass of lemonade, Sophia
drew in a long breath, then softly released it. 'They look
like they're having fun,' she commented, her glance
cautiously alighting on Jarrett.

'Labradors and small boys were meant to be together,' he agreed, silently owning to feeling more content at this moment, in this lovely woman's company,
than he could remember having felt in a long time. The
revelation was an unexpected and tantalising gift that
made the idea of wooing her even stronger.

Several guests had moved outside with their refreshments onto the patio, he noticed, and immediately the
sight put him on his guard. Every now and then they
glanced over at Jarrett and his companion, clearly speculating on their apparent closeness. He made a point
of deliberately meeting their glances and staring right
back.

'It's a shame that Beth and Paul haven't got kids that
can play with Dylan,' he commented, seeking to divert
Sophia from the realisation that his sister's guests were
paying them an inordinate amount of attention.

'How long have your sister and her husband been
married?'

'About ten years, I think.'

'Do they want to have children?'

'They've said many times that if it happens it happens…but in the meantime they'll concentrate on their
careers and just enjoy each other's company.'

'Are they happy?'

Pausing, Jarrett gave the question proper consideration. He had straight away registered the apprehension,
hope and even *envy* in the arresting emerald eyes that
studied him so fervently, and he guessed the answer
was important to her. 'I think so.' He shrugged, smiling, then added, 'Although anyone can present an image
of happiness, contentment and togetherness, can't they?

In truth, only the individuals concerned know if they're happy or not.'

'I agree. Unfortunately if they seem happier than you, then you can feel a bit of a failure.'

Intrigued, Jarrett leaned forward a little.

'Have you ever asked yourself why happiness seems to come so easily to some and not to others?' she pondered. 'Do you think it's got anything to do with *deserving* it?'

'No. I don't think it's got anything to do with deserving it,' he replied. 'There are too many examples in the world to disprove that. Why? Has someone told you that it has?'

'No. Maybe I just feel too guilty about the wrong turns I've made.'

'It sounds to me as if you're much too hard on yourself. Maybe if you could just dump all the guilt that weighs you down and try to be more optimistic things might get a little easier for you, Sophia? I know you can't control everything that happens in life, but I must confess I'm a strong believer in creating your own luck…being captain of your own ship.'

'Oh.'

'Do you have other views on the matter?'

Working her even white teeth against her plump lower lip, Sophia lightly shook her head. 'I do—but I think they might be somewhat prejudiced. I started out being very optimistic about life…convinced that I knew which road to take to make me happy. But although I remained optimistic and hopeful I made some very poor decisions that made me anything *but*. Let's just leave it at that, shall we?'

'We all make poor decisions and mistakes from time

to time. It comes with the territory of being human. It doesn't mean that you won't ever make a good decision again and achieve some level of satisfaction and happiness.'

'I'm sure you're right.'

'Going back to your original question about my sister and her husband—what's your impression? Do *you* think that they're happy?'

'Well, I've only just met them, but if this extremely tidy garden is any indication I get the impression that they live a very ordered and potentially happy life together.'

'Beth and Paul are both very practical people. I'd never call them dreamers, if that's what you're getting at.'

Hunching forward to rest his elbows on his knees, he examined the neat borders with new eyes, almost guiltily recalling Beth's account of her several visits to a local garden centre for advice on creating the perfect lawn. The very concept had bemused him.

'And, yes, they don't appear to leave very much to chance,' he agreed cautiously.

'Dreamers or not, life has a way of subverting even the most carefully laid plans.'

Sophia gazed off into the distance, as if preoccupied by some disturbing recollection that still haunted her. Turning to observe her, Jarrett felt his insides submerged in a wave of sympathy.

A second later Charlie called out to her to watch him throw the ball, and her lovely face broke into an unguarded smile, the disturbing memory temporarily banished. 'That's wonderful, darling!'

'You should learn to play cricket, Charlie,' Jarrett called out. 'You're a natural bowler.'

'Will you teach me, Mr Gaskill?'

'I'd be delighted to…but only if you call me Jarrett.'

The small boy gifted him with a self-conscious grin. 'Okay!'

'That's settled, then.'

'You shouldn't promise him things that you don't have the time or the intention to follow through on,' Sophia scolded him, her cheeks flushing pink. 'He has a memory like an elephant. He forgets nothing…even the things I wish he *would*.'

It was the last part of her statement that perturbed Jarrett the most. Now wasn't the time, but very soon he fully intended to ask her exactly what she meant by it. He also wanted to ask why she'd commented that she wasn't sorry she was a widow. That discussion they'd just had about happiness was already taking on a significance that he wanted to explore.

Depositing his glass of wine on the small wrought-iron table in front of them, he suddenly pushed to his feet. 'What makes you think I wouldn't keep my promise?' he asked, irked that she would doubt him.

'He's been let down by people breaking their promises to him before, and I don't want him building up hopes only to have them dashed again.'

'Not everyone breaks their promises. Maybe you need to learn to trust a little bit more?'

'Trust *you*, you mean? I barely know you.'

'That can be remedied.'

She lifted a slim, nonchalant shoulder to indicate her ambivalence, but Jarrett saw her lips duel unsuccessfully with her natural inclination to smile. Satisfied at the sight, he grinned, then hurried down the veranda steps, calling out to the boy on the lawn at the same time, 'Throw me that ball, Charlie, and we'll see how good you are at catching!'

Returning to the kitchen a while later to replenish their drinks, he found his sister standing at the sink, staring out of the window into the garden as she expertly rinsed some used glasses.

'I've been watching you playing with Charlie. You looked like you were really enjoying yourself,' she remarked.

'Why so surprised? I *do* have the ability to enjoy myself, you know.'

'It's just that you looked quite bored until Sophia arrived...then you lit up.' Beth turned to give him an affectionate smile. 'I'm pleased that you seem to enjoy their company so much.'

'I don't deny it. She intrigues me, and Charlie is a great little boy.'

Walking forward to rinse the empty glasses he'd brought with him, Jarrett wasn't surprised when Beth took them from him and set them down on the drainer.

'You don't have to wash the glasses. Just leave them and get some fresh ones.' Frowning, she dried her hands on a teatowel, then patted down her hair. 'I've just been standing here thinking about Sophia. She strikes me as quite a troubled person. I wonder what's behind that sad look in her eyes. She seems very protective of her son.'

'And that's a crime, is it?'

'Don't be silly. Of course it isn't. But everybody who heard her hesitate about letting him play out in the garden thought it was a little over the top.'

'Ah.' Folding his arms across his chest, Jarrett endeavoured not to let irritation get the better of him. 'So it's a case of the majority rules, is it?'

'It's only natural that people speculate. Think about it. Sophia appears out of nowhere and moves into the most coveted house in the district when the place wasn't even up for sale. Is there some family connection? If so, why not let it be known? It arouses suspicion when people are so secretive. My guess is that there was some kind of tragedy in her life before she came here. Something to do with Charlie's father, perhaps.'

Jarrett was so taken aback by this observation that for a moment words deserted him. Then he sighed, disturbed because Beth was probably right. *What if, for instance, Sophia's husband had done the unthinkable and taken his own life?* Maybe he'd suffered from depression and that was why she'd alluded to the fact that the marriage had been unhappy?

'If that turns out to be the case then all anyone can do is offer sympathy and kindness and not judge her. Don't you agree?' he said.

Lifting her shoulders in a somewhat chastened shrug, his sister visibly softened her expression. 'You're right.' But, clearly unable to put the matter to bed entirely, she added, 'Has she said anything to you?'

'No, she hasn't. It's not likely that she'd confide in *me* about anything, is it? Since we've only just met?' Quirking an eyebrow, Jarrett made his way across to the counter that was laden with cartons of juice and bottles of wine. 'I'd better get our drinks and get back to her.'

'It's not just because she owns High Ridge that you find yourself attracted to her, is it?'

'What?' He spun round, his heart drumming a dizzying tattoo inside his chest.

'Don't be mad at me for asking. It's just that I know you've always loved the place. Perhaps you're hoping that if you become friends she'll consider selling it to you?'

'I think we'd better end this conversation right here.'

He'd been seriously intent on wooing Sophia, but Beth's comments made him fear that she was viewing him solely as the hard-headed landowner he was reputed to be. A man who wouldn't hesitate to be mercenary if it suited him, rather than the amiable brother she loved. Her good opinion mattered to him. The bright afternoon was suddenly soured.

Irked, Jarrett left her in the kitchen, shouldering past the guests outside on the patio and deliberately ignoring any attempts to engage him in conversation. Surprised glances followed him into the garden as he made a beeline across the grass to the pretty woman still sitting on the bench outside the veranda.

Catching hold of her hand, he pulled her to her feet. 'I think it's time that we left.'

'Why? What's wrong?'

Instantly regretting being the instigator of what looked like fear in her eyes, Jarrett abruptly let go of Sophia's hand and took a deep breath to compose himself. 'It's my fault. I should never have persuaded you that it was a good idea to come here today. How do you feel about my taking you and Charlie to the seaside instead? There's still plenty of daylight left. If you want to stop off at home to collect your camera so that you can take some pictures you can do that. We'll drive down in my car.'

Regarding the earnest expression on his handsome face, and trying hard to ignore the bolt of electricity that had shot through her insides when he'd grabbed her hand, Sophia couldn't deny that Jarrett's impromptu suggestion was appealing. But, even so, the memory of past wrong decisions aroused her caution.

'Do you really think I should risk going with you anywhere when I hardly even know you?' she asked.

He held her gaze with a long and steady stare. 'You're getting to know me…you know my name and who I am. You also know who my sister is and where she lives, and there are plenty of other people here who could testify to seeing us leave together. Isn't that enough to reassure you that I'm no sinister stranger with unsavoury motives?'

Sophia was indeed reassured. She smiled. 'Okay, I'll go to the seaside with you…Charlie will be ecstatic at the idea. But first I want you to tell me what's made you suddenly decide we should leave.'

Dropping his hands to his lean jean-clad hips, Jarrett glanced down at the ground, as if to glean inspiration as to how best to answer, then raised his head and scowled. 'Excluding yourself and Charlie, let's just say the company isn't as charming as I thought it would be.'

Now it was Sophia's turn to be dismayed. Someone must have said something unflattering about her. But even though she was curious to know what had been said, she knew it was a pointless and self-destructive exercise to find out. After what she and Charlie had been through what could it possibly matter what anyone thought of her? *Especially* people she didn't know and who didn't know her?

'Let's get out of here.' Obviously impatient to be

gone, Jarrett glanced over at Charlie, who was still throwing the ball for an excitable Dylan to fetch.

Sophia touched his sleeve to get his attention. 'If someone's running me down I'm quite capable of standing up for myself, you know. You don't need to act as my protector.'

'No one's running you down. People are just curious about you, and I don't want you to feel inhibited by what you imagine they think of you.' Shaking his head, he hunted her with his azure gaze so that there was nowhere for her to hide. 'I've sensed since we met that something bad happened before you came here... something you want to escape from. You told me that you're a widow but that you aren't sorry about the fact. I'm not asking you to reveal the details about what happened right now, but all I'll say is that if you've been hurt by someone I don't intend for you to be hurt again by people's narrow-minded suspicions.'

'I see.'

Whilst she'd already told him that she didn't need him to act as her protector, Sophia couldn't deny the wave of warmth that his compassionate defence stirred inside her. It was an exhilarating feeling, and she wondered what she had done to deserve it. Having dealt with her problems single-handedly for so long, it was irresistibly comforting to have someone exhibit compassion towards her.

Just when Jarrett seemed about to make another plea for them to leave, she lifted a slender brow, smiled, and asked lightly, 'Does our little trip to the seaside include food? It's just that you're dragging us away from that incredible-looking feast up there on the patio and I'm feeling rather hungry.'

'I'll treat you both to a five course meal at a swanky restaurant, if that's any inducement?'

'You don't need to go that far. Charlie and I are extremely partial to a bit of fish and chips at the seaside.'

With a cheeky grin that squeezed Jarrett's heart, Sophia swept past him to inform her son about the sudden change of plans.

Not only had Sophia collected her camera by the time Jarrett had followed her and Charlie home in his Range Rover, but she'd also picked up her son's swim-trunks, towel, and a bucket and spade.

When they got to the beach she made a foray into the frigid sea in her rolled-up jeans and shirt—with a shrieking Charlie splashing about beside her—whilst Jarrett stood barefoot in the sand calmly watching them, declaring that they must be mad to even *think* of immersing themselves in such freezing cold water. Though she didn't turn round to check, Sophia sensed his eyes on her as though they were twin suns burning into her skin. Just the thought of him observing her was enough to make her temperature rise, despite the cold of the sea.

To distract herself from the realisation, she dipped her hands into the water, spun round and aimed what she'd collected at Jarrett. The water hit him straight in the face.

'I can't believe you just did that.' He rubbed at his dripping eyelids and scowled.

Laughing out loud at his shocked expression, Sophia couldn't prepare herself for his reaction. Never mind that he was going to get soaked, Jarrett raced up beside her, grabbed her by the waist and lifted her high into his arms.

Charlie could scarcely contain his delight. 'What are you going to do with my mummy, Mr Jarrett?' he squealed.

'All's fair in love and war, Charlie.' Directing the comment at Sophia, Jarrett gave her an unashamedly roguish grin.

Her heart thumped in alarm when she realised that he was probably going to dump her fully clothed into the sea, so she fastened her arms round his neck and made her expression as fierce as she was able. 'Don't you *dare*! If you do I'll take you with me, I swear!'

'That's a puny threat. I'm twice your size. You're hardly strong enough to take me down with you.'

'Try me!' Sophia warned.

But as her furious gaze locked with his the volatile tenor of the situation changed completely to something far more exciting and disturbing to her peace of mind. His nearness, along with the sexily musky aroma of his cologne, made her feel dangerously weak. Not just weak but *aroused*... Straight away she saw by Jarrett's darkened pupils that she was having the same effect on him.

'Maybe I'll save the dunking for another day,' he commented huskily, then abruptly returned her to her feet and the freezing water that lapped the shore.

Murmuring, 'In your dreams...' to hide her embarrassment, Sophia directed her full attention back to her son. 'Come on, Charlie, let's run towards the waves and run back again before they reach us!'

By the time she and Charlie ran back onto the shore, a few minutes later, Jarrett was waiting with the gener-

ous sized bathtowel she'd brought from home. Catching
her eye, he smiled as if to reassure her he held no
grudges about her splashing him with ice-cold seawa-
ter. Then he unhesitatingly wrapped the towel around
Charlie, as if genuinely concerned that he get warm
and dry again as quickly as possible.

Sophia was certain that anyone observing them
would assume that he was the boy's father. Their colouring—apart from the eyes, of course—was practically identical. The notion gave her the strangest most
unsettling pang. Jarrett was bigger, leaner and more
muscular in build than her husband Tom had been...
taller too. It wasn't likely that Charlie would reach a
similar height. Yet he would undoubtedly be handsome
when he was grown.

Ruffling her son's damp corkscrew curls, Jarrett
stood aside so that Sophia could finish off the drying
and help him get dressed. With his T-shirt and shorts
on again, Charlie was eager to collect some seashells,
so he skipped a little bit further on down the beach with
his red bucket and spade, his mother's clear instruction to not wander out of her sight ringing in his ears.
Deliberately avoiding glancing directly at Jarrett, because his commanding masculine presence was making
her feel painfully self-conscious, she lifted her long,
drenched plaits off the back of her neck, arranged the
towel round her shoulders and stooped to pick up the
straw bag with the spare set of clothing that she'd left
lying on the sand next to her sandals. Her jeans and
shirt were plastered icily to her skin where Charlie had
splashed her.

'I'm going over by those rocks to change,' she told

Jarrett, finally meeting his arresting cobalt gaze. 'Would you keep an eye on Charlie for me?'

'No problem. I'll go and join him to help collect seashells.'

Even though they'd spent a thoroughly enjoyable afternoon together on the beach, and at the small seaside restaurant where they'd had fish and chips, Jarrett honestly hadn't expected Sophia to invite him in when they reached High Ridge. But fate was on his side. Charlie had fallen asleep in his car seat.

Sophia got out of the car, peered in at him, then glanced round at Jarrett with an almost apologetic shrug. 'Would you mind carrying him into the house for me? I'll grab our things and open the door.'

On entering the hallway, he saw the ceiling with its old-fashioned cornices was far loftier than he'd anticipated, but the overall impression Jarrett got was that the place was as dark and dingy as Miss Havisham's decaying manor in *Great Expectations*. The remaining evening light that did manage to stream in through the front door's decorated windowpanes was nowhere near illuminating enough to make the place remotely welcoming. Underfoot was an equally dingy, well-trodden maroon carpet that in his view ought to be replaced, or at least given a professional clean.

As he followed Sophia into the house, carefully transporting her still-sleeping little boy in his arms, he couldn't help reflecting that he'd love to help restore the place to its former beauty. But even as the thought stole into his mind Jarrett's sight was helplessly waylaid by the graceful sway of the lithe yet shapely hips of the pretty woman in front of him. Her long slim legs along with the peach-like derrière snugly enclosed in a pair of almost shabby blue jeans suspended any further reflections bar the realisation that he *wanted* her. From the moment he'd seen her lissome shapely figure outlined by the clinging jeans and shirt at the beach, and briefly lifted her into his arms, he'd ached with every fibre of his being to be intimate with her—and soon.

'You can put him down on the couch,' his lovely companion instructed him, her porcelain cheeks flushing a little as her emerald eyes warily met his.

He willingly complied—but not before thinking how much he'd love to free her beautiful chestnut hair from the plaits she'd worn all day, knowing that it would ripple down her back like a pre-Raphaelite beauty's. Jarrett had a powerful compulsion to comb out the long silken skeins with his fingers, then gently smooth them back so that he could more closely examine the sublime contours of her lovely face.

'I can carry him up to bed if you'd prefer?'

Sophia declined the offer. 'He'll be fine right here on the couch. We don't use the bedrooms upstairs. There's a lot of work to be done to make them anywhere near habitable, I'm afraid. Charlie and I sleep in what was once the parlour. I've cleaned it up a bit, got rid of the dust and cobwebs—that sort of thing. I've put up some new curtains and arranged our beds in there. There's even a fireplace that we can use in the winter if need be. The house doesn't have the luxury of central heating, and I'm sure the temperatures will be bitter by then.'

After gently pulling the colourful crocheted blanket that lay folded at the end of the antique sofa over Charlie's sleeping form, Jarrett straightened to give her his undivided attention. 'I don't mean this unkindly, but did you even know what you were doing when you bought a place like this?'

Sophia dropped the straw bag she'd taken to the seaside onto a nearby Edwardian chair and folded her arms. Then she lifted her chin in a gesture that clearly illustrated her defensiveness. 'I didn't buy it. Do I look like the kind of person who could afford to buy a house like this?'

He shrugged. 'What *does* a person who can afford to buy an expensive period property look like? If you didn't buy it, then how did you come to be here?' Sensing this wasn't the kind of information she readily wanted to share, he almost held his breath as he silently willed her not to keep it a secret.

Absently freeing the two covered red bands that secured her plaits, she started to loosen her hair. *Jarrett's mouth turned helplessly dry as he watched her comb her slender fingers through it.* Just as he'd imagined, the luxurious fall of rippling dark strands might have come straight out of a pre-Raphaelite painting.

'My aunt left it to me.'

'Mary Wingham was your aunt?'

'My great-aunt.'

Taken aback for a moment, he rubbed a hand round his jaw. 'Did you visit her much when she was alive?'

She looked downcast. 'No. I didn't. The last time I was here was when I was about twelve years old.'

'Yet she bequeathed you this house?'

'Yes.'

'She must have been very fond of you.'

'Hmm.' The soft green eyes glimmered wryly. 'My dad always told me she didn't exactly like our family... although I think she secretly had a bit of a soft spot for him. Anyway, the last time I personally set eyes on her was at his funeral, and I remember her looking pretty upset. But I still don't know why she chose to leave the place to me. Of course I'm very grateful that she did.'

'But—'

'I'm tired, and I really think I've answered enough questions for one day.'

Even though he yearned to hear more, the expression on Sophia's face was determined enough to make Jarrett conclude he shouldn't push his luck—and neither should he forget that for a woman who had an obvious tendency to be reclusive she had at least let her guard down enough to allow him to spend time with her and her son.

CHAPTER FOUR

TELLING herself it would be rude not to offer Jarrett a cup of tea when he'd so thoughtfully taken her and Charlie to the beach for the afternoon, Sophia fought down her wariness at his curiosity about her and led the way into the lofty-ceilinged kitchen. With its dulled terracotta tiled floor and tall curtainless windows overlooking the currently wild and untended back garden, it was hardly inviting.

Seeing the daylight was fading fast, she flicked on the light switch. But the pool of dreary yellow light emanating weakly from the single bulb hovering above the scrubbed pine table in its nondescript cream shade hardly helped matters. It was hard for her not to feel painfully embarrassed that the room wasn't more hospitable.

'How do you take your tea?' she asked her guest, almost flinching as his penetrating gaze interestedly examined his surroundings. There was no way they'd make a favourable comparison with his sister's ultra-modern fitted kitchen, she thought. Not unless his preference was for genteel old buildings in urgent need of a major makeover.

'I like it strong, thanks…no sugar. What an incredible kitchen—great for a large family. Beautiful too.'

'It certainly could be. Of course I plan to renovate it, along with the rest of the house, but I can't afford to do it all straight away. It's going to take an awful lot of money and time to do it justice. It's clear that my aunt got rather frail towards the end of her life and couldn't take care of the place like she used to. When I visited here as a child it always seemed so grand. It was like a palace, and the garden was a fairy princess's magical kingdom.'

One corner of Jarrett's lips hitched up into his cheek. 'That's a nice memory. You know, Sophia, some things are worth waiting for. With a house like this it makes good sense to take your time mulling over what you'd like to do room by room. Just do what you can when you can. One step at a time, would be my advice.'

'Why don't you sit down?' Making a cursory nod towards one of the straight-backed chairs round the table, Sophia was a little taken aback by Jarrett's measured comments, but she also felt reassured that he sympathised and understood.

'Sophia?'

'Yes?' Glancing round as she stood at the deep ceramic butler sink, filling the copper kettle at the single tap, she was slightly unnerved by the intensity of his gaze. He was standing behind the chair rather than sitting down, and his big hands curled round the dark wooden back as though he were indelibly stamping his presence on everything he touched…disturbingly on her *senses* too…whether she liked it or not.

'You seem a little on edge,' he observed. 'Why don't you try and relax?'

'I'm afraid it's become rather a habit…*not* being able to relax, I mean.'

'Because of what happened to you before you came here?'

The sonorous chiming of the grandfather clock in the hallway just then drowned out any other sound. It also gave Sophia some precious moments to collect her thoughts. 'What do you mean?'

'I think you know what I mean… But I'll ask you plainly so that there's no confusion.'

Turning off the tap, she lifted the kettle with a less than steady hand, then set it down on the wooden draining board. She turned to face him. 'Go on, then.'

'You told me that you were a widow. But the comment you made straight afterwards about not being sorry about it definitely suggested your marriage wasn't a happy one. Was that the reason you came to the village and moved into your aunt's house rather than selling it?'

'You think I was running away from a bad marriage?'

'I'm not suggesting that wouldn't have been the right thing to do if you were dreadfully unhappy.'

'Look, I want you to know that I'm not comfortable with you so freely expressing your opinions about my life, and nor am I happy about you asking all these questions. Perhaps you should respect my right to privacy a little more?'

Jarrett sucked in a breath through his teeth. 'Maybe if you were just someone I ran into now and again— someone who meant nothing to me—then I most definitely *would*. But I'm sure you've guessed by now that I've become quite intrigued by you.'

His statement might have quickened Sophia's heart if she'd been in a good place mentally and emotionally, but she knew she was far from feeling good enough about herself to accept it even for a second. The sensation of the cold ceramic sink pressing into her back added to her sense of feeling utterly chilled right then... desolate at the idea that life might never be good again, no matter how hard she prayed it would be. Now that her wonder and gratitude at her eleventh-hour reprieve of being gifted this beautiful house had started to fade a little, a sense of battle fatigue after what she'd endured had begun to seep into her bones.

'Well, you're wasting your time being intrigued,' she snapped, knowing that she was only being curt because she feared him getting too close and pursuing the idea of a relationship. 'I have nothing to offer you, Jarrett. I mean it. I really don't...particularly friendship. I'm in no position to be a friend to anybody—*even* myself. If you knew my unerring ability to take wrong turns and make disastrous decisions, trust me, you'd avoid me like the plague. You'd be much better off directing your interest towards the kind of women that were at your sister's party today...women who are completely at ease with making social small talk, who are undemanding and uncomplicated and no doubt come from the kind of comfortable world where what everything looks like is far more important than being remotely real. That way at least you'd know *exactly* what you'd be getting.'

Glowering, Jarrett angrily pushed away from the chair, and the ear-splitting sound of wood scraping against the red stone flags made Sophia gasp. Breathing hard, he planted himself directly in front of her. One glance up into his hot and fierce blue eyes made her head feel as if it was spinning. Above the pounding of her heart she could hardly hear her own panicked thoughts.

'I might be materially comfortable, but I'm not superficial. Where did you get that unflattering impression from? Do you think you're the only person who's ever made a mistake or a disastrous decision? And, for your information, I neither want nor desire *any* of the women you've just described. They might be my sister's friends but they're not mine. And the fact that you've immediately intuited what they're all about must surely tell you *why* I wouldn't be interested in them.'

Despite her heart hammering at his nearness, and also because for one dreadful moment his action had brought back a sickening memory of Tom, furiously lashing out at her because she'd displeased him in some way, Sophia schooled herself to stay calm. The man standing in front of her *wasn't* Tom. And, even though she'd obviously hit a raw nerve by describing the world of his sister's friends as 'superficial', she somehow knew that Jarrett wasn't the kind of man who would use his superior strength to intimidate or wound a woman.

The breath she exhaled was undoubtedly relieved— but then another disturbing thought struck. 'Perhaps you're not interested in them because you're already involved with someone?'

'If you were interested in my relationship status then why didn't you ask me about it before? Do you think I'd offer to take you and Charlie to the seaside if I was involved with someone else?' As he crossed his arms over his chest, Jarrett's scowl turned into a perturbed frown.

Sophia heard what he said, but just then her attention was helplessly captured by the way the clearly defined muscles in his upper arms bunched and flexed beneath the loose-fitting material of his cotton shirt. The sight made her feel hot and bothered in a way that she hadn't experienced since she was eighteen…*before* Tom Abingdon had crushed all her innocent hopes and dreams of a happy, loving marriage deep into the dirt with his proclivity for cruelty and licentiousness.

'I'm sorry. Clearly my social skills aren't what they once were. I didn't mean to offend you.' Turning away in a bid to hide her heated reaction to him, she gasped when Jarrett fastened his hand lightly round her forearm.

'You haven't offended me.' His voice rolled over her senses like a warm sea of honey. Along with his touch, and the simmering heat in his gaze that he didn't trouble to disguise, it completely electrified her.

'Just so that you know, there's only one woman I'm interested in, Sophia, and that's *you*.'

'I already told you that I can't offer you anything. Weren't you listening?'

'I heard what you said. But I'm not a man who gives up easily when I sense something or *someone* might potentially be important to me.'

His riveting gaze made her feel as if she was diving into a molten blue lake. When he lifted his hand from her arm, Sophia knew the sensuous tingling imprint that he left on her skin would not easily vanish when he had gone. Apart from being immensely pleasurable, the thought of what it might mean…where it could lead should she succumb to his touch more fully…made her quake inside…

* * *

Putting a lit match to the tinder she'd arranged between the split ash logs in the once grand fireplace, it was with a real sense of satisfaction that Sophia watched the dry wooden limbs and scrunched-up newspaper catch fire. Her father had always loved a real fire in winter, or when the weather was sufficiently cold to warrant one, and they unfailingly reminded Sophia of home and of *him. Sometimes it was too much to bear to remember he was gone and that he'd left the world believing that his only daughter was in safe hands with her new husband.* But she'd often counted her blessings that he *hadn't* lived to see the misery Tom had inflicted on her, because it would have broken his heart. He would also have been furious that any man would treat her with anything but the utmost respect, and would have fought tooth and nail to extricate her from a marriage that in truth had been *doomed* even before the ceremony.

What she would give now to have had the common sense to see it for herself. Yet her union with her husband had not been a total disaster, because it had given her Charlie…the little boy who had helped Sophia cling to hope even when times had been unremittingly dark and frightening… The depth of love she felt for her son went way beyond any love she could ever imagine. She glanced over at him now, to check that he was still sleeping. Satisfied that he was, she allowed herself a pleased smile, then returned her gaze to the fire.

Flashes of blue flame were licking hotly round the fragrant logs, denoting the fire had taken firm hold, and she rose to her feet from her kneeling position in front of it, dusted her hands over her jeans and returned to the worn maroon armchair opposite her guest. Charlie continued to slumber blissfully in his curled-up position on the couch, his plump cheeks rosy as the sweetest red apple even though the warmth of the fire had not yet permeated the room. Sophia moved her glance to Jarrett. The long muscular legs in faded black denim were stretched out in a relaxed pose as he sipped at the mug of tea she'd made him, and she couldn't help admiring his apparent ability to be so at ease.

'Great idea of yours to light a fire,' he remarked, and his sinfully velvet-rich tones elicited an outbreak of goosebumps up and down her skin.

'It's cold enough for one,' she said and smiled. "Cast not a clout 'til May is out" my grandmother used to say—and it's true. Funny how the old sayings are such a comfort…even when you're little and don't understand them.'

'I know what you mean. Was the grandmother you mentioned your father's mother or your mother's?'

Making herself as comfortable as she could manage in the hard-backed armchair—not easy when the seat cushion beneath her was worn flat as a pancake from use and old-age—Sophia took a careful sip of her hot sweet tea, then lowered the mug to rest it against her denim-covered thigh. 'She was my dad's mum. My mother was an orphan. I didn't know any of her family. And, before you quiz me about that, don't you think it's time you told me a little bit about yourself?'

'Fair enough.' He leant forward a little, glinting blue eyes watching her with the same deceptively languid curiosity of a cat. 'What do you want to know?'

'Have you always lived round here?'

'No. I moved to the area about ten years ago, when my sister got married and set up home in the village.

Before that I lived in lots of different places…mainly
abroad.'

'I take it that you and Beth are close, then?'

Despite being irked that Beth had suspected him of
trying to get close to Sophia in order to persuade her
to sell him High Ridge, and hadn't entertained the idea
that he genuinely liked her, Jarrett couldn't deny that
they were indeed close.

'We lost our parents when we were in our teens. That
kind of tragedy helps to forge a close-knit bond with
a sibling. Beth is a couple of years older than me, and
I suppose she took it upon herself to be my guardian.
Unfortunately—even though I'm thirty-six and have
been independent for a hell of a long time—she occasionally still likes to assume the role. Needless to say
I hardly welcome it.'

'So you came back from your travels to be near her?'

'Perhaps.' Feeling uncomfortable at admitting as
much, Jarrett was wary of Sophia judging him and
making the assumption that he wasn't psychologically
strong enough to get on with his life without Beth being
close by. 'I think most people are always looking for a
point of reference—a sense of belonging somewhere
where they're unconditionally accepted and known…
don't you?'

'You mean like home?'

His companion's voice softened audibly and her
small, perfect hands curved round the cheerful yellow mug of tea as if to try and contain her feelings.
'Yes,' he answered, intuiting that her mind had wan-
dered back into the past…perhaps back to the series
of events that had led her to come to High Ridge and

into a whole new mode of existence where she had to raise her son on her own.

The pretty green eyes that still glanced cautiously at him from beneath dark brown lashes were full of painful shadows, Jarrett saw. In that instant the compulsion to offer comfort was so strong that he scarcely knew what to do with it. But the last thing he wanted was to scare or overwhelm her. In the end he simply put down his mug of tea and bided his time until she started talking again.

'I'd like to make a home here too,' she confided at last, her tone wistful, 'for me and Charlie. But the truth is I don't know if I'll be able to. Not in this house anyway.'

'Why?'

'Look at the size of this place...the responsibility is overwhelming. You've only glimpsed how much work needs doing—and that's just the gardens and the downstairs. Upstairs there are eight rooms...*eight*! Thanks to my great-aunt Mary I own the house outright, but that doesn't mean I can afford to keep it.'

'You don't earn enough from your photography to maintain it and pay the bills?'

'You must be joking! I'm only starting to build my career after a long period of not being able to pursue it. I've managed to secure a couple of potentially lucrative commissions, thanks to some old contacts, but nowhere near enough work to be able to relax and not worry.'

Jarrett frowned. 'Didn't your late husband leave any provision for you and Charlie? At the very least he must have had life insurance?'

Sophia reddened and lowered her gaze. 'The answer is no to both those questions.' When she glanced up again, her expression easily revealed that memories of her husband still had the power to cause her tremendous pain. 'The only person he ever provided for was himself.'

'I see. I'm sorry.'

'The truth is, as much as I love the idea of spending the rest of my days living in this beautiful old house, maybe I should be a bit more realistic. Maybe what I need to do is just sell it and buy something a lot smaller and more manageable for Charlie and me.'

Jarrett could hardly believe what he was hearing. But even as his heart leapt at the possibility of making an offer to Sophia to buy High Ridge from her—the house that he'd long dreamt of owning—in all conscience he found he suddenly *couldn't.* It was already clear as crystal to him that she was looking for a safe haven from her painful past, and right now he intuited that this historic old house was *it.* She'd had family here…blood ties. That sense of an ancestral link, of familial continuity, more importantly of *belonging,* must be important to her and Charlie right now, given their situation.

Wasn't that why Jarrett himself had made his permanent home here? Just so that he could be near his sister? Because at the end of the day there was no one else who cared if he lived or died. Despite their sometimes vociferous differences of opinion, and her perhaps not-so-flattering speculation on his intentions earlier today, he firmly believed that family was important.

If his competitors ever learned that he hadn't leapt at the chance to secure High Ridge Hall, he didn't doubt they would seriously think that he'd lost that renowned single-minded steely edge that had helped make him one of the wealthiest landowners in the county. But right then Jarrett didn't care. For maybe the first time in his life he was genuinely considering someone else's wellbeing above his own. The truth was that Sophia Markham had *disarmed* him. The defences that he'd kept stoically intact for so long were swiftly and devastatingly crumbling every time he saw her…

'Jarrett? Did you hear what I said?'

'Hmm?' Distracted because his feelings had stolen a march on him, he stood up and crossed to the now blazing fire. 'If you want to make a home here for you and Charlie, then in my opinion I don't think you should give up on the idea of keeping the house simply because of finances. In the meantime I could make you a loan, if that would help? Then you wouldn't be reliant on getting more photographic commissions straight away. You could take your time sourcing more work. You could also pay for some of the essential repairs and renovation to be done on the house.'

Turning back to survey his companion, he didn't expect to find her expression so crestfallen. The glitter in her beautiful eyes immediately alerted him to the fact that she was crying. Jarrett's mouth dried in alarm.

'What on earth's the matter?'

'Even presuming that you can afford to make such a substantial loan, why would you do that for me?'

'Because I want to.' He shrugged, knowing there was no point in pretending otherwise. 'I want to help you in any way I can. Trust me…I can more than afford it.'

'You barely even know me.'

'You keep saying that. But I've got great hopes that you *will* let me get to know you better, Sophia.'

Wondering how on earth he managed to contain the in-flammatory urge that scorched through his blood right then, to haul her to her feet and kiss her, to taste the sweetly seductive strawberry lips that had unwittingly been taunting him all day, every time he so much as glanced at her, Jarrett exhaled a frustrated sigh. 'Then you won't be able to use the fact that we don't know each other well enough as an excuse.'

'No, Jarrett.' Firmly wiping away all trace of tears with the heel of her hand, Sophia rose to her feet and approached the mantelpiece. Leaving her mug of tea on the white marble shelf, she crossed her arms over her navy wool cardigan and turned to face him. 'I ab-solutely won't accept a loan from you. I either find my own way to finance this place or I *don't*.'

'It's admirable that you're so determined...but if you love this house as much as I'm guessing you do then it makes sense to accept some help when it's of-fered, doesn't it?'

The emerald eyes flashed. 'Can't you *see*? Can't you *tell* that I find the idea of being beholden to anyone for mine and Charlie's welfare abhorrent?'

Jarrett could indeed see that, and whilst he under-stood her very human need to remain independent—and honestly admired it—he guessed things weren't as simple or straightforward as that. More than once he'd witnessed fear in her eyes...*dread* even. It made him determined to discover why. He'd already gleaned that her husband hadn't been the best example of mas-culinity on earth, but was there more to it than that?

'Putting that topic aside for a minute, what about my getting to know you better?' He forced himself to ask the question, even though he feared her response wouldn't be the one he wanted. It had already dented his confidence that she'd refused his offer of a loan.

'You mean as a friend?'

'That would be a start, I suppose.' The wry quirk of his lips along with his slightly uneasy tone revealed that he hoped for much more than friendship…*so* much more.

Sophia's mesmerising emerald glance was absolutely steady. 'If I had met you years ago, Jarrett…before I met my husband Tom…perhaps we would have been a good match. Who knows? You seem to have a lot of the qualities and attributes I used to hope to find in a man. But my experience of being in a relationship has been irredeemably damaged by Charlie's father. I don't have the hope or the innocence I once had to trust in another relationship or believe that it could work. Nor do I want you to think that there's the slightest chance that I'll change my mind, because I know that I won't.'

As Jarrett silently observed the bewitching planes and contours of Sophia's lovely face in the flickering firelight inside he was cheering—because she'd remarked that if she'd met him before she'd met her husband they might have been a good match. She might also have asserted that she wouldn't change her mind about entering into a relationship with him, but quite frankly that cut no ice. Because he wouldn't be deterred…not when he knew that it was the outcome he craved above all else—*even* above owning High Ridge. And when it came to determination in achieving a goal…*any* goal…his ability to follow through and not be dissuaded was second to none.

'One day soon,' he said, 'I hope that you can tell me exactly what happened between you and your husband.

I want to know what put that look of cold dread in your eyes that I sometimes glimpse. It's my opinion that you deserve to be free of whatever haunts you, Sophia. Not just for your own sake, but for Charlie's too.'

Curling her hair behind her ear, she left the ghost of a wan smile briefly curve her lips. 'Some hurts that we're haunted by are too deep to ever be free of,' she answered softly, 'but I *will* tell you my story. Not tonight, because it's getting late and I'm tired, but soon— I promise.'

'Fair enough... How about tomorrow afternoon?' Jarrett suggested boldly, somehow knowing that if they left the topic alone for too long she might again retreat into herself and not tell him anything. 'I'll bring my cricket bat and teach Charlie how to play, then afterwards you and I can talk.'

There was a very brief flash of concern in her mesmerising eyes, but then to his relief her expression softened. 'Okay. Come over tomorrow after lunch—around three o'clock. You can stay for tea.'

'Perfect.' He grinned. If he'd been on his own Jarrett would have punched the air with joy...

CHAPTER FIVE

'COME in. It's so good to see you!' Standing back to allow the tall fair-haired young man entry into the hallway, Sophia smiled up into eyes that reflected the same soft green hue as her own.

Her brother David hugged her hard, not hesitating to express his heartfelt love and affection. He was without a doubt pleased and happy to see her. He'd rung her on her mobile only a couple of hours ago, to tell her that he was driving down from Suffolk on his way to visit an antiques market in London and wanted to pay her a flying visit to see how she and Charlie were settling into the house—did she mind that it was at such short notice?

Of course she didn't.

Sophia simply felt blessed that she was able to renew their relationship after being separated for so long by the unhappy restrictions of her marriage. Tom had been so possessive of her that towards the latter months of his life he'd even banned David from visiting her. The only reason that her brother hadn't fought harder for the right to do so was because he'd feared the consequences for her and Charlie if he did.

'I've missed you, Sophia...I can't begin to tell you

how much.' Holding her at arm's length, so that he could make a thorough reconnaissance of her face, her handsome sibling smiled a dazzling smile that had the look of a child on Christmas morning having just opened the gift he'd been hoping to receive above all others. 'You're looking really well…the best I can remember seeing you look for a long time. I'd almost forgotten how pretty you were! Did the two rooms I got ready for you work out all right? I'm sorry that I didn't have more time to make them a bit more welcoming.'

'They worked out just fine. After what I'd endured, trust me…a tent pitched in a field would have been welcome if no one had access to disturb me or try to control me and tell me what to do.'

They both knew who she was referring to with that comment, and some of the colour in David's face drained away a little. He dropped his hands down to his sides.

'I'm so sorry, Soph. So sorry that I didn't try and get you and Charlie away from him long before the bastard went and died.'

'Please don't beat yourself up about that. I know you must have been thinking of us. But the truth is the situation was a nightmare, with no easy solutions to bring it to an end. I know you would have done more if you could have. Besides, you had your wife and child to think of—and you know how vindictive Tom could be. I wouldn't have wanted you or your family to be at risk in any way. Look, let's not talk about this today, hmm?' She laid her hand on the soft suede of his jacket sleeve and lightly squeezed his arm. 'Let's just enjoy our time together knowing we've at last got the freedom to be brother and sister again without interference—agreed?'

He scraped his fingers through the cropped fair hair
that highlighted his strong square-cut jaw and glanced
back a little uncertainly into her eyes, as if debating
whether anything he ever said or did could help take
the sting out of the horrors of the past, no matter how
much he wished that they could. 'Okay…I only want to
do whatever makes you feel safe and secure again. God
knows that's long overdue. Why don't you tell me how
you and Charlie are doing? Where is he, by the way?'

'In the garden…he practically lives out there when
the weather's fine. I'll call him in shortly to come and
say hello to you.'

'As long as he's well and happy—that's the main
thing. This place must seem like a veritable castle to
him it's so big! You've certainly got your work cut out
if you're planning on eventually renovating the place.'

'That's an understatement.' Sophia grinned. But then
she frowned as she remembered something she'd badly
wanted to address since being left the house by their
relative—something that had been playing on her mind
ever since she'd heard the news. 'Did you mind very
much that Great-Aunt Mary left High Ridge to me instead of to us both?'

'Did I mind?' Her handsome brother was already
shaking his head in disbelief. 'Are you mad? I was absolutely delighted. Especially when I knew that that
poor excuse of a husband of yours had left you and
Charlie practically destitute and I found out that you
had to sell your home to pay off his debts. As for myself, I'm fortunate to have a place of my own as well
as a good income with which to maintain it and to live
on. Nothing could have pleased me more than to hear
that some good fortune had come your way at last.'

Sophia's anxiety over the matter thankfully eased, to be happily replaced by a wave of the most profound relief. 'Thanks for that. I don't think I could have borne it if you'd been at all resentful. And, in answer to your question, Charlie *is* well and happy. He's starting his new school in a couple of weeks, and he's looking forward to making some new friends. I'm not doing too badly either, though it still feels a bit like I've been let out of jail. How are Lindsay and Oscar doing?'

'Oscar's seven going on sixteen!' David answered wryly. 'And if his current stroppy moods are anything to go by Lindsay and I will have our work cut out when he becomes a teenager, that's for sure'

'Why don't you come into the kitchen and we'll have a cup of tea and a chat? I was going to make some lunch for me and Charlie very soon—just something simple. You're welcome to join us if you're not in too much of a hurry to get to London?'

Even as she issued the invitation Sophia remembered with a jolt that Jarrett was paying her a visit after lunch, and that she'd promised to tell him the whole story of her bitterly unhappy marriage. She wouldn't put off the visit, but she'd rather her brother left before he arrived. All morning, whenever she'd reflected on seeing him again, she'd felt almost sick with nerves. Yet underneath the nerves was growing a distinct sense of excited anticipation, and it was that pleasurable expectation that worried her *far* more than being judged on making such a terrible marriage and enduring it for so long, when she should have found the courage to get herself and Charlie away from the situation as soon as possible…*whatever* the threatened or imagined consequences.

Jarrett had hardly slept. He'd risen early and busied himself with inconsequential activities, like browsing the Sunday newspapers, surfing the internet and drinking enough coffee to raise a person from the dead, simply to kill the time before he could drive over to High Ridge Hall and see Sophia. *It was as though someone had put a spell on him.* He could hardly think about anything else but her beautiful face, and the realisation that he was a different man when he was in her company—a man who was far more in touch with his feelings than he usually managed.

The mere idea of being so vulnerable to a woman would have normally had him running for the hills. God knew he'd had a lifetime of doing just that, fooling himself that long term relationships were best avoided because he didn't want to deal with the grief he might feel if things didn't work out. Losing his parents in a car accident when he was young had taught him that loving someone wasn't always enough to keep them by your side. Better to not risk being hurt, should that ever happen again. Yet what was happening to him now as far as Sophia was concerned was completely out of his control. And while it was undoubtedly frightening, it was also the most wonderful thing that he'd ever experienced.

Now, drawing up outside the familiar manor house, he reached over to the back seat of the car to collect the enormous bunch of flowers he'd brought for Sophia. They were all hand-picked from his own well-planted gardens. He and his gardener had walked the stone paths between the colourful beds together to select and cut them. Jarrett smiled to himself, shaking his head in bemusement as the heady floral perfume drifted up to him.

Even his gardener—the elderly but still sprightly Alfred—had winked knowingly up at him when he'd asked him to help choose some of the most beautiful blooms for a 'friend'. As the gnarled hands had reverently cut stalks with secateurs, the gardener had said, 'Your friend is a very lucky young lady indeed, Mr Gaskill. I hope she knows that.'

Stepping out onto the pavement, Jarrett walked up to the rusted iron gate that was positioned between tall hedgerows scattered with pink and white blossoms. It opened directly onto the house's path. Inside his chest, his heart was infused with optimism and hope for a good outcome to his visit—an outcome that would herald the start of what could be a genuinely meaningful relationship between him and Sophia Markham. But as he put his hand out to open the gate, up ahead the front door opened and a tall fair-haired young man stepped onto the stone porch with Sophia. His thoughts suspended in shock and surprise, Jarrett froze as he observed the man envelop the small slender brunette in a tight bear-hug and pull her head down onto his chest. He then proceeded to stroke his hand lovingly over her hair.

A harsh breath that was akin to the aftermath of being punched exited his lungs. *She'd lied to him.* Above the white noise that drowned out all other sounds that was the thought that pounded Jarrett's brain. Was she even a widow, as she'd claimed? If she was, then she obviously hadn't wasted any time in finding herself a replacement for her husband.

Engulfed by jealousy and rage, he felt his heart thunder hard. When he saw Sophia step back to cup the man's face tenderly between her hands, and smile up at him as if he was infinitely dear to her, it became too much for him to linger there a second longer. His mind teeming with desperately furious thoughts about what an idiot he was to be taken in by her beautiful face and bewitching company, he turned away and strode quickly back to the car—the need to escape that hurtful, bitter scene was paramount. On the way, he deliberately let the lovely bouquet he'd brought her fall carelessly onto the ground, as though the carefully handpicked blooms were nothing but an unwanted and ugly bunch of weeds.

'Why didn't Jarrett come and teach me to play cricket today, Mummy?' her small son asked plaintively as Sophia tucked him into bed.

Her hand shook slightly as she smoothed it over the patterned eiderdown, thinking hard what to say. In truth, she'd begun to believe that Jarrett had reneged on his agreement to visit because he'd suddenly got cold feet. The thought was hard to bear after he'd been so kind the evening before, and as the day had worn on she hadn't been able to help becoming close to despondent when she'd realised he wasn't going to show.

He could have at least dropped a note through the letterbox to tell her that something else had come up. He could even have made up some not too hurtful excuse as to why he'd changed his mind, Sophia reflected. But could she blame him? After all, what man in his right mind would seriously contemplate taking on a woman like her? A woman who wore the battle scars of her bitter experience in her eyes every time she met anyone's glance?

It didn't matter that she'd resolved never to put herself in the path of such a dangerous liaison again—that she would stay alert and awake round anyone who had the slightest propensity to mistreat her. Somehow Jarrett Gaskill had got under her skin—even made her long for something she could never have.

Her self-confidence had already been shattered by the hard and lonely years spent with Tom, and her ability to trust had been severely tested—perhaps *beyond* repair. It had taken a huge leap of faith on her part even to invite Jarrett into the house, let alone contemplate deepening their association. She'd become used to assuming a shield as strong as toughened steel to fend off anyone who tried to get too close or pry into her business. Protecting herself and her son from harm or hurt had taken priority over everything, and rightly so. She should definitely take it as a warning that she'd dared to relax her guard round Jarrett so soon, only to be paid back by his letting her down.

Why had she done such a thing?

The answer came immediately. She'd risked trusting him because hope had started to stir in her heart that he was cut from a finer cloth than her husband, and now it hurt all the more that he'd disappointed her. It was a fruitless exercise, but Sophia couldn't help wondering *why* again. Was it because he'd concluded that she just wasn't worth the risk or the potential heartache?

'I don't know why he didn't come, my darling, I really don't,' she answered, tenderly stroking back her son's corkscrew curls from his forehead. 'Perhaps he wasn't feeling well. Anyway, I don't want you to worry about it, because I'm sure we'll find out what happened very soon. In the meantime, you've got your stay with Uncle David and Aunt Lindsay to look forward to. You're going to have so much fun, spending some time with your cousin Oscar, I'm sure. Now, get some sleep, my angel. You've had an exciting day, what with building a den in the garden and seeing your uncle again. I can see that you're tired. I love you so much, Charlie.' Affectionately brushing her lips against her son's soft cheek, Sophia got up from his bedside and moved across to the door.

'I love you too, Mummy...more than anybody else in the whole wide world!'

As she quietly closed the door behind her the distressing sting of tears pressed against her eyelids like a painful burning brand.

Jarrett had been in a foul mood all week. Each day he'd risen practically at dawn to seek refuge in work, and he lingered late in his office when he didn't have to— just to escape the mocking reality of his empty home. However desirable the executive-style house might appear from the outside, with its panoramic windows, the Ferrari, vintage Bentley and Range Rover parked on the drive outside the garage, and its landscaped gardens encompassing almost three acres of prime countryside, there was no getting away from the fact that inside it had suddenly become too cavernous and empty for him to tolerate being there on his own. With nothing but his despairing thoughts to keep him company, it had become a prison.

Even when his sister had rung to apologise for offending him with her remark about him wanting to get close to Sophia only so that he could buy High Ridge, he'd been too disheartened and impatient to forgive her. Beth's speculation about the woman he desired rankled even more now that he had discovered that she did indeed have secrets that she'd taken pains to conceal from him.

His mind couldn't seem to dislodge the disturbing image of her tender expression when she'd gazed up into her lover's eyes and gently cradled his face between her hands. Up until he'd witnessed that heart-knifing scene Jarrett couldn't deny that he'd been longing for Sophia to gaze up at *him* in a similar loving way one day soon. And, even though she'd so cold-heartedly deceived him, he couldn't totally kill that longing.

At least choosing to work even longer hours had helped ensure he wouldn't run into her by chance and perhaps be driven to express publicly his anger and disappointment at her deception. He imagined her soft husky tones explaining who the man was, and maybe a beseeching look in her green eyes that begged his understanding and forgiveness. *How in hell was he going to deal with that?*

About to climb out of the car and step onto his drive, he cursed vehemently, tunnelling his fingers furiously through his hair. At the same time the ominous sound of rumbling thunder made him glance up at the sky, to see the darkening grey dome above him turn to a dramatic blackened violet. Barely a few seconds later heavy rain began pelting everything in sight like indiscriminate machine gun fire.

The fresh string of curses that issued from Jarrett's

lips was even more vehement than the first. Tugging
his jacket collar up towards his ears, he hurriedly exited
the car and slammed the door shut. *He'd be drenched
long before he reached the front door.* Fine! It suited
his already bleak mood to be soaked to the skin and
made even colder in body, mind and spirit than he was
already.

'Jarrett!'

For a frozen second he thought he'd imagined
Sophia's voice calling out his name. But when he
glanced over his shoulder towards the end of the drive
he saw that his imagination *wasn't* working overtime.
Her slim, rain-coated figure was huddled on the other
side of the wrought-iron gates. Her hands were jammed
into her pockets and her braided hair was plastered to
her head by the violent downpour. Her lovely face was
so pale that the exquisite cheekbones seemed to jut
through the porcelain skin.

In spite of what she'd done to him Jarrett's heart
slammed against his ribs, and in those arresting few
moments his desire for her surmounted all doubt. He
took a deep breath in to steady himself.

'What is it you want from me, Sophia? You'd better
tell me quick, before we both drown in this monsoon!'

Through the deluge of heavily falling rain he saw
her bite her lip and lift her sodden braids away from
her face. 'Just tell me one thing. Why didn't you show
up on Sunday? Charlie was so upset. You could have at
least have had the decency to let us know you weren't
coming.'

'I'm sorry I let your son down. I really am. But
though I fully understand why *he* was upset, clearly
you didn't suffer the same regret, did you?'

'What do you mean?'

'You know damn well what I mean!' He glared at her, clenching his fists down by his sides and shaking his head. 'You'd better come in. This is ridiculous. We can't talk out here'

He pressed a button on his keypad to open the electronic gates, refusing to contemplate for a moment that she might refuse his invitation to follow him inside and talk. *She owed him that much.*

Although her hair and outer clothing were clearly soaked, in no way did Sophia cut a forlorn figure. In fact, as she walked through the open gates towards him she held her head up high as if she didn't have a damn thing to hide.

He moved quickly towards the smart beechwood front door. Although outside the rain pounded at the building with almost uncanny force, inside the light and airy hall it was suddenly as quiet as a church. Shrugging off his jacket and hanging the soaked garment on the coat rack inside the door, where it dripped into an umbrella stand, Jarrett impatiently stretched out his hand to take Sophia's coat. Seeing the hesitation in her glance, he bit back his impatience and trusted his expression was benign enough not to make her nervous. Even if she *had* lied to him, he would never descend to intimidation to vent his anger.

When she didn't remove her coat, he lowered his hand. 'Wait here. I'll go and get a towel for you to dry your hair.'

'Don't bother about that. Just answer the question I asked you outside and I won't take up any more of your valuable time.'

There was a hurt, resentful edge to her tone, and

Jarrett wrestled with the sense of injustice it provoked inside him. It beggared belief that she was acting so aggrieved when it was *her* that had played him for a fool.

'All right I'll tell you why you didn't see me. Although as a matter of fact I *did* call round.' Feeling the talons of what he believed was justifiable anger dig into him at the expression of surprise on her face, he slowly crossed his arms over his chest, praying that she wouldn't try and maintain her innocence to the point of embarrassing herself when she realised he knew the truth. 'I was about to open the gate when I saw you step outside the house with a man,' he said, low-voiced. 'A tall, fair-haired chap. Is he your lover, Sophia? Or perhaps he's the husband you told me had died?'

'What?' Her face had turned the colour of parchment. 'You say you called and saw me come out of the house with a man?'

'Yes, I did. I was about to open the gate when I saw him. Who was he? I don't want any lies. Just tell me the truth.'

Sophia's limbs were almost too weak to keep her upright for another second. The cold, damp material of her raincoat clung to her, making her shiver hard. She'd left the house in a hurry, unable to stand for a moment longer the torment of not knowing why Jarrett hadn't called round last Sunday. But it was the bitter disappointment and fury now reflected in his crystal blue gaze that made her tremble even more.

'For your information, I didn't consider telling you anything *but* the truth,' she insisted, and saw a muscle in the side of his strongly defined cheekbone flinch, as if denoting that he didn't believe her. 'The man who you saw me with is not my lover. He's my brother.'

Her companion's lightly tanned skin actually blanched, and she saw him swallow hard. 'Your *brother*?'

An icy drip of water slid down the back of her neck from her sodden coat collar, but her blood was pumping so hard through her veins that the heat it poured into her body right then meant that she barely even registered it. 'Yes, he's my brother. And if you'd had the guts and good manners to open the gate and walk in, instead of skulking outside and jumping to the worst possible conclusions, then I would have introduced you to him.'

'My God.'

'Now you know the truth, there's no need for me to hang around any longer.'

'Please wait. Look, I'm truly sorry. You can't know how much I mean that. I made a terrible mistake.'

'That's all that you can say? I thought you were a good man…a *fair* man. But then you go and shatter my illusions by behaving just like everybody else in this godforsaken place, with their small minds and unfair suspicions. I would have told you everything if you'd stayed. I see now what a bad error of judgement that would have been. Anyway, I am going to leave now, and I think it's best if we don't see each other again.'

Even as the words left her lips Sophia knew she didn't mean them. Having not set eyes on Jarrett for almost a week, she'd yearned to see him so badly that the image of his handsome face had seared itself onto her brain practically to the exclusion of all else. But she also knew it was unlikely she'd be able to trust him again, after he'd jumped to the wrong conclusion about David.

'Don't go.' He stepped towards her and stilled her

escape by catching her hand and holding it. His expression mirrored his distress. 'At least give me the chance to make amends. You're right. I was a small-minded idiot not to give you the chance to explain who he was. But I was so intent on seeing you that I reacted like a jealous fool when I saw you with someone I thought must be a rival.'

'That's still no excuse for staying away without even contacting me to tell me why.'

'You're right. It isn't.' As he lifted one broad shoulder and dropped it again in a shrug a rivulet of rain slid down his sculpted cheekbone from his still wet hair. 'I suppose I thought the longer I stayed away, the longer I could delay hearing you tell me that there *was* someone else in your life after all.'

The tenor in his voice conveyed genuine regret, and in spite of her reservations Sophia sensed some of her anger and tension subside. Hearing Jarrett tell her that he'd acted like a jealous fool made her realise how much it must have meant to him to see her again that Sunday, and how shocked and disappointed he must have been when he'd believed she was seeing someone else.

He still hadn't released her hand, and it was as though an electrical current was shooting through it simply because his big palm enfolded it. 'There's nobody else.' She lifted her head, intensifying her gaze to emphasise the point. 'But that doesn't mean I'm looking for a relationship either.'

His lips split into a disarming grin. 'You know it's going to be my mission to make you change your mind about that?'

'By all means try. But don't say I didn't warn you when you fail.'

Letting go of her hand, he drove his fingers through his damp ebony hair. 'Will you still share what you were going to tell me before I made such a colossal fool of myself on Sunday? I honestly want to hear your story, Sophia. And before you say anything else, I'll make you a cast-iron promise that I won't share the content of what you tell me with another living soul.'

'Not even your sister?'

'Not even her.'

She saw from his unwavering stare that he meant it.

'By the way, where's Charlie?' he asked.

She gave him a brief smile. 'With my brother and his family. They've invited him to stay with them in Suffolk for a short break before he starts school. David has a son just a couple of years older than Charlie, and they haven't seen each other for a long time. I'm glad that he wanted to go, but I'm going to miss him like crazy.'

Just the thought of being without her precious child for even a *day* made Sophia feel tearful. They'd always had the strongest bond, but they'd become even closer since the shadow of Tom had no longer loomed over them.

Jarrett's glance was warmly reassuring. 'You'll be fine,' he told her. 'I know you'll miss the little man, but you could probably do with a bit of a break too.'

'I suppose it's a good opportunity to get on with doing some work...both my photographic assignments *and* the house.'

The man in front of her looked thoughtful. Then with another warm smile he said, 'Why don't you let

me hang up your coat? Then we'll go into the kitchen
and have a hot drink.'

With fingers still icy-cold from the rain that had
drenched her, Sophia slowly started to unbutton her
damp raincoat.

CHAPTER SIX

THE hot mug of tea helped to dispel the chill that seemed to have seeped right through to her marrow.

Not since her father had Sophia known a man who knew his way confidently round a kitchen, and it had been an unexpected bonus to have Jarrett make the tea and then bring it to her at the table, along with an inviting plate of custard creams. As she'd watched his eye-catching physique garbed in a black fitted cashmere sweater and black trousers move with arresting masculine grace round the luxurious bespoke kitchen—a kitchen that was a million miles away from her own rather spartan one at High Ridge—Sophia hadn't been able to help but be transfixed.

Her heart was still thudding inside her chest because she'd at last found out why he hadn't turned up on Sunday. It had been the biggest shock to learn that he'd arrived just as her brother was saying goodbye and had immediately assumed that David was her *lover*. Although she'd forgiven him, it still hurt that he'd believed for even an instant that she was the kind of woman who would deceive him like that.

'Is your tea all right?'

Her host's arresting voice broke through her reverie.

As he dropped down into the seat opposite her at the round glass-topped table, for a moment the close proximity of his arresting presence made it almost impossible for Sophia to think straight. His sexy but classy cologne made a devastating foray into her senses first. But then she met his gaze. His dark-lashed eyes were so blue that it was as if God had especially reserved the perfect portion of sunlit summer sky to make them. Entranced, Sophia hoped that the neutral expression she aimed for adequately concealed the effect he was having on her.

'It's perfect. Just the way I like it. Where did you learn such a mundane but *vital* domestic task?'

'My sister always told me that the way to a woman's heart was through the perfect cup of tea.'

'Did she really?'

'No. I'm only joking.' His lips formed an unabashed grin. 'Living by myself, I've learned to do most things. I draw the line at wearing an apron, though. Wouldn't be at all good for my street cred if my family or friends were to see me in one.'

'Why don't you just pay someone to look after the domestic side of things for you?'

'Ah…' Jarrett knowingly tapped the side of his perfectly shaped aquiline nose. 'Now you're veering very close to discovering my Achilles' heel.'

'Which is?'

'Clearly you believe in living dangerously.'

The lowered husky voice that came back to her made the tips of Sophia's breasts inside her bra surge and sting. 'Don't tell me, then.' She endeavoured to sound nonchalant when she was feeling anything *but*.

'I'm a boring perfectionist, I'm afraid,' Jarrett admitted wryly. 'I somehow always come round to thinking that I may as well do it myself rather than hire someone who won't live up to my standards.'

'You're a bit of a control freak, then?'

'That accusation is not unknown to me.' He took a sip of his beverage, then grimaced. 'But I hope I'm not controlling in a way that puts me in the category of typically macho male. With the right woman I'm sure I could learn to be a lot more flexible.'

His glance was sheepish, and too endearing for her to take umbrage with, and she lightly shook her head as if to break free from the spell he so effortlessly cast. 'It's entirely up to you how you conduct yourself. One thing puzzles me, though. This house and the expensive cars on the drive, plus the fact that you're not exactly ugly...women must view you as quite a catch. It makes me wonder why you're still single.'

'Clearly not *all* women think I'm such a catch. You're not particularly impressed by my wealth *or* my looks. I know I'm risking denting my ego even further by asking, but why is that, Sophia? I'm feeling a little insecure here, knowing that none of my supposed assets can entice you.'

Bravely she met his searching gaze, her mouth drying at the weight of hurtful memory that backed up inside her like a swelling wave, knowing that she could no longer let it recede. 'I was married to a man who had wealth and good-looks—and it was like being married to the *devil* himself,' she admitted softly.

'Why? What did he do?' Jarrett's eyes were wild for a moment—the very thought of any harm coming to her was abhorrent to him.

Glancing away, Sophia desperately tried to garner

every ounce of courage she could find to continue. 'There's more than one way to skin a cat, as my dad used to say, and my husband knew them all. He was a virtuoso in the art of being cruel. Unfortunately it wasn't just *me* who bore the brunt of it.'

Her companion's sharp intake of breath was clearly audible. On his face, the shock that mingled together with disbelief was vivid too. 'You mean he hurt Charlie?'

'Not physically, thank God.'

She quickly moved her head from side to side, wishing they could talk about anything but *this*. However, she had promised her companion that she would tell him everything. She had never even shared the full extent of what she'd experienced at her husband's hands with her brother. To her mind, David had suffered enough, knowing that she lived with such a brute and that if he'd tried to take action to bring an end to her misery it might have made the situation worse for her and Charlie. There was no reasoning with a man like Tom Abingdon.

'Mental cruelty was his speciality,' she said out loud, 'and he could be as sulky and petty as a spoilt child. He regularly demanded that Charlie pay him more attention, because our son naturally came to me if he wanted or needed anything. He'd go ballistic at him for doing that. It was an affront to him that our boy needed his mother. After all, *he* was the one who was clever and educated—as he so often reminded me. He was the one with friends who admired and envied him, whereas I was a nobody. A picayune from a very average, nondescript family. He even told Charlie that I was a useless mother as well as a useless wife to him, and that they both deserved better. In a bid to prove it, he brought his mistress home.'

Sophia saw Jarrett's jaw slacken in disbelief and bit down heavily on her lip. 'I can see in your eyes that you're wondering why on earth I would put up with something like that if I had any self-respect at all.' Anger—defensive and bitter—crept into her voice. 'Well…perhaps you'll hold back your judgement until you hear the whole story. I hope that you will, because I'm *so* sick of being judged.'

Somehow she made herself continue. 'One evening when he brought this woman home—he'd been besotted with her for quite a while, I gather—he tried to convince our son that she would make a much better mother than me. She knew how to teach a boy to become a man, he said. She wouldn't turn him into some "namby-pamby Mummy's boy" like I was doing.'

She swallowed hard across the burning cramp in her throat. 'Tom thought he was justified in having affairs because after I'd had Charlie I locked him out of our bedroom. But I did that *because* he was always making eyes at other women, and when he didn't come home nights I knew he was messing around.' She freed a despairing sigh.

Jarrett gave her a quizzical look. 'He *let* you lock him out of the bedroom?'

Sophia's short burst of laughter was harsh. 'I think that was the first time I made him realise that I wasn't the gullible little schoolgirl he thought I would stay for ever when he married me. I was so furious with his behaviour that I didn't care if he hit me. I discovered it's a powerful thing to meet your fear instead of running away from it. But then he got back at me by other demoralising means. The worst thing of all was when he insisted on taking Charlie out for the day…away from my "despicable' influence", he used to say. I knew he'd be with his so-called friends. Friends who were as self-destructive and immoral as he was. I fought against him taking Charlie every time, and suffered not only verbal but sometimes physical abuse too for my protests.'

Taking a deep breath in at the dreadful memories that flooded back—at the humiliation and hurt of being hit and disparaged, along with her growing fear at the time that her son would grow up to be just like his father if she didn't find a way to get him away soon— Sophia laid her hand over her chest in a bid to calm her thudding heart.

As soon he saw the gesture, Jarrett moved across to the sink and poured some water into a glass tumbler. Returning swiftly, he pressed it into her hand.

Gratefully, she took a few sips and her companion moved back to his seat. Setting the glass down on a coaster, Sophia darted out her tongue to lick the moisture from her lips. Then she resumed her story. 'Leading up to the time when Tom died—his heart stopped beating one night in his sleep—Charlie was clearly being adversely affected by his father's behaviour. And why wouldn't he be? He was wetting the bed at night, having nightmares that made him scream out loud, and hitting me if I said no to something he wanted. I'm afraid it was making him ill.'

Jarrett scowled and looked disgusted. 'The man must have been absolutely deranged.'

'He was. He was addicted to everything that was harmful…alcohol, drugs, gambling, prostitutes. He had an utter lack of self-control and no self-respect whatsoever, and he didn't care who he contaminated—certainly not his wife and son. His death was a blessing, not just to me and Charlie...but to *him* too. I'm sure.'

'Why didn't you leave him long before it got so bad?'

Sensing an excruciating throb of guilty heat surge through her, Sophia abruptly left her seat and walked across the kitchen. There was an elegant glass wall cupboard full of pristine white crockery and, catching sight of her ghostly pale reflection in it, she quickly looked back to the dark-haired man whose uncomprehending and furious gaze seemed to burn right through to the very core of her vulnerability. He was clearly waiting for her explanation.

'I did leave him once. I went to a women's shelter in a nearby town. It was only meant to be a temporary measure. I'd planned to move further away, but Charlie and I had only been there barely a fortnight when Tom's father turned up and demanded we leave. As well as being a top QC, he comes from landed gentry...he's a very powerful and influential man. He must have brought the full weight of his powers down on the women who ran the shelter, because by the time they regretfully asked me to leave they looked quite shaken. They told me he'd threatened to have the shelter shut down if they didn't let me go, and that was the last thing that any of us wanted. So I went back with him...back to my husband. I wouldn't jeopardise the other women's security by staying, no matter how desperate I was. Back at home, things didn't improve. And the situation wasn't helped by Tom's father. Whenever he visited us they had the most terrifying rows. He regularly accused Tom of being a disgrace to the family name, but worse than that he threatened to take Charlie away if he didn't pull himself together and change his behaviour. Ironic, really, when the man was even more of a bully than his son.'

She crossed her arms over her chest to contain the icy shudder that ran through her. 'It didn't even seem to cross his mind that I was Charlie's mother and would fight him tooth and nail on that. He believed that his son had married beneath him, so consequently he had very little regard for me. Tom's behaviour didn't change. He warned me he would take Charlie away from me himself if I told his father that his drinking, drug-taking and womanising had got worse. He was spending every penny we had on his destructive habits. He was pinning all his hopes on his inheritance. He said if I jeopardised his birthright by trying to leave then he would find me, come hell or high water. And then I would *really* see what he was capable of.'

Shaking her head in despair, Sophia lifted her now brimming eyes to Jarrett, incapable of holding back the emotional tide that swamped her. 'Both my husband and his father made it impossible for me to turn to anyone for help—even my brother. They blocked every avenue I could take. They didn't want me to talk to *anyone*. My father-in-law feared losing his reputation if anyone found out the truth about what was going on, and my husband was terrified he'd lose his inheritance. His debts escalated wildly—as I found out when he died. Because of their threats, because of my terrible fear that somehow they would snatch Charlie away from me if I *did* manage to escape—that was why I stayed in the marriage longer than I should have… *Not* because I wanted to, or because I had no self-respect, but because I honestly believed I had no choice.'

'You should have gone to the police…told them everything.'

'If I'd filed a report then they would have conducted an investigation. If Tom hadn't hurt me even more because I'd dared to do such a thing, then I've no doubt that his father would have done everything in his power to take Charlie away from me and make me pay for disgracing him and his son. Can you see why I couldn't do that? My son means everything to me…*everything*!'

'Don't cry, sweetheart…please don't cry.'

On his feet, Jarrett was by her side in an instant. Enfolding her in his arms, he pulled her head down onto his broad muscular chest. In the midst of her distress, a jolt of surprise ricocheted through Sophia. The wonderful sensation of being held so tenderly instantly made her feel warm and protected. She hadn't experienced such a feeling since she'd lived at home with her dad—before she'd met and married Tom Abingdon. But what surprised her most of all was the realisation that Jarrett's heart was beating as wild and as fast as her own beneath the soft wool of his luxurious cashmere sweater.

She lifted her face up towards him. 'Before my husband died I vowed to myself that I *would* find a way to get Charlie and me out of that horrendous situation. I'd even started making discreet enquiries about going abroad…somewhere far-flung where Tom's father's influence carried no weight. But then Tom died in his sleep…just like that. When I found him he looked almost peaceful. It doesn't seem right somehow, does it? That a man can put his family through such hell and then abdicate all responsibility by simply dying?'

'I don't want to make you feel even more upset—but why did you marry such a man in the first place?'

Jarrett's big warm hand cupped her cheek as he glanced intently down into her eyes. The guilt she still suffered made Sophia struggle to find adequate words to explain. 'I was young and naive and flattered by his attention. He was good-looking, funny and clever, and because he'd been given everything on a silver spoon he was supremely confident too. When it came to getting what he wanted he knew exactly how to go about it, and when he decided that he wanted *me* I was too young and stupid to see that I might be walking into a trap. I was so dazzled by him that I relinquished every ounce of common sense I may have had. When he asked me to marry him I didn't even hesitate. Even when I started to hear rumours about his drinking and chasing women I told myself not to worry...that he would soon learn he'd made the right choice in making *me* his lifelong partner. I thought I could reform him, make him change some of his less attractive qualities when he saw what a good life we could have together.'

'How did you meet him?'

'I went to school with his younger cousin, and I met him at a party at her house.' Feeling suddenly uncomfortable beneath Jarrett's intense scrutiny, she removed his hand from her cheek and glanced away. 'No doubt I was easy prey. I was only eighteen—hardly a woman of the world. I'd just got into studying photography, and I wanted to go on to university. Meeting Tom put a stop to all that. It wasn't as though nobody warned me. My dad told me early on to cool things off and not rush into anything. But I was deaf to his advice. My husband-to-be even managed to fool *him* into thinking his intentions were good…that he loved me and wanted to take care of me. In the beginning I believed it, too. But it didn't take long for my fiancé's true nature to surface. I thank God that my dad didn't live to see what he put me through.'

The silence that pervaded the room after she'd finished speaking felt like a smothering blanket, and Sophia wanted to escape into the open air. Moving out of the intimate circle of Jarrett's protection, she lifted her glance to stare forlornly out of the window at the still pounding rain. She shivered.

'I'd better go. I'm trying to convert one of the downstairs rooms into a darkroom, and there's a lot to do. I have to get on. Thanks for the tea…and for listening.'

'Don't go. It can't have been easy to share what you've just told me. It was very brave. It's only natural that you might be feeling vulnerable and exposed. I made you a promise that I wouldn't share your confidences with anyone, remember? I want you to know that you can trust me, Sophia. I would never harm you or Charlie.' Catching her hand, Jarrett gently impelled her towards him. 'You've been through a terrible ordeal,' he acknowledged huskily, 'but given time things will slowly but surely get better—believe me. This is a new start for you and your son. Your husband is dead, Sophia…he can't hurt you or Charlie any more.'

'What about his father? Why do you think I reacted the way I did when you came up to me that day by the stream? After Tom died I had to sell the house to pay off his debts, and his father suggested that Charlie and I move in with him instead of finding somewhere else to live. Can you imagine it? The thought filled me with absolute horror. I had to run away so that he wouldn't try and force me. That day, when you first saw me, I thought you were someone he'd hired to come and find me and snatch Charlie. If he ever finds out where I am he could—he might—'

'Hey...'

Jarrett drew the pad of his thumb down over her cheek, and the look in his intense blue eyes along with the enticing flare of heat that his touch instigated inside her made Sophia sway a little closer towards him.

'Stop scaring yourself. You and Charlie are safe now,' he told her. 'I'll do everything in my power to make sure of that.'

'Why? Why would you do that for me?' The lid she'd tried so hard to keep firmly shut down on her emotions when she was with other people suddenly flew open, and she couldn't stop the slow track of scalding tears that started to spill down her face.

'You don't really need to ask me that...do you?'

His carved masculine mouth formed a knee-trembling smile that could melt a heart of stone, and although bruised and battered Sophia's heart was neither stony *nor* hard. She was ripe for a little tenderness, even though she'd sought to arm herself against it.

No further reflection was necessary as Jarrett laid his lips over hers in a kiss that started off on a slow-burning simmer and then quickly turned into a conflagration of passion and need. Again and again she gasped breathlessly into his mouth, needing to taste him, needing to feel the ravenous demand of his warm lips and hot tongue, meeting it with her own helpless craving, almost swooning with pleasure as his big hands dived into her hair and freed her still damp plaits.

In response, her arms wound themselves round his lean hard middle to keep her steady.

The realisation that hit her like a tidal wave was that her sexual need hadn't been completely deadened by her husband's cruel behaviour, as she'd believed. His cutting taunts and profligate behaviour had killed her desire very quickly once they were married. By the time she'd learned she was pregnant with Charlie the mere idea of her husband's hands coming anywhere *near* her body had been like agreeing to imbibe poison. Now, with Jarrett, she felt like a neglected flower in a shaded part of the garden that had unexpectedly caught a shower of glorious summer rain just in the nick of time. If he had wanted to become more intimate with her there and then Sophia would have let him. Her usually highly maintained defences had been demolished by that first exquisite contact with his lips and the sensation of his body pressing hungrily against hers. He made her feel like a real woman again.

It was Jarrett who poured the first drops of ice-cool water on the fire they'd made. Breaking off their passionate kiss with a rueful smile, he held her gently at arm's length, and she knew that the sound of his fast and heavy breathing and the look of stunned pleasure on his face easily matched her own.

'As much as I desire you—and it must be obvious to you by now that I do—I won't take advantage of you when you're clearly feeling vulnerable,' he asserted, his glance flicking concernedly over her face. 'When you're feeling calmer, and know what you want without your thoughts and feelings being clouded by emotion...then—if you decide that's what you want—we can have a more intimate relationship.'

Her heart was thudding so hard inside her chest that Sophia couldn't get an immediate grip on her emotions. Humiliation and shame slammed into her that she'd so stupidly exposed her need and vulnerability to Jarrett. Would he think it was no wonder that she'd ended up with a brute like her husband when she was clearly so desperate for love and affection...for *sex*?

Twisting out of his arms, she shakily rubbed her face dry of tears. 'Thanks for keeping a level head when I was clearly losing mine. I appreciate it. Now I'd better go. I have things to do at home. Like I said—I've started to convert a room into a darkroom to print my pictures and I really need to get on with it.'

'Sophia?'

'Yes?' The command in Jarrett's tone ensured her feet stayed firmly rooted to the spot when her preference was to escape as quickly as she could, so that she could go home and lick her wounds in private and examine why she had so eagerly let down her guard around him.

'I *want* you... Make no mistake about that. But it's not just sex that I want. What I want most of all is a relationship with you. I'd like to start by taking you out to dinner tonight.'

'I don't think that I—'

'Don't turn away from me. It's time you returned to the land of the living and started to enjoy life again.'

'The concept of enjoying my life feels like a million miles away right now,' she confessed quietly as she ventured to meet his piercing gaze.

'Well, maybe you can start by at least entertaining the thought. And by agreeing to go out to dinner with me tonight.'

The tumult inside Sophia started to subside a little, so that she was at last able to think more clearly. After Tom she'd been certain that she would steer clear of men—particularly *handsome* men—for the rest of her life.

With a trembling hand she brushed back the long waving hair that clung damply to the sides of her face. 'All right. I'll go out to dinner with you tonight. Satisfied?' she added with a touch of feistiness. Because although she wanted more than anything to go out to dinner with Jarrett she had to be careful not to seem too eager.

'After *that* kiss?' His face assumed an exaggeratedly pained expression. 'Not by a long chalk, sweetheart. Not when I think I've just discovered the true meaning of the word frustration!'

'You were the one who put a stop to it.'

'Very true.' A muscle hitched in the side of his sculpted cheekbone, and this time his expression was deadly serious. 'But I'm glad that I did. I want to get to know you, Sophia. I want you to get to know *me*. Isn't that how all good relationships are meant to start out? With friendship?'

She stared. The concept was alien to her...that a man and a woman could be *friends* before they were lovers.

CHAPTER SEVEN

IN THE softly lit restaurant, with candlelight flickering between them, at the beautifully laid corner table that he had specifically reserved, Jarrett formed his hands into a steeple and rested his chin on it to study his companion more closely.

It wasn't just the muted lighting and candlelight that rendered her features beautiful. It was a face that he could never imagine growing tired of looking at. Just one glance into eyes the colour of new-mown summer grass with sweeping chestnut lashes was enough to kindle a lifelong fascination. But it didn't hurt that Sophia's other features were equally compelling—from the small, elegant nose, the strongly defined pretty mouth, right down to the gentle cleft in a firm chin that denoted an uncommon strength of character and resolve. And, by God, she must have had to employ both of those attributes in spades during a marriage that had surely been made in hell.

He was still reeling at what she had told him. The truth had turned out to be much worse than he'd anticipated. The thought of her suffering at the hands of the sort of man her husband had been was enough to make a peaceable man like himself commit violence. In his opinion Tom had done her and Charlie a favour by dying suddenly like that. Still, it bothered Jarrett that Sophia would probably carry the psychological wounds of that terrible experience for the rest of her life.

That was why he had gently held her off in the midst of that incredible kiss they'd shared. He didn't want her to feel as if he was taking advantage of her in any way, even if his decision to cool things down a bit had been one of the hardest things he'd ever done. Now he planned to woo her properly…to let her know that he would put respect for her feelings, needs and wants above his own desires. He'd waited a long time for the right woman to come into his life, and Sophia was already too important to him to scare her off with any kind of rash move. You didn't rescue a bird with a broken wing and expect it to fly again without tending to it first, without allowing it time to heal.

'What are you thinking about, I wonder?' Sophia smiled, breaking into his thoughts.

'I was thinking about you.' There was a helpless, smoky catch in his voice.

'Boring subject…been there, done that. Earlier today, as a matter of fact—remember?'

She made a face and for a moment the child in her surfaced—a child who had been unbearably wounded. It made Jarrett's heart constrict. It was becoming clear to him that she went on the defensive at the least provocation. He didn't doubt her bitterly unhappy marriage had ripped into her sense of safety.

Leaning forward a little, he caught her gaze. 'How could you think yourself boring when the whole village is buzzing with speculation about you? You're not like anybody else round here… And although people are naturally suspicious because you're an unknown quantity, they're also envious.'

'You should know by now that they have nothing to be envious of. Besides, do you *think* I want that kind of attention? I'd rather live like a hermit in a cave. All I want is to be able to go about my business unnoticed and be like everybody else. Just to be ordinary. I'm not asking for the world. I have the same aspirations as most women round here, I'm sure… To be a good mother, be well paid for the work that I do, and to have a comfortable and affordable home. I love High Ridge, but I'd be a liar if I said that it doesn't keep me awake nights wondering if I haven't bitten off more than I could chew because I'm living in a house straight out of one of Dickens's novels!'

Jarrett smiled, wondering if she had any idea how beautiful she was in her simple wrap-around blue jersey dress, with her long chestnut hair glossy as dark fire as it flowed down over her slender shoulders. 'Those are reasonable and commendable aspirations indeed,' he answered thoughtfully. 'Except that I'm perturbed you haven't included the desire for a meaningful and happy relationship on your list. I was hoping you might include that one.'

Sophia's returning gaze was steady. 'Maybe that's because past experience has demolished all the optimism I once had.'

He was still soberly absorbing this comment when two smartly dressed waiters arrived with their food. The Italian restaurant Jarrett had driven them to was about ten miles from the village, deep in the heart of the surrounding countryside. The chances of bumping into anybody local were slim, and he'd hoped that might help Sophia to relax. Glancing down at the pasta dishes they'd selected from the menu, he didn't think either he or his companion would be disappointed with their choices. Not if the tasteful presentation and delicious aroma that wafted tantalisingly beneath his nose was anything to go by. And he knew the food was particularly good here because he'd eaten there on the odd occasion with his sister.

His stomach growled. The only sustenance he'd imbibed all day was a slice of nearly burnt toast and a cup of strong black coffee at breakfast. In fact his appetite *and* his sleep had been poor all week, due to his belief that Sophia was seeing another man.

'Let's eat, shall we?' he suggested lightly, giving her a broad smile as their attentive waiters left them alone again. 'I don't know about you, but I could eat the proverbial horse!'

'So, not only don't you have someone to clean for you, you obviously haven't succumbed to hiring a cook either?' Picking up her fork, Sophia expertly twirled some strands of spaghetti round it, guiding it into place with her spoon.

For a moment Jarrett was too transfixed by the sight to even think about satisfying his own appetite. She somehow managed to make the most commonplace actions look sexy, he mused, as a pleasant buzz of heat infiltrated his insides, 'Are you putting yourself forward for the job? Because if you are then I'll happily forego the interview and appoint you straight away.'

She moved her head to indicate no. 'I won't consider it right now, because I need to put my energies into my photography, but ask me again in a month or two when the coffers aren't exactly spilling over with coin and I might accept.' She popped a forkful of pasta with its accompanying fragrant sauce into her mouth and squeezed her eyes shut in a demonstration of un-restrained pleasure. 'Mmm…' she groaned. 'This is really, *really* good'

Jarrett almost let his fork clatter back onto the table. The look on her face was straight out of a candid scene from an erotic movie. Helplessly shifting in his seat as an arrow of flame zeroed straight into his loins, he suddenly found it wasn't food that he was hungry for.

'Aren't you going to eat?' Sophia asked innocently. 'I thought you were starving?'

He cleared his throat. 'I am. I'm afraid I just got a little distracted.'

'Oh.' She brushed off the comment with a careless shrug, but nonetheless he saw the swathe of hot pink that swept into her cheeks.

Feeling undeniably pleased, Jarrett watched her tuck into her meal for a few seconds longer before hungrily attacking his own.

By the time coffee arrived Sophia was feeling much more relaxed and at ease. Tonight, in this lovely restau-rant, she was like any other diner enjoying the company of her date, and nobody either knew or cared about her painful past. That gave her a sense of freedom and au-tonomy that she'd long craved.

Adding some cream to her coffee, she stirred it in, and when she looked up again Jarrett was studying her, an enigmatic smile lifting the corners of his mouth. A frisson of intense pleasure rippled through her as she recalled his urgent passionate kisses just a few short hours ago. There was no doubt in her mind that the man could win a trophy for his ability to kiss a woman and render her weak with instantaneous desire. In fact, there was so much about him that was wonderful that it was hard to fathom why he hadn't already met and married someone, Sophia mused.

'My turn to ask what *you're* thinking,' he remarked, just as her mind was in the middle of listing the qualities of his that she found the most appealing and attractive.

She smiled with a guilty blush. 'I was remembering that I once asked you why you were still single and you didn't really give me an answer. Have you ever had a long-term relationship?'

'No.' He shifted a little uncomfortably in his seat, settled again, then paused to take a sip of his strong black coffee.

Sophia was intrigued by his apparent reticence. 'Why not?' she asked bluntly.

'I guess up until recently I've never felt the desire to commit to anyone. No doubt there are many people who would think that's extremely selfish. My sister has despaired of me from time to time,' he said candidly, shrugging his shoulders. 'Don't get me wrong,' he added quickly, seeing her frown, 'I don't play the field…nothing like that. It's just that I've never met anyone that I wanted to be with for more than a few dates. And I've devoted most of my time to building my business.'

With a little flare of satisfied heat warming her insides at the realisation that he'd been referring to her when he'd stated that 'up until recently' he'd never felt the desire to commit to anyone, Sophia leaned forward a little, unconsciously inviting more candid revelations about his feelings and his life. 'And what *is* your business, Jarrett?'

'In simple terms, I buy and sell land.'

'Locally, you mean?'

His arresting smile was modestly wry. 'All over the world,' he confessed.

'Goodness…no wonder you haven't had time for romantic relationships. Such a global undertaking must surely demand a huge amount of time and energy? How will you manage things if you ever *do* settle down with someone?'

She almost held her breath as she waited for his answer, wishing that it didn't suddenly matter quite so much as it did.

His returning glance was completely frank. 'It's fortunate that I have several very competent and skilled people working for me, so it wouldn't be a problem to delegate a little more in order to free up more time. Especially if I'm ever lucky enough to have a family.'

The unexpectedly revealing comment had the effect of silencing the next question that hovered on Sophia's lips and it made her heart gallop. Reminding herself to get a grip, and not to let her hopes run away with her, she unconsciously added another lump of brown sugar to her coffee and took a deep sip. It was far too sweet and she couldn't help grimacing.

Jarrett laughed, and Sophia blushed to the roots of her hair when she realised he had seen her sour-faced expression.

'I was wondering if you usually made a habit of putting five lumps of sugar in your coffee. I surmised that you clearly just had a very sweet tooth,' he teased.

'I'm afraid I lost count of how many I put in,' she murmured, colouring hotly.

'I'll order you a fresh cup.' About to beckon a waiter, Jarrett hesitated when Sophia reached out and touched his hand.

'Please don't,' she said earnestly. 'It would probably keep me up all night anyway, and I need my sleep.'

'In that case I'll pay our bill and we'll go.'

Brushing back her hair from the side of her face, she nervously let her eyes meet his as she wondered what the protocol was these days on dating a man if he'd bought a woman a meal. *Was he going to expect much more than a goodnight kiss?*

A short while later, as they were sitting in the car in the impressive shadow of High Ridge, Sophia turned to her handsome companion and sighed. 'So there really hasn't been anyone you've been serious about in the whole of your romantic history?'

'That's right,' Jarrett answered. A thread of anxiety rippled through him that she might not believe him—that she might think he was just making it up to pique her interest.

'And you've never been lonely? Being on your own, I mean?'

The question made Jarrett smile. He knew perfectly well what she was asking him. 'If by lonely you mean have I ever felt the need for some female company to share my bed, then, yes. I have.'

'And presumably there's been no shortage of takers?'

Even in the dimly lit interior of the car, her blush was endearingly delightful. From the roots of his hair to the tips of his toes, Jarrett's whole body tightened. 'Can we talk about something else?' he suggested lightly. 'For instance, are you going to invite me in for a coffee? I know you implied that too much caffeine keeps you awake, but I wouldn't say no to another cup if you're offering.' He knew his smile was boyishly hopeful.

Sweeping her hair behind her ear, Sophia was suddenly wary. 'Can we do that another time, maybe? I really am feeling rather tired tonight.'

'Why didn't you mention that earlier?'

'Because I was feeling fine then...it's only just hit me now we've arrived home. By the way, I've really enjoyed our evening together and the lovely meal. Thank you. It was so nice to be taken out to dinner. I can't remember the last time I did such a normal thing.'

'It was my pleasure. My hope is that we'll have many more evenings like this together. Are you okay?' he asked, frowning. The wary look hadn't retreated, he saw.

'Yes, I'm fine. A good night's sleep will sort me out, I'm sure.'

'I'll walk you to your door, then.'

'There's no need...thanks all the same.'

Sophia was already taking her keys out of her purse. As she glanced up again, Jarrett saw she appeared to be thinking hard about something.

'Do you still see any of the women who kept you company when you were lonely?' she quizzed him.

He might have known she wouldn't let him off lightly. She was behaving like every other woman who had the bit between her teeth about something. But in Sophia's case her need to know about this particular facet of his past was entirely justified, he thought—because she knew only too well the pitfalls of being with someone who couldn't be relied upon except to *hurt* her.

'No, I don't. I already told you I never dated anyone for very long, but neither did I cold-heartedly desert them. When we parted it was always mutual. The kind of women I saw were usually from the corporate world, as time-poor as me because they were immersed in their careers, wanting to make a name for themselves. Having a romantic relationship was never going to be top of their list of priorities.'

There had been one liaison where the woman in question had got a little bit too attached to the idea of deepening her association with him, Jarrett recalled wincingly, but he had told her as diplomatically and as kindly as possible that he couldn't consider it. She hadn't guessed that he was holding out for the woman of his dreams, and he wondered if she would have been surprised that he secretly harboured such a romantic ideal.

'Did you ever want more than just a mutually satis-fying fling with anyone in particular?' Sophia asked, just as though she'd read his mind.

He heard the slight condemnation in her voice and flinched inwardly. 'No, I didn't,' he admitted, low-voiced. 'And I don't want you to think that's because I'm some kind of devil-may-care playboy, because I'm not. The truth is I just never met anyone I fell for in that way. But that doesn't mean I haven't had a desire to. To fall in love, I mean.' He hardly knew how he kept his hands off of her as he said this, because she was becoming more irresistible and important to him every time he saw her.

Like now, when her face was so bewitchingly il-luminated by the gentle rays of moonlight drifting in through the windscreen.

The smooth skin between her brows puckered in thought. 'I'm sure if it's meant to happen it will,' she commented, and then, leaning towards him, dropped a light kiss at the corner of his mouth.

A purely *chaste* kiss, Jarrett thought in frustration. Every masculine instinct he had clamoured for him to haul her into his arms and kiss her *properly*...to taste and ravish her mouth in the way that he yearned to do...to run his hands down over her lithe, beautiful body and build up a storm—a storm that he'd sensed had been brewing between them ever since he had first set eyes on her.

Yet he couldn't bring himself to succumb to such a raw, elemental need when the woman he desired was still wrestling with so many fears from her past. He would just have to learn to be patient.

Already out of the car, Sophia dipped her head to give him a smile. Her long hair fell softly around her face and framed it. 'If you want to drop round tomorrow some time and have coffee then I'd be glad to see you,' she said.

His relief was off the scale. For a moment there he'd worried that she might put him off indefinitely.

'What time?'

'Don't you have to work?'

'Yes, but tomorrow I'm working from home... How about eleven o'clock?'

'Eleven is fine. I'll see you then.'

Jarrett didn't respond with goodnight or goodbye. He merely gave her a brief nod. He guessed he wanted to avoid any reference to the fact that they were going to be parted—even if it *was* only until tomorrow...

* * *

A devastating nightmare had shocked Sophia awake. The icily threatening quality of the dream disorientated her, and for a moment or two she was completely unaware of where she was or even her own name.

Breathing hard, she sat up and swung her legs over the side of the bed. It jolted her to realise that she wasn't back in the expensive London house she'd once shared with Tom Abingdon, and neither was this her bed. She hardly remembered electing to sleep on Great-Aunt Mary's threadbare old couch, but now it came back to her. When she'd finally decided to turn in—just like on the previous three nights—it had hit her that she was all alone in the house *without* Charlie. It was too hard to sleep in her own bed when on the other side of the room her son's endearing little cabin-bed with its Paddington Bear quilt was empty, and above her the rest of the cavernous rooms were full of imagined ghosts that her imagination was only too eager to make real.

The fire that she'd left alight in the grate to keep her warm during the night was down to a few glowing embers, and the large stately room she'd been sleeping in was now so cold that it frosted her breath.

In the horrible nightmare that had visited her she'd been running barefoot through eerily menacing dark woods, with Tom chasing after her, threatening all kinds of dire consequences when he caught up. When the white-hot rage that he was still tormenting her had suddenly spilled over, giving Sophia the courage to turn and face him, the cruel face that had gaped back into her eyes hadn't been her deceased husband but his *father*...

A chill and queasy sensation lodged like congealed porridge in the pit of her stomach and made the inside of her mouth dry as sand. Reaching for the glass of water she'd left nearby on a table, she gulped the contents down. Before she finished the drink, the hot tears burning at the backs of her eyes were streaming in an unchecked flow down her face. She hadn't even undressed. She was still wearing the blue wraparound dress she'd worn out to dinner with Jarrett.

With stoic determination she scrubbed away the moisture streaking down her face with the heel of her hand. Just the thought of him sent a tropical heatwave sweeping through her blood and made her ache almost beyond bearing to see him again. And, for a blessed few moments even the memory of his reassuring presence drove out the cold and fear that gripped her. Simply recollecting his sculpted handsome face, haunting blue eyes and the richly sensual quality of his mesmerising voice was enough to make her yearn to have him appear. Not only was he the most attractive man she had ever seen, to Sophia's mind his best asset was his unquestioning ability to be kind. She'd seen plenty of evidence of that. Jarrett epitomised the very best of masculinity, where her deceased husband had epitomised the *worst*.

With all her heart she wished she could turn back the clock and invite him in for coffee, instead of walking into this lonely old house on her own. But her emotions had been in a distressing state of turmoil after her revelations to him about her marriage, and she'd feared she had told him too much. Confessing the details of her personal horror story had left her feeling uncomfortably exposed, and fear of Jarrett's unspoken judgement had made her want to distance herself from him for a while.

If only she hadn't succumbed to that painful impulse so quickly, she thought now. If she hadn't, he might still be here...

Jarrett had lain down on his bed fully clothed, thinking hard about the evening he'd just spent with Sophia. His mind simply refused to let him dwell on any other subject. It had done his heart good to see her tuck into her meal with such enjoyment, and he wondered how many meals she'd left uneaten or barely touched because she'd been consumed by the threat of harm her malicious ex-husband regularly seemed to have menaced her with?

His hands curled into fists down by his sides. He made himself think about something far less likely to arouse his fury. Apart from her undoubted beauty, there was so much that he admired about this lovely woman. For instance her ability to be brave in the face of the most horrendous adversity and not lose hope. Even now she was putting on a brave face, because her little son was away from home staying with his uncle and she was spending her nights at High Ridge alone.

Cursing out loud, because that particular thought was apt to inflame him and rob him of his sleep entirely, Jarrett got up, quickly shed his clothes, then got back into bed again, dragging the duvet up over his head to block out any disturbing glimpse of light. Then he turned his face into the pillow and willed sleep to rescue him from the too tempting images of Sophia that his mind seemed determined to taunt him with...

Jarrett wake up...you must wake up. I need you!

Sophia's voice—urgent and low—was right against his ear, shockingly stirring him from the deep, dreamless slumber that he'd fallen into. Immediately turning on his side towards her, Jarrett's heart hammered hard. Feeling as if he'd been cruelly cheated of the one thing that he longed for above all else when he realised the space beside him was empty, he reached towards the bedside lamp, almost knocking it over in his haste for illumination. Impatiently he switched it on. As light flooded the room, he sat up, scrubbing the sleep from his eyes with his knuckles.

The sound of her voice had been so *real*. Even more disturbing to his peace of mind was that it had sounded so frightened—*desperate*, even. Was she in trouble? *I need you*, she'd cried. Had that bastard of a father-in-law discovered her whereabouts and was right now threatening her?

Not even taking time to dwell on the sense of the action he intended, or be remotely concerned that it was the dead of night, Jarrett rushed into the dressing room adjacent to his bedroom, grabbed a pair of jeans and a sweatshirt from out of the bank of mirrored wardrobes that contained his clothes and quickly dressed. Returning to the bedroom, he pushed his feet into the pair of loafers he'd left by the bed, then grabbed the leather jacket he'd thrown onto a chair and hurriedly exited the room as though the hounds of hell themselves were snapping hungrily at his heels...

CHAPTER EIGHT

THE sudden thumping on the front door reverberated warningly through the house like the violent rumble of thunder heralding a storm. Clutching the folds of her dress anxiously to her chest, Sophia's blood turned to ice. *Who on earth would bang on her door like that in the middle of the night unless something was terribly wrong?*

Her thoughts naturally flew to her son. But surely if something untoward had happened to Charlie, her brother would have notified her with a phone call first? He wouldn't just turn up out of the blue and knock her door down! The next fear following close on the heels of the first one was that her father-in-law had found her and was waiting outside to confront her with a demand to see his grandson…to take him away from her. *What if he'd brought help with him to do just that?* She wouldn't put it past him to hire a couple of heavy-set thugs to accomplish what he was too cowardly to accomplish himself.

When she rose to her feet a surge of adrenalin pumped through her veins, rendering her almost too weak to stand. Quickly slipping her feet into the plain black leather pumps she'd worn to dinner, she stole a cursory glance at the fire now blazing brightly in the grate, thanks to the fresh ash log she'd added, and on the spur of the moment grabbed one of the heavy iron tongs in the stand beside it. Squeezing her eyes shut tight for a moment, she murmured a quick heartfelt prayer beneath her breath, then left the room to step out into the dark, cavernous hallway that led to the front door.

The porch light there had automatically come on, and she nearly fainted with fright at the sight of the tall shadow that loomed up behind the decorated glass panels.

'Sophia! Sophia, are you there? It's me, Jarrett.'

'Oh, my God.' Her reaction was as though someone had careened into her back with a battering ram. Her body felt weak and winded all at the same time.

Trembling hard, but this time with relief instead of stark cold fear, she laid the heavy iron tongs carefully down on the floor, glad to be free of their threatening weight now that she knew that she wouldn't have to employ them in self-defence. But her heart still pounded at the realisation that her night-time visitor was Jarrett... the man whose presence she'd been desperately longing for ever since she'd decided not to invite him in for coffee.

With fumbling fingers she undid the latch and the bolts at the top and bottom of the door. By the time the cool night air rushed in to greet her and she came face to face with her visitor Sophia hardly had the strength to hold herself upright. The shock she'd received at the pounding of the door had robbed her of every ounce.

'Are you okay? Tell me!'

Jarrett's face looked pale, haunted almost...as if he

too had received the most disturbing shock. The dim porch light highlighted the hard cobalt glitter of his mesmerising gaze.

Fastening his hands round her slim upper arms, he stared down into her face as if to make an urgent assessment of her state of mind. 'I heard you call out my name as if you were right there beside me. I wasn't dreaming, Sophia…your voice was as real as can be and you sounded distressed.'

'What did I say?'

'You said…you said, "I need you."'

Had her longing been so powerful that it had transcended time and space and transmitted itself straight to Jarrett?

But even before he'd confessed what he had heard Sophia had already been overwhelmed by the heat and solidity of his reassuring male body, and she couldn't help breathing out a heartfelt sigh as she gazed steadily up into his eyes. 'How strange that you heard that. It's true. I *do* need you, Jarrett. I had the most terrible nightmare. I dreamt that Tom and his father were coming after me. I haven't had a dream like that for a long time, and it was even harder to bear after such a nice evening. It really shook me up.'

Her legs buckled a little with the force of emotion that swept through her at the memory of the distressing dream and also at Jarrett's timely but altogether unexpected appearance…all because he'd had some kind of psychic intuition that she needed him.

Her handsome visitor didn't hesitate to catch her as her balance faltered, and he lifted her up high into his arms to hold her safely against his chest as though she weighed nothing. Then he carried her into the dimly lit hallway. Its scant illumination came from the warm light that drifted out through the open drawing room door at the end of it. Inside, Sophia had left one small lamp burning, and the fire she had lit to chase away the chill of her nightmare still emitted a welcoming bright blaze.

Kicking the front door shut with the heel of his boot, Jarrett made a beeline for the softly lit room. Once inside, he headed straight for the old-fashioned couch where Sophia had left her quilted eiderdown to drape over her as she slept, and dropped her carefully down onto a cushion, still cradling her in his arms.

'I'm glad you lit the fire. The warmth and light will help—especially after that nightmare,' he said with gentle authority, his fingers tenderly brushing back some long skeins of silky chestnut hair that had partially drifted over her face.

His touch was *divine*. Straight away Sophia sensed a delicious melting sensation in the nether region of her stomach. The scent from his body was sexy, warm and compelling, and the tough denim of his jeans couldn't disguise the iron hardness of his strong, muscular thighs. He'd already intimately acquainted her with how strong he was, making light work of lifting her up into his arms and carrying her, and since he'd swept her up against his chest even the icy tentacles of the dreadful nightmare that had visited her had lost most of their power to hold her in their chilling grip. Right now the only thing that was unsettling her—but in a *good* way—was Jarrett.

'I'm sorry if I frightened you, banging on your door like that, but when I thought you might be in danger I had to come to you.' The palm of his big warm hand settled against her cheek and tenderly cupped it.

'I'm glad that you did.' Her soft voice was a little breathless.

'Do you want to tell me about the dream? It can sometimes help to dispel the memory if you talk about it rather than just bottle your feelings up inside.'

'I'd rather not, if you don't mind. I'm already feeling better because you're here…honestly.'

A muscle flinched in the side of his unshaven cheek. 'I'm glad about that. I really am. But you must know that sooner or later you're going to have to confront this bully of a father-in-law of yours, or else he'll be intimidating you for the rest of your life…and maybe Charlie's too.'

'I know—and you're right.' Sophia agreed with a sigh. 'I *do* need to confront him, and to let him know that I refuse to be bullied by him any longer. God knows I spent enough miserable years being bullied by his son! The thing that worries me is that he'll bring the whole weight of the judicial system down on my head until he gets the outcome that he wants—and that's Charlie.' She laid her hand over her chest to calm her racing heart. 'If the case goes to court I can't afford a good defence lawyer, and trust me…it's going to take someone very special and clever to face the intimidating might of Sir Christopher Abingdon.'

'Christopher Abingdon?' Jarrett's blue eyes visibly widened. '*He* was your father-in-law?'

'You know him?'

He shook his head, grimacing. 'I don't know him, but I know *of* him. I've seen him on enough political talk shows to know that he's perfectly odious and reprehensible. Don't worry about affording legal fees, my angel. I happen to have a very good friend in the legal realm—a man who is particularly dedicated to stamping out injustice wherever he finds it. If he can't represent you then he'll know someone who will. We'll find you the best damn lawyer money can buy, and that's a promise. Just don't tell me that you won't accept my help. It would mean a lot to me if you let me.'

As she absorbed the passionate intent of his words she relaxed against him in the realisation that, for the first time since she'd lost her father, she felt safe and secure in the presence of a man—a man she was slowly but surely beginning to allow herself to trust. To have Jarrett's sincere regard made Sophia feel more valued than she'd felt in a long, long time. It also lifted her spirits to know that at last someone really wanted to help her.

Raising her head, she knew her smile was a little shy, but she couldn't hide how much his words had meant to her. Before she could say a word Jarrett's hand had moved round to the back of her head to bring her face closer to his. *Then his mouth covered hers.* She had already had an example of how his kiss could make her dissolve, but *this* kiss—gently coaxing at first, then inexorably gathering in heat—was so gloriously seductive that she wondered how on earth she'd lived without his touch for so long.

The sultry caress quickly turned into a helpless, hungry demand that she couldn't help but rise to. As Jarrett's tongue melded hotly with hers and the roughened prickle of the beard that studded his jaw scratched against her skin his sensual ministrations sent her spinning. Suddenly she was caught in the eye of a storm that she didn't want to escape from.

When he cupped her breast through the thin jersey of her dress and teased the already rigid nipple between finger and thumb the force of the pleasurable groan that eased huskily from her throat didn't sound like the repressed and lonely woman of her hard, embittered marriage. *It didn't sound like her at all...* And when he carefully but firmly moved her off his lap to lay her on her back next to him she had not one single thought in her head about protesting. On the contrary, she just about contained herself from ripping his jacket and shirt from off his back so keen was her desire and need for him to love her.

As if reading her mind, he kicked off his shoes, then shrugged off his jacket. In less than a heartbeat he was leaning over her, his mouth continuing its exciting barrage on her senses, mind and body with luxuriously hot and exploring kisses to die for. But then came the dizzying point when even the most combustible kisses weren't enough...

'If you want me to stop then you have to tell me now, sweetheart. Although I'm strong I'm only human— and you're driving me wild.' Lifting his head, Jarrett threaded his fingers through Sophia's hair, smiling wryly down into her eyes.

'I don't want you to stop.' Her reply was a broken whisper of long-suppressed need and remembered heartache, but she knew there was no way on God's good green earth that she wanted to put an end to what they both so urgently desired.

'That's what I'd hoped you'd say,' Jarrett murmured,

already reaching towards her to help her remove her dress.

In the flickering firelight as she lay down again, shivering in anticipation of what was to come, she was treated to a candid view of his fit male body as he disposed of his shirt. There was not one ounce of spare flesh on his hard-muscled chest with its smattering of ebony hair. And his strong arms with their silky, toned biceps were in a mouth-watering category all of their own. But her appreciative musings were instantly laid aside when he hungrily claimed her lips yet again and ran his hands lightly but expertly down over her body.

'You're so beautiful,' he murmured, his riveting blue eyes glancing passionately down into her face.

'So are you,' she answered.

'Does that mean that you now find me more appealing than when we first met?'

'I'm not going to encourage your vanity by saying anything further.'

'Good. Because I think the time for talking is past... at least for now. Don't you?'

He bent his head and put his lips to her breast. A spike of molten heat shot through her, rendering her boneless and making her tremble. The sensation was so off the scale of any barometer of pleasure she could have imagined that Sophia's eyelids drifted closed in order to deepen the deliciousness of the experience... to lose herself in a sensual world that for so long had been denied her. The moan that left her throat was soft and low, and as Jarrett's warm lips and beard-roughed jaw moved down over her heated skin, she drove her fingers through his silky cap of ebony hair.

For a moment she went rigid when his mouth dipped

lower to caress the more sensitive skin between her thighs. After his long, lazily exploring kisses, the urgency that was building inside her was at breaking point, and suddenly she couldn't wait to hold him close and feel his body moving over hers, skin to skin...

'Jarrett...' His name left her lips on a breathy sigh, and he immediately responded by lifting his head and giving her a heart-stopping smile.

'What is it, sweetheart? Tell me what you need.'

Utterly transfixed by his devastating blue-eyed stare in the firelight, for a moment Sophia couldn't think straight. *Tell me what you need...* To answer the sexily-voiced command was almost beyond her powers, so alien was the sensual request.

'I need—I need you to love me,' she breathed.

In just a couple of effortlessly fluid movements Jarrett moved up, sat back and tugged off his jeans. Before he let them fall onto the floor he extricated his wallet and a small foil packet therein.

Her cheeks burned red at the impressive sight of his aroused sex, and in her mind she immediately scolded herself. *For goodness' sake, Sophia...it's not as though you're some untried virgin!* But the thought gave her no comfort, because it made her remember that she'd given her virginity to a man who had despised her.

As if intuiting that just such a thought had stolen into her mind, her would-be lover sheathed himself with his protection and carefully straddled her, stroking back her hair as he gazed deep into her eyes. 'Don't let the past spoil this time we have together,' he urged. 'Because everything's going to be all right.'

'It is?'

Any further speech she might have been going to

utter was silenced by the warm pressure of his mouth against hers. As she lost herself in the spell of the intimate duelling of their lips and tongues his hand deftly moved to the apex of her thighs to prise them apart, and in one smooth, urgent stroke he drove himself into her.

His possession was dizzying. More than that if felt so *right*. Tears surged hotly into Sophia's eyes. When Jarrett started to move rhythmically inside her she wound her arms round his neck to invite even more of his incendiary kisses, but he glanced down at her with surprised concern when he saw the moisture that slid down her face.

'What's wrong? Am I hurting you?'

'Nothing's wrong. Everything's *perfect*, in fact... promise.'

'But—'

Now it was *her* turn to silence him with a lingering and sexy open-mouthed kiss. She sensed his pleasure straight away, because he began to move inside her with more purpose and intent, anchoring his hands round her hips and urging her to wrap her thighs round him as he rocked into her more deeply. Catching her breath, Sophia dug her nails into his back and held him to her with all her strength. Suddenly the powerful waves of pleasure that were transporting her to only one destination crested, and the resultant erotic laps of blissful heat that throbbed through her entire being made her gasp out loud.

The lovely emerald eyes that glanced up at him had never appeared more beautiful, Jarrett thought, even though it was the heart-rending glitter of tears that rendered them especially bewitching tonight. But all further thought was suspended as he sensed her muscles clasp him hotly and contract. Clasping her arms about his neck even more tightly, she murmured his name with what sounded very much like a sob.

Dear God! He could lose himself in this woman's charms for ever and not regret a single moment he spent with her whether he lived to be a hundred or died tomorrow. No other woman had made him feel this good, this glad to be a man...*ever.*

As his lover's breathy little gasps died away he could no longer keep a grip on the wild storm of need that held him in thrall, and as his desire peaked and soared beyond the point of no return his body convulsed hard. The fierce shout that left his throat was inevitable. The only sound he heard straight after that was the creak of the old couch's springs as he lay down in his lover's arms. With her gentle fingers tunnelling in and out of his hair, Sophia's warmly velvet lips pressed tenderly against his cheek.

'Are you all right?' she enquired softly.

Jarrett raised his head to examine her with a mixture of amusement and disbelief. '"All right" doesn't even begin to describe how I feel. I'm ecstatic...in heaven. Can't you tell?'

Her cheeks dimpled with pleasure. 'My great-aunt Mary would be scandalised if she knew what we had just done on her antique couch.'

'Maybe she would...maybe she wouldn't.'

Her green eyes widened in surprise, 'Are you suggesting that Great-Aunt Mary *wasn't* the terribly proper, stiff-upper-lipped lady that she presented to the world?'

Grinning, Jarrett waggled his eyebrows. 'I haven't a clue what the lady was like, but don't forget appearances can be deceptive. Don't you think it might be nice to imagine that underneath her very proper exterior she yearned to let her hair down and have a little fun? You said she lived on her own. Was she ever married?'

Thinking back over the scant history her father had told her, Sophia lightly shook her head and sighed. 'No. She stayed single all her life. My dad once told me it was because she didn't particularly like men.'

'That doesn't mean she didn't have any lovers... does it?'

'I suppose it doesn't.' She reddened a little. 'Anyway...she's gone now, and if she found some pleasure in the arms of someone, good luck to her! She's been very good to me, leaving me this incredible old house, and I'll never forget her.'

The fire spat and hissed in the grate, and the robust log that Sophia had laid at its centre cracked and settled deeper into its fiery bed. Gazing down into her flushed beautiful face, Jarrett moved, tugging the prettily patterned eiderdown over them both. Lying down again, he arranged a cushion behind his head, then put his arm protectively round her slender shoulders. As she willingly rested her head on his chest her silky hair felt like the softest down against his skin, and, his body throbbing warmly in the aftermath of their lovemaking, he marvelled at the sense of perfect rightness that rolled over him.

There was no doubt in his mind that being with Sophia was the best thing that had ever happened to him. And now that he'd made love to her Jarrett made a silent vow that if it was at all in his power he would never let any danger threaten her again. The gentle glow of the firelight and the lamp on the small mahogany side table hadn't been able to hide the fading scars he'd glimpsed here and there on her supple, slender body, and he'd had to tamp down the anger that had threatened to choke him at the sight. Men who hit women were the lowest of the low in his book.

A sense of urgency gripped him to help her deal with the despicable father-in-law who was still intimidating her and get him out of her hair for good. What he and her worthless husband had put her through was nothing less than criminal, and the remaining perpetrator shouldn't get off scot-free. *Not if Jarrett had anything to do with it.*

As Sophia settled herself more comfortably against him, she covered her mouth to suppress a yawn. 'I'm sorry,' she apologized. 'I guess my broken night's sleep has caught up with me.'

'There's no need to apologise. Why don't you just let yourself drift off? I'll stay here with you until the morning.'

'Will you really? It's not exactly the most comfortable couch in the world to sleep on.'

'I give you my word. Now try and get some sleep.'

Sophia was still sleeping when Jarrett peered out between the closed red velvet drapes at the window and saw that it was daylight. The fire in the grate had long gone out, and the temperature in the lofty room was icy enough to make him wince.

Making his way back to the couch, he carefully arranged the quilt more snugly round Sophia's pale shoulders. She stirred a little, but didn't wake. In repose, her lovely face looked peaceful and young. A faint smile raised the corners of his mouth. Rubbing his hands to warm them, he turned on his heel and moved across to the fireplace to rebuild the fire. He didn't want Sophia waking up to a cold room. After that he made his way to the kitchen.

Ten minutes later, sitting at the old-fashioned breakfast table with its dented and scratched oak surface, revived by a steaming mug of strong black coffee, he searched for his lawyer friend's phone number on his mobile and rang him. He knew for a fact he would already be at his desk. After a long, heated conversation he ended the call and got restlessly to his feet. He hadn't mentioned Christopher Abingdon's name, but it had been enough for him to tell his friend that Sophia's father-in-law was a renowned QC for him to get the bit between his teeth and promise to do all he could to help just as soon as Sophia personally instructed him to act on her behalf. The case was 'potential dynamite', he said.

Staring out of the window at the shadowy back garden, where a large portion of the light was cut off by the untamed shrubs growing wild, he was deep in thought when—still attired in the pretty blue dress of the night before and with her hair endearingly tousled—the lady herself appeared at the kitchen door tiredly rubbing her eyes.

'Good morning.'

'Morning, sleepyhead.'

'You made up the fire in the living room. Thanks for that.'

'The temperature put me in mind of Siberia when I woke up, and I didn't want you to be cold. Want some coffee? I hope you don't mind, but I made a pot.'

'Of course I don't mind.' Her smile was a little uncertain, almost as if she didn't quite know how to proceed after the passion that had erupted between them last night. After tucking some hair behind her ear, she crossed her arms over her chest as if to warm herself. 'I thought you might have had to dash off. I didn't mean to lie in so long. I'm normally up at the crack of dawn, and I'm a light sleeper. If I hear so much as a sparrow cough it wakes me up.'

Jarrett chuckled. 'I've no intention of dashing off— if that's okay with you? It's not even eight in the morning—surely you're entitled to have the odd lie-in? Especially when Charlie's staying at his uncle's.' In truth, he had plenty of work to get on with at home, but he'd already decided that it wouldn't take priority over being with Sophia today.

'I'd really like it if you stayed for a while. But I'll say no to your offer of coffee, thanks. What I'm most in need of right now is a shower and a change of clothing. No doubt you feel the same?'

'Are you suggesting that we take a shower together?' Keeping his tone teasingly light, he moved to stand in front of her. At first Sophia seemed to find it inordinately difficult to meet his glance. But then Jarrett lifted her hand and raised it slowly to his lips, leaving the warm imprint of his mouth against her fingers. His senses were already rioting at her touch and her sweetly addictive scent.

His romantic gesture brought the smile to her face that he'd hoped for. 'Maybe…maybe we could do that some other time? Right now I'd just really like to freshen up. You're welcome to jump in after me, though.'

'Fair enough…but you don't know what you're missing.' He grinned.

Sophia's emerald eyes visibly darkened. 'That's not true after last night. I don't think I'll ever forget what you did for me, Jarrett.'

'What I did *for* you?' He was puzzled.

'I mean the way you turned up in the middle of the night like that…just when I needed you.'

He suddenly realised that he was still holding her hand. He used it to impel her firmly into his arms. 'Don't you know that I needed you too, Sophia?'

The last thing he registered just before he kissed her was the gentle quiver of her lips as he lowered his head and helplessly and hungrily crushed his mouth to hers…

CHAPTER NINE

JARRETT had showered, and apart from knowing that Sophia had used the cramped cubicle before him it had not been the most salubrious experience of his life. Clearly her great-aunt had not considered a little luxury in the bathroom high on her list of priorities, and the addition of a shower stall in the Victorian bathroom looked to have been installed somewhat grudgingly.

At any rate, it had forced him to be somewhat creative with his use of the slow trickle of barely warm water that emanated from the shower head. It had taken a long time to rinse Sophia's vanilla and honey scented shampoo from his hair, so he'd simply spent the extra time recalling every sensually intimate detail of their lovemaking the night before. Maybe he should have tried harder to persuade her that they ought to shower together?

Abruptly turning off the water, he stepped out of the cubicle. Brusquely drying himself with the generous-sized white bathtowel that had been thoughtfully left folded neatly over the back of a rattan chair for his use, he scowled when he realised there was no radiator to warm it.

Other than dwelling on his sexual frustration, and

the fact that the temperature in the room was cold enough to give him hypothermia, he forced himself to think about topics less apt to make him irritable.

Examining the room, he observed the tired furnishings and fittings that predominated. The space was generous and high-ceilinged, with beautifully moulded carved cornices, but in Jarrett's opinion it cried out for the decor and fittings that would enhance the property's stately appeal. It made him eager to call an interior designer friend of his and arrange for his company to fit a completely new bathroom for Sophia and her son. One that would have all the modern day accoutrements and luxury anyone could desire but would be sensitively done to enhance the grandeur and history of this beautiful old house.

One step at a time, he told himself. Even though he genuinely had her wellbeing at heart, he had to be careful not to make assumptions about her needs.

Dressed again in the jeans and black sweatshirt he'd worn on his three a.m. dash to the house, he returned downstairs to the kitchen, quietly whistling some bars of Puccini. There was no sign of the lady of the house. Curious as to where she might be, because after her shower he'd left her in the drawing room combing out her long damp hair in front of the fire, Jarrett proceeded along the corridor outside the kitchen, knocking on doors, calling out her name and opening them if there wasn't a reply.

Right at the back of the house he heard sounds that suggested furniture being moved or rearranged. He approached the wide open door he'd seen, and came to a standstill in the doorway at the surprising sight that met his eyes. Sophia appeared to be vainly trying to shift a tall metal cabinet on her own, and the task was obviously getting the better of her. She'd tied back her newly dried chestnut hair into some kind of loose top-knot, and was clearly hot and a little bothered from her physical exertions. She impatiently blew some gently drifting strands of hair out of her eyes and cursed softly.

The picture she made was utterly endearing…sexy too. Dressed in the faded blue jeans with the ragged hole in the knee, and an old green and white checked shirt that might have been a man's, she could easily have graced any men's 'lifestyle' magazine with her arresting image.

Charmed and amused, and not a little turned-on all at the same time, Jarrett folded his arms and grinned. 'What are you doing, wrestling with that metallic monster? Moving it or beating it into submission?'

The emerald-green eyes in front of him flashed with enough electricity to start a fire. 'Very funny… Instead of making fun of me you *could* give me a hand, you know!'

'I wasn't making fun of you.' His mood immediately sobered. 'Where do you want this archaic monstrosity moved to?'

'I want to move it out into the corridor for the time being.'

'Let's do it, then.'

'I'm sorry. I'm apt to be a little tetchy in the mornings.'

'No need for an apology. What are you intending to do in here?'

'Remember I told you that I was going to create a darkroom for my photography? Well, this is going to be it. It will be such a boon to have my own instead of paying a photographic company to print my photographs for me. Once upon a time this must have been some kind of utility room, but I think my aunt must have used it as a repository for junk mostly. The great thing is it's got an old ceramic sink in it with running water, which can be my wet area for processing. But first of all I have to move all the old furniture out and clean the place up. Then I want to scrub down the walls and paint them white.'

'That's a new one on me…white for a darkroom?'

'That's right.'

Sophia dropped her hands from round the metal cabinet as Jarrett took over and carefully stood it upright again. He paused to hear what she had to say next before he transferred the furniture out into the corridor, catching the faint tantalising drift of her perfume as he did so.

'I've learned that white is the best colour for a darkroom. It helps save time trying to block out light spills.'

'Well…if you need a hand with the painting…or anything else for that matter…I'm your man.'

'Are you indeed?'

Sophia took the wind out of his sails with a teasing little smile that all but cut him off at the knees. If she thought he could stay immune to such a provocative gesture then Jarrett was sorry—but he was only human. It was tantamount to expecting bees to keep away from a dripping honeypot.

Brushing the dust from the cabinet off his hands, he caught her by the waist and impelled her firmly into his arms. The heat in him was already on simmer even before he held her. 'If I'm not already…then I want you to know that I fully intend to be.'

'You're very sure of yourself!'

'I told you before. When it comes to the things that are important to me I state what I want and go for it. It's always been a policy of mine to err on the side of confidence.'

'Well…if you're feeling so confident perhaps you'd like to cook us some breakfast? I don't know about you, but I'm starving. I have to confess that any kind of physical work never fails to stimulate my appetite.' Her lips shaped another saucily provocative grin.

Before he answered Jarrett paid her back by delivering a slow, no-holds-barred sexy kiss on her open mouth, drowning in her sweetly honeyed flavours. His passionate siege made her go limp in his arms. Satisfied he'd got the response he wanted, he made a Herculean effort to manfully resist further arousing temptation and smiled lazily down into her stunned green eyes instead.

'I'll happily cook us breakfast—but only if you promise to stay with me in the kitchen and keep me company. That way at least I can look at you from time to time. Then, after we've eaten, I'll make a start helping you with the darkroom.'

'Are you usually so amenable when a girlfriend asks you to do something?'

His hands moved from either side of her slim waist down to the trim, shapely hips encased in softly napped denim and he held them fast, rocking her even closer into his body. The intimate contact almost made him groan out loud. It was still a thrill to him that Sophia allowed him such liberties—especially when her trust in men could very easily have been rendered obsolete by her deceased husband's cruel exploits.

'So you're my girlfriend now, are you?' He almost held his breath as he waited for her reply, even though he'd kept his tone teasingly light.

In answer, Sophia endeavoured to give a nonchalant shrug, but the sparkle in her eyes betrayed her. 'I suppose I must be…since we've slept together. I'm old-fashioned like that, I'm afraid. I've never seen sex as a form of recreation. I don't think it should ever be taken lightly.'

'Well…' Bending his head, Jarrett lifted her hair to place a provocative kiss on the enticing juncture between her shoulder and neck. The combination of her silkily warm skin and her body's naturally sexy scent instantly hardened him. 'It's lucky that I have a penchant for old-fashioned girls like you, isn't it?'

Jarrett wasn't the only one finding it hard to resist temptation. A small gasp of breathily-voiced pleasure escaped Sophia's lips. 'Didn't you—didn't you say that you were working from home today?' she asked, a small frown puckering her brow.

As she met his smiling gaze her pretty face was rosily flushed, and the tantalising rise and fall of her chest beneath the checked shirt she wore illustrated that she was nowhere near as calm and unaffected as she might be endeavouring to portray.

'I did. But if the choice is between working and being with you then I'm afraid there's no contest. I'd much rather spend the day here, being your odd job man, than trying to get my head around work…that is if you have no objection?'

'That's…that's fine with me.'

'Good. So the first thing on the agenda is cooking breakfast, is it? I mean, you wouldn't like to take a little

R&R first?' His fingers were busy slipping the buttons of her shirt through their buttonholes even as he talked.

'As lovely as that sounds—*ahh*—how am I supposed to even think straight when you—when you—?' Her even white teeth clamped heavily down on her plump lower lip as Jarrett slipped the final three buttons free from their buttonholes and, curling his fingers round the two cotton sides of her shirt, opened them to reveal the prettily embroidered white bra she wore underneath. 'You don't play fair.'

Her hand clamped onto his wrist to halt his eager aim to slip her shirt off of her shoulders, and with satisfaction he sensed it tremble.

'But playing is exactly what I have in mind before I cook you the best breakfast you'll ever eat,' he told her, meaningfully lowering his voice.

'I'd love to, but—'

'I don't like the sound of *but...*'

'Jarrett...I've honestly got to crack on with this dark-room. It's important for my livelihood. Please try and understand.'

A second or two passed as he strove to get his amorous mood in check. Then he started to refasten the buttons on the shirt that he'd hoped would be just the *first* item of her clothing that he removed. 'I do understand—but can I help it if you're just too damn tempting for words?'

'That lascivious look could tempt a nun from her vows, and I'm sure you know it, but luckily for me I have a will of iron,' Sophia quipped back.

'Lucky, is it? Forgive me if I can't agree. Oh, well... I suppose I'd better try and distract myself by cooking that breakfast. At least it will keep me out of mischief for a while. But I can't promise that I won't try to get you naked later.'

When he started to move away, with a rueful smile playing about his lips, Sophia laid her hand on his arm, her expression suddenly serious. 'Jarrett? It's not that I don't want to make love with you again, because I do. Last night was—well, it was incredible. You made me feel like a woman again, instead of just an empty husk of the girl I used to be. It's just that while Charlie is away this is too good an opportunity to make some real progress with my darkroom.'

'You're right. Of course it is. With my help you can get a fair amount done, too.'

'Thanks.' She smoothed back some drifting stray hairs that had escaped from her loosely fashioned top-knot and the smile she gifted him with was intimately warm. 'I also wanted to say thank you again for coming to my rescue in the middle of the night, and for agreeing to stay here with me today.'

'It's me who should be thanking *you*.' Jarrett's response was instantaneous and heartfelt. He deplored the idea that she might have even momentarily doubted he would want to stay. Catching her hand, he turned it over in his palm, then lifted it towards him to gently touch his mouth to her softly folded fingers. 'And I'm here because I want to be, Sophia. I'd rather be here with you than anywhere else. Now, I suppose I'd better let you lead me to the kitchen before you accuse me of trying to starve you into submission.'

'I would never try to coerce you into anything you didn't want to do...by fair means or foul. If you think I would then you really need to get to know me better.' Finishing her comment with a grin, and with her hand still in his, she spun round to pull him firmly towards the door. 'But I have to tell you I'm highly intrigued to know whether you can cook half as well as you kiss, Mr Gaskill, and I'm warning you…you'd better not disappoint me!'

Jarrett had indeed cooked Sophia the best breakfast she'd ever eaten. She shouldn't have been at all surprised, because it seemed that the man could undertake any task given him and make it look like a masterclass in effortless ease. And when they'd both moved back to her great-aunt's old junk room to start work on transforming it into the darkroom she craved they'd worked alongside each other in complete harmony— moving furniture out into the hallway, briskly sweeping the stone-flagged floor clean after every item was removed.

As if by unspoken consent they kept their conversation light, with a fair amount of mutual banter. But it wasn't long before Sophia became aware that they were both trying hard to resist the powerful undercurrent of electricity that sparked between them whenever their gazes inadvertently met and held. *She felt like an excited bride-to-be on the eve of her wedding day.* And it wasn't just Jarrett's compelling dark looks or his tender lovemaking that fuelled her growing attraction towards him. His unfailing good humour was a powerful incentive too. Although sometimes she found herself holding her breath, in case his light-hearted teasing turned into a cruel or unkind barb, it never did.

It bitterly saddened her to realise yet again that the desolate and painful years with her husband had set up a belief in her to *expect* to be treated badly by a man.

Was she really going to let that soul-destroying experience dictate the pattern of the rest of her days? What effect might such a way of being have on Charlie? *It hardly bore contemplation.* No. If she wanted to change such a damaging belief then she had to be more determined to learn to trust…to anticipate love and respect instead of the hatred, mockery and deceit she'd lived with for far too long.

'Jarrett?'

'Hmm?' He was halfway across the room, moving the last item of unwanted furniture—a squat gate-legged table—out into the corridor. He set it down on the stone flags and dusted off his hands.

To Sophia's amusement she saw that he had acquired a fair amount of dust on his sculpted cheekbones, as well as in his curling ebony hair. Crossing over to him she reached up on tiptoe to plant an affectionate kiss on his mouth.

'What's that for?' The timbre of his voice was a little husky and his gaze became more intense.

'You indicated when we first met that you were rather partial to apple pie.'

'I did?'

'Yes, you did. You came up to me at the market, remember? You asked me if I wanted an extra guest for tea.'

'So I did.' His hands settled lightly either side of her hips as his beautifully carved lips quirked a smile. 'My mother always taught me that if you don't ask you don't get.'

'I thought I'd nip out to the corner shop and buy some cooking apples to make you one…as a reward for all your help. Sound good?'

'Sounds very good…except for the fact that I don't want you to go.'

'I'll only be gone about twenty minutes.'

'Trust me—it will feel like a lifetime.'

Dipping his head towards her, Jarrett delivered a melting kiss that buckled Sophia's knees the instant his lips touched hers. As his tongue dived hotly into her mouth, eliciting a helpless moan from her, it made her think about the exciting possibility of whiling away the rest of the afternoon in bed with him. The thought made her tremble. Funny how the imperative to get on with her darkroom suddenly waned in light of such a provocative alternative…

Consequently it took every ounce of will-power to extricate herself from his enticing embrace so that she could carry out her mission to bake him an apple pie. 'I won't be long,' she said, and with her heart racing she smiled cheerfully and headed for the door. 'I promise.'

Rowena Phillips—the middle-aged brunette with the rather severely pencilled-in eyebrows who ran the local corner shop—had never exhibited the least bit of friendliness towards Sophia before. In fact there were times when she'd been downright unhelpful—hostile, even. As far as Sophia knew, all she'd done to warrant such an attitude was to arrive in the village as a stranger and keep herself to herself. But now, as the door swung shut behind her with the tinkle of a melodic bell to announce her entrance, the older woman's small dark eyes widened with peculiar interest as she recognised her customer.

'Hello, dear. What can I do for you today?'

Her voice had acquired the kind of fake cheeriness

that immediately put Sophia on her guard. Her glance honed in on the basket of cooking apples in the aisle opposite the newspapers, and she helped herself to one of the brown paper bags that hung suspended from a small nail above. 'I'd just like three or four cooking apples, thanks,' she answered distractedly, wanting to pay for the fruit and get out of there as quickly as possible.

'Baking an apple pie, are we?'

'Yes, I am, as a matter of fact.'

Flustered by the unwanted attention, Sophia quickly slipped three large green apples into a paper bag and approached the counter. As the woman relieved her of the bag to weigh them on the scales, Sophia saw that she was deliberately taking her time about it. It quickly became obvious that she had something on her mind that she wanted to share.

'I see that you've become very friendly with our local landowner, Mr Gaskill,' she remarked. 'Wasn't that his Range Rover that I saw parked outside High Ridge this morning?'

For a dizzying moment Sophia was dumbstruck. Feeling her cheeks flush hotly in embarrassment, she agitatedly closed the purse she'd just taken from her jacket pocket and opened in readiness to pay for the apples. 'What possible business is it of yours or anyone else's who I'm friendly with?' she answered through numbed lips, suddenly wishing that she'd ignored the spontaneous urge to bake Jarrett an apple pie and stayed home with him instead.

'I was only being neighbourly, Ms Markham... But you keep yourself to yourself, don't you? A small village like this...well, we're apt to notice things like that.'

'That I value my privacy, you mean?'

'No. That one of our most successful local business-men is parked outside your house in the early hours of the morning.'

'I'd like to pay for the apples, if you don't mind. I'm in a hurry.'

In response Rowena Phillips curtly stated the price, holding out her hand at the same time. Sophia opened her purse and counted out the right money. Lifting up the bag of apples, she dropped them into her hessian shopping bag. Intent on leaving, she was about to turn away when the shop's presumptuous proprietor added another barbed aside.

'You *do* know that Jarrett Gaskill has always wanted to own High Ridge Hall, don't you? I heard he made several attempts to try and buy it when Miss Wingham died, but you obviously pipped him to the post.'

Inside her chest Sophia's heart was thundering so hard that she suddenly felt quite faint. She struggled to make the words teeming in her brain leave her lips. 'Exactly what are you trying to say, Mrs Phillips?'

The woman folded her fleshy arms across her tur-tleneck sweater. 'All I'm saying is that perhaps you should be wary of getting to know him, Ms Markham. A wealthy property developer might use any means possible to get the property or land that he wants... don't you think?'

'What I think is that you really should keep your nose out of other people's business.'

As she walked back down the country road to where she'd parked her car several distressing thoughts ran through Sophia's mind all at once. Jarrett had already told her that he was a rich *landowner*—but he'd said nothing about buying property, too. To learn of his interest in High Ridge had come as a great shock. The obnoxious shopkeeper had said he'd made several attempts to purchase it. Why had he never told her? Surely it was obvious that she'd be interested?

She felt sick to her stomach. She'd been utterly foolish to trust him. If only she'd stuck to her initial suspicions when they first met that it was the house that drew him and not her! What was she going to do now? As well as entrusting him with the distressing and painful details of her doomed marriage she'd also made love with him…and that had been no insignificant thing. Because during their short association she'd lost her heart to the man. *Dear God.*

She murmured ,as she turned the key in the car door with a hand that wouldn't stop shaking, and by the time she'd arrived back at the house and walked up to her front door she was so angry and fearful that she'd been duped that she left the shopping bag with the apples in on the back seat of the car along with her intention to bake a pie.

As soon as she turned her key in the lock the door was wrenched eagerly open from the inside and a smiling Jarrett—dust still evident in his curling dark hair and on his cheek—appeared in front of her. Before he uttered a single word, she passionately burst out, 'Why didn't you tell me that you'd tried to buy High Ridge?'

The words came out on a broken sob as she blindly pushed past him into the hallway.

CHAPTER TEN

'WHO have you been talking to?' Scraping his hand through his hair in bewilderment, Jarrett spun round on his heel and tore down the corridor. He caught up with Sophia just as she stepped through the drawing room door. His heart threatened to burst out of his chest as he grabbed her arm to halt her flight. 'Who told you that I wanted to buy High Ridge? I wasn't trying to keep it a secret from you, but I'd like to know who told you.'

Her expression was more distressed than he'd ever seen it.

'So it's true, then? In that case does it matter who told me?' Shaking her arm free from his hold, she stared up at him with emerald eyes that shimmered with tears. 'What I want to know is, are you here because you really like me, Jarrett, or is it merely because you hope that I'll sell High Ridge to you? I hear you made several attempts to try and buy it before I arrived. Is that also true?'

Telling himself to remain calm, and not let some interfering busybody's spin on his intentions cloud his reason, Jarrett dropped his hands to his hips and shook his head. 'I wanted to buy this place when I heard the owner had died. As someone who's always

admired beautiful architecture, I had a yen to restore
it to its former glory and perhaps one day live in it myself. But buying it ceased to be important after I met
you, Sophia. If you honestly think I'd be so conniving
that I would *pretend* to be attracted to you for the sole
purpose of getting the chance to purchase your house,
then I'm pretty devastated. If you'd rather believe some
stranger's incriminating story about me than my own
testimony I honestly don't know how we can regain the
trust that I thought we were building. I know you've
been badly hurt in the past, but I'm not a liar or a cheat
or a bully. The last thing—the *very* last thing I would
ever do is use you or abuse you. I'm shaken to my core
to think for even a second that you could believe that
I would.'

'But why didn't you tell me that you'd been interested in the house?'

'What was the point? It's *your* house…you inher-
ited it from your family. If I was so intent on persuad-
ing you to sell it to me then why would I offer to make
you a loan to help you keep it?'

Sophia hung her head for a moment, clearly busy
processing what he'd said. When she raised it again to
study him, he could see by her quivering lip and desolate gaze that she was even more distraught than before.

'You're right…it doesn't make sense. But I reacted
the way I did because it was my worst fear, you see…
that you only wanted the house and not—and not me.'

Although Jarrett ached with every fibre of his being
to take her in his arms, to hold her tight and reassure
her, he didn't. The idea came into his head that perhaps
he had pushed too hard too soon to persuade her to
enter into a relationship with him. Seeing how shaken

she was after listening to some gossip put damning beliefs about him in her head, he suddenly knew that he needed to back off a little and give her some space. Given time, would she come round to realising that he honestly *did* have her best interests at heart and would never deceive her? *He really hoped so.* He had felt sick to his stomach when she'd looked at him so accusingly just now. After spending that one incredible night with her in his arms he already knew that he would never want any other woman but *her*. But it was clear that the bird with a broken wing he'd likened her to still needed more time to heal.

'You should stop scaring yourself. Try to realise instead how much you have to offer any man, Sophia. You should also believe and trust in your ability to discern truth from lies. Does your heart tell you that I've been deceiving you?' he asked.

She shook her head, her hand rubbing away the moisture that glistened on her cheek. 'No, it doesn't. When I heard that I'm afraid I just panicked. Fear has had such a hold on me for so long that I've fallen into the habit of waiting for the other shoe to drop…for something to go wrong. I always think that if something good happens then I'll have to pay for it in some way. It's like I don't deserve it. That's all I can say in my defence, Jarrett. I'm so sorry that I was angry with you. I truly regret it.'

This time Jarrett *did* pull Sophia into his arms. As he enfolded her she shuddered and laid her head against his chest. Lifting his hand, he gently stroked his fingers up and down the back of her velvety-soft neck. 'You blame yourself too much,'

'You're probably right about that. I promise I'll try to change and be less unkind to myself…more optimistic.'

'That would be good. But don't change too much.' He slid his fingers beneath her chin so that he could gaze down into her long-lashed emerald eyes. 'There's nothing wrong with the way you are. You react the way you do sometimes because you've been hurt. It's perfectly understandable. In light of that, it makes sense that you need to give yourself some proper time to heal, to regain your self-confidence.'

With a thoughtful sigh, Jarrett drew the pad of his thumb down over her damp cheek. 'That's why I want to honour that need. You're still the only woman I want to be with, Sophia, but if our relationship is going to have a chance at all then you need time to work things out for yourself. To reach your own decisions about things without my influence. What I'm leading up to is that I suggest we have a break from seeing each other for a while.'

The shock that registered in her eyes tore at his heart, but Jarrett steeled himself against changing his mind. He was convinced this was the right thing to do. To act in any other way would be to put his own wants and needs before hers, and he'd already vowed not to do that. That was what her brutish husband had done, and he'd seen for himself the damaging effects.

Slowly but surely Sophia extricated herself from his arms. When she was satisfied that there was enough space between them, she folded her arms tightly over her chest. Her lips quivered. 'All right, then. I agree. I see where you're coming from. I didn't trust you— I'm not surprised you want a break. Maybe even a permanent one.'

'I don't want a permanent break. I'm genuinely thinking of *you*, Sophia. And while we're apart if you need me for anything—anything at all—I'm there for you. I give you my word on that.'

'Thanks.' She shrugged. Her discomfort was painful to witness.

'I mean what I say. There's just one other thing I wanted to mention.'

'What's that?'

Hearing the slight catch in her voice, Jarrett had to steel himself for a second time not to take back his suggestion. Reaching into the back pocket of his jeans, he took out a small notebook and pencil and wrote down a number, which he handed to Sophia. 'This is the number of a lawyer friend of mine. I've already spoken to him and outlined the problem you've been having with your ex father-in-law. Needless to say I've mentioned no names, but my friend was instantly interested in helping you. He's a good man, and if anyone can bring about an end to this intimidation he can. I want you to give him a ring, and I want you to do it soon. You've lived with the threat of losing Charlie for far too long.'

Examining the slip of lined paper Jarrett gave her, Sophia thought it was a wonder she could make out a letter or digit through the hot blur of tears that clouded her gaze. *Jarrett was breaking off their liaison and it was all her fault.* She'd elected to believe some stupid comments she'd heard from a mean-spirited gossip over the kindness and generosity of a man who really cared for her. How could she have been so short-sighted and stupid?

She folded the note and slipped it into the pocket

on the front of her shirt. 'I promise I'll ring,' she murmured.

'Sophia?'

'Yes?'

'Don't put off ringing him because you're worried about how much a consultation will cost. I've already arranged with my friend for him to send the bill to me. And if it transpires that you decide to sue Abingdon for damages then I'll foot the bill for that, too.'

Swallowing hard, Sophia made herself bring her glance level with Jarrett's. His blue eyes glittered like incandescent sunlight over a still lake, and she could swear she heard her heart crack. 'One day I'll pay you back for all the kindness you've shown me…that's my promise to you, Jarrett.'

'You owe me nothing.' His voice was slightly gruff, as though he was struggling with emotion.

'Let me be the judge of that, will you?' She offered him the most tenderly loving smile that she could manage. It was a poor reflection of the torrent of love and longing that poured so helplessly into her heart.

Three days after she'd tearfully said goodbye to Jarrett, Sophia found herself on a train to London. She'd taken his advice and had an appointment with his lawyer friend. Now she was intent on facing one of her worst fears—holding her ex father-in-law to account not just for his own vile intimidation of her, but his son's too.

She'd done a lot of thinking since Jarrett had suggested they take a break, and their being apart had made her realise that she didn't want the themes of regret and loss to be the pervading story of her life. Nor did she want anyone else to have power over her. So, instead of running away and hoping for the best, she would face her fears head-on instead. She refused to spend one more night in fear that Christopher Abingdon might exploit some loophole in the law to take Charlie away from her.

The buildings that housed the elite coterie of lawyers in Lincoln's Inn were grand and imposing, with a long and distinguished history, but as Sophia mounted the stone steps of one of the grandest buildings in the tranquil urban enclave she refused to be intimidated. And if she wavered for an instant all she had to do was think of her son and how he deserved a mother who was courageous, who would do anything to ensure his wellbeing now and in the future, no matter what the cost to herself.

In the opulent waiting room, with its stately antique furniture and solemn portraits of imperious-looking lawyers of bygone days, she flicked through a copy of *Tatler* magazine to while away the time. But she barely registered the glossy contents because the adrenaline pumping through her body made her impervious to anything but the all-important and possibly life-changing interview that lay ahead of her.

When Jarrett had endured his first self-inflicted separation from Sophia—after he'd wrongly mistaken her brother for her lover—he had been sullen and ill-tempered with anyone who'd happened to rub him up the wrong way. And it hadn't taken much—just a glance that lingered a little too long had been enough to ignite his temper. That was until she'd confronted him with the truth. But their being apart this time had made him turn in on himself rather than inflict his bad temper or desolate mood on anyone else.

At first he chose to bury himself in his work, but when he wasn't distracting himself with that he returned to missing Sophia unbearably, and the interminable ache in his heart grew worse. Had Charlie returned from his visit to his uncle? If he had, Jarrett hoped that his presence might help ease the pain in her eyes that he'd witnessed when he'd suggested they spend some time apart for a while. Even now he wondered how he had been strong enough to make such a suggestion. It barely consoled him that he'd done it for her own good, so that she might take the proper time out to heal.

Today, three days into their separation, he'd received a dinner invitation—or rather a *command*—from his sister Beth. Unsure whether he could face another long evening on his own, with nothing for company but his increasingly desperate desire to see Sophia, he'd reluctantly elected to go. Besides, he told himself, they hadn't spoken since she'd rung to apologise for suggesting he was getting close to Sophia purely because he wanted High Ridge. It didn't sit right with him that they hadn't properly made up yet.

'Hello, stranger!'

Beth threw her arms round Jarrett in a waft of her favourite Dior perfume, and he couldn't help but hug her back. Tonight she looked relaxed and pretty in an uncharacteristically casual ensemble of pink sweatshirt and faded blue jeans. In contrast, he still wore the Armani suit he'd donned for a board meeting in London. Not wanting to appear as uptight as he felt inside, he reached up and loosened his navy silk tie.

'Dinner's about half an hour away,' she informed him cheerily. 'Why don't you come and join me in the kitchen and we can chat as I put the finishing touches to it?'

'Okay,' he agreed, wondering why all the house lights were off apart from in the hallway and kitchen. 'Where's Paul?'

Beth rolled her eyes. 'Gone to see his mother in Exeter. He'll be gone for a few days. I'll miss him, but I actually think it's good for couples to have some time apart. It makes the heart grow fonder, as the saying goes. Anyway, I thought it would be a good opportunity for us to catch up with what's been happening.'

'Hmm…' Suddenly wary, and knowing he'd have to take a view on how much or how little to share as the evening progressed, Jarrett stood the bottle of fine red wine he'd brought on the marbled surface of the kitchen counter. 'Shall I open this?'

'Yes, please.' His sister was suddenly at his side, examining the vintage of the bottle. 'Impeccable taste, as usual. Mind if we keep it simple and eat in here?' She nodded towards the white marble island where she had set two places.

'Good idea. I'm all for keeping things simple,' he murmured, unable to keep the irony entirely out of his tone.

'Well, you pour the wine and I'll get my ingredients together for custard to go with the apple crumble. We're having beef bourguignon for the main, and I thought I'd make your favourite dessert to go with it rather than anything fancy.'

'Thanks.' He opened the wine and left it to breathe as he collected two slim-stemmed glasses from the cabinet on the other side of the room—all the while painfully remembering that Sophia never had made the apple pie she'd promised him. All because some poisonous gossipmonger had made her doubt his sincerity.

'Jarrett?' His sister was giving him one of her deeply penetrating looks that he knew prefigured an uncomfortable query into his private life.

Tensing, he kept his gaze focused on the two elegant wine glasses he'd set down side by side on the counter. 'Yes?'

'You seem a little subdued this evening. Is everything all right? I mean, there aren't any hard feelings about what I said at the party?'

'You mean about my reason for getting to know Sophia?'

'Yes. You are still friends with her, I take it?'

'Yes. We're still friends.'

The heavy sigh Beth released made Jarrett immediately lock his reluctant gaze with hers. 'I'm getting the distinct feeling you want to be more than just friends with her. Am I right?' she gently quizzed him. 'You *can* talk to me about it, you know. Contrary to what you might believe, I can be discreet.'

'I'd like to believe that—I really would—but having recently experienced the damaging effects of idle gossip I'm not in a hurry to share my thoughts or feelings with anyone...even *you*.' Suddenly restless, he waved his hand towards the bottle atop the marble counter. 'Shall I pour us a glass of wine?' he suggested.

'Sure.'

Her expression thoughtful, his sister moved back to the oven to check on the progress of the fragrant apple crumble she was baking. When she'd completed the task, she turned back to him with a frown, her blue eyes clearly reflecting both regret and concern about what he'd just shared. Having poured the wine, he handed her a glass.

'Thanks. Look, Jarrett, I'm so sorry about how I behaved when Sophia was here. I don't know what got into me. My only defence is that—as is my habit—I wanted to protect you. I know you're all grown up now, and you've achieved the kind of success that our parents probably dreamed of for us both when we were kids, but you're a rich, good-looking guy and I'm sorry to say that there are plenty of unscrupulous women out there who wouldn't hesitate to take advantage of you.'

'Weren't you suggesting that *I* was the unscrupulous one—trying to get to know her in order to persuade her to sell the house?'

'Yes, but that was before—'

In no mood to be either diplomatic or polite, Jarrett exploded. 'Before *what*? For your information Sophia Markham is a million miles away from the kind of woman you think she is. If you knew what she'd survived then you wouldn't be so quick to imagine that she's some kind of mercenary man-eater!'

Dragging his fingers impatiently through his hair, he strode across the room and back again in a bid to try and dispel the red mist of fury that had stealthily crept up on him. When he returned to stand in front of his sister once more, much to his indignation he saw that she hadn't taken his outburst at all seriously—instead, she was smiling...*smiling*, for goodness' sake!

'You're in love with her, aren't you?' she commented in wonder. 'That's what I was going to say to you... that I realised you didn't just want to get to know her to purchase the house. The real reason was because you'd fallen in love.'

Jarrett stared at her in open-mouthed surprise. Then he clamped his teeth together and made a dismissive jerk of his head. *But there was no point in denying it.* He knew that there were times when he could be obtuse, but this wasn't one of them. All Beth had done was put a name to the alternately painful and exhilarating intensity of the feelings he had for Sophia. But somehow to hear it declared out loud like that made it all the more real and incontrovertible.

'Yes, I am…' Now it was his turn to express his wonder.

Immediately closing the gap between them, Beth flung her arms around him for the second time that evening. 'I'm so happy for you. Honestly I am. Have you told her? Does she feel the same? If she doesn't then I want to know why!'

Lightly fastening his hands round her slim upper arms, he gave her a rueful smile. 'The answer to whether she feels the same is I don't know. But I do know that she's the only woman I've ever loved—and the only woman I ever *will* love.'

'And have you told her that?'

He sighed. 'We're taking a break from seeing each other at the moment.'

'You are?'

'She has some things she needs to deal with…baggage from the past that still haunts her—' He broke off from what he'd been going to say to take in a deep steadying breath. 'She's had the most horrendous time of it. That's all I'll say. I wanted to give her the time and space to take stock and find a way to put it behind her so that she can truly move on.'

'So you were the one that suggested you have a break?'

Doubt and guilt suddenly pulsed through him. 'Yes.'

'She must have been dreadfully upset if she cares about you as much as you do about her. It's my experience that most women want love and support when they're going through a hard time...not space,' Beth remarked astutely.

Dropping his hands from round her arms, Jarrett irritably spun away. 'You really know how to kick a guy when he's down, don't you?'

'I'm not trying to make you feel bad. I was only expressing an opinion.' Folding her arms, she nibbled thoughtfully at her full lower lip. 'And it doesn't mean that I'm right. Maybe Sophia *does* need a break to sort things out in her head. I don't know her well enough to comment.'

Impatiently rubbing his hand round his jaw, he sensed his heart constrict with sudden dread. 'What if she doesn't?' He frowned. 'What if she did prefer that I stay with her and show her how much I care instead of suggesting we take a break from seeing each other? What if I've done the completely wrong thing?'

'Go to her,' Beth advised gently. 'Go to her and tell her exactly what you've just told me...that you love her and want to be with her come what may. I guarantee she won't ask you to leave.'

'You can go in now,' the receptionist advised Sophia.

She rose from her seat in such haste that the glossy

copy of *Tatler* slithered off her lap and fell to the floor. Flustered, with her heart throbbing like a drum, she quickly retrieved it and returned it to the polished table in the centre of the room. As she walked through the brass-handled mahogany door the receptionist held open for her she made sure she inhaled a good lungful of air to bolster her courage.

The man she'd come to see was standing with his back to her by the huge plate-glass window. Its only adornment was the plain net curtain that allowed a good portion of very welcome light to flood into what was otherwise a quite sombre room. Attired in an immaculate charcoal-grey pinstriped suit, he cut a tall, imposing figure. When he turned round to focus his hard berry-brown eyes on her Sophia's legs buckled a little… but *only* a little. His long face was much more lined and careworn than she remembered, she observed, and his mouth still curved down at the edges, denoting that he rarely ever smiled.

Lifting her chin, she met his forbiddingly stern countenance with an equally unwavering stare of her own. 'Hello, Sir Christopher,' she said coolly.

'You've led me a merry dance, young lady. I've scoured the country looking for you,' he answered irritably. 'You weren't using either your married or your maiden name according to my sources.' Nodding curtly towards the leather-backed chair in front of the desk he scowled. 'You had better sit down. I want to make sure you're listening very carefully when I say what I have to say.'

'What you have to say is neither here nor there. I haven't come to hear one of your lectures on my conduct, and neither have I come to hear you set down terms for our future association. As far as me and my son are concerned, there *isn't* going to be one.'

'You can't keep me from seeing my grandson. If this is how you intend on proceeding then I will issue a court order immediately for his custody.'

'No, you won't.' Sophia's voice was almost chillingly calm. Coolly she brushed away a piece of lint that clung to her jacket sleeve. 'You won't do that, Sir Christopher, because if you do my lawyer will slap a writ on you for substantial damages on my behalf. Not only that, but tomorrow morning you'll find a very interesting and revealing article about you and your despicable son in your copy of *The Times*.'

'You're bluffing. You can't afford a lawyer. My son left you with—'

'Nothing?' Sophia suggested helpfully. 'You're absolutely right, of course. And *why* did he leave his widow and his son with nothing? I'll remind you. He left us destitute because he spent every penny that came his way on drink, drugs and any other seedy pursuit you care to mention. I even had to sell our home so that I could pay off the horrendous debts he'd accumulated. And of course that played right into your hands, didn't it? You didn't step in and offer to help pay his debts yourself, did you? Oh, no. Instead you arrogantly insisted that Charlie and I come and live with you, so that you could maintain control over us both. Do you know what, Sir Christopher? I'd rather drill nails in my knees and crawl along the ground in agony for the rest of my life than ever contemplate such a repellent thing! Your precious son was a vain, cruel man, who made my life hell from the moment he married me, and it's hardly a surprise when he had the example of such a man as yourself as his father.'

The barrister in front of her looked visibly shocked. His pale cheeks had turned quite florid and the veins in his temple throbbed warningly. Still standing, Sophia clenched her fists down by her sides so that her nails bit into her palms and refused to allow herself to be remotely intimidated.

'And if I *do* decide to press charges,' she continued, 'I have to tell you that I've kept the vile letters you wrote me when you were still my father-in-law, warning me that if I ever told anyone what your dear son was putting me and Charlie through the consequences would be *dire* indeed. I would guess that they would be evidence enough for me to bring a very strong case, wouldn't you? My lawyer thinks so. In fact, he can't wait for me to give him the go-ahead so that he can start proceedings against you.'

'Who *is* this damned lawyer you say you've hired? Give me his name.'

'I don't need to give you his name. At least not until I instruct him to bring a case. Suffice to say he's got an impressive record in dealing with similar cases of marital abuse from the wives of men in the public eye.'

'You damn little bitch!'

The man behind the desk was shaking so hard with fury that spittle flew out of his mouth along with the insult. Sophia did flinch then—but only because she was disgusted. 'You can call me any names you like, Sir Christopher, but frankly I'm immune to them. I'm standing up for myself after five sickening years of un-believable cruelty meted out by you and your son. If you want to maintain the esteemed reputation you're

so proud of, I suggest you think carefully about what
you're going to do. When I leave here it will be to
visit the office of my lawyer. Whether I instruct him
to prosecute you or not depends on your signature to
the agreement I've had him draw up for me. The first
thing I want you to agree is that you will never make
any attempt, either now or in the future, to take Charlie
away from me, or to interfere in his life or mine. If he
chooses to see you when he's grown up, then that will
be up to him. Do you want to read the document, or do
I simply tell my lawyer to go ahead and press charges?'

In answer the barrister took the perfectly ironed
handkerchief from his pocket and mopped the beads
of sweat gathering on his face. He slumped down into
his throne-like chair behind the desk with a defeated
sigh the like of which Sophia had never heard him emit
before in the entire time she'd known him.

CHAPTER ELEVEN

THE apple pie she'd made sat cooling on the sill by the open kitchen window. A tantalising breeze stirred outside, reminding her that it was late spring and soon the longer days would come. But tonight even the dark of the evening seemed kind.

Sophia hugged herself. It had been many years since she'd felt content enough to contemplate nature without fear tainting her musings. Her daily life had been full of such unbearable hardships and challenges she hadn't allowed herself much time for hopes and dreams. It had been too bitter to think that they would never come true.

But today, after her late husband's father had signed the agreement she'd given him, Sophia was free. Free at last from the chains of a destructive relationship that had imprisoned her mind, body and spirit for too long. At last she could make plans for her and her son's future. Not only that, she could restore High Ridge Hall to the beauty it deserved—because Sir Christopher had made out a substantial cheque for damages to her and, as he'd gruffly added, 'So that my grandson can be taken care of in the manner in which he deserves.' It was probably the closest thing to an apology she would ever receive from that hard-hearted man.

Yet she wasn't quite as happy as she yearned to be.

It had only been three days since she'd seen Jarrett, but each day had felt more like a year without sight of his handsome face, twinkling blue eyes and the sound of his resonant deep voice. Just how long did he intend them to be apart? Had these past three days helped him conclude that because of her damaged past she just wasn't worth the stress and strain that a relationship with her might entail?

Not wanting to dwell on too many negatives, Sophia restlessly got up from her place by the table where she'd been sitting sipping her tea to move across to the open window and take a breath of the soft night air. Once there, she paused to admire the tantalisingly aromatic apple pie she'd made, with its perfect golden crust and delicate decoration of leaf-shaped pastry. Her sole reason for making it was so that she could take it over to Jarrett and ask him to reconsider his suggestion about them taking a break. She was also eager to share the good news of her triumph today.

But, glancing over at the kitchen clock, she saw that it was nearing nine in the evening. What if she'd left it too late for visiting or he wasn't there? What if he was out for the evening or still at his office? Even waiting until tomorrow for the chance to see him again was too much to be endured...

The harsh sound of the door-knocker suddenly filled the air, piercing her reflections. Scarcely pausing to think, she flew down the corridor, praying hard that by some miracle the caller was Jarrett.

To her joy...*it was.* He was wearing a black cashmere

coat over his stylish suit, and the spicy scent of his cologne mingled with the mild night air made Sophia's tummy flip. He looked simply wonderful.

Her first instinct was to immediately throw her arms around him so that she could feel the reassuring strength of his body against hers. She'd so yearned for the opportunity to do that again. But just then she saw what she thought was a flicker of doubt and maybe even reticence in his deep blue eyes, and she froze. In that interminably frightening moment Sophia wondered if he'd come to tell her that he was breaking their association off for good.

'Hi.' Her greeting was helplessly uncertain.

'Hi, yourself.' In the fading evening light Jarrett's unreserved smile was like the sun coming out. 'I know I suggested we should spend some time apart, but I'm afraid I've come to tell you that I just can't keep to my part of the agreement after all.'

'You can't?' She desperately wanted to smile back at him, but it was hard to control the quiver in her lips. 'Why not?'

'Why not?' he echoed, ruefully shaking his head. 'Perhaps you'd better invite me in first so I can tell you.'

'Okay. Please come in, Mr Gaskill.'

'It will be my pleasure, Ms Markham.'

'Will you come into the kitchen with me first? I have a surprise waiting for you...*two*, in actual fact.' Confident now that she had nothing to fear, Sophia caught Jarrett's hand as she slammed the door shut behind them and guided him into the long dim hallway. The firmness of his grip as he curled his fingers round hers thrilled her right down to the marrow. 'Shut your eyes and don't peep,' she playfully instructed him as they stood on the threshold of the kitchen rendered cosily warm from her baking.

Jarrett obediently closed his eyes. 'Has Charlie come back home?'

'He's coming home tomorrow afternoon. Did you think that was the surprise?'

'I did,' he admitted. 'I've missed not seeing the little man.'

'You have?' Sophia could have kissed him for that.

'Yes, I have. Now, just how long do you intend to keep me in suspense before you give me my surprise? There's a seriously tantalising aroma in here, and it's making my mouth water.'

Retrieving the pie in its still warm dish from the windowsill, she set it carefully down on the table in front of him. 'You can open your eyes now.'

He gave a throaty chuckle when he saw the pie. 'You made this for me?'

Sophia's cheeks flushed with pleasure. 'I promised that I would—remember?'

He didn't reply straight away. Instead he slipped off his cashmere coat and laid it over the back of a ladder-backed chair. Then he turned round to her and circled her tiny waist with his big hands to impel her gently but firmly against him. 'Want to hear why I couldn't keep to my part of the deal?' he challenged.

With her heart thudding hard inside her chest, her glance locked joyfully with his, she answered softly, 'Yes, I do'

'I couldn't stay away because I love you, Sophia. I love you with everything in me that's good and noble and honourable, and I want to spend the rest of my life showing you just how much I adore you. I know that you probably need plenty of time and space to heal the pain of your past but I was hoping I could help you by being the one you turn to when things get rough. I don't want you to have to cope with your troubles on your own. I'll always do whatever I can to make your path a little easier, I promise.'

It wasn't easy to form a reply because her heart was full to overflowing with a great swell of love for him. In her wildest dreams Sophia had never imagined a man would ever say such wonderful things to her—and mean them. But she only had to see the truth and concern in Jarrett's eyes to know that his declaration was utterly genuine.

'I guarded my heart against you, you know,' she admitted softly, laying her hand over the lapel of his fine wool jacket and sensing the heat from his body that permeated it. 'But somehow…somehow you managed to storm all my defences and reach me. I think I'll spend the rest of my life being glad that you did. These past three days without you have felt like a prison sentence. Just in case you haven't already realised…I love you too.'

She heard the sharp intake of breath he emitted before he lowered his head and kissed her. His warm lips moved over hers with a kind of savage hunger that electrified her, and she responded with an equally voracious desire, her hands moving urgently over his hard male form as if she wanted to climb right inside him. It made her realise that the youthful fascination she'd once had for her husband was nothing but a short sharp breeze when compared to this urgent, quiet storm that tore through her whenever Jarrett was near.

Tearing at the buttons on his shirt to free them, she

moved her hand inside the material so that she could feel the throb of his heartbeat and the warmth of his skin, even as he made a similar move and palmed her breast through her sweater. She released a ragged moan when his fingers teased and then pinched her nipple, a spear of scalding erotic heat flashing right through her core.

It became quickly evident that their urgent fumbling was not enough for either of them, but it was Jarrett who articulated his frustration first.

'We need a bed.' Breathing hard, he grinned as his gaze lit on her animated flushed face. 'I adore you, my angel, and will always treat you with the utmost respect, but that doesn't mean that I don't lust after you like crazy. Any time that I don't have you in my arms… in my *bed*…is wasted time as far as I'm concerned.'

'Well…' Sophia dimpled as she lovingly touched her hand to his cheek. 'Will *my* bed do for now, do you think?'

'That answer is music to my ears. But first I have a question to ask you.'

'Oh?' Already weak with anticipation of making love with him again, she tried hard to stem her impatience to head straight for the bedroom. 'What's that?'

'Will you marry me?'

'Are you serious, Jarrett?' The question drove away every other thought in her head. Now she wasn't just weak, she was breathless too.

'Haven't I just told you that I want to spend the rest of my life showing you how much I adore you? It stands to reason that I want to marry you, doesn't it? Besides, I need a good woman like you to make an honest man out of me.'

'You *are* an honest man—a good man I can trust…
and they're two of the qualities I love about you the
most.'

Beneath his lightly tanned skin he flushed a little.
'Thank you.'

'But marriage is a big step, Jarrett. Are you really
sure you want to take it? And don't forget you'd be taking Charlie on as well as me.'

'It *is* a big step, my darling, and one I never contemplated until I met you. But now that I'm head over
heels in love with you nothing else will do. And as
for becoming stepfather to your fine little son…I'd be
honoured.'

'That's a good answer. Go to the top of the class.'
Sophia grinned. 'So your bachelor days will be well
and truly over if we marry?'

'And I thank heaven for that. Haven't you guessed
that you're the woman I've been waiting for most of
my life? One look into those incredible eyes of yours
and I was smitten. I can remember leaving you by the
brook with Charlie in your arms, somehow knowing
that my life would never be the same. Now, for God's
sake, put me out of my misery and give me your answer,' he pleaded, and this time there was a real flicker
of doubt in his eyes.

Not wanting him to suffer unnecessarily, Sophia
stood up on tiptoe and planted a loving, lingering kiss
on his lips. 'My answer is yes, Jarrett. I *will* marry you.
I'm sure there are plenty of people who would probably advise me to take longer to think about it after my
first marriage—but I honestly don't think I have anything to fear this time round. I feel absolutely certain

that I'm meant to be with you, and I'd be honoured to be your wife.'

Cupping her jaw, Jarrett moved the pad of his thumb across her naked mouth to tenderly trace her lips. 'That's settled, then.'

It was the most understated yet most profound response Sophia could have wished for, because she easily detected the catch in his voice that told her just how much her agreement meant to him.

'Remember I told you that I had two surprises?' she reminded him, suddenly anxious to share the immensity and importance of her trip to London earlier that day. 'Do you want me to tell you about the second one?'

Gently, she extricated herself from his warm embrace so that she could think straight and breathe more easily. She was apt to feel too intoxicated to do either with ease when she was in his arms.

'Go on.' He was shrugging off his suit jacket as he spoke and, briefly turning to the chair where he'd left his coat, he hooked the jacket over a corner. Then he removed his tie.

Sophia's mouth went dry. The collar and a good part of the top of his shirt were already partially undone where she'd torn at the buttons, giving her a tantalising glimpse of the fine curling dark hairs on his chest, and as he stripped away the corporate persona he wore for work he looked very warrior-like, she thought—like a seasoned campaigner home from the wars whose most urgent need was to bed his woman and bed her *soon*.

Heat suffusing her, she let her tongue nervously moisten her lips. 'I took your advice and rang that lawyer friend of yours,' she declared, her words spilling out in an anxious rush.

When Jarrett received this information in silence, standing perfectly still as if his every sense was on high alert, she breathed in deeply before continuing.

'He more or less told me to come and see him straight away. He postponed a couple of other appointments, because he knew that you'd asked him for help on my behalf.' Tendering a lopsided smile, she carried on. 'So I went up to London, and when I gave him a full account of my story he was really helpful and supportive...just like you said he'd be. He told me I had a practically cast-iron case against Sir Christopher. I was overwhelmed that he believed me and didn't suggest I was making it up. I suppose I'd worried about that. Anyhow, before I made any decision to prosecute I rang Sir Christopher's office and arranged to see him too.'

Jarrett frowned deeply, as if expecting to hear the worst, but nevertheless he held his tongue and remained silent.

'You would have been proud of me. For the first time in all the years that I've known him I stood up to him and refused to be intimidated or made to feel small. He didn't expect that. I think he thought that I'd come to him hoping for a hand-out and to admit that I had been wrong to run away. I can't tell you how incredible it made me feel to disappoint him. But the most empowering thing of all was being able to say at last exactly how I felt about his son's mistreatment of me as well as his own. I told him that if he didn't stop harassing me and threatening to take Charlie away then I'd give a statement to *The Times* exposing his family's cruelty. He was shocked that I'd even *dared* to threaten such a thing. Bullies never expect their prey to fight back, do they? I could see that he was seriously rattled…*scared*, even. In that moment it was as though a cold heavy stone had been rolled away from inside my heart and I was free to be myself again…to stand up for my rights and fear no one.'

'That was a truly brave thing you did, confronting him like that. And I *am* proud of you, Sophia…immensely proud. So what happened after you threatened him with taking your story to the newspapers?'

Sophia's smile was wide. 'He signed the agreement that your lawyer friend helped me compose, stating that he wasn't to pursue any association with me or Charlie ever again. At the end of the day an egotistical man like him was never going to risk his reputation or have a bad word said in public about his son…even though he was such a bastard. Everything was conducted in a professional manner, and his signature was witnessed and countersigned by a solicitor who practises in an office down the hall. When the man was curious as to the content of the document Sir Christopher brushed him off, telling him it was just a "small' family matter" that he needed to attend to. I have a copy of the agreement for myself, and I took a second one back to your lawyer friend for him to keep in his records before I came home.'

'That was a good move.'

'Thank you so much for speaking to him about me. I felt much more secure talking to someone that you personally know and recommended.'

'It was my pleasure to help you, sweetheart, and you don't need to thank me.'

'Oh, but I do! In the short time that I've known you you've done so much for me, Jarrett, and I want you to know that I appreciate it and take nothing for granted.'

'Do you think Charlie will ever want to see his grandfather again?'

She shrugged. 'If he wants to make contact when he's grown up, then that will be entirely down to him. Anyway, the meeting ended with him writing me a substantial cheque for damages... Hush money, I think they call it in the movies. Anyway, the amount was more or less what I sold my house for to meet Tom's debts. And to be honest—without taking him to court—it was a bonus I didn't expect.'

'A bonus, you call it?' Jarrett scowled fiercely. 'It was the least he could bloody well do after the hell he and his son put you through!'

'But *he's* the one in hell now, when you think about it. Not only has he lost his only son, but his grandson too. I'm sure as he gets older—especially if he continues living alone—he'll reflect more and more on both losses and bitterly regret it. I genuinely feel sorry for him.'

'You are one in a million—you know that?' Wrapping his arms around her, Jarrett gazed tenderly down into her eyes. 'I don't think there are many people that would be so quick to feel pity for someone who'd mistreated them as badly as you've been mistreated.'

'I can feel pity for him because he's now firmly in my past and no longer features in my present. The same goes for Tom.' Anchoring her arms more firmly round his waist, Sophia breathed out a contented sigh.

'So, after your hard-won triumph, you're in the mood to celebrate, I take it?'

'Yes, I am. I tell you what—I'll make us a nice cup of tea and cut us both a slice of that pie I made you.

How about that?' she replied, pretending she didn't understand the hopeful and lascivious glint in his eye.

'Tempting as it sounds...that's *not* how I want to help you celebrate.' Without further preamble, Jarrett tipped her up into his arms, and he did indeed put her in mind of a warrior again, with the fiercely purposeful expression he wore on his handsome sculpted face. 'I have something much more satisfying in mind than apple pie...delicious as I'm sure it undoubtedly is.'

'Are you perhaps suggesting that I show you where my bed is located?'

'Your ability to read minds is seriously impressive, Ms Markham,' he said wryly. And without further ado he followed Sophia's happily voiced directions to her bedroom along the hall...

Jarrett propped himself up on his elbow to study his lover's gently slumbering form. In the soft glow of the lamp he saw that one slender arm was flung out over the rumpled red and cream quilt, and her long chestnut hair flowed unhindered down her back like a rippling fire-lit river.

Freed from the dark history that had entrapped her spirit for so long, she'd lost any inhibitions she might have had to fully express her desire, and their passionate lovemaking on this night would be an experience he would never forget. Even now, when a good hour had passed since their rapturous union, his body still throbbed. He just about suppressed a groan at the memory. Never in his thirty-six years had Jarrett guessed or even *imagined* that loving a woman with all his heart could be so ecstatic...could bring him more joy and satisfaction than anything he'd ever experienced before.

More wondrous still was the pride and delight he felt that Sophia had agreed to become his wife.

He was so grateful to his sister that she'd urged him to go to her tonight. There was no doubt in his mind that she would be over the moon at the outcome.

Having spent a long time privately yearning to experience the sense of truly coming home to a woman who loved him as deeply as he loved her, now that he'd incredibly got what he'd wished for he vowed passionately to himself that he would guard and protect Sophia with his life. And at the same time he would always give her the freedom and encouragement to do whatever made her happy.

His musings turned to her son Charlie. A thrill of pride shot through him when he thought about becoming his stepfather. After the boy's natural father had mentally abused him, and let him down so badly, Jarrett would make it his mission to help replace his hurtful memories of the past with much more loving and positive ones. He would show him what a difference it could make to his life to have a man who really cared about him and his mother as his parent.

Stirring, Sophia turned onto her back, blinking up at him with quizzical green eyes. 'Can't you sleep?'

'Not really.'

'Why?' She was immediately concerned.

'I'm just too happy to go to sleep, I guess. I was just sitting here admiring you, and thinking that I've never seen you look so relaxed and at peace.' Lifting her hand, he tenderly pressed his lips to the centre of her palm. Coming into contact with her matchless silken skin again, he sensed the blood in his veins quicken and heat.

Her lips split into a grin. 'Well, I've honestly never *felt* this relaxed or at peace before...I suppose that's why. Plus I'm basking in the glow of our wild and passionate lovemaking, don't you know?'

Turning towards him, she trailed her fingers down over his bare chest, letting them glance provocatively against the skin an inch or two below his belly button.

Jarrett sensed himself instantly harden. 'You're playing with fire, woman,' he growled, then threw back the rumpled quilt and straddled her.

Her teasing grin instantly vanished. Instead her glance became much more focused, and her pupils turned inky jet with desire.

'And things are about to get even hotter,' he told her huskily, 'because that was only the warm-up.'

'Really?'

'Yes...*really*.' He entered her with one smooth powerful stroke, and was gratified to hear her whimper of pleasure.

After that, Jarrett had no further need or desire to talk any further...

EPILOGUE

One year later...

IT HAD been a long time since the gardens at High Ridge
had appeared so beautiful. It had been hard work restoring it, but surveying it today, in the bright sunshine,
Sophia thought it had been more than worth every bit of
toil and sweat she and Jarrett had expended. Believing
that it was important for a sense of pride and achievement to have a personal input into the restoration of the
gardens and the house, and not just hire professionals
to come in and do the job, together she and Jarrett had
tended to the myriad of plants and flowers with every
spare moment they had, as well as implementing the
ongoing work on the major restoration of both the interior and exterior of the house.

Along with the very professional darkroom she'd
dreamed of, so far they had a bathroom and spa to die
for, newly designed bedrooms, and a drawing room
with several seriously comfortable and beautiful sofas
and armchairs. And having developed a sentimental
fondness for her great aunt Mary's rickety old couch,
after initially storing it in one of the unused bedrooms

Sophia had recently had it despatched to a professional upholsterer's where it was being restored.

Since they had married last year, and Jarrett had moved in with her, they had both become keen to transform the genteel old house into their own vision of a beautiful family home they could be proud of. But even with that aim firmly in mind they both knew what the most important values that made a real home were *love and family*. And today they had invited their friends and family to help them celebrate not only their first wedding anniversary and the restoration of the gardens but the news that they were most excited about of all…that she and Jarrett were expecting their first child together.

'One fresh apple juice, made with apples from our very own orchard, for the ravishingly beautiful Mrs Gaskill!'

Sophia called a halt to her surveying of the gardens from the newly installed drawing room patio with a start, and spun round to find her husband, casually attired in jeans and a black roll-necked sweater and looking more handsome than ever, theatrically brandishing an antique silver salver with a single glass of juice on it.

'Now, that's what I call service,' she said, smiling and lifted it off the tray.

'I aim to please,' he replied with a wink, setting down the salver on a side table and returning to lightly lay his hands either side of her waist. 'By the way, I love what you're wearing today.'

She had on a vintage white dress, and had teamed it with a pretty daffodil-yellow ribbed cardigan. She had to admit she did indeed feel pretty in the outfit. Perhaps it was because of the news she was all but bursting to share with their family and friends? It didn't matter.

All Sophia knew was that she was happier than she'd ever been in her life. The harsh life that she'd led with Tom Abingdon no longer haunted her as much as it had used to. Her only sadness was that her dad couldn't be there to witness her joy.

'You always know just what to say to make me feel good,' she remarked, and received a long, lingering kiss from Jarrett in return.

'If I do,' he replied, lifting his head, 'it's only because when I look at you I can't help but speak from the heart.'

'Well, you look pretty good yourself, if you don't mind my saying so. I really like you in that black sweater. Makes you look vaguely mysterious...sexy too. Your sister hasn't invited any of her predatory friends to our little party, has she?'

'She wouldn't dare. In any case, even if she has I wouldn't notice them. Not when I'm married to the loveliest and most alluring woman in the world.'

Sophia emitted a soft groan. 'Stop saying such provocative things or I'll be waiting for everyone to go just so that we can get to bed.'

Her husband grinned with pleasure. 'Once Charlie's asleep—going by our record so far—that will be our first destination anyway. Are you looking forward to seeing your brother and his troupe today?'

'Very much so!'

'Do you think he'll be pleased about the baby?'

'Of course he will, my darling. He'll be overjoyed. How many times has he told us that we ought to have a brood of kids? Five or six at the very least! Talking of kids...do you know where Charlie is? I left him in the kitchen eating chocolate ice cream just ten minutes ago, and I'll probably have to get him to change his shirt and jeans before our visitors get here because no doubt they're covered in the stuff by now.'

'He wasn't in the kitchen when I poured your drink a minute ago.'

'Then where is—?'

Before Sophia had finished speaking the boy in question tore into the room and out onto the patio, pursued by the rapidly growing light cream Labrador puppy that Jarrett had adopted for him on the day they'd got married. Right now, both boy and dog wore the evidence of the chocolate ice-cream on their faces and on their bodies—and in Charlie's case all over his previously clean white shirt and jeans.

'What on earth—?'

'Sorry, Mum, but Sam wanted to share my ice cream and I wanted him to have some. I couldn't be mean and not give him any, could I?' Spinning round, her small son gazed hopefully up at Jarrett, as if searching for an ally. 'I'm right, Dad, aren't I?'

Jarrett's colour visibly rose beneath his cleanly shaved jaw and Sophia's heart turned over, because she knew how much it meant to him to hear Charlie refer to him as 'Dad'. She almost held her breath as she waited for him to respond.

'Yes, son…you are right. I agree,' he answered, and when his eyes next met hers they had never seemed more crystal blue…like the finest-cut diamonds glinting in the sun.

Her heart swelled with love and pride for the two men that meant the most to her in the world…

* * * * *

THE LOST WIFE

CHAPTER ONE

SHE ran to the window when she heard the muffled engine sound of the car coming up the drive. When it pulled up in front of the cottage, the smart silver-grey SUV that belonged to her ex-husband looked like a snowmobile, blanketed in several layers of thick white frosting. And still the crystalline flakes fell relentlessly from the sky, as if poured through some divine sieve.

The snowy display hadn't let up all day. Ailsa would have succumbed to the magic of it if she hadn't been so concerned about Jake returning their daughter safely home. Living in an English country idyll had lots to commend it, but when severe winter weather kicked in the hilly narrow roads could be utterly treacherous. She stood waiting with the front door open as the driver of the vehicle stepped out and walked across the snow-laden path towards her.

It wasn't Alain—the slim, smart-suited chauffeur she'd been expecting. Usually it was Jake's French driver that brought Saskia home from her fortnightly trips to London to visit her father, or from the airport when Jake was working in Copenhagen and she stayed with him there. When Ailsa saw the once familiar diamond-chipped blue eyes staring back at her through the relentlessly falling snow, her heart stalled.

'Hi,' he said.

She hadn't seen her ex-husband face to face in a long
time…not since his chauffeur had become a reliable go-
between. The impact of confronting those carved, unfor-
gettable features hadn't lessened one iota, she discovered.
He'd always had the kind of effortlessly handsome looks
that guaranteed major female interest wherever he went.
Even with the cruel scar that ran down his cheekbone. In
truth, it made his already compelling visage utterly and
disturbingly memorable—and *not* just because his beautiful face carried such a vivid wound. But the sight of that
wound now made Ailsa's heart pound and her stomach
clench with remembered sorrow at how it had occurred.

For a long moment she got lost in the dark cavern of
memory, then realised that Jake was staring at her, waiting for her greeting. 'Hello…it's been a long time, Jake.'

Even as she spoke, she was thinking he should have
warned her that there'd been a change of plan.

Her insides jolted. 'Where's Saskia?'

'I've been trying to ring you all day but there's been
no damn signal! Why in God's name you would choose
to live out here in the middle of nowhere is beyond me.'

Ignoring the irritation in his voice, which bisected her
heart with knives, Ailsa pushed back her hair and crossed
her arms over her thick Arran sweater. Just standing on
the doorstep inside the peg-tiled porch, she was already
freezing from the blast of icy air that had hit her when
she'd opened the door.

'Has something happened? Why isn't Saskia with you?'
Peering over his shoulder at the snow-covered vehicle, she
willed herself to see her daughter's pretty heart-shaped
face staring back at her through a window—*any* window
so long as she was there. When she realised the car was
empty the bones in her legs morphed into limp spaghetti.

'That's what I've been trying to call you about. She

wanted to stay with her grandmother in Copenhagen for a while…she pleaded with me to let her stay until Christmas Eve. I agreed. Because she was worried that you might be upset about that I agreed to travel here myself and give you the news. I'd heard the weather was bad but I had no idea it was as grim as this.'

His hand impatiently swept the snow from his champagne-blond hair, but the white flakes quickly settled again to render the gesture pointless. For a long moment Ailsa couldn't summon the words to reply. Shock and disappointment rolled through her in a sickening hurtful wave as she thought of all the plans she'd made for the lead-up to Christmas Day with Saskia. *The plans that now wouldn't be materialising.*

They'd been going to make a special trip to London for shopping, then stay at a nice hotel for the night so they could go to the theatre and out to dinner. Only yesterday the Norwegian pine she'd ordered had arrived, and was standing bare and alone in the living room just waiting for the shiny baubles that would transform it into a magical seasonal emblem. Mother and daughter were going to decorate it together, with carols playing joyfully in the background either on a CD or from the radio. It was inconceivable that her beloved child wouldn't be home again until Christmas Eve.

In Ailsa's mind the days leading up to that date would only serve to remind her of how lonely she could feel without the family she had once counted upon… *Jake and Saskia*… She'd barely got through the past week without Saskia as it was.

'How could you do this to me? How? You and your mother have already had her staying with you for a week! You must know that I was counting on you bringing her back today.'

The broad shoulders beneath the stylish black overcoat now smothered in snow shrugged laconically. 'Would you deny our daughter the chance to be with her grandmother when she's so recently lost my father? Saskia lifts her spirits like no other human being can.'

Knowing her daughter's warm, bubbly nature, Ailsa didn't doubt her ex-husband's words. But it didn't make her absence any easier to bear. And underneath her frustration her heart constricted at the thought that Jake's father was gone. The senior Jacob Larsen had been imposing, and even a little intimidating, but he had always treated her with the utmost respect. When Saskia had arrived in the world he hadn't stinted on his praise, proclaiming his new granddaughter to be the most beautiful baby in the world.

How sad for his son that he was gone. Their relationship had had its challenges, but there was no doubt in her mind that Jake had loved his father.

The swirling snow that was rapidly turning into a blizzard added to her misery and distress. 'I'm sorry you lost your dad…he was a good man. But I've already endured Saskia not being here for too long. Can't you understand why I'd want her back with me when it's so close to Christmas? I'd made plans…'

'I'm sorry about that, but sometimes whether we like it or not plans are hostage to change. The fact is that our daughter is safe with my mother in Copenhagen and you don't need to worry.' Sucking in a breath, Jake blew it out again onto the frosted air. He thumbed towards the bank of snow-covered cedars edging the road at the end of the drive behind him. 'There was a police roadblock on the way here, warning drivers not to go any further unless they absolutely had to. They only let me through because I told them you'd go crazy if I didn't make it to the house to let you know about Saskia. I only just made it—even in the SUV. I'd be mad to try and make it back to the airport tonight in these conditions.'

As if waking from a dream, Ailsa realised he looked half frozen standing there. Another few minutes and those sculpted lips would surely turn blue. As difficult as the prospect of spending time with her estranged husband promised to be, what could she do but invite him in, make him a hot drink and agree to give him a bed for the night?

'Well, you'd better come in, then.'

'Thanks for making me feel so welcome,' he answered sardonically as he stepped towards her.

His brittle reply cut her to the bone. Their divorce hadn't exactly been acrimonious, but coming less than a year after they'd suffered the terrible car accident that had robbed them of their longed-for second child, it hadn't been amicable either. Words had been flung…corrosive, bitter words that had eaten into their souls. But even now thinking of that horrendous time, of how their marriage had shockingly unraveled, was almost a blur to her because her senses had been so frozen by pain and sadness…like a delicate scallop sealed inside its shell after being relentlessly battered against the rocks.

Four long, hard years she'd lived without Jake. Saskia had been just five when they'd parted. Her daughter's poignant question, 'Why did Daddy leave, Mummy?' replayed itself over and over again in her mind most nights, disturbing her sleep and haunting her dreams…

'I didn't mean to be rude.' She grimaced apologetically. 'I'm just a little upset, that's all. Come in out of the cold and I'll get you a drink.'

He passed her into the hallway and the familiar woody scent of his expensive cologne arrowed straight into Ailsa's womb and made it contract. Inhaling a deep breath to steady herself, she hurriedly shut the door on the arctic weather outside.

The sixteenth-century beamed cottage that Jake had never been inside before was utterly charming, he mused as his senses soaked up the cosy ambience that greeted him. The lilac-painted walls of the narrow hallway were covered in a colourful array of delicate floral prints, intermingled with delightful framed photographs of Saskia as a baby, then a toddler, and a couple of more recent shots of her as a nine-year-old, already showing signs of the beauty she was becoming. And on the wall by the polished oak stair-case the French long-case clock with its floral marquetry, its steady ticking peacefully punctuating the stillness...the stillness and peace that constantly seemed to elude *him*.

The snug little house felt so much more like a real home to Jake than the luxurious Westminster penthouse he rat-tled around in alone when he was in London, and even the smart townhouse he lived in when he was in Copenhagen. Only his mother's white-painted turn-of-the-century house just outside the city, which backed onto magical woodland, could match Ailsa's home for cosiness and charm.

When she had bought the cottage not long after they'd separated Jake had been seriously disgruntled by her re-fusal to let him purchase something far more spacious and grand for her and Saskia. *'I don't want something grand,'* she'd replied, her amber-coloured eyes making her look as though she despaired of him ever understanding. *'I want something that feels like home...'* The house in Primrose Hill that they'd bought when they'd married had no lon-ger felt like home for either of them, Jake remembered, his heart heavy. *Not when the love they'd once so passionately shared had been ripped away by a cruel and senseless ac-cident...*

'Give me your coat.'

His icy fingers thawing in the warmth that enveloped him, Jake did as she asked. As he handed over the damp wool coat he couldn't help letting his gaze linger on the golden light of her extraordinary eyes. He'd always been mesmerised by them, and it was no different now. She glanced away quickly, he noticed.

'I'll take off my shoes.' He did just that, and left them by the door. He'd already noticed that Ailsa's tiny feet were encased in black velvet slippers with a black and gold bow.

'Let's go into the front room. There's a wood-burner in there. You'll soon get warm.'

Fielding his turbulent emotions, Jake said nothing and followed her. His fingers itched to reach out and touch the long chestnut tresses that flowed down her slim back, he shoved his hand into his trouser pocket to stem the renegade urge.

The compact front room was a haven of warmth and comfort, with a substantial iron wood-burner at the centre throwing out its embracing heat, its funnel reaching high into the oak-beamed rafters of the roof. There were two red velvet couches laden with bright woollen throws and cushions, and the wooden pine floor was generously covered with a rich red and gold rug. Just one Victorian armchair was positioned by the fire. Two sets of pine shelves either side of the burner were packed with books, and in one corner—its roots embedded in a silver bucket—sat an abundant widespread Christmas tree waiting to be decorated. Jake's insides lurched guiltily.

'Sit down. I'll make us a hot drink…that is unless you'd prefer a brandy?'

'I don't touch alcohol any more. Coffee will be fine… thanks.' Now it was *his* turn to glance quickly away. But not before he'd glimpsed the slightly bewildered furrowing of Ailsa's flawless brow.

'Coffee it is, then.' She left the room.

Lowering his tall, fit frame onto a couch, Jake breathed out at last. For a while he watched the increasingly heavy snow tumbling from the skies outside the window, then fell into a daydream about his daughter playing on that sumptuous red and gold rug with her dolls. She'd be chatting away non-stop to them, he mused, her vivid imagination taking her far away from this world—a world that until she was five had promised a safe and secure day-to-day existence as she grew up, a comforting life that had abruptly changed beyond all recognition when her mother and father had separated.

He didn't realise Ailsa had returned until she stood in front of him, holding out a steaming mug of aromatic black coffee. Gratefully Jake took it. 'Just what the doctor ordered.' He tried for a smile but knew it was a poor effort.

'How is your mother coping since she lost your dad?'

He watched his pretty ex-wife walk across the room in that graceful, mesmerising way she had that made her look as if she glided. She'd always had that balletic quality about her, and the blue denim jeans she was wearing highlighted her slender thighs and tiny waist—especially with the broad leather belt she wore around her sweater. As she sat down on the other couch he tried to curtail his irrational disappointment that she'd chosen not to sit beside him. Her slender ringless fingers wrapped themselves around a mug of tea. From memory, Jake knew it was rare that Ailsa drank coffee. But he didn't dwell long on that. Inside he was reeling at the unexpected sight of the missing wedding band on her finger—another painful demonstration that their marriage had well and truly ended.

Clearing his throat, he garnered the defences that he'd fine-honed during the past four years without her. 'Outwardly she seems to be coping well,' he replied. 'Inwardly is another matter.' *He could have been talking about him-self...*

'Well, then, perhaps it's a good thing that Saskia stays with her for a bit longer. It's been, what...? Six months since your dad died?'

'About that.' Sipping the too-hot coffee, he grimaced as the beverage scalded his tongue. If it was Ailsa's aim to hold out an olive branch by not making a fuss about their daughter staying with her grandmother and spoiling her plans for the lead-up to Christmas, then he didn't intend to take it. He couldn't seem to help resenting the fact that she was clearly getting on with her life quite well without him.

'And how about you?' she persisted, low-voiced, lean-ing slightly forward, amber gaze concerned.

'What about me?'

'How are *you* coping with the loss of your dad?'

'I'm a busy man, with a worldwide property business to run...I don't have time to dwell on anything other than my work and my daughter.'

'You mean you don't have time to mourn your father? That can't be good.'

'Sometimes we all have to be pragmatic.' His spine stiff-ening, Jake put the ceramic mug down on a nearby side-table then flattened his palms over his knees. Ailsa had always wanted to get to the heart of things and it seemed that nothing had changed there. Except that he didn't feel like spilling his guts to her about his feelings any more... *been there, done that.* He had the bruises on his heart to prove it.

'I remember that you and he had your differences, and I just thought that his passing might be an opportunity for you to reflect on the good things about your relationship, that's all.'

'Like I said...I've been too busy. He's gone, and it's sad, but one of the things he taught me himself was to rise above my emotions and simply get on with whatever is in front of me. At the end of the day that's helped me cope with the "slings and arrows" of life far more than wallowing in my pain. If you don't agree with such a strategy then I'm sorry, but that's how it is.'

He sensed his temper and his unreasonableness rising. Privately he had nothing but contempt for such a tack. Leaving his father's death and his regret that they hadn't found a way to communicate more healthily aside, he reminded himself that he wasn't the only one in this one-time marriage who had been to the depths of hell and back. In the four years since their divorce Ailsa had grown noticeably thinner, and there were faint new lines around her sweetly shaped mouth. Perhaps she wasn't getting on with her life *that* well? He yearned to know how she was really coping. Saskia had told him that her mother worked long hours at her arts and crafts business, even at the weekends. *There was no need for her to work at all.* The divorce settlement he'd made for her was substantial, and that was the way he wanted it.

Jake frowned. 'Why are you working so hard?' he demanded, before he'd realised he intended to ask.

'What?'

'Saskia told me that you work day and night at this arts and crafts thing.'

'Arts and crafts *thing*?' She was immediately offended. 'I run a thriving local business that keeps me busy when I'm not doing the school run or tending to Saskia, and I love it. What did you expect me to do when we broke up, Jake? Sit around twiddling my thumbs? Or perhaps you expected me to spend my divorce settlement on a chic new wardrobe every season? Or the latest sports car? Or get interior designers in with pointless regularity to remodel the house?'

Wearily he rubbed his hand round his jaw. At the same time her words made him sit up straight. When he'd met her and married her he had never envisaged Ailsa as a businesswoman in the making. 'It's good to hear that your business is going well. And as regards the settlement, it's entirely up to you what you do with the money. As long as you take proper care of Saskia when she's with you—that's all I care about. I've noticed that you look tired, as well as the fact you've clearly lost weight…that's why I asked. I don't want you wearing yourself out when you don't have to.'

Her expression pained, Ailsa tightened her hands round her mug of tea. 'I'm not wearing myself out. I look tired because sometimes I don't sleep very well, that's all. It's a bit of a legacy from the accident, I'm afraid. But it's okay… I try and catch up with some rest whenever I can—even if it's during the day.'

If a heavyweight boxer had slammed his fist into his gut right then Jake couldn't have been more winded. It took him a few moments to get the words teeming in his brain to travel to his mouth. 'I told you years ago that you should get some help from the doctor to help you sleep better. Why haven't you?'

As she shook her head, her long chestnut hair glanced against the sides of her face. 'I've seen enough doctors to make me weary of ever seeing another one again. Besides…I don't want to take sleeping pills and walk round like a zombie. And unless the medical profession has found an infallible method for eradicating hurtful memories— because it's those that keep me awake at night—then I'll just have to get on with it. Isn't that what you advocate yourself?'

'Dear God!' Jake pushed to his feet. How was he supposed to endure the pain he heard in her voice? The pain he held himself responsible for?

Yes, they'd been hit by a drunk driver that dark, rainy night when their world had come to an end, but he still should have been able to do something to avert the accident. Sometimes at night, deep in the midst of troubled sleep, he still heard his wife's heartrending moans of pain and shock in the car beside him... He'd promised in their marriage vows to love and protect her always and that cruel December night he *hadn't*... He hadn't. He just thanked God that Saskia had been staying with his parents at the time and hadn't been in the car with them. It didn't bear thinking about that his child might have been hurt as badly as her mother.

He must be a masochist, he reflected. Why had he come here to tell Ailsa himself that Saskia was prolonging her stay with his mother? He could so easily have got his chauffeur Alain to do the deed. Wasn't that what he'd done for the past four years, so he wouldn't have to come face to face with the woman he'd once loved beyond imagining? Wasn't it a situation he'd willingly engineered so he wouldn't have to discuss the deeper issues that had wrenched them apart perhaps even more than the accident?

Sighing, he tunnelled his fingers through his hair. He was only staying the night while he was snowbound. As soon as the roads were passable again he would drive to the airport and return to Copenhagen. After spending a precious day or two with his daughter and mother he would get back to the palatial head offices of Larsen and Son, international property developers, and resume his work.

'I've got an overnight bag in the car. I brought it just in case. I'll go and bring it in.' When he reached the door he glanced back at the slim, silent woman sitting on the couch and shrugged his shoulders. 'Don't worry…I promise not to outstay my welcome. As soon as the roads are cleared I'll be on my way.' *Not waiting to hear her reply, Jake stepped out into the hallway.*

As hard as she bit down on her lip, Ailsa couldn't prevent her eyes from filling up with tears. 'Why?' she muttered forlornly. 'Why come here now and shake everything up again? I'm doing all right without you…I *am*!'

Frustrated by the unremitting sorrow that rose inside her whenever Jake or the accident were mentioned, let alone having him near, she stoically put aside any further thoughts on the matter and instead made her way up to the spare bedroom to put clean sheets on the bed for her ex-husband's unexpected overnight stay.

On the way there she pushed open her daughter's bedroom door and glanced in. The pretty pink walls were covered in posters, from the latest Barbie doll to instantly recognisable children's programme characters. But amongst them were two large posters of the latest male teen movie idol, and Ailsa shook her head in wonder and near disbelief that her daughter was growing up so fast…*too* fast, in her book. *Would it be easier if Saskia had both her parents taking care of her together instead of separately?*

In the time-honoured habit of caring parents everywhere, she wondered yet again if she was a good enough mother—if she was perhaps *failing* her child in some fundamental unconscious way? Was she wrong in wanting a career of her own? To stand on her own feet at last and not feel as if she was depending on her ex-husband? At the thought of Jake she wondered if she hadn't been utterly selfish in pushing him away emotionally *and* physically, and finally driving him into asking for a divorce. She should have talked to him more, but she hadn't. Relations between them had deteriorated so badly that they'd barely been able to look at each other, she remembered sadly.

Hearing the front door open, then slam shut again, she quickly crossed the landing to the spare room. The pretty double bed with its old-fashioned iron bedstead was strewn with all manner of knitting and materials from her craft business, and she scooped them up and quickly heaped them on top of the neat little writing desk in the corner. She wouldn't stop to sort them all out right now. Tomorrow she would venture out to the purpose-built heated office in the garden, where she created her designs and stored her materials, and she would store the colourful parapher-nalia away properly. Right now she would concentrate on making the bed, so that Jake could bring up his overnight bag and unpack.

As she unfolded the pristine white sheets she'd retrieved from the airing cupboard Ailsa noticed that her hands were shaking. They might not be sharing a bed tonight, but it was a long time since she'd slept under the same roof as her ex-husband. Once upon a time they had been so very close—as if even an act of *God* couldn't tear them asun-der. She'd often fallen asleep at night after they'd made love enfolded in his arms and woken the next morning in just the same position... *Her insides churned with grief and regret at what they had lost.* The haunting memories that Jake's appearance had brought to the surface again were so intense that it felt as if they might drown her.

'It's all right,' she muttered to herself. 'It's only for one night. Tomorrow he'll be gone again.' But as she glanced out of the window at the cascade of white flakes still steadily falling her stomach clenched anxiously. She might well be wrong about that...

* * *

Jake had gone upstairs to take a shower and get a change of clothes. Ailsa took the opportunity to retreat to the kitchen to mull over what to cook for dinner. She'd planned on having a simple pasta dish with a home-made sauce for Saskia and herself that night, but she was concerned that it wouldn't be enough to satisfy a healthy male specimen like Jake. He loved good food and the finer things in life, and was a surprisingly good cook himself. It was another reason why she was slightly nervous about cooking for him again. She was no domestic goddess, and during their marriage her husband had patiently tolerated her culinary attempts with great good humour—even if more often than not he had ended up suggesting they go out to eat at one of his favourite restaurants instead. Many times he'd suggested they hire a full-time chef or cook, but Ailsa had always insisted she loved to cook for her husband and daughter. At heart she was a traditionalist, and would have felt as if she'd somehow failed her family if she hadn't prepared their meals.

Having grown up in a children's home, it was inevitable that her greatest longing had always been to have a family of her own.

A heavy fall of snow rolled off the eaves outside the window and fell to the ground with a crash. Snapping out of her reverie, Ailsa reached for the kitchen telephone and listened intently for a dial-tone. *Nothing...* The lines were obviously still down. She was longing to hear Saskia's sweet voice and find out for herself if her little girl was happy with her grandmother in Copenhagen. Knowing how warm and loving Tilda Larsen was, she didn't doubt it, but she would have liked confirmation from Saskia herself.

Biting down on her lip, she reached for the apron behind the larder door and turned on the oven. She scrubbed and rinsed a couple of generous sized potatoes, pricked the skins with a fork and popped them in the oven on a baking tray. Then she retrieved some minced beef from the fridge, a couple of onions and some garlic, and arranged a chopping board on the counter. She would add the prepared pasta sauce to the ingredients in the frying pan, along with some kidney beans and rustle up a quick *chili con carne*, she decided. *At least it was a recipe she knew well, and therefore there was less chance of her having a disaster.*

'You look busy.'

The huskily male voice behind her almost made her jump out of her skin. Turning, Ailsa glanced into a sea of glittering iced blue, and her whole body suddenly felt dangerously weak. 'I'm—I'm just preparing our dinner.'

'Don't go to any trouble on my account.'

'It's no trouble. We've both got to eat, right?'

His gaze scanning the ingredients on the marble-topped counter, Jake shrugged. 'Need any help?'

'I'm fine, thanks.' Turning back to the job in hand, she picked up the waiting sharp knife to dice the onions. But it was hard to keep her hand perfectly steady when the image of Jake in a fitted wine-coloured sweater and tailored black trousers, his hair damply golden from his shower, kept impinging on her ability to think straight. 'I know when we were together my cooking wasn't great, but I've gotten better at it over the years and you might even be pleasantly surprised.'

The man standing behind her didn't immediately reply. When Ailsa heard him exhale a heavy sigh, she tensed anxiously.

'Why did you think your cooking wasn't great?'

'Well…you always seemed to end up suggesting we go

to a restaurant whenever I made anything. Perhaps that was a clue?'

Saying nothing, Jake moved up beside her and gently removed the ivory-handled knife from her hand. Laying it down on the chopping board, he turned her round to face him. 'I don't remember ever suggesting we go to a restaurant when you'd already spent hours in the kitchen cooking a meal. And when I suggested we eat out it was only ever to give you a break, so that you wouldn't stress over preparing something. You made some great food when we were together, Ailsa. You must have, because I'm still here...right?'

What special ingredient did he possess that made that crooked smile of his so heartbreaking? His eyes so penetratingly, flawlessly blue? Her breath hitched and her heart started to race...

CHAPTER TWO

IT PAINED Jake that Ailsa had harboured the belief all these years that he'd thought her cooking unpalatable. *Yes, he had on occasion smiled at her earnest efforts when they hadn't quite worked out, but he hoped he'd conveyed that he was appreciative too.* He'd eat burnt offerings every day if he could turn back the clock to the time when they were together, before the shattering event that had torn them apart.

He breathed out slowly. As he examined her thoughtful amber gaze a ripple of undeniable electricity hummed between them.

'Yes, you're still here,' she quietly agreed with a reticent smile.

'Battle-scarred, but still alive and kicking,' he added, joking.

Ailsa's smile fled, as did the beginning-to-melt look in her eyes. 'Don't joke about that,' she scolded. Her tone was softer as she looped some silky strands of hair behind her ear. 'Does it still bother you? The scar, I mean?'

His heart thudding—as it always did whenever his scar came under scrutiny—Jake mentally strengthened his defences, hammering in iron nails to hold them fast. 'Do you mean am I worried that it's spoiled my good looks?' he mocked. Spinning away from her, he jammed his hands into his pockets, but quickly turned back again before she had a chance to comment. 'It's been over four years since I acquired it. I've quite got used to it. I think it gives me a certain piratical appeal…don't you? At least, that's what women tell me'

'Women?'

'We've been divorced four years, Ailsa. Did you imagine I would stay celibate?'

'Don't!'

'Don't what?'

'Be cruel. I don't deserve that. When I asked you if your scar bothered you, I meant does it still give you pain?'

'The only pain I get from it is when I remember what caused it…*and* what we lost that day.'

She fell silent. But not before Jake glimpsed the anguish in her golden eyes.

'Well,' she said after a while, 'I'd better get on with the cooking or we won't have a meal tonight at all.' Clearly discomfited by what he'd confessed, Ailsa returned to the counter to continue dicing onions. 'Why don't you go and make yourself comfortable in the living room and just relax?'

'Maybe I'll do just that,' he murmured, glad of the opportunity to regroup his feelings and not blurt out anything else that might hurt her. Gratefully, he exited the room.

The charming dining room had terracotta walls, exposed beams on the ceiling, and a rustic oak floor. In the centre of the sturdy table—also oak—several different-sized white and scarlet candles burned, lending a warm and inviting glow to the room now that the day had turned seasonally dark. The window blinds were not yet pulled down, and outside snowflakes continued to float past the window in a never-ending stream. In the past, when they'd been married

and in love, Jake might have considered the atmosphere
intimate. But something told him it wasn't his ex-wife's
intention to create such a potentially awkward impression.
She'd always lit candles at dinner, whatever the season.
She simply loved beauty in all its forms.

She'd once told him that the children's home she'd
grown up in had been bare of beauty of any kind and her
soul had longed for it. Quickly he jettisoned the poignant
memory, but not before berating himself for not encouraging her to talk more about her childhood experiences
when they'd been married.

Now, at her invitation, he drew out a carved wooden
chair, then tried to relax as she briefly disappeared to get
their food. When she returned he watched interestedly as
she carefully placed the aromatic meal she'd prepared in
front of him, noting how appealing she'd made it look on
the plate. He hadn't realised how hungry he was until he'd
scented the chilli, and he tucked into it with relish when
Ailsa told him to, 'Go ahead and eat…don't wait for me.'

'What do you think?'

The slight suggestion of anxiety in her tone made his
gut clench. Touching his napkin to his lips, Jake grinned
in a bid to help dispel it. Sitting opposite him, her long
hair turning almost copper in the light of the gently flickering candle flames, she was quite utterly bewitching. A
little buzz of sensual heat vibrated through him. 'It's delicious. I can't begin to tell you how welcome it is after a
long day's travelling,' he answered huskily.

'That's all right, then. Would you like some juice or
some water?' She was already reaching her hand towards
the two jugs positioned on the raffia place-mat between
them.

Jake nodded. 'Water is fine…thanks.'

They seemed to have an unspoken agreement not to

talk during the meal. But then, just as he finished every last scrap of the chilli she had prepared, Ailsa took a deep breath and brought an end to the silence.

'Was it snowing in Copenhagen when you left?' she asked conversationally.

'We've had a few heavy snow showers over the past couple of days, but nothing like you've got here.'

'Saskia must be pleased, then. She loves the snow. She's been praying for a white Christmas.'

Leaning back in his chair, Jake met her gaze warily. 'I'm sorry I didn't bring her home today.'

Ailsa didn't reply straight away and reassure him that she was okay with it. Behind her soft amber glance he sensed deep disappointment, and perhaps some residue of anger too. He blew out a breath to release the tension that had started to gather force in the pit of his stomach.

'I know you don't want to hear it, but I had so many plans for Christmas. I even told my customers to get their orders in early because I was taking an extra week off before Christmas Day to spend some time with my daughter. I'm really sorry that your mother lost your father, Jake, but she's not the only one grieving.' She was fighting hard to contain her emotion, and her beautiful eyes misted with tears.

'Grieving?' he echoed, not understanding.

'Have you forgotten what day it is today?' Her steady gaze unflinching now, she curled her fingers into the pristine white napkin now lying crumpled by her plate. 'It's the anniversary of our baby's death...the day of the accident. That's why I needed Saskia home today. If she was here I'd be focusing all my attention on her and wouldn't let myself dwell on it so much.'

For the second time since setting eyes on Ailsa after so long Jake felt winded. Then a plethora of raw emotion gripped him mercilessly, almost making him want to crawl out of his own skin. An intense feeling of claustrophobia descended—just as if someone had shoved him inside a dark, windowless cell and then thrown away the key...

'I've never noted the date,' he admitted, his dry throat suddenly burning. 'Probably because I don't need some damned anniversary to remind me of what we lost that day!' Pushing to his feet, he crossed to the window to stare blindly out at the curtain of white still drifting relentlessly down from the heavens. Vaguely he registered the scrape of Ailsa's chair being pushed back behind him.

'We haven't talked about what happened in years...not since the divorce,' she said quietly.

'And you think now's the right time?' He spun round again, feeling like a pressure cooker about to blow. Ailsa was standing in front of him with her arms folded, her expression resolute. Yet he easily noted the giveaway tremor in her lower lip that revealed she was nervous too.

'I'm not saying I want to dwell on what happened just because it's the anniversary of Thomas's death, but I—'

'Don't call him that... Our son wasn't even born when he died!'

At the reminder that they'd given their baby a name, Jake felt his knees almost buckle. If he didn't think of him as having a name then he couldn't have been real, right? He couldn't have had an identity other than that of an unborn foetus in the womb. It was the only way he'd been able to cope with the tragedy all these years.

The delicate oval face before him, with its perfectly neat dark brows, looked faintly horrified. 'But we *did* give him a name, Jake...a name and a gravestone, remember? Before the snow got really bad yesterday I took a bouquet of lilac asters and white anemones to the graveyard where he's buried. I do it every year at this time.'

The graveyard that housed the tiny remains of his son was situated in the grounds of a picturesque Norman church tucked away behind a narrow street not far from the Westminster offices of Larsen and Son. But Jake hadn't visited it since the day of the funeral. *That had been a bitter winter's day, when icy winds had cleaved into his wounded face like hot knives, and it was a day that he wished he could blot from his memory for ever.*

Pressing his fingers into his temples, he drove them irritably back into his hair. 'And that helps, does it?'

'Yes, it does, as a matter of fact. I know I was only seven months pregnant when he died, but he deserves to be remembered, don't you think? Why do you seem so angry that I've brought the subject up? Did you really expect to stay here the night and not have me talk about it?'

Feeling utterly drained all of a sudden, as well as a million miles away from any remedy that could soothe the pain and distress he was experiencing at the memory of the longed-for son they'd lost so cruelly, Jake moved across to the dining room door that stood ajar.

'I'm sorry...but I really don't think there's any point in discussing it. What can it possibly achieve? You have to let it go, Ailsa. The past is finished—*over*. We're divorced, remember? We've made new lives for ourselves. Who would have thought the shy young girl I married would end up running her own business? That's quite an achievement after all that's happened. Not everything ended in disaster between us. We've still got our beautiful daughter to be thankful for. Let's leave it at that, shall we?'

'Yes, we have Saskia—and I count my blessings every day that we have. And, yes, I run my own business and I'm proud of it. But do you really believe that if we don't discuss it the shadow of that dreadful time we endured will magically go away? If it was so easy to just let it go don't you think I would have done it by now? I thought that the divorce would help bring some closure after our baby's death—help us both put it behind us and eventually heal. But somehow it doesn't feel like it has. How can it when I've lost half of my family and can't even hope for more children in the future? The accident robbed me of the chance. Perhaps because we're not together any more it helps you to pretend that it never happened at all, Jake? "Out of sight, out of mind", as they say?'

Ailsa was so near the truth that Jake stared at her. He hadn't really wanted a divorce at all, but he had finally instigated it when the agony and the blame he'd imagined he saw in his wife's eyes every day began to seriously disturb him. *He just hadn't been able to deal with it.*

'How can I pretend it never happened, hmm? I only have to look in the mirror every time I go to the bathroom and see this damned scar on my face to know that it did! Anyway...'

He swallowed down a gulp of air and his thundering heartbeat gradually slowed. It gave him a chance to think what to do next...to try to blot out the torturous memory of Ailsa being so badly injured in the accident that she'd slipped into unconsciousness long before the surgeons had performed a ceasarean to try and save the baby. The head surgeon had told Jake afterwards that her womb had been irreparably damaged and their infant hadn't survived. It was unlikely she'd ever be able to bear a child again.

'I've brought some work with me that I need to take a look at before I turn in. My father's death has meant that I've become CEO, and inevitably there's a raft of problems to sort out. Thanks for dinner and the bed for the night. The food was great. I'll see you in the morning.'

Even though his excuse was perfectly legitimate, there

was no escaping the fact that it made him feel like a despicable coward.

'If you need an extra blanket, you'll find a pile of them in the oak chest at the end of the bed.'

Ailsa's tone made her sound as if she was determined to rise above her disappointment at his reluctance to yet again deal with the past. He silently admired this new strength she'd acquired, and was moved to hear the compassion in her voice…compassion that he probably didn't deserve.

'Sleep well,' she added with a little half-smile. 'Don't sit up too late working, will you? You've had a long day's travelling and you must be tired.'

Obviously not expecting an answer to her remarks, she gracefully moved back to the table, then methodically started to clear away the detritus of their meal. Knowing already that his unexpected appearance had disturbed and upset her, Jake fleetingly reflected again that he should never have come here. *Then he would have avoided this agonising scene.* His throat locked tight with the guilt and regret that made him feel, and he swept from the room. In the prettily furnished bedroom he'd been allocated, he glanced despairingly over at the neat stack of paperwork he'd left on the hand-stitched patchwork quilt that covered the bed and angrily thumped his chest with a heartfelt groan…

Knitting at the fireside, as was her usual habit before retiring to bed—*she was always working on something beautiful and handmade for a customer*—Ailsa took comfort from the rhythmic click of her needles along with the crackle of fresh ash logs she'd added to the wood-burner. After that altercation with Jake earlier she was feeling distinctly *raw* inside—as though her very organs had been scraped with a blade. Already she'd resigned herself to another sleepless night. Sometimes she didn't vacate the high-backed Victorian armchair until the early hours of the morning. What was the point when all she did most nights if she went to bed early was toss and turn? Sleep was still the most elusive of visitors. It wasn't usually until around five a.m. that she'd fall into an exhausted slumber, then a couple of hours later she'd wake up again feeling drugged.

She often wondered how on earth she survived on such a relentlessly punishing lack of sleep and was able to take care of Saskia and work too. The human capacity to endure never ceased to amaze her.

But she was even more unsettled tonight by the fact that Jake was occupying the spare room upstairs. Seeing him again had been wonderful and dreadful all at the same time. *But the sight of him had always made her react strongly.* The deeply grooved scar on one side of his chiselled visage made him no less charismatic or handsome, she reflected. She was grief-stricken at the idea he believed that it did. And. yes…she privately admitted it *did* make him look rather piratical—although she hadn't wanted to hear that other women thought so too. It nearly killed her that he seemed to have forgotten the passionate love they'd shared and moved on. There was no such 'normal' pattern of existence for her. How could she even *look* at another man with the prospect of a relationship at the back of her mind after someone like Jake Larsen?

She'd been a trainee receptionist in the Larsen offices when they'd first met. Only nineteen, yet brimming with determination to better herself after her difficult start in life, she'd been so grateful for the chance of such a 'glamorous' job when she'd barely had any qualifications under her belt. But she'd been studying hard at her local adult education facility to remedy that. When Jake had walked through the revolving glass doors one day, wearing a single-breasted black cashmere coat over his suit, his lightly tanned skin and blond hair making him look like some kind of mythical hero from one of those magical folk tales that had at their roots the trials and travails of life and the story of how the handsome hero and beautiful heroine overcame them together, Ailsa almost forgot to breathe.

As he'd walked up to her and her colleague, her much more confident fellow employee had whispered under her breath, *'It's the boss's son....Jake Larsen. He's come over from Copenhagen.'* But even before her colleague had told Ailsa his identity her heart had already turned over inside her chest at the arresting sight of all that sculpted Viking beauty and the spine-tingling charisma that Jake exuded. She'd *never* been so fascinated by a man before. And especially not a man who was clearly light years out of her league, who wore the mantle of authority and power as though it was a natural component of his DNA. Yet he'd warmly introduced himself to her, the most junior and inexperienced of his staff, as though she were no less important than one of the firm's directors, she recalled. When he had followed up his welcome to her with a near-incandescent smile—a smile that had wiped every thought clean from her head—she'd found herself well and truly under his spell…

'Blast!' She dropped a stitch, patiently unravelled the multi-coloured wool, then cast on again. The logs in the burner hissed and spat and she glanced mournfully across at the beautiful Norwegian pine standing in the corner. It poignantly reminded her of a shy young girl at a party, waiting to be noticed by a boy and asked to dance… Once upon a time, in another life, Jake would have happily volunteered to help her dress the tree, singing lustily along to the carols playing in the background and teasingly increasing the volume of his voice when she protested he was singing out of tune.

It hurt that he wouldn't discuss the baby's death with her. Ailsa had hoped such a discussion would help them be a little easier around each other and truly be able to move on. They hadn't had a prayer of being able to do that after the accident and then leading up to their divorce, when they'd both been so wounded, hurt and angry, blaming each other for everything. She'd even hoped that such a mutually frank discussion might at last help her to sleep better at night.

'Oh, well…' Murmuring under her breath, she sighed softly. *When he leaves tomorrow I'll just carry on as normal. It's not all bad… I've still got Saskia. And the business is doing well…better than ever, in fact.*

She bit her lip, trying hard not to cry. Sniffing determinedly, she wiped her eyes and lifted her gaze to the tree again. Her daughter might not be around to share in the joy that decorating a Christmas tree could bring but it wouldn't stop Ailsa from taking on the task herself. After all, it was something she excelled at. She ran a very successful business designing and making beautiful things—everything from tree decorations to hand-knitted sweaters and patchwork quilts. Plus, she and Saskia had been collecting and making decorative odds and ends the whole year for this season.

Feeling her spirits lifting a little, she put her knitting away and instead of dozing in the armchair, as she normally did, for the first time in months she went upstairs to bed…

His hand fumbling for the clock beside the bed, Jake groaned when his sleep-fogged brain registered the time. Realising that he must have slept the sleep of the dead, he tried to fathom why. Like Ailsa, he had become a veritable insomniac over the years following the accident. Sitting up and arranging a plump pillow against the iron-bedstead to support his back, he was just in time to hear the radiator in the room click and hum into life. Breathing out deliberately heavily, he wasn't surprised to see the plume of steam that hit the icy air.

Was the house usually this perishingly cold in the morning? He couldn't help feeling a spurt of annoyance shoot through him at the thought that Ailsa could have chosen to live in much more luxurious surroundings, with underfloor heating and every available comfort. Instead she had stubbornly opted for this too isolated cottage. Charming as it was, it wasn't the home he wanted his daughter to grow up in...

Rubbing his hands briskly together to warm them, he diverted this disturbing line of thought by wondering how soon he could get a flight back to Copenhagen today. Mulling over the possibilities—or *not* as the case might be—he shoved aside the patchwork quilt that covered the silk-edged woollen blankets and strode over to the window. Lifting a corner of the heavily lined floral curtain, Jake stared out at the incredible scene that confronted him with a mixture of frustration, disappointment and sheer bewildering astonishment.

As far as the eye could see and beyond everything was deeply blanketed in brilliant diamond-white. And fierce gusts of wind were making the still falling snow swirl madly like dervishes. Unless he could sprout wings and fly there'd be no getting out of here today. In any case, all the planes at the airport would surely be grounded in such Siberian weather.

'Damn!'

He stood there in black silk pyjama bottoms, his

hard-muscled chest bare, and willed himself to come up with a plan. But even as he seriously considered phoning his helicopter pilot back in Copenhagen he remembered the lack of service yesterday for both landlines and mobiles in the area. The current extreme weather conditions didn't bode well for the service returning any time soon. The helicopter option was clearly off the agenda. As he bit back his increasing frustration, a tentative knock at the door made Jake's heart race.

'Jake, are you up and about yet? I was wondering if you'd like a cup of tea?'

Instead of answering, he crossed to the door and pulled it wide. Her dark hair flowing down over her shoulders, slightly mussed as if she'd had a restless night, Ailsa stood in front of him like some wide-eyed ingénue in a kimono-style red silk dressing gown. She barely looked out of her teens, let alone the mother of a nine-year-old. Disconcertingly, that old sense of fierce protectiveness that he'd always felt around her came flooding back.

'Never mind me. You look like you could do with a hot drink to warm *you* up,' he told her gruffly. 'Why doesn't your heating come on earlier? Have you seen the weather outside? It's freezing in here.'

'The boiler is on a timer. And, yes, I have seen the weather. I don't think the snow has let up all night. But it's not surprising you're cold, standing there with barely a stitch on!'

Jake couldn't prevent the grin that hijacked his lips. 'You know I don't sleep with much on. Or had you forgotten that?'

'You didn't say whether you wanted a cup of tea or not,' she persisted doggedly, clutching the sides of the silk dressing gown more closely together and concealing her face by letting her hair fall across it.

But not before Jake saw that she was blushing. He experienced a very male sense of satisfaction at that. It was good to know that he could still get a reaction from her, despite all the muddied water flowing under the bridge between them...

'I definitely wouldn't say no to a hot drink of some kind. But let me take a shower first and dress before I join you downstairs.'

'Okay.' The slim shoulders lifted, then fell again before she turned away. As Jake closed the door on Ailsa's retreating back, she swung round again. 'Shall I cook breakfast for you as well?'

He hesitated. Purely because he'd just noticed the smudged violet shadows beneath her eyes that clarified his belief that she probably hadn't slept. 'I don't want to put you to any trouble,' he said huskily.

A fleeting smile curved the pretty lips he'd so loved kissing—still *dreamed* of kissing from time to time, whenever he tortured himself with thinking back to what they'd had.

'It's no trouble.' She continued on her way down the landing and the gentle womanly sway of her hips made Jake's heart ache.

CHAPTER THREE

EMERGING from the living room, flustered and hot after making up the fire with some freshly cut applewood logs, Ailsa brushed her dusty hands down over her jeans and glanced up at the very same moment that Jake descended the staircase. No matter how many times she'd seen him… lived with him, loved him…it still gave her heart a jolt to be confronted with the sheer physicality of his presence. He was dressed much more casually this morning than yesterday, his long muscular legs encased in softly napped light blue denims, and he wore a white tee shirt beneath a black V-necked wool sweater. His sun-kissed hair looked as if it had been finger combed rather than brushed, and when he turned towards her and smiled his clear blue eyes were no less a magnet for her than they'd always been.

She didn't even notice the cruel scar on his cheek because her attention was so consumed by his gaze.

'I'll put the kettle on again and make some tea. I'm sorry if I'm a bit behind with the breakfast but I had to make up the fire. Did you sleep all right?'

'Like a baby,' he drawled. 'That's one hell of a comfortable bed.'

'When you consider that most people spend half their lifetime in bed, a comfortable one has got to be pretty essential, don't you think?' *Argh! She was babbling because she was suddenly inexplicably nervous around him.* And, however innocent, the last topic in the world she wanted to discuss with her charismatic ex-husband was bed!

When Jake merely grinned instead of commenting, as though he knew very well how uncomfortable she was, Ailsa quickly tore her glance away and headed down the hall to the kitchen. Her house guest followed her. She quickly washed her hands, then flicked on the switch to boil the kettle again. She was reaching for a couple of pottery mugs from the dresser when Jake pulled out a chair at the breakfast table and sat down. Knowing that his interested gaze trailed her every move, she grew more and more discomfited. Although she was tense and on edge in his company, she knew that if she turned round right then her ex wouldn't be displaying any such similar tension. When he *did* relax he turned it almost into an art form. His athletic body knew how to lounge to mouthwatering effect…even in a hard-backed kitchen chair.

Ailsa bit back a sigh. Deciding to bite the bullet, she made herself bring up the subject that had been at the forefront of her mind since waking that morning and seeing the breathtaking result of last night's heavy snowfall.

'If you were hoping to get to the airport today I don't think much of your chances.'

'Neither do I,' he agreed. The smooth skin between his brows puckered. 'Have you checked to see if there's a phone line yet?'

Ailsa grimaced. 'Yes, I have…it's still out, I'm afraid.'

'Damn!'

The harsh-voiced comment didn't do a lot for her confidence. *Had he come to dislike her so much that the thought of spending any more time than necessary in her company was abhorrent to him?*

'I feel just as frustrated that I can't talk to Saskia,' she murmured. Realising that the kettle had boiled, she swallowed down her hurt, then busied herself making the tea. She took Jake's over to him at the table. 'Help yourself to sugar. I'm going to get on with cooking your breakfast.'

'Are you going to join me?'

'I don't eat much in the morning. I'll probably just make myself a slice of toast.'

'Just toast? Is that all you have for breakfast?'

'Usually, yes.'

'Then it's no wonder you've lost weight.'

'Anything else you've noticed about me?' she asked, stung. It hardly made sense since they weren't together any more, Ailsa knew, but the notion that he might find her skinny and unattractive upset her. Yes, she'd always been on the slender side, but before the accident she'd had some nicely rounded curves too. Curves that he'd professed to *adore*. And when she'd been pregnant with Saskia, and then their son, he'd loved her womanly shape even more.

Did he spend his time adoring some other woman's curves these days?

Jake's steady, unwavering glance told her he was considering the question deeply. 'Yes. You're even more beautiful than I remember.'

'No, I'm not.' Her arms went protectively around her middle. 'Events have inevitably shaped me, and I'm very aware that I'm a little too thin and tired-looking. I'm twenty-eight, but sometimes I feel more like a hundred.'

'That's just crazy talk.'

'It's not that I even mind really.' She shrugged. 'As long as I have the energy to work and take care of Saskia, that's all that matters.'

Ailsa hadn't realised that he had risen to his feet until he stood in front of her, tipping up her chin to make her look at him. His eyes were such a searing sapphire-blue they were nearly the undoing of her. Had his lashes always been that long and lustrous? He was standing so close that surely he must hear the sound of her galloping heart?

'You might be tired, but you're not too thin and you certainly don't look old before your time. As a matter of fact I thought when I saw you yesterday how incredibly young you still are. Perhaps you were too young when I married you, hmm?'

Softly smoothing back her hair from her forehead, the palm that glanced against her skin was slightly rough edged, yet infinitely soft at the same time. *Like velvet.* Along with his deep, mellow voice, it almost lulled her into believing that everything that was wrong between them could be set right again.

Where had *that* dangerous notion sprung from? *The idea was as self-destructive as hoping for sanctuary in a burning house...*

As if coming out of a trance, Ailsa stepped back from Jake to cross her arms protectively over her chest, almost as if guarding her heart. 'Are you saying that you regret our marriage?'

He raised an eyebrow. 'I'm not saying that at all. Why do you always have to go on the defensive and believe the worst?'

Now *her* gaze was unwavering. 'Because some days it's hard to believe in anything good any more,' she told him honestly.

'It grieves me that you feel like that.' Sighing heavily, Jake narrowed his gaze. 'We had some good times when we were together, don't you remember?'

'We did… But then we made the painful mistake of believing we had a wonderful future in prospect…you, our children and I. Look what happened to that particular little fantasy.'

Why did she do this? Go for the jugular every time?
Hearing the despair in her voice made Jake feel as though
his heart was being slashed to ribbons again…just as his
hands had been in the accident, when he'd reached for
Ailsa to protect her from the splintering glass and jagged
metal that the drunken driver had recklessly and devastatingly reduced their car to, killing their beloved baby in
the process. He'd already had to bear the unbearable…how
long did the fates intend him to suffer?

In an agony of pain and frustration he squeezed his eyes
momentarily shut. When he opened them again Ailsa had
already moved back to the stove to cook breakfast. Staring at the glorious waterfall of long dark hair that waved
down her back, he wanted to step up behind her, pull her
too-slender form hard into his body and never let her go.
Instead he glanced out of the window in front of her to
see an even heavier curtain of snow descending from the
cobweb-grey skies.

'Is there to be no end to this godforsaken weather today?'

He made no attempt to disguise the anger and despondency in his tone, and Ailsa glanced round at him. 'I
know you can't wait to be gone, to be back in Copenhagen again…but you're going to be utterly miserable if you
can't accept the fact that right now you're stuck here for
a while. Just as I have to accept the fact that Saskia won't
be with me for another week.'

'Make me feel even worse than I do already, why don't
you? Don't you think I feel bad enough, showing up here
without her? My mother and she were so adamant they
wanted to be together for a little while longer, and I thought
why not? Where's the harm? I thought surely you'd understand for once, but instead you're regarding me like I've
committed the crime of the bloody century!'

'Jake, I—'

There was a loud hammering on the front door that made them both start.

'Who the hell is that?'

There was only one person it could be in this unbelievable weather, Ailsa realized. *And she knew his appearance probably wasn't going to help ease the current friction between her and Jake.* Wiping her hands down the front of the apron she wore, which was patterned with tiny red robins in honor of the season, she hurried out into the hall.

Stamping his feet on the doorstep, trying to shake off some of the frost and snow that caked his boots and fur-lined parka, was the handsome, dark-haired son of the farmer who was her closest neighbour.

'Good morning, Ailsa.'

'Linus, what are you doing here?'

'I've brought you some eggs, milk and bread to help tide you over until you can get to the shops again. Nothing can move out there except the tractor. Are you okay? I was worried about you and Saskia being here all on your own.'

'I'm absolutely fine, thanks—and Saskia's still with her grandmother in Copenhagen. It's very good of you to come and check up on us like this.'

'What are neighbours for?' A friendly grin split his lips, showing well-tended white teeth. 'Just a second and I'll go and grab those provisions.'

As she waited for him to return to the impressive red tractor that was steadily being drowned in even more layers of thick snow Ailsa clapped her hands together to warm them. The frosted air was literally like *ice*.

'Shall I take it through to the kitchen?' her visitor suggested, returning with a medium-sized cardboard container.

'Yes, please.' Forcing a smile to her lips, Ailsa sensed apprehension seep into the pit of her stomach at the thought that he was going to come face to face with her ex-husband.

There was nothing but casual friendship between her and the farmer's son—she'd never even remotely felt like advancing their association into anything more mean-ingful—but somehow, even though they'd been apart for a long time, she knew Jake would immediately jump to conclusions. The *wrong* conclusions... He'd always had a propensity to be jealous. But, although *he* had clearly entertained the possibility of another relationship, after that reference he'd made to women thinking he looked 'piratical', Ailsa *hadn't*. How could she *not* welcome in a friendly neighbour who had been so thoughtful? That was just plain bad manners in her book. The least she could do was make Linus a cup of tea to warm him up before send-ing him off on his journey home.

But as soon as they arrived in the kitchen Jake's aloof air easily conveyed his suspicion and even his annoyance at the presence of the other man. His glacial glance was colder than the icy weather outside as he silently surveyed the stranger who followed Ailsa in.

'Jake, this is my neighbour Linus—he's very kindly brought me some provisions from his farm. Linus, this is Jake Larsen...Saskia's father. He came to let me know that Saskia was staying with her grandmother a bit longer and now he's stranded here.' She subconsciously gnawed her lip at the realisation that Jake might well be annoyed that she'd given the other man a little *too* much information.

'I've heard a lot about you.' Linus frowned before quickly setting the box of provisions down on the table. He stole a brief glance at Ailsa before recovering his sur-prise and politely extending his hand towards the other man. 'From Saskia, I mean. She talks about you all the time.'

'Is that a fact?'

Although Jake paid deference to good manners and shook the other man's hand, the gesture was clearly reluctant. For a second all Ailsa could hear was the beating of her heart in tandem with the stolid ticking of the antique clock on the mantelpiece. Lightly touching Linus's arm, she made herself smile, as though everything was perfectly normal and her ex-husband *wasn't* wearing an expression that would repel even the most dogged comers.

'It is.' Her visitor's smile was awkward.

'Why don't you sit down, Linus, and I'll make you a nice cup of tea?'

He shrugged, clearly discomfited by Jake's frosty reception. 'That's kind of you, but I'd better not stay…there's still plenty to do on the farm before the daylight goes. But thanks for offering. Maybe I'll drop in again to see how you are in a day or two?'

'Are you sure you don't want a hot drink? It's freezing out there.'

'I'll be okay. I'm used to working in all weathers, and I've had a big breakfast this morning to help sustain me.'

'All right, then.' One eye on Jake, Ailsa clamped her teeth anxiously down on her bottom lip. 'Thanks so much for bringing those provisions. That was thoughtful. I owe you.'

'Don't be daft. It was my pleasure. To tell you the truth it was nice to have an excuse to drop round and see you. Sometimes work is relentless, and I don't get the time to visit as much as I'd like.'

His awkwardness had vanished, and now Linus's smile was broad. She was a little taken aback by it—especially

in front of Jake—but she privately owned to feeling pleasure too at being so warmly regarded.

His glance briefly moved across to her ex. 'It was good
to meet you,' he said.

'You too.'

The reply was uttered without expression, and Ailsa
thought it was just as well that Linus wasn't staying longer, because she definitely sensed that her brooding ex-
husband had hardly welcomed the idea.

'If we don't meet again I hope you have a safe journey
home.'

This time Jake said nothing at all. He simply looked at
the other man as if he wished he would disappear.

Linus smiled faintly at Ailsa, then turned and went out
into the hallway. When she returned to the kitchen, after
waving him goodbye, she clenched her fists down by her
sides and stared hard at Jake. There wasn't so much as an
ounce of remorse on his striking face for his distinct cool-
ness towards the other man, she saw. Her blood pumped
with indignation.

'Did you have to be so aloof? Linus is a good man. He
only came to check up on me and Saskia to make sure we
were all right. He even brought us some supplies because
I can't get to the shops.'

'Are you telling me that you're in need of another man
around these days to look out for you and my daughter?'

In sheer disbelief at what he was assuming, Ailsa
clenched her teeth. 'He's not "another man" in the way
that you're insinuating. For your information, Jake, I don't
need another man for anything! I can take perfectly good
care of myself. Linus is just a friend and neighbour.'

Rubbing his forehead, Jake momentarily glanced down
at the floor. When he lifted his gaze the crystalline blue
eyes glinted dangerously. 'You're telling me you can't see

that he wants to be much *more* than just a friend and neighbour?'

'What?'

'Perhaps things have progressed beyond friendship and neighbourliness already?'

'We've had an occasional cup of tea and a chat together and that's all. I've certainly never encouraged anything more personal than that. And even if I had it's none of your business who I spend my time with...not any more. Did you forget that we're divorced?'

'No.' For a moment his expression bordered on tortured. 'I didn't forget.'

The annoyance and indignation that had threatened to overwhelm Ailsa a few moments ago deflated like a burst balloon. Now, instead of annoyance, the predominant feeling that coursed through her veins was compassion. They'd both been badly injured in the accident that had killed their longed-for baby, and if that wasn't enough they'd also endured the devastating end of their marriage. On top of that, Jake had recently lost his father. He had to be hurting.

Was his anger towards her over the thought that she might be seeing someone else a cover for that hurt? More than ever she realised they needed to talk. Somehow during this enforced stay of his at the cottage they had to find a way to start resolving their shared agony from the past.

Her gaze came to rest on the sturdy cast iron frying pan she'd left on the stove. 'I'll get on with cooking your breakfast. Do you want another cup of tea? That one's probably gone cold by now.'

Returning to sit down again at the pine table, Jake pulled the mug of tea that Ailsa had made earlier towards him and took a sip. 'It's fine,' he murmured.

She was by his side in an instant, taking the mug from

his hands and cupping her hands round it to glean if the beverage was still sufficiently hot. 'It's practically cold. I'll make you another one. It's no trouble.'

'Why are you being so pleasant towards me when I've just upset you with my less than warm reception of your friend?' Disturbingly, Jake trapped her with his unflinching gaze.

'Is it going to help us if I'm *unpleasant*?' she asked reasonably.

A faint smile curved his lips. 'I guess not.'

'Then I'll get on with the breakfast.'

Opening the cardboard container Linus had left on the table, Ailsa retrieved a box of eggs. 'The eggs from the farm are amazing. They're new laid every day and better than anything I can get at the supermarket.'

'How lucky that you can get them from Linus.'

The comment was a bit more than lightly sarcastic, and she sensed the ground she thought they'd just gained slipping away. 'He *is* just a friend, you know. I wouldn't lie to you about that. I have Saskia's happiness to consider, as well as my own, and while she's still young I won't be in the market for a romantic relationship with anyone.' Her brow furrowing, she didn't draw away from Jake's interested glance. 'How about you? Are there any important new relationships in your life that I should know about?' Even as she asked the question her stomach lurched sickeningly in case he said yes.

To her relief, he shook his head. 'Like you, I don't intend to get seriously involved with anyone else until Saskia's grown. But nor have I resigned myself to some monastic existence either.' A muscle flexed in the plane of his cheek, just to the side his scar. 'I'm only human, and my basic human needs are no different to anyone else's.'

It took Ailsa a couple of seconds to find her voice after

that incendiary comment, because she was busy fielding the giant wave of hurt that washed over her at the idea of Jake having his sexual needs met by another woman… maybe even *more* than one woman. They'd been divorced for four years now, after all, and it was hardly the first time the thought had crossed her mind. Most times she quickly pushed it away. But she intimately knew her husband's needs in that department. *He had always been the most incredible lover.* That part of their marriage had fulfilled every dream of love and passion she had ever had *and then some…*

'What about *my* needs?' she asked, struggling to keep her voice level. 'Do I have the same freedom there as you do, Jake? Or don't you think I have such needs any more since the accident rendered me unable to bear children? Perhaps you think it's made me less of a woman?'

'Don't say that!' The flash of shock and dismay in his compelling blue eyes took Ailsa aback. 'Don't even *think* it, let alone say it. You're more a woman than any other female I know, and even though we're not together any more nothing will ever change that.' Getting to his feet he pushed back his chair. It was easy to detect he was breathing hard. Wordlessly, he lifted the box of eggs out of her hands and left it on the table. Then he slid his palm over her cheek, slid his thumb beneath her jaw to hold it steady. 'Saskia always says she has the most beautiful mama in the world, and she's right.'

'She would say that. She's biased.'

'Didn't you hear me?' His fingers tightened a little round her jaw…tightened *and* trembled. 'I said she's right.'

Twin desires of wanting him to say more, just to hear the smoky inflection in his voice at close quarters—a voice that could both comfort and seduce at the same time—and of longing to know what it would be like to feel his commanding lips on hers again swept through her. But Ailsa knew it wasn't wise to crave either of those things…not when she'd worked so hard to recover from the hurt and rejection that had come so close to breaking her. She'd lost her baby and then she'd lost Jake.

He might have instigated their divorce in a moment of black despair to finally escape the pit of despondency they had both sunk into, but Ailsa had readily concurred with it. The situation between them had become intolerable. They'd both needed breathing space. But even as she'd heard herself agree to legally ending their marriage she'd been utterly heartbroken at the prospect. *She didn't ever want to need him so much again.* She'd told herself over and over that Jake should be free to love again, to father a son with someone else. *Why hadn't he?*

Dangerously close to tears, she firmly removed his hand from her cheek and turned away. Then she turned back to collect the box of eggs from the table. 'Would you like one egg or two with your bacon?'

'You know what? I think I've lost my appetite.' The bleakness in his eyes moved through her like a knife.

'I'm not pushing you away, Jake. I just—' She breathed out a long slow breath, fighting to get her feelings under control. 'I just don't want to get hurt again, and neither do I want to hurt *you*. We've got no choice but to be together right now, so let's not spoil it, hmm? I'm totally open to talking about things, and maybe by the time it comes for you to leave we'll have resolved some of the issues that have bothered us so we can be more at peace with the choices we've made. What do you think?'

'Have you got a shovel?'

'What?' Not comprehending, Ailsa frowned.

Combing his fingers through his hair, Jake moved restlessly over to the window to glance outside. 'The path badly needs clearing. I'll go and see to it now…work up an appetite so that I can eat that breakfast you keep promising me.'

The unexpected humour in his tone gave her hope that he might at last be going to meet her halfway, so that they could talk freely about the past without blaming each other. 'Do you think it's worth doing right now? If it keeps on snowing it's going to be a thankless task. You'll have to go out and clear it all over again later.'

'If you were to step outside for any reason and take a fall, it's not something I want to have on my conscience when I leave. Just tell me where the shovel is, will you?'

Biting back *God forbid you should have me on your conscience,* Jake, and remembering she really *did* want to stop blaming him, Ailsa shrugged. 'Okay. Go out through the back door to the garden. You'll find one in the tool shed there,' she told him.

'Good. Can I put in my breakfast order? I think you'd better make it *two* eggs with my bacon. It could be hungry work,' he remarked wryly, crossing the stone-flagged floor to go outside.

CHAPTER FOUR

JAKE was honestly glad of the physical exercise as he put his back into clearing the snow laden path. The icy wind that stung his cheeks and made his eyes water—*just* occasionally—helped divert his mind from dwelling on Ailsa. It had been an almighty shock to the system to meet her neighbour Linus. If ever a man had a hopeful look in his eyes where a woman was concerned then Ailsa's farmer friend's look epitomised it. It wasn't that Jake was shocked that the man wanted Ailsa—what man in his right mind *wouldn't*?—it was *more* the fact that his beautiful ex-wife clearly had no idea that he desired her. That made her vulnerable. Sometimes she was just too naive for her own good.

It was funny that Saskia had never mentioned him to Jake—especially when he often asked her if her mother had any new friends. Clearly their young daughter didn't consider the farmer enough of a good friend to warrant talking about him to her father. Still…the man had no business casually dropping round, trying to sweeten Ailsa with his gifts—practical or otherwise.

Grim-faced, he stopped shovelling snow for a couple of minutes to stare up at the house. It was a compact, charming little cottage, chocolate-box perfect—especially as viewed now, dressed in its raiment of pristine white snow.

In truth, it was a million miles away from the luxurious houses and apartments his company sold across the globe to the rich and famous. But if they were happy here instead of somewhere more urban and expensive then what could he do? It had been clearly demonstrated to him by Ailsa over the years that she wanted as little interference and help from him as possible, and even though Jake didn't like it he couldn't blame her.

When that out-of-control car had hit theirs that stark December day he should have protected what was most precious to him against all the odds—even if it meant surrendering his own life to do so.

From deep within his soul an arrow of despair pierced him—so great that it almost made him double up with grief. Why had she told him that she visited their son's grave? *It wasn't as if he needed reminding that he hadn't survived.* His wife had been able to display her sorrow openly—to rant and rail at the heavens and shake with grief if she felt like it. In contrast, Jake had had to mourn his loss in silence, as well as appear as if he was handling it 'like a man'. In terms of being a great businessman, a good provider and a loyal husband to his wife, his father Jacob could definitely be regarded as a success, but when it came to expressing warmth and emotion he had been far too shut down for Jake to get close to. Consequently he had never truly felt he'd been loved by him.

Sometimes he cursed the pattern he had unconsciously adopted from the man who had raised him. To keep his emotions inside...not to show that his heart was breaking when he was hurt and to pretend that everything was okay.

Ailsa and he had lost so much. She believed they should talk. Did she really think they could overcome the tragedies that in the end had defined their once passionate union by merely *talking*? Jake's learned proclivity of keeping his feelings to himself was so ingrained that maybe it was too late to try and get past it?

Tasting salt on his tongue, he realised the tears that had been burning the backs of his eyes had tracked down his face. Furiously wiping them away—almost appalled at the emotional display that no one else was witness to anyway—he began shovelling the mound of snow on the path with extra zeal.

'Would you like some more bacon?'

'Are you kidding me? If I eat another bite I won't be fit for anything.'

'Are you sure?'

'Sure. Why don't you come and sit down for a minute?'

Jake's invitation was like being tempted with her favourite Swiss chocolate after Ailsa had vowed to give up the indulgence for good...

A silent war of attrition was already taking place inside her when his compelling glance mercilessly captured hers, and she sensed her defences pathetically crumble. 'Just for a minute, then.'

Carrying her toast and cup of tea across to the table, she sat down opposite him, her back to the large cream dresser that was laden with a colourful assortment of porcelain collectables. Outside the snowfall was gathering momentum but inside the house it was warm, snug and cosy—much more conducive to a little conversation than tearing around doing housework.

'I'm honoured.' His reply was gently mocking.

'Thanks for clearing the path, but I'm afraid it won't be long before it needs doing again. Not that I'm saying you should go out and do it,' she added quickly, her face growing hot.

'Anything physical is infinitely preferable to doing paperwork or gazing at a computer screen.'

Determinedly shoving aside the taunting images his smoky-voiced remark conjured up in her head, Ailsa smiled awkwardly and took a bite of her toast.

'You still enjoy doing crafts?' Cupping his hands round the cup of coffee she'd made him, Jake bestowed upon her the charming, slightly crooked smile that she'd always found so appealing, 'I guess that's a stupid question, considering you've turned it into a business,' he added.

'I do enjoy it…very much. It's only a small enterprise, but it's growing bit by bit. Some nice compliments from customers have helped. They're very loyal, and they tell their friends about me. Advertising online has boosted interest too. I was recently asked to do an interview for one of the top homes and interiors magazines.'

'Well done. That must mean a lot to you.'

'It does.' She lightly pursed her lips. 'When I think of where I came from it's a bit of a miracle, to be frank. I never thought I'd manage to accomplish anything worthwhile…at least in terms of a career.'

'Why would you believe that?'

'The conditions of my childhood, I suppose. Knowing that I was abandoned as a baby didn't exactly help. I've never quite been able to shake off the feeling that I was unwanted…therefore not good enough.'

'You've never told me that before.'

Feeling hot, and ill at ease because she'd unwittingly raised the topic, Ailsa nonetheless forced herself to meet the sudden intensity of Jake's examining stare. 'You never really asked about my childhood. I sensed it made you slightly uncomfortable—the fact that I came from a world so at odds with your own, I mean. That's why I never talked to you about it.'

Linking his hands together, he shook his head as if in surprise and disbelief. 'I'm sorry...sorry I didn't discuss such an important aspect of who you are and ended up having you believe I was uncomfortable with it. And I guess most of all I'm upset at the idea you thought you weren't good enough. I always knew how capable you were, Ailsa...how talented. Instead of just keeping it to myself I should have told you.'

There was a glow inside her at his words. But, even more than for what he'd said, she was just so glad that they were really talking at last...*connecting*. 'Anyway, I'm doing my best not to feel not good enough any more. Starting the business has really helped me in that department. It's also given me a boost to know that I can earn a reasonable income from my endeavours.'

Jake's scowl denoted that he didn't appreciate her answer. 'You're not short of money, and you don't have to depend solely on what you can earn for yourself.'

Hurt that he didn't appear to understand, Ailsa suddenly lost her appetite for even the single slice of toast she had made. 'I know you left me well provided for, Jake—and don't think I don't appreciate it. But it's important for me to know that I can support myself. I use the money you gave me for anything Saskia needs, but when and where I can I like to rely on my own income. Is it so hard for you to comprehend that I like being independent?'

'You were married to me once, and the money that was settled on you in the divorce is rightfully yours. Doesn't what most people would regard as a fortune make you independent enough?'

'I...' Feeling suddenly choked, Ailsa couldn't speak. Jake couldn't see that it wasn't the money *or* the amount that was important. It was what it represented to her...the death of their beloved baby and the end of their marriage.

At least the money she earned independently for herself came with no such painful or onerous baggage.

'Does that farmer friend of yours know that you're a wealthy woman?'

Her eyes widened. 'What are you suggesting? You think he only calls round because I've got money? Thanks, Jake. You really know how to make a girl feel special!'

Snatching up her plate, she shoved back her chair and strode away. She was leaning against the granite worktop, trying desperately to calm down, when Jake set down his coffee and came to stand in front of her.

'I didn't mean to suggest he only likes you because you have money. I just want you to be careful, that's all. I wouldn't want you taken advantage of. Sometimes you're too trusting for your own good.'

'And if I am why should you care?'

'Do you have to ask?'

'Is it because I'm the mother of your child? That's the only reason I can think of that you would care a jot about me.'

He actually *flinched*...just as though Ailsa had physically attacked him. Why, just then, did the scar on his face move her more deeply and terribly than it had ever done before? Before she'd realised, she had lifted her hand to gently trace its raised edge with her fingertips.

'Don't!'

She ignored the steely command and spread out her palm to cover his entire cheek. The bristles round his jaw made his skin feel like roughened velvet. 'I'm sorry I hurt you with what I said,' she told him softly.

Firmly circling her wrist, just as she had feared he would, Jake lifted her hand away.

'And I'm sorry that you really believe I couldn't give a damn about you. It's not true...'

As Ailsa's heart started to pound with regret and sorrow at the cruel events that had driven them apart, she found herself impelled hard against his seductive iron strength, her senses drowned by his compelling male warmth and deluged by memory, hurt and desire.

It was *desire* that took precedence. It touched her blood with fire, mercilessly scorching through her veins as he hungrily, without finesse, took possession of her lips. *The most disturbing thing of all was that she didn't try to stop him.* Just one taste of him was enough to remind her of what she had missed...what she had *pined* for when he'd left. Jake was like an opiate she still craved, even though she knew renewing such an addiction was a road that could only lead to further pain.

As his lips and tongue stoked the passion already consuming her his hands moved through her hair and then down her body, where they settled round her hips, hungrily bringing her closer. His belt buckle bit into Ailsa's belly even as she registered the steel-like evidence of his desire pressing against her. But even as her pelvis softened and the tips of her breasts surged against her bra beneath the sweater she wore shock rippled through her. She realised exactly what she was inviting...the *madness* and soul-destroying stupidity of such an act. Did she really believe that such reckless behaviour could fix anything? She was delusional if she did.

Breaking off the kiss, she wiped her hand across her still throbbing lips, breathing hard. 'This isn't a good idea, Jake.'

'It feels like a very good idea to me.' The grin that accompanied his smoky voice made her legs feel dangerously weak.

'Well, it's not. Do you really think succumbing to a

steamy grope in the kitchen will help us resolve all the problems of the past?'

He looked appalled. Then he looked angry. 'That sounds disturbingly cold. You might not need some human warmth from time to time, but *I* do—and I'm not ashamed of it either. And actually I wasn't thinking that what just happened between us might help us. I simply got lost in the moment. Once upon a time you liked that about me...my spontaneity, I mean. I'm going up to my room to do some work. I would tell you to call me if you need anything, but as I very much doubt you would forget I even mentioned it.'

At the door he briefly turned back, blue eyes mocking. 'On second thought, perhaps you'd prefer to call on your farmer friend? You certainly don't seem to mind accepting help or gifts from *him*!'

Shaken by the hurt that had deluged her at Jake's sardonic parting shot in the kitchen, Ailsa stood blankly in front of the pine tree in the living room, wondering how on earth she would even summon the energy never mind the *enthusiasm* to decorate it. Inside she was quietly devastated that Jake believed she didn't need or desire human warmth like he did. If he had known how much she'd loved the feel of his strong arms around her just now... If he had guessed how much being held by him and kissed by him felt like coming home...

He might think that she was more amenable to receiving Linus's help than his, but the other man didn't have a hope of ever getting a warm response in that way from her because she didn't *desire* him. *Not the way she desired Jake.*

Fighting back her tears at their sorrow-ravaged relationship, she moved across to the wood burner to add another applewood log. After stoking the simmering flame that licked round the previous incumbent, she carefully closed the small glass doors as a flash of electric blue heralded the fire fiercely taking hold again. *Christmas was traditionally a time for families,* she thought achingly, missing her daughter afresh. What would Saskia think if she could see her mother now, hesitating over decorating the Christmas tree with all the trinkets and baubles they had had such fun making together? *Come on, Mum,* she'd say, *It's nearly Christmas! Don't be sad...*

Spurred on by the idea of not disappointing her child, Ailsa hesitated no more. Her darling girl would return home to a Christmas tree *beyond* wonderful, she vowed.

At the back door that led onto the garden she braced herself to face the still swirling snow, pulled on her boots, coat and hat, then determinedly negotiated her way down the thickly frosted path to the purpose-built shed that housed her craftwork. Bringing back the large box of decorations she'd stored there, along with two generous strings of white lights, Ailsa quickly disposed of her outdoor clothing, then returned to the living room with her container of goodies in tow. Along with the delicious heat from the fire, the scent of warm apple immediately suffused her senses as she entered. It definitely made the atmosphere feel Christmassy.

Stowing the box of decorations by the tree, she crossed to the discreetly placed music centre on one of the bookshelves to switch on the CD that was already in there. As an orchestral rendition of 'Silent Night' filled the air, accompanied by a cathedral choir, she breathed a satisfied sigh and then returned to the elegant Norwegian Pine to start decorating…

Sitting on the bed with his arms around his knees, Jake

couldn't summon the slightest interest in working. The urgent mail his secretary had handed to him before he'd left Copenhagen would just have to wait. Right then he didn't care about the consequences.

He turned very still when he heard the notes of his favourite Christmas carol drift up the stairs. Positioning his arm behind his head, he lay back against the stack of plumped up pillows. The poignant music invited him to turn to more peaceful contemplation, but it wasn't easy. He'd been so angry with Ailsa just now, for all but pushing him away and rejecting him, that he'd allowed his hurt to consume him. *Steamy grope indeed!* He hadn't intended to kiss her, but the feelings that had been building inside him ever since he saw her yesterday morning had been growing more and more difficult to contain. Like a dam about to burst.

The kiss he'd stolen had been inevitable, the gesture totally spontaneous…spontaneous and *wonderful*. Even now Jake's body was in a heightened state of painful readiness to make love to her. For a long time after they'd parted his clothes had smelled of Ailsa. It had been a slow, sweet torture to scent her body and not be able to reach out and touch her. Every day had been an agony to him because he couldn't be with her… No other woman since had even come *close* to making him feel like she did. *So much for peaceful contemplation…*

Groaning, he turned over on his side and for a long while just watched the glittering white flakes drifting down outside the window. Then long-held fatigue—both physical and psychological—finally got the better of him and he fell asleep…

The third CD of carols had almost come to an end when Ailsa stepped back to take a proper look at her handiwork.

The handmade decorations that she and Saskia had been creating throughout the year looked a treat. At last the tree was dressed. Along with the glittering coloured baubles and bells, the twinkling white lights gave it the essential magical finish. As soon as daylight started to fade the full, enchanting effect would be apparent.

More than pleased with her efforts, she hummed along to the final track on the CD. It was 'In the Bleak Midwinter'. Not exactly the most uplifting of carols, but she loved it nonetheless. The head carer at the children's home she'd grown up in had always teased her that it was probably the Irish predilection for tragedy in her blood that made her love it so.

The only thing Ailsa knew about her mother was that she had been just sixteen when she gave birth to her and was Irish. Years later, when she'd tried to trace her whereabouts, all she had got was several dead-ends. Many times during her marriage to Jake he had suggested they hire a first-class detective to try and find her, but Ailsa had always declined. After trying to locate her for a while and having no luck she'd decided it wouldn't help her to dwell on the woman who was her mother. It was enough to know that she'd been abandoned—ergo *unwanted.* If her mother had wanted to find her then she would surely have tried years ago, she'd told Jake. *The truth was Ailsa was scared to find her in case she was rejected all over again.* She couldn't have borne that.

Shaking off the unhappy reflection, she started to gather up the odds and ends she hadn't used and began piling them neatly back into the cardboard container.

'Personally I much prefer "The Holly and the Ivy" or "Silent Night". This one is too much like its title…*bleak.*'

Her back to him as she stood up with the box in her arms, Ailsa jolted at the sound of Jake's voice coming from the doorway behind her. She swung round. The first thing she noticed was that his hair was more than a little bit awry, making him appear as if he'd just got out of bed. The second thing she realised was that his compelling deep voice was friendly—as if he wanted to make amends for his earlier irritation with her. Her heart skipped a beat at the mere idea.

'I was playing "Silent Night" earlier,' she replied.

'I know. I heard it. It sent me to sleep.'

'You must have needed the rest. Do you like the tree?'

He studied it for a few moments then smiled...*warmly*. 'It's magnificent. I wish Saskia was here to see it.'

As soon as the words were out of his mouth there was something in his expression that suggested he regretted them. Ailsa wondered if it was because he feared an emotional backlash. But for once, instead of allowing her emotions to get the better of her, she made herself smile.

'She'll see it when she gets home on Christmas Eve. Besides, I'm sure your mother will make her own tree equally if not more beautiful.'

'You're right—she will. If only because her granddaughter is there.'

'It's going to be tough for her...her first Christmas without your dad.'

Jake came right into the room. 'For sure,' he agreed readily, his blue eyes far away for a moment. 'But having Saskia there until the day before will make all the difference.'

Ailsa's disappointment and hurt that he hadn't brought Saskia home when he'd said he would dissipated. She almost couldn't bear the thought of the warm and gracious Tilda Larsen being on her own at Christmas without the man she'd loved since she was a girl beside her, and suddenly she was genuinely glad that her daughter was with her grandmother.

'Are you going to be with your mum on Christmas Day?' she asked.

'That's the plan—if this arctic weather ever clears.'

The box in her arms started to get a little heavy, and she put it down on the rug in front of her. Just as she was about to straighten up again she caught a glimpse of some spangled gold material. Reaching inside the colourful contents of the box, she retrieved the small figure of an angel that Saskia had lovingly made a dress for. A flood of warmth suffusing her chest, she smilingly held it up so that Jake could see it.

'The fairy that goes on the top of the tree... I know you only have a star in Denmark, but here we always have a fairy. Saskia spent ages choosing the material to make her dress with. It's a bit ostentatious, I know—but, hey...it's Christmas.'

'Do you think our little girl has pretensions of grandeur?' Jake suggested wryly.

Smiling fondly in agreement, Ailsa shrugged. 'She's a "girly" girl... She loves dressing up and adores anything pretty. Not like me as a child at all. I was a real tomboy— never happier than when I was dressed in jeans and tee shirt and covered in mud and dirt from the bottom of the garden, where I'd usually be found closely studying the population of worms.'

'And after you'd studied them...what did you do?'

'I took them back into the house to show everyone, of course!'

'You must have been a real handful for those who raised you.'

'The carers at the home, you mean? I certainly can't have been easy for them. I was never a "sit in the corner" type of child. I was always into something I shouldn't have been...a real rebel. I got a prospective adoption placement once, but I kept running away. The people who wanted to adopt me were good and kind, but by then I was so used to the home that I kept trying to break out of the house... even at night. Eventually they decided they simply couldn't handle a girl who rejected every bit of love they tried to give her.'

Saying nothing, Jake rubbed his hand over his chest.

Twisting a long silken strand of chestnut hair round her finger, Ailsa allowed her gaze to fall into his. *It was like diving into a bottomless blue lake.* 'That's probably why it wasn't easy to find anybody else to adopt me. I was a regular tearaway, by all accounts—not the sweet, malleable little girl everybody wanted me to be.'

'No doubt you had a lot of anger inside... It's understandable under the circumstances.'

'Who knows? It's in the past, isn't it?'

'Yes,' Jake agreed soberly. 'It's in the past. Do you want me to put that fairy on the top of the tree?'

'Would you?'

He was tall enough not to need a chair to stand on, and as he reached up to position the bright little figure on the central branch his sweater and tee shirt rode up his muscle-ridged torso. Ailsa gawked. He'd always taken care of himself, but he looked even leaner and fitter than before. She almost had to bite back a groan. His taste still lingered on her lips, in her mouth and on her tongue... The memory of their passionate kiss taunted her. Now her whole body was suddenly taken over by a deep carnal ache.

As Jake turned round again she strove hard to keep her expression neutral. 'That's great,' she told him. 'Just perfect. Saskia's going to love it.'

'Anything else you'd like me to do to help add to the festive atmosphere?'

'No.' She gritted her teeth and smiled. 'I don't think so.'

'What about stringing some lights up in front of the house? We always used to do that…remember?'

The memory was so bittersweet that tears immediately sprang to her eyes. Seeking refuge from his knowing glance, she gathered up the box of discarded decorations and moved to the door. Realising she was starting to distance herself from him again, she stopped to glance back over her shoulder. 'I remember. But it's freezing out there. Do you really want to go outside and do that?'

'I think it would be a nice welcome home for Saskia… don't you?'

That was enough to make Ailsa believe it was a good idea—a *very* good idea. When they'd been married they could easily have hired professional interior designers or decorators to make the house look stunningly festive, but each year, when the most magical season of all had come round, Jake had always insisted on stringing the lights outside the house himself.

'I'll go outside to my workroom and get some extra lights, then,' she told him.

'No, you stay here. Tell me where they are and I'll go get them.'

Her arms were still around the cardboard container, and her heart started to bump hard when Jake came to stand in front of her, smiling down with that ever so slightly crooked smile of his… It affected her so much that somehow she lost her grip on the box and it dropped to the floor, its contents spilling in a kaleidoscope of colours at her feet.

'I'm so clumsy!' she exclaimed, dismayed, instantly dropping down to her haunches to pick them up.

'Don't say that. You're not clumsy at all.' Helping her gently but firmly to her feet, Jake's hands were like a burning brand round the tops of her arms, and Ailsa was so captivated by his nearness, along with the blazing need she saw reflected in his brilliant blue eyes, that she was powerless to free herself...

CHAPTER FIVE

'You're beautiful and graceful.'

It was almost too hard for her to hear a compliment from him when they had seemed to be at war for so long. 'Don't say such nice things to me.'

'Why not, in God's name?' Looking perturbed that her amber eyes were awash with tears, Jake slid his hand beneath her jaw.

'Because if you say nice things then I can't stay mad at you,' Ailsa whispered back brokenly.

Almost unconsciously she'd been leaning towards him, and she didn't know or care right then who made the first inflammatory move but as soon as their lips met she knew she was lost…swept up in a maelstrom that she didn't have a prayer of resisting. Allowing the power of it to suck her under, she didn't protest when Jake held her face so that he could plunder and ravish as she ached for him to do. There was no doubt in her mind about letting desire have its way. She supped and drank him in with equally passionate ardour, hardly noticing that his beard-roughened jaw scraped her skin and would probably leave it feeling tender. Winding her arms round his lean, hard middle, she secretly thrilled at his indomitable male strength…the rock-solid physicality of him, the rugged warmth and scent that made her want to jump right inside him. It was, perhaps, the aspect of his presence that she'd missed the most.

It was actually Jake who regained his sanity first. With his hands still cupping her face he lifted his lips away from hers, his head making a rueful motion. 'You know where this is going to end if we don't call a halt to it right now, don't you? Are you ready for that, Ailsa? Is that what you want?'

She hadn't wanted him to give her a choice. If he had just continued kissing her until her lips were numb and she was too weak with desire to stand then she would have definitely succumbed to being seduced by him. But Jake *had* given her a choice, and now that sanity had prevailed she was moved to act on it.

'I'm sorry,' she murmured. Her face burned with guilt and embarrassment as she shakily stepped out of his embrace. 'Call it a weak moment.'

'What we had between us was never weak or half-hearted, baby. It was always like a lightning storm. It seems that some things haven't changed as much as we thought they had.'

'I can't deny it.' Regret was like a heavy blanket smothering her—regret that Jake had stopped kissing her and regret that an accident had destroyed all their hopes and dreams and torn them apart. Ailsa wished she knew a way to throw off that smothering blanket for ever. Unfortunately she didn't. 'But I know that if we give in to it,' she continued across the ache in her throat, 'it might satisfy a momentary urge but it's not going to mend anything. How can it? We've built separate lives Jake. They may not be perfect, but living apart has kept us from blaming each other for what happened and being angry all the time. Towards the end we were so bad to each other, and I really regret that. We added to our suffering by making each other feel guilty. At least we both get a little peace now, and so does our daughter.'

'Peace? Is that what you call it?' His mouth twisting with derision, Jake muttered a curse. 'The memory of that accident is like being hunted day and night by a pack of rabid wolves. No matter what I do, no matter where I go, I'm never free of the darkness it brings. I'm glad that you feel peace sometimes, Ailsa. I really am. But I can't say that I ever do. I was going to string the lights. I'll go and get them.'

He was out through the door before Ailsa could call him back…

Adding another sweet-smelling applewood log to the wood-burner, Ailsa sat back on her heels. Glancing up at the clock on the mantelpiece, she noted that Jake had been outside stringing lights in freezing temperatures for at least a couple of hours now. Earlier, remembering that he didn't touch alcohol these days, Ailsa had taken him a warming mug of non-alcoholic mulled wine. He'd reached down from the ladder he'd rested against the cottage's sturdy stone walls, murmured 'thanks', then climbed back up the ladder without so much as a backward glance.

The chasm of hurt and tension between them was like an icy splinter embedded in her heart. By the time the weather let up sufficiently for him to be able to travel home would that chasm have grown even wider? Swallowing down her concern that it might, and worrying about the implications for their daughter, she impatiently rose to her feet and headed for the kitchen. Somehow they had to make peace with each other—for Saskia's sake if not their own.

As she entered, the back door opened and Jake put his head round the door. 'I've finished. Do you want to come outside and take a look?'

As his wary glance scanned her, she was struck near-speechless by the dazzling glitter of his piercing blue eyes. It was so easy to fall into a trance looking into them sometimes.

'Give me a minute. I'll just get my coat.'

At the front of the house sparkling white lights dropped in concentric arcs just like a stunning diamond necklace. Even though she was good at crafts and had an eye for design Ailsa knew she could never have come up with anything nearly as beautiful or exquisitely elegant. She was touched that Jake had taken so much time and trouble—and in weather that would have driven most people to hurry back indoors just as soon as they could.

Turning round to study him, she saw how the icy wind had seared his cheeks red raw and felt a leap of concern. 'You've done a wonderful job. Saskia will be over the moon when she sees it.'

'They'll look even better when we switch them on later.'

'They will. But you should come inside now and get warm. You look half frozen. Are you hungry? I'll make some sandwiches and coffee.'

'That sounds great.'

Shucking off his boots on the mat inside the door, Jake hung up his fur-lined jacket and made a cursory attempt to dislodge some of the ice and snow that clung to it. Shivering hard, he clapped his freezing hands together to try and restore his circulation. It was hard to remember when he had last felt so deathly cold. Fixing the lights had been intricate work, and gloves would have rendered the task impossible so he hadn't bothered with them. But it had been worth enduring the stinging snow and icy wind to hear the pleasure in Ailsa's voice at what he had done—to imagine his daughter's delight when she saw the sparkling display.

God, how he missed his little girl... All he wanted to do at Christmas was watch her tear open her presents and then sit with her and hug her tight. Sadly, that wasn't going to be possible, when she would be here in England with her mother and he would be back in Copenhagen. Jake had spent the last four Christmases alone. He'd even declined the usual loving invitations from his mother to spend the holiday with her and his father. The relationship between the two men had become more and more strained due to Jake's desire to bring new innovation into the company—not just to stick to the traditional Larsen way of doing business. Instead of being pleased at his son's ideas, his father had seen his efforts as a bid to somehow usurp him. It seemed that no matter what he'd done Jake had never managed to gain the older man's approval. Spending Christmas with his family would only have exacerbated his unease and pain.

He sighed. It had become a tradition for Ailsa to have Saskia with her over Christmas…especially on Christmas Day…and because of his guilt about past wrongs he'd simply allowed the tradition to continue. But the truth was he didn't want to be with anyone else but his child at that time, and if he couldn't be with her then he would rather be alone.

As he stepped into the warm and cosy kitchen, to find Ailsa humming another familiar carol beneath her breath as she stood at the counter slicing bread, he suddenly knew that it wasn't just his daughter that he wanted to spend that day with. Knowing the very *idea* would just exacerbate the heartache he already endured daily, he quickly jettisoned the thought to the furthermost corners of his mind.

'I'll make the coffee, shall I?'

'Could you?' She threw him an absent-minded smile that all but cut him off at the knees. Even though he'd just spent a freezing couple of hours outside, putting up the lights, his body still ached with the kind of heat that could spark a forest fire—to hold her close and make love to her again one last time…

'Jake? Are you okay?'

'Loaded question.' Grimacing, he moved towards the other end of the counter to switch on the kettle. 'Where do you keep the coffee?'

'I bought a new Colombian blend. Do you want to give it a try? It's in the white porcelain jar…the one from Denmark that your mother gave me our first Christmas together.'

Wincing at the bittersweet memory of his mother's gift, Jake lifted the lid on the aforementioned jar and appreciatively sniffed the coffee grounds contained inside. 'Smells good. Are you going to join me in a cup, or would you prefer your usual tea?'

'I'll have a cup of coffee with you. You can make it in the large cafetière, if you like.'

'Breaking routine, I see?'

As she paused in her careful spreading of butter on the bread, Ailsa's glance was prickly. 'I do occasionally enjoy a cup of coffee, you know. I don't always have tea. You make me sound very boring and predictable.'

Amused by her tetchy defence of her choice, Jake stretched his lips into a grin. 'I wasn't suggesting you were boring or predictable. That's not something I would ever accuse you of. In fact, your unpredictability definitely kept me on my toes during our marriage.'

'That sounds very much like I was unreliable. Anyway, *how* did it keep you on your toes?' Her amber gaze was both quizzical and slightly irritated.

'I didn't mean to suggest you were unreliable. I just meant that sometimes you said you were going to do one thing and then at the last minute you preferred to do something else. Do we have to go over the details?' Carefully he measured out two generous scoops of coffee into the cafetière. 'Isn't it enough that I was charmed by your maverick nature? I wasn't complaining about it.'

'That's all right, then.' With a sniff, she turned back to making their sandwiches.

He didn't know why, but on some level Jake was encouraged that Ailsa still minded what he thought of her. He might be grasping at straws, but right then he didn't care.

'Did you warm the pot before you put the grounds in?' Waving a vague hand, she cut the sandwiches into triangles, then arranged them on two daintily scalloped white plates and carried them across to the table.

Staring at the grounds he'd already scooped into the cafetière, Jake ruefully dropped his hands to his hips. 'No, I didn't.'

'Never mind. I don't always remember to do it either.' She flashed him a genuinely warm smile, and suddenly the winter inside him was supplanted by tantalising summer.

'Thank the Lord for that. I thought you were about to throw me out into the snow in disgust!' he returned jokingly.

'I would never do— Come and eat your sandwiches.' Colouring a little, and looking discomfited, she sat down at the table.

'I'll make the coffee first.'

When he finally sat down opposite Ailsa, Jake rested his elbows on the table and linked his hands, making no move to touch either the food or the coffee—not when he'd much rather contemplate the exquisite features in front of him that made his heart jump every time he gazed at them.

'You're miles away. What are you thinking about?'

She'd always used to ask him that, he remembered, and usually he'd have been thinking about *her...* How lovely she was, how lucky he was to have found her and married her, and how much he adored her. *It was a shame he hadn't spoken those thoughts out loud,* he thought now. *Especially when he'd since learned that she hadn't felt good enough.*

'I was thinking how much Saskia resembles you,' he said instead. It wasn't a lie. Sometimes his daughter's smile stole his breath because it reminded him of Ailsa so much...

'She has your amazing eyes,' she replied softly, following the comment up with a self-conscious shrug.

The warmth in Jake's belly increased tenfold. 'Blue eyes are ten a penny where I come from.'

'But there are many shades of blue...yours is particularly unusual. The colour is like the blue you get at dusk.'

Silence fell between them as their glances met and clung—magnetised by a longing that had somehow miraculously escaped untarnished from the ashes of the past. He hardly dared inhale a breath in case he somehow caused it to vanish.

'Shall I pour the coffee?'

Already lifting the cafetière, Ailsa deposited some into the two slim scarlet mugs Jake had brought to the table. He noticed that her hand shook slightly as it curled round the handle.

'I'm afraid I need some milk and sugar. I can't drink it without.' She rose up quickly from her chair, leaving the hauntingly rich and melancholy trail of her own particular fragrance behind.

His stomach clenched so tight that Jake covered the clutch of iron hard muscles with his hand in a bid to ease the ache.

'Has Saskia told you what she'd like from Father Christmas this year? I suppose we ought to compare notes in case we double up.' Returning to the table, she stirred milk and sugar into her coffee, then took a tentative sip. 'Mmm, that's good.' She smiled.

With a guilty pang, Jake remembered the envelope he'd thrown into his overnight bag. His daughter had given it to him just before he'd left. 'I've got a few things I thought she might like, but before I left she scribbled down some of her own recommendations in a letter addressed to both of us. We could look at it together later on, if you like?'

'Good idea…although she never asks for much.' Ailsa's amber eyes seemed faintly troubled for a moment. 'I know children are resilient… God knows they have to be sometimes, with the things they have to endure…bereavement, illness, divorce… But I worry that Saskia doesn't always tell me if something is bothering her. Do you ever get that impression?'

Because her observation echoed his own feelings about his daughter sometimes, Jake breathed out a long, considered breath before replying. 'I do. In fact, that was why I thought it was a good idea for her to spend some extra time with my mother. I think it's more likely that if she's troubled about anything she might find it easier confiding in her grandmother than telling us.'

'Sometimes it's so hard raising a child. I mean it's wonderful too, but when you're in bed at night you lie awake wondering if you've got it all wrong… You worry that you might have missed something vital that will significantly impinge on their lives later on. Do you know what I mean?'

It wasn't the easiest question in the world for him to answer, even though they had joint custody, because the lion's share of Saskia's care fell upon Ailsa. With every fibre of his being Jake wished it could be different. If only they had been able to ride out the terrible storm that came in the aftermath of the accident…if only they had— He cut the thought off short, impatient and angry with himself for even going there, because it was a soul-stealing exercise.

'I do… But at the end of the day it seems to me that all any parent can do is the best they can. If they love their child unconditionally, whatever happens, then it will work out.'

'I'm sure you're right.' Handing him his plate, Ailsa managed the briefest of uncertain smiles. 'Have your sandwich,' she urged. 'It's only ham and mustard—nothing terribly exciting. You must be famished.'

'You should eat yours too. You barely ate anything this morning.'

'Are you trying to fatten me up?' she joked.

He levelled a serious gaze at her. 'I wouldn't care what size you were as long as you were well and happy,' he said, low-voiced.

Responding with a sigh, Ailsa awkwardly dragged her glance away. 'I am well and I'm not unhappy… It's just that— Never mind.'

'What?'

'It's nothing…really.'

'Tell me.'

'I wish we had talked more when we were together, that's all. You were always so driven to make the family business even more successful that often it felt as if there wasn't room for much else in your life. Anyway… I don't want us to argue again, so I'll leave the subject alone for now. Let's just eat our food and drink our coffee, hmm?' Glancing out of the window, she gave an exaggerated shiver. 'All we have to do is just sit here in the warmth and look out at that winter wonderland, knowing we don't have to go anywhere or do anything very much.'

Uneasy at her disturbing admission of what she'd been musing on, Jake reluctantly agreed. 'Okay…if that's what you want.'

'You never were very good at relaxing.'

He lifted an eyebrow. 'Oh? And you *were*?'

'At least I could sit and knit—do something productive and relax at the same time.'

'I suppose you're going to suggest I take up knitting now?'

About to sip her coffee, Ailsa quickly put the mug down again, her hand against her chest as she fought to control the laughter that bubbled up inside her. *She failed.* 'That would have to be the funniest sight in the world,' she giggled.

'I'm glad you think so.' His lips twitching with the urge to give way to laughter himself, Jake just about managed to keep his expression on the stern side—but it wasn't easy.

As he stared back into the sparkling golden eyes across the table the sight of this pretty woman's enjoyment was more effective at demolishing his defences than anything else he could think of. It reminded him how often in the past a dark mood had been rescued by her humour. *It was another precious facet of her that he missed…* These days—except for when he was with his daughter—the dark moods were sadly more and more prevalent.

'Don't be so serious,' she scolded him cheerfully. 'Apparently men who take up knitting are on the increase.'

'Now you're going too far.' This time Jake couldn't hold back a grin. 'Besides…I don't have elegant, nimble fingers like you. My hands are too big to wield knitting needles!'

'Let me see.'

Before he could stop her, Ailsa reached for both his

palms and turned them over to examine them. The sharp intake of breath she exhaled made his heart turn over. She was staring at the vivid patchwork of scars that decorated his skin—some deep and jagged, others pale and thin.

'I'd forgotten about these,' she murmured softly.

He wanted to drag his hands back, keep them out of sight so as not to remind her of what had happened to them both, so as not to remind himself that he had failed in not keeping her and their baby safe. But Ailsa wouldn't let him drag them away. Instead she was lightly smoothing her fingers over the scars, and the touch of her infinitely soft skin was just too soothing and mesmerising for him to want to be free of it just then.

'I've always loved your hands, you know?' She looked straight into his eyes. 'It doesn't matter that they're scarred. They don't diminish you in any way, Jake. You got these scars because you were protecting me…they're heroic.'

His heart thumped hard. For a long moment a sensation of *white noise* prevented him from thinking straight. When he finally could, he snatched his hands away rubbing them almost with distaste. 'Heroic is the last thing they are,' he muttered angrily. 'Because at the end of the day I *didn't* protect you, did I?'

Ailsa's expression was stricken. 'It all happened so fast… It was like some horrific dream…a nightmare. What more could you have done? You did everything you could to protect me and the baby. You risked your life for us and got badly hurt in the process.'

Reaching for a sandwich, Jake took a bite—but it might as well have been cardboard, because his tastebuds were so deadened by anguish and regret that he couldn't even taste it.

Returning it to the plate, he shoved his chair away from the table and got up. At the door, he threw up his hands in a gesture of apology. 'I can't do this. I can't keep revisiting what happened. I only end up feeling like the whole of my life's been a waste of time.'

'That's dreadful. How could you even think such a terrible thing for even a moment? What about your daughter? How do you think *she'd* feel to hear you speak like that? As if you'd given up on everything? To maybe think she could never even have a chance of making you happy?'

Knowing that he'd hate for Saskia to hear him sounding so low, or to believe that her existence didn't mean the world to him, Jake forced himself to rally as he regarded the increasingly troubled look in Ailsa's eyes. 'Some hero, huh?' He grimaced. Then, turning away, he made his way back upstairs to his room…

CHAPTER SIX

Some hero, huh? Jake's self-deprecating comment hung in the air long after he'd left the room, making Ailsa feel like weeping.

He was a hero…he *was*! Fresh panic gripped her that she had been too hard on him at the time of the accident and during the long recuperation period they'd both endured afterwards. All her grief and anger at the loss of their baby and the realisation that she would never again bear children had been targeted at Jake. No wonder he'd wanted a divorce!

Her heart thumped hard. But then the difficult memory returned of how even before the accident their marriage had been in trouble. It had been just as she had described it to Jake earlier. They hadn't talked nearly enough because he was always working so hard. They'd never discussed what was most important to each other—never found out who they really were, what had shaped them into the people they were. They had simply left it to chance that somehow any difficulties would work themselves out and things would be good again.

The only place that Jake had truly revealed his feelings had been in bed. As wonderful as that had been, it hadn't been enough to help their relationship endure. They'd needed to build a foundation of honesty, respect and truth that would carry them through the hard times. They *hadn't*. One look into the desolate valley of his glance was enough for Ailsa to realise that he had suffered greatly— perhaps *beyond* endurance. She had no doubt that his father's death had added to that suffering.

She lightly thumped her breastbone to help release the distress that threatened to gather force. If she did nothing else, she decided, Jake would walk away from here knowing that she wasn't going to add to his suffering any more—if Ailsa could just convince him that in future she only wanted the best for him, that she forgave him for the way things had worked out between them and genuinely regretted everything she'd ever said or done that had wounded him, then maybe…maybe this time they could at least part as friends?

Restless now, she wrapped the uneaten sandwiches and stored them away in the refrigerator. Tonight she was determined to cook them a delicious meal that they would both eat and enjoy. Maybe she could suggest it was a peace offering—a new start for them both as friends? But even as Ailsa turned the idea over in her head her stomach roiled in protest. *She didn't just want to be Jake's friend… She wanted… She wanted…*

With a heartfelt sigh she remembered the delicious warmth of his seductive lips, how his hard body fitted hers so perfectly—as if they'd been created just for each other and nobody else. Then, like a blow she hadn't been quick enough to duck, the memory of their baby growing inside her—of Jake pressing his lips to her belly each night before they slept—cruelly returned and devastated her all over again.

Choking back a sob, she found her anguished gaze captured by the fresh shower of delicately drifting snow outside the window. Hugging her arms over her chest, she let

her thoughts immediately turn to her living child...darling
Saskia. Her racing heartbeat steadied. In a few more days
she would be home again. And, however her daughter was
spending the time with her grandmother, she hoped she
was enjoying herself.

Adding a quick heartfelt prayer that she and Jake could
somehow find a way of making the remaining time they
had together before he left for Copenhagen less traumatic
and much less wounding for them both, she reached for
her favourite recipe book on the shelf above the fridge, already decided on the appetising dish she would make for
dinner...

Opening his eyes to the darkened room, Jake realised he
must have fallen asleep again. One minute he'd been lying
on the bed, staring up at the beamed ceiling with his stomach churning and his thoughts racing, then the next...*bam!*
He'd been out like a light. The emotional exhaustion that
had regularly visited him since the accident had caught up
with him again with a vengeance. It had laid him out with
a punch worthy of a prize-fighter.

Sitting up, he scraped his fingers through his hair, then
rubbed his chest because his heart ached. The dark and
heavy sense of loss that sometimes imprisoned him when
he awoke returned. *'Dear God...'* The harsh-voiced utter-
ance sounded desolate even to his own ears. Accompanying his return to consciousness was another disturbing
element. He might have been comatose but his heavy sleep
hadn't been dreamless...not by a long chalk. His mind had
been full of arresting images of Ailsa...of her incandescent amber gaze, her lustrous long hair, her 'pocket Venus'
figure and flawless velvet skin. The most disturbing thing
of all was that the images had been so erotically charged.

Right then Jake knew that if the roads weren't cleared

soon then he was going to be in trouble. Lusting after his beautiful ex-wife had not been one of the problems he'd envisaged when he'd decided to make this trip. *Why had she said those things to him, as if she still held some residue of feeling for him?* 'I've always loved your hands…' she'd admitted, then gently touched his scars as though she was far from repelled by them…as if they signified something almost precious…

Shaking his head with a groan, Jake swung his long jean clad legs over the side of the bed. The night was already drawing in, and he reached towards the lamp to turn it on and illuminate the gloom. If the temperature in the room hadn't been quite so chill he would have taken an ice-cold shower to help quell the searing ocean of need that his erotic dreams of Ailsa were making him drown in. As it was, now that he was fully awake he found himself concerned that she didn't have a better heating system in place.

For a few distracting seconds sexual need was overshadowed by irritation and frustration that she hadn't used some of the money he'd given her to live more comfortably. After all, there wasn't just herself to consider. Didn't their daughter deserve to benefit from her father's wealth too? he thought angrily.

She was cooking again. The most sumptuous aroma he could imagine was emanating from the kitchen as Jake walked down the stairs. His empty stomach growled hungrily. Ruefully he recalled that he hadn't eaten the sandwich Ailsa had made him earlier. She was stirring something in a generous-sized cast iron pot on the range cooker, her slim back to him as he entered the cosy, much warmer room.

But the first thing Jake asked didn't concern her cooking. 'Have you tried the phones again to see if there's any service?'

Laying down her wooden spoon on a nearby saucer, then smoothing her hands down over her ridiculously cheerful apron, Ailsa turned to him with a frown. 'I have. It's no-go, I'm afraid.'

'Pity.' The comment was uttered with more force than he'd intended.

'I'm sorry it's such disappointing news. Were you rest-ing?' she asked lightly, clearly attempting to divert his sullen mood and proffering an unexpected smile. A near-*angelic* smile that made Jake feel like the very worst boor. 'You look a lot less tired than you did earlier.'

'What have you done to me? Drugged my coffee? Woven some kind of spell? I don't think I've slept so much in my entire life!'

Her smile didn't disappear. She gave a slight shrug of her slim shoulders, her serene expression the personifica-tion of kindness itself. 'Then it must be exactly what you needed. I'm envious. Don't knock it. I'm making us *coq au vin* for dinner tonight. I thought something more sub-stantial as well as perhaps a bit more adventurous would be good.'

'I don't want you to spend all your time cooking for me. I'm not helpless. I can easily rustle something up for myself.'

'I'm sure you can.' Now her smile was a little tight-lipped, as if he had offended her. *He found himself curs-ing his boorish inability to be more amenable.* 'But I'm making a special meal as a kind of truce between us,' she continued, 'When the time comes for you to leave, I want you to know that you're welcome here if you should ever want to visit again.'

'Well, it doesn't look as if that time is coming any time soon…at least not tonight.'

Standing in front of the uncurtained window, Jake glanced up at the darkening skies and the lacy fall of snow that showed little sign of abating. It took him aback that Ailsa had asserted he was welcome if he ever wanted to return. Yet frustration gnawed at him that he wasn't yet able to head back to Copenhagen, as he'd planned, and sign off his work so that he could go and spend some time with Saskia and his mother. Even more frustration reigned because he wasn't able to corral the desire that automatically seized him whenever he was in the same vicinity as Ailsa. Just being in the same room was becoming a physical and emotional *torment* that tested him to the very edge of his reason.

'Dinner will be ready in about half an hour. The chicken is in the oven and I'm just making some vegetable soup for a starter. Would you mind going into the dining room and lighting some candles? If you need any spare you'll find them in the sideboard drawer.'

Did she know that he'd do anything she asked him right then—*even climb onto the roof and howl like a wolf*—just for the chance of a repeat showing of that sweet angelic smile she'd given him earlier?

Deliberately holding her gaze, Jake couldn't help grinning at the wild reaches of his imagination. 'Sure.'

'What's so funny? Have I got dirt on my nose or something?' Rubbing her face with the edge of her sleeve, she sounded vaguely upset.

'No. Your face is fine…perfect, in fact. I was just amused at what I'd be prepared to do to be on the receiving end of one of your smiles again.'

'Really?' Her voice dropped to an entranced whisper,

and the already slow and heavy primal beat in his blood throbbed even harder and headed devastatingly south.

'*Really*... Are the matches in the sideboard drawer too?'

'Yes, they are.'

'I'd better go and light the candles, then.'

Switching on the light as he entered the dining room, Jake moved towards the heavy mahogany sideboard where a pair of elegant silver candelabra stood. Blinking at them unseeingly for a moment, he took some deep slow breaths to reorientate himself. If he'd ever forgotten that Ailsa had the power to hold him in thrall with just a simple innocent glance, then he was forcefully reminded of that power now.

Distractedly, he opened a drawer to retrieve the box of matches that she'd told him he would find there. He'd just struck one when the dining room was suddenly plunged into darkness. An answering jolt leapt in the pit of his stomach. Touching the flame in turn to the candle-tips in front of him, he watched the fire's sensuous shadows weave and dance against the wall for hypnotic seconds before transporting the candelabra out into the hallway, almost bumping into an agitated Ailsa, who'd come to find him.

In the glow of the candle flames, her beautiful almond eyes were as bright and golden as a cat's. 'It must be a power cut. We haven't had one in ages, but we do get them out here from time to time.'

'Why doesn't that surprise me?' he answered. Because he hadn't been able to keep his growing desire for her in check, Jake failed to keep the irritation from his tone. 'Have you checked the fuse box?'

'It was the first thing I did. None of the switches have tripped, so it must be a power cut.'

'Take this.' Handing her one of the candelabrum, with its flickering trio of candles, he turned back into the

dining room to collect its twin. Back in the dimmed hallway, he said brusquely, 'Let's get back into the kitchen,
shall we?'

'Thank goodness for the range cooker.' Returning to
the stove, Ailsa resumed her stirring of the fragrant soup
she was cooking. 'At least dinner won't be ruined.'

Setting his candelabrum down on the table, Jake moved
to stand beside her. 'Is the stove oil-fired?'

'Yes.'

'So it supplies the central heating too?'

She stopped stirring the soup. Her smooth brow was
distinctly worried as she turned to face him. 'I'm afraid
not… But I've got the wood-burner in the living room. We
can go and eat our dinner in there to keep warm, if you
like?'

'When you've had these power cuts before, have they
lasted long?'

'The last one lasted a whole day. It was a bit of a nuisance because I lost all the food in the freezer. Apart from
that…we managed.'

Jake bit back an accusing retort. He didn't have any say
about where or *how* Ailsa chose to live any more—he knew
that. But Saskia was a different matter. 'I can't say I'm enamoured of the idea of you and our daughter just "managing". Don't you think that it's crazy, choosing to live in
such an isolated place where you could potentially be cut
off from the rest of the world for days in bad weather, and
are prey to inconvenient losses of power that could leave
you without heat and light for God knows how long?'

'That's a bit dramatic. They have power cuts in the city,
as well you know. Besides…I've lived here for a long time
now. I'm used to it and I like it.' Looking as though she
wanted to embellish upon that statement, she chewed down
on her lip instead and said nothing.

Jake sighed. 'You should at least see about getting your own generator, so you'll have back-up if this happens again. Look…this probably isn't the time to get you to think about moving somewhere less remote, but now that I've experienced what you and our daughter have to contend with for myself, I can't promise I'm going to leave the subject alone.'

Dropping down to a low cupboard next to the cooker, Ailsa retrieved two plain white dinner plates, along with a pair of matching soup bowls, and put them on the lowest oven shelf to warm them. As she straightened again, her previously pale cheeks were rosily flushed, Jake noticed. Was she angry at what he'd just said? If so, she'd clearly decided not to express it. *He wondered why.* The Ailsa he had known after the accident used to explode at the least little thing.

'We'll eat in here, shall we?' she suggested. 'The heat from the stove will keep us warm for a while.'

As she stole a furtive glance at the strong-boned, scarred, but still handsome visage on the other side of the table where they sat eating dinner, Ailsa was glad she hadn't irritably responded to Jake's declaration that she and Saskia should be living somewhere less remote. Having promised herself that she wouldn't add to his store of unhappiness, she meant to keep that vow. By the time he came to leave she wanted him to know that living 'out in the sticks', as it were, wasn't nearly as dreadful or inconvenient as he imagined. She also wanted him to realise that she was much more together than she'd used to be…that she was capable and strong and forging a good life for herself and their daughter after the unspeakable tragedy that had wounded and demoralised them all.

'I don't know what you saw in me when we first met.'
The admission was out before she realised.

Laying down his fork, Jake steadily met her gaze across
the candle flames. The midnight-blue lake that confronted
her was so compelling that Ailsa's heartbeat all but thun-
dered in her chest.

'That's easy. I saw a beautiful young woman who was
shy and uncertain in an environment she clearly wasn't
used to,' he answered, 'but who was so intent on doing a
good job that it was endearing.' His rich voice was so low
that she had to lean in to hear him.

'Shy and uncertain just about sums me up back then. I
was so afraid of making a mistake that I practically jumped
out of my skin every time the phone rang.'

'You left out beautiful.'

'What?'

'I said you were beautiful as well as shy and uncertain.'

She knotted her hands together. 'I never felt very beautiful…and I'm not looking for you to reassure me about that.
The truth is I was stunned that someone like you would
even glance at a girl like me.'

'Someone like me?'

'Yes—someone who seemed to have it all…looks,
money, position. It really was hard for me to understand
your interest in me.'

'You didn't see the eyes of the other men that followed
you whenever you walked into a room?'

'No…I didn't.' *I only saw your eyes*, Ailsa admitted silently. From the very first time, when Jake had introduced
himself to her, she'd been completely captivated by him.
The other men that had walked through her days had been
relegated to ghostlike figures of little substance in comparison.

'Why don't we take our drinks into the living room?

It's getting a little chilly in here and we can add another log to the burner,' he suggested, already on his feet.

Glancing distractedly down at her barely touched glass of wine, Ailsa felt her senses roar at the idea of spending the evening sitting by the fire with Jake, with nothing but the light of the dancing flames of fire and candle to illuminate the blackout.

Her hand shook a little as she curled it round the glass's crystal stem and stood up. 'Are you sure you only want to drink orange juice? You wouldn't prefer a glass of wine?' she asked, a husky catch in her voice.

A glimmer of a smile visited Jake's well-cut lips but was quickly gone again. 'I'm sure.'

'You don't enjoy it any more?'

'No.'

'Can I ask why?'

'I don't touch alcohol because I can't find pleasure in something potentially so destructive.'

The seductive warmth that had been curling deep into Ailsa's belly was suddenly replaced by ice-cold steel. She snatched her hand away from the wine glass as though a piece of it had sheared off and cut deep into her skin. 'You mean because that driver was drunk when he ploughed into us?'

A muscle flinched clearly in the cheek that was still smooth and unscarred. 'Yes. But I'm not saying that *you* shouldn't enjoy it. I'm sorry if I was too blunt.'

His meant-to-be consoling words didn't help. 'You weren't too blunt. I'd rather have the truth, no matter how hard it is to hear. I think there are too many sorrys between us...we've blamed each other for so much, Jake.'

He looked to be considering this comment for a long time. Then he breathed out a sigh and said, 'Let's go into the living room, shall we? You take that candelabrum and I'll bring the other one. Bring your wine too.'

'I don't want it now.'

'Bring it.' He lifted a gently chastising eyebrow.

Once they'd arranged the candles in the best positions to light the room, Jake sat on one supremely comfortable couch and Ailsa on the other. The mere fact that they'd done that so automatically grieved her more than she could say. Cradling the glass of wine she no longer had the slightest inclination to drink, she focused her sights on the fire blazing in the burner rather than on her charismatic ex-husband—even though her secret wish was to gaze at his compelling features for the longest time. A disturbing thought struck her. What if when they woke tomorrow morning a thaw had taken place during the night, melting the snow? *If so, there'd be no further need for him to stay...*

'Come back to me, Ailsa.'

'What?'

The smoky-voiced command jolted her. So much so that she almost spilled her wine. In her heart, wild hope tussled with a more pragmatic desire to be sensible.

'You went to a place where I couldn't reach you. I don't like it when that happens. It worries me.'

'I—I was thinking what a shame it is that we can't switch on the Christmas lights,' she lied. 'You worked so hard fixing them up.'

'We'll switch them on tomorrow. It's not the end of the world if we can't turn them on tonight.'

'No... It isn't. We've seen the end of the world, haven't we?' Her voice faltered, dropped to a bare murmur.

The fresh applewood log Jake had added to the fire crackled and hissed, and suddenly Ailsa was staring at long straight legs in velvet-napped, expensive blue denim as he came and planted his feet in front of her.

Gently, he took her glass and set it down on a nearby surface. 'Come here.'

She didn't argue. She didn't have the heart. Besides, how could she argue with the man she had built every dream of love and hope around? It felt like heaven having him so close, sensing his warm breath brush her face, having his long-lashed blue eyes command her attention like no one else's could.

As his glance roved across her fire-warmed features, it was perhaps the most intense that she'd ever seen it. The heat from his hands burned through the denim of her jeans as they settled round her hips. 'I wish you didn't hurt so much. It near kills me to think of you in pain in any way.'

'It's not your fault. It's just that sometimes—sometimes the most dreadful feelings wash over me…feelings stirred by the terrible memory of that car hitting us. I can still hear the ear-splitting sound of the car tyres skidding in the rain. Even when I tell myself that one day the memories and feelings will fade, because this hurt can't last for ever, I don't think I really believe it. Most of the time I try and stay positive…not let things get me down…especially for Saskia's sake. But then something reminds me, and the pain comes back and makes a liar of me.'

Jake's hands firmed round her hips and Ailsa swallowed hard.

'I just wish it was spring again, so that I could throw open all the windows and breathe more freely—do you know what I mean? Sometimes I feel so trapped it's as though I couldn't run far enough away to escape.' She sniffed, knowing that inside her emotions were helplessly unraveling. 'But of course I'm only trying to escape from myself.'

He didn't reply. He didn't have to. It was enough for her to know that he listened and understood. She exhaled a breath that wasn't quite steady. Then he was kissing her—kissing her as though the desire had erupted pure and undiluted straight from his soul. If there was the slightest inclination in her to regain control then Ailsa willingly surrendered it. Beneath the onslaught of devastating emotion and the wild, hungry need that her heart and body easily matched she felt like the fragile frond of a willow, borne on a hurricane into the drowning rapids of a thunderous waterfall...

CHAPTER SEVEN

JAKE drew Ailsa down onto the couch behind them and never—not even for a moment—separated his mouth from her lips or his hands from her body. Hunger and desire long denied could no longer be contained. They cleaved to each other as though fearful another storm would batter them, separating them for ever this time…

Finding herself positioned beneath Jake's hard, heavier body, Ailsa greedily drove her fingers through the short silken strands of his hair, her senses bombarded by the twin scents of his arresting cologne and the deliciously musky male warmth that was his own personal blueprint. He raised his head to look at her. This time he didn't ask her if this was what she wanted. *There was no need.*

In the softly waving candlelight the strongly hewn features mesmerised her. Even his scar was beautiful, because it was an integral part of him now. And in spite of all that had happened he exuded such tenacity and strength. Ailsa sensed it. So how could even the cruellest wound mar or lessen such an indomitable presence?

She gently touched her palm to the side of his face. 'Jake…I want this as much as you do…I really do. But I haven't—I mean it's been a long time since I— What if I can't manage it any more?'

Her hand fell away and she curled it round his iron hard

bicep instead. The force of how much she wanted him took her breath away. Her blood was on fire just at the mere anticipation of him loving her as he'd used to. Yet the blunt truth was that she was scared...so *scared* that it would hurt or be too uncomfortable for her to endure. Her body had not healed overnight after being injured in the accident and losing the baby. It had taken weeks before she'd had the strength and confidence even to try to meet the normal demands of day-to-day life. If she now found herself physically unable to go through with this most intimate of acts between a man and a woman then she would disappoint and demoralise them both.

Her heart drummed hard as she waited for Jake's response. When she saw that his expression was the epitome of tenderness itself a huge weight lifted from her heart. The kindness reflected back at her softened the harsher contours of his face, turning his eyes to liquid silver in the dimmed light.

'We'll take it slowly,' he promised. 'The last thing in the world I want to do is hurt you. And if at any point you want to change your mind...well, that's okay too.'

Ailsa breathed a relieved sigh. Then she simply surrendered to the melting sensations that seemed to be intensifying deliciously inside her.

Item by item Jake carefully undressed her. In between removing her clothing he tenderly kissed every inch of flesh that was revealed. She shivered and shook with the sheer joy and pleasure of it. When he removed his own sweater and the tee shirt underneath, her gaze appreciatively luxuriated in the jaw-dropping male physique whose mouth-watering appeal had not dimmed at all in the passing years. Yes, there were a few nicks and scars that hadn't been there before the accident, but—like the healed gash on his face—they didn't detract one iota from his powerful attraction.

His shoulders and torso were lean and muscular—like an athlete's—and he had a very light dusting of dark blond hair crossing his chest. As she had glimpsed before, when his tee shirt had ridden up, Ailsa saw that even though Jake was a businessman—by dint of his career working in offices most days—he kept himself in good shape.

All thought was dizzyingly suspended when he touched his lips to her breast and drew the aching, rigid tip deep into the molten cavern of his mouth. Her womb gave an answering leap. He slid his hand down over her ribcage, the provocative trail his fingers took leading straight to the apex of her slender thighs. Gently but firmly he nudged them apart. When he started to explore the moist heat at her core she immediately tensed and grabbed his hand.

'Is it too much too soon? Am I hurting you?' Jake husked, lifting his head to examine her face concernedly.

Unable to relax and completely enjoy an experience she'd privately longed for and fantasised about throughout the years—even though fireworks were exploding inside her at his touch—Ailsa pursed her lips. She shook her head. 'No. I'm just a bit tense in case—in case it does hurt,' she confessed anxiously.

He emitted a grated breath. 'Did the doctor tell you that it might?'

'She told me I might be sore…but that was about three months after the accident. And by that time we'd stopped being intimate, so I never—I never found out whether it hurt or not.'

'It's been over four years since then.'

The silvery-blue eyes boring down at her were like haunting starlight, and Ailsa's stomach turned over at the sorrow she saw glinting in their depths. That ravaged glance made up her mind.

'I know,' she whispered. Carefully cupping her hand behind his neck, she pulled his face back down to hers. 'Try again,' she urged softly, tracing the outline of his lips with her fingertip. 'Everything will be okay.'

He hesitated. 'Are you sure?'

'Yes.'

As if to confirm her decision, her hips automatically softened and her body relaxed. This time when Jake explored her she sensed urgency and a need for fulfilment take hold of her almost straight away. There was no pain, as she'd feared there might be. Instead there was a sensual and erotic blaze of heat that built and built, until her teeth clamped down on her lip because it was almost too incredible to bear, and as the sensations reached a crescendo a throaty moan of pleasure she couldn't hold back escaped her.

Before she recovered Jake kissed her again, his silken tongue gliding into her mouth with a similar urgent need to experience the bliss and fulfilment that Ailsa had just enjoyed. Dizzingly giving herself up to his wonderful kiss without reservation, she sensed him press himself inside her and then thrust deeply upwards. Again there was no pain—just an amazingly pleasurable fullness she knew straight away she'd missed and achingly mourned. She wrapped her slender legs round his lean, hard middle to welcome him in even deeper. As he thrust into her again and again her hands clung onto the broad banks of his shoulders and her fingernails bit into the smooth muscle of his back. For a second time she came undone. Only a few moments later Jake anchored her head with his hands and with a harsh-voiced groan helplessly joined her...

As soon as he came back down to earth and the reality

of what he'd just done hit it wasn't the fact that he'd spilled his seed unprotected inside Ailsa that was Jake's concern. Because sorrowfully, to his cost, he knew that she couldn't become pregnant. He was concerned that he'd maybe been too forceful and hurt her. But then he saw that her sweet, entrancing lips were curved into a wistful contented smile, and it raised his hopes to the skies.

With growing wonder he cupped the side of her face beneath the silken waterfall of her lovely hair to tenderly stroke the pad of his thumb across her cheek. 'You look happy,' he said.

'That's because I feel good...*very* good.'

'I didn't hurt you, then?'

'No, you didn't. My body feels like it's healed completely. It's just such a wonderful revelation that I can function normally again. I suppose the worry that I couldn't has been playing on my mind for a long time now.'

'Maybe you should have gone to a doctor to have her properly check you over and reassure you?'

'You know how I feel about doctors.'

'Even so, having an examination could have saved you a lot of heartache.'

'Point taken.'

'I'll drop the subject, then.'

On the wall behind them, the sinuous shadow of the candle flames continued to dance and weave, and the fire in the wood burning stove seemed to blaze more brightly than before. With a silent prayer, Jake thanked the powers that be for the unexpected gift of a blackout. Then he carefully withdrew from the incomparable delights of Ailsa's body and reached for the substantial plaid woollen throw on the back of the couch to pull it over them both.

'Cosy, huh?' he said, grinning as he urged her close into his side.

'It feels seriously decadent,' she agreed, screwing up her nose.

Her amber-coloured eyes were delightfully mischievous. *It had been a long time since Jake had seen her looking so untroubled...like the Ailsa of old that he had fallen head over heels in love with a lifetime ago...*

'So when was the last time you felt as decadent as this, hmm?'

'I think it was when you whisked me away from work in the lunch hour one day and took me to the Hilton where you'd rented a room for just the afternoon.' Her lashes lowered shyly for a moment. 'We made love for the longest time. Normally I would have feared being sacked, returning to work so late, but seeing as I was with the boss's son...'

'Didn't I promote you after that?' he teased.

She playfully slapped him on the arm. 'No, you didn't! And if you'd tried I would have vehemently protested.'

'No, you wouldn't.'

'Yes, I would.'

'I agree. You probably would have. You were always far too conscientious for your own good.' He dropped a lingering warm kiss onto her mouth and she went very still. 'We had fun together once upon a time, didn't we?' he mused softly.

'You were very passionate.'

'I still am.' He noticed wariness creep into her eyes at that comment, but in the next instant it was gone again.

'Jake?'

'Yes?'

'Why did you wait so long to meet up with me again? I mean...four years of telephone calls making arrangements for Saskia to stay with you every other weekend, then sending Alain to pick her up and bring her home instead of doing it yourself. I know you have to work, but would it have been so inconvenient for you to collect her and bring her home to me?'

'It's not that it was inconvenient. It was that— Look, do we have to talk about this right now?'

Fiercely resisting breaking the spell of these precious intimate moments, Jake feared another soul-destroying disagreement if they fell into discussing how they'd conducted things in the past. He really didn't want to reveal the guilt and shattering disappointment that dogged him still for not protecting her and the baby that terrible night. Neither did he want to confess that he saw it as his punishment to stay away from her. That was why he employed Alain to act as go-between—not because it was too inconvenient for him to get away from work.

He and Ailsa had just made love, and it had been beyond wonderful, but he knew it didn't make everything all right. *How could it when his mind, body and spirit were weighed down with enough crippling guilt to sink a battleship?*

With a sleepy smile, Ailsa dreamily stroked his arm. 'No. We don't have to talk about it now if you don't want to. But I'd really like us to talk tomorrow and maybe clear a few things up.'

'Okay.' Jake fought the reluctance that her suggestion inevitably caused, containing his feelings to try and protect himself and silently conceding that maybe it *was* time to tell her a bit more about himself and why he struggled so hard with expressing his emotions. He brought her fingertips up to his lips and kissed them. 'Why don't you close your eyes for a while, hmm? You look a little tired.'

Letting her head rest against his chest, she concurred. 'I *am* tired—though goodness knows why, when I've done very little today. Don't let the fire go out, will you?'

she murmured, already drifting off into a land where he couldn't follow.

'I won't.' Swallowing down the ache inside his throat, he settled his arm around her shoulders. Then, staring over at the wood stove, he surrendered to the hypnotism of the still dancing flames...

'What was that?' Staring wildly round in the semi-dark a few hours later, Ailsa pushed herself up. The haunting sound that had pierced her sleep still echoed disturbingly in her mind. 'It sounded like a baby crying.'

'It wasn't a baby.' Crouched low in front of the burner, where he'd obviously been stoking the fire, his torso bare, Jake got to his feet. 'I think it was a fox,' he said, turning to face her.

His jeans were riding low across his hips, highlighting the ridged toned muscle of his flat stomach, and his voice was 'just woken from sleep' husky. She couldn't imagine any other man looking more dangerously sexy. In a disturbing flash she remembered why they were still there in the darkened front room, sensed the places on her body where he'd intimately touched her. That instigated a deep and powerful ache for more of his passionate attentions.

Then, realising she was as bare as a newborn babe beneath the throw, she tugged the cover self-consciously up around her shoulders.

'A fox?' She rubbed her eyes and blinked at him.

'We're deep in the heart of the countryside. It's not unusual. We even have them in London.'

'That's why I don't keep chickens.'

'Really? You mean you *wanted* to keep chickens?'

Ailsa saw that Jake was shamelessly grinning, perhaps mocking the notion that she had such ordinary, mundane ambitions these days. *It certainly didn't sit easily with the luxurious lifestyle she'd once enjoyed as his wife.*

'I did. What's wrong with that?'

His expression sobering, Jake lifted his shoulders and dropped them again. 'I didn't say there was anything wrong with it. You're quite the little country girl these days, aren't you?'

She felt her face heat at the observation. 'It's quieter here than the city, and consequently I feel less stressed.'

'Well…talking of lessening your stress, I think you should try and get a bit more sleep. It's only just after three a.m.'

'The power hasn't come back on yet?'

'I haven't checked. I've just been enjoying the candle-light and the glow from the fire.'

His concentrated sleepy-eyed glance instigated an out-break of goosebumps all over her body. 'I prefer that too,' she murmured, snuggling back down under the throw.

Immediately crossing the carpet to the light switch, Jake flicked it on. The electric light failed to register. Shaking his head, he made his way back to the fire. 'If the phones are back on in the morning I'll make some calls and see about organising that generator.'

'You don't have to do that.'

'I know I don't *have* to. I *want* to… There's a differ-ence.'

'Yes…' Ailsa agreed sleepily, nervously wondering if he was going to rejoin her in their makeshift bed on the couch any time soon. She realised she'd be very happy if he did… 'There is a difference.'

As if intuiting her secret wish, he dropped down beside her, at the same time raking his fingers through hair that had clearly received similar rough treatment earlier.

'I like this "just got out of bed" look,' she teased him.

Unable to understand why it should happen right then, Jake stared into Ailsa's smiling beautiful face and felt a powerful resurgence of grief at what he had lost. Sometimes he seriously wondered if sorrow was the price he had to pay for this life even for the briefest moment of pleasure. If so, the trade-off was a cruel one. *For him, the death of their baby and the death of his marriage had signalled the end of love...period.*

Coiling a gleaming strand of her chestnut hair round his finger, dredging up a smile from God only knew where, he stayed where he was for only a minute more, suddenly knowing that he wouldn't be spending the rest of the night there on the couch with her. He wouldn't renege on his silent promise to reveal to her why he found it so hard to express his true emotions, but right now he knew he needed some space to think things through.

'Rock stars would give their eye teeth for inside information on how I do it so effortlessly,' he replied drolly.

'Are you okay? Why were you up? Did the sound of the fox wake you too?'

'No. I just naturally woke up, then saw that the fire was dying.'

'You look tired, Jake. Why don't you come and join me under the covers...lie down for a while?'

Feeling as though he had lead in his heart, he shook his head. In another second he was up on his feet again. 'I think I need to get back to my bed upstairs...we'll both sleep better if I do. I've stoked the fire, so it should keep you warm for a while yet. Like I said, in the morning, if the phone lines are working, I'll sort out getting you a generator. Goodnight, Ailsa...try and get some more sleep, hmm?'

Collecting the remainder of his clothes from where they lay strewn on the carpet, he exited the room without so much as a backward glance. But the disturbing memory of Ailsa's surprised and saddened face weighed heavily on his tread as he climbed the staircase in the dark to return to his room…

A dazzling ray of sunlight arrowed through the window, and outside, where a blanket of snow covered everything in sight, it had the dramatic effect of making the crystalline white carpet shimmer like diamonds. And even as she stood there in the kitchen, gazing out at the magical wintry scene, Ailsa heard the sound of ice dripping from the eaves. *It was beginning to melt.*

She ought to be overjoyed, but she wasn't. The possibility of the chill weather changing for the better left her feeling raw and empty inside. *When he left, would it be another four years before she saw Jake again?* She'd found a note from him on the kitchen table. It read that the electricity had returned, and so had the service on the house phone. He'd gone out for a walk, but would be back soon to sort out the business of a generator and to make some calls home to Copenhagen.

He must have got up especially early, Ailsa realized, because by the time she'd arrived in the kitchen to sort out the detritus from last night's dinner the dishwasher had been almost at the end of its cycle. She had to confess it was a pleasurable surprise to find everything cleared and tidied away.

Moving across to the table, to lay out the crockery for breakfast, she grimaced and rubbed her back. Her muscles were seriously stiff from her night spent on the living room couch. *Pocket sprung mattress it was not!* But the main discomfort she was suffering was in the region of her heart, because Jake had left her there alone. *Why hadn't he stayed with her?* Was he afraid that now that they had been intimate she would make some sort of unreasonable demand on him?

To bring a temporary end to the string of apprehensive thoughts that were gathering with disturbing momentum as she stood there, she made a beeline for the telephone. Less than a minute later the warmly reassuring voice of Tilda Larsen sounded in her ear. Taken aback by the pleasure Jake's mother expressed at hearing from her, Ailsa once more conveyed her condolences on the death of her husband and asked how she was coping. Hearing that she was just taking one day at a time—because what else could she do?—Ailsa felt her heart go out to her. Then, unable to wait a moment longer, she asked to speak to her daughter.

'She's right here beside me,' Tilda replied affectionately. 'The little angel has been longing to talk to you.'

'Hello, Mummy—I've really missed you!'

'Hello, my darling. I've missed you too…so much. But the snow has been so heavy here that we couldn't get the phone to work and ring you. Are you all right?'

'I'm fine. I've been having a lovely time with Grandma. You don't mind me—staying a bit longer, do you?'

Ailsa's throat swelled. 'Of course I don't mind. I'm sure it's been a great help to her to have you there'

'Is Papa still with you?' Saskia asked.

Picking up on the longing in the childish tones, Ailsa sensed her stomach clench tight. 'Yes, he's still here, sweetheart. He's had to stay with me because the snow is so bad that he can't make it back to the airport. That's why he hasn't been able to return to Copenhagen yet.'

'You haven't been fighting?'

The question was like a thunderbolt, arrowing down out of the sky, exploding shards of electricity at her feet. 'Why do you ask that?'

At the other end of the line there was a brief pause, followed by a lengthy sigh. 'It's just that whenever you talk about Papa you get sad, and whenever he talks about you he sounds angry. I hope you don't get in a fight. It's nearly Christmas and I want you both to be happy.'

'Darling, I—we're neither of us unhappy, I promise you. And nor will we get in a fight.' Biting back the near-overwhelming urge to cry, Ailsa started in surprise when at the very moment Jake came in through the back door.

Having already divested himself of his outdoor clothing, he clapped his hands together to warm them and threw her a disarming grin. His cheeks were ruddy from the biting winter wind and his eyes mirrored the electric blue of a cloudless summer sky. A second lightning strike exploded through her insides.

'Mummy, are you still there?'

'Of course I am, darling. Papa is back from his walk. Do you want to say hello?'

'Yes, please!'

'It's Saskia,' she said quietly, her hand over the phone's mouthpiece.

Jake was at her side in an instant, and all but snatched the receiver from her. 'Is that you, baby?' she heard him ask huskily, and knew she didn't imagine the slight break caused by emotion in his meltingly rich voice.

CHAPTER EIGHT

UNABLE to keep the hurt and anxiety from her tone after they'd both completed their conversations with Saskia, Ailsa tackled Jake about the worrying comment their daughter had made expressing her concern that they might 'get in a fight'.

'Why would she say something like that?' she demanded, hugging her arms round the hip length, black angora sweater she'd matched with leggings. 'She said that you sound angry when you talk about me.'

'She's never mentioned that to me before.' His expression was immediately guarded, she noticed, almost drawn, as if this was an added complication he didn't want to discuss. 'If I've ever sounded angry it was probably because I was tired or stressing over something at work. I've certainly never been aware that I've conveyed anger towards you in her presence.'

'Well, Saskia is a very intuitive child. I'm sure she wouldn't have imagined it.' Her fingers were trembling a little as they brushed her hair back from her face, and beneath her ribs Ailsa's heart was galloping. 'She also said that I sound sad whenever I talk about *you*.'

His lips twisted ironically. 'Now, *there's* a surprise.'

'What do you mean?'

'I'm sure the thought of me doesn't exactly fill you with

joy. You must have plenty of regrets about how things worked out. In truth, apart from giving you Saskia, I must be the biggest mistake you ever made! All you ever wanted was a family, you told me once…but I even managed to screw that up for you.'

His tone was savage, his expression bleak. Shock eddied through her as though she'd stumbled into a ravine. She was dizzy with fear that the situation would only deteriorate if she didn't find a way of rescuing it somehow. The need to talk things out had never been more urgent.

She swallowed hard. 'I've never seen being with you as a mistake…*ever*. How could you believe such a crazy thing? And you didn't screw anything up either. Was it *your* fault that that man was over the limit that night? Of course it wasn't! Look, Jake…whatever personal hurts or damaging beliefs we're carrying around about each other, don't you think it's time we aired them so that we can let them go and move on? It was a dreadful thing to lose our baby, but does that mean we should stop fully living? Stay static in some kind of frozen animation for the rest of our lives and never enjoy happiness again? I don't think so. Besides…we have a daughter to think about as well as ourselves. I don't know about you, but I've had enough of grief and sadness. I want to find a better way. I certainly don't want our daughter growing up thinking that all we've done since the accident is blame each other for everything going wrong. That would be a horrible legacy.'

'I don't blame you for anything.'

'No? Then why would you be angry with me? Why did you go back to your own bed in the middle of the night? That looks very much like you weren't happy about something. Was it something I said? First you make love to me—then you shun me.'

'I didn't shun you.'

Jake looked distinctly uncomfortable. As if he might walk out at any second. In her mind, Ailsa implored him to stay. In the next instant the tension that emanated from his whole being seemed to dissipate—just as if he'd overcome his resistance for a deeper conversation and was now resigned to at least *some* discussion on the matter.

'It wasn't about anything you've done or said, Ailsa...I want you to know that. If I blame anyone for the situation between us it's myself, and if it's distressing Saskia because she's picking up vibes that I'm holding on to some kind of anger about the past then clearly we have to do something about it... *I* have to do something about it... I agree.'

The silence that followed Jake's surprising remark prickled with assorted tensions. He might have agreed they had to reconcile the past in some way, but Ailsa easily sensed the wealth of pain behind his words and the feeling that he was struggling to get a grip on it. She realised she would have to steer the ship.

'Jake? We'd run into problems in our marriage long before the accident. Let's be honest about that. That's probably why you're still angry. We never got to the bottom of our unhappiness then and we're still avoiding the issue now. The accident just brought things to a horrible head.'

'You're right.' His glittering gaze held her in a trance for several electrifying seconds before she reminded herself to breathe again. 'You know what I think part of the problem was?'

Ailsa stared. 'Tell me.'

'I put work before my family. I worked hard not for more money, position or acclaim, but because I craved my father's love and approval above all else. I never felt like I'd ever really had it...even as a child. He was a tough man to get close to. The hoops I'd put myself through to even win a smile from him you wouldn't believe! I'm afraid I got so blinded by the need to win his regard that I thought that if I worked harder, became more important to the success of the business than anyone else, then that would help me reach my goal. When you used to try and get me to talk about things, to tell you how I was feeling...I resisted at every opportunity. Even though I sensed the tension between us getting worse, I somehow convinced myself that things weren't really as bad as I imagined... I told myself that I could carry on behaving like some...some driven automaton and everything would still turn out all right. My father was a workaholic and I adopted the same soul-destroying pattern.

'Why couldn't I see it? Why couldn't I see that my obsession was hurting my family? Hurting *us*, Ailsa? I loved you so much. Except I didn't really demonstrate that to you, did I? Even when you found out you were pregnant with our son I still didn't take the time to get closer to you...except in bed, of course. I'm so sorry. I behaved like the classic emotionless macho male and I want you to know that I'm not proud of it.'

Ailsa was so overcome by what he'd said that she didn't know how to respond. Her body had no such dilemma. Unbidden, a purely primal desire for him to take her to bed drowned out any other thought or feeling. In all the years she had known him Jake had never spoken to her so frankly and honestly about his feelings. Suddenly the behaviour he'd exhibited during the dying days of their marriage—even before the accident—made so much sense. Having been raised without the love or approval or a parent herself, it wasn't hard for her to understand why Jake had been so constantly driven to win his father's regard. He was right. Jacob Larsen had been a good man, but he had definitely kept up a shield in front of his emotions.

How she wished that Jake had really been able to understand the depth of her love…had realised how it might have
helped him. It probably wouldn't have healed his sense of
hurt around his father, but it might have gone some way
to helping him make peace with it and letting him concentrate on the people in his life he meant the world to instead.
A wave of heat suffused Ailsa at the spine-tingling memory of the candlelit passion they'd shared last night. But,
as compelling as the idea of making love was, she didn't
want to bring their frank conversation to an end just yet.

'I'm sorry too, Jake. If you'd shared some of this with
me back then we might have been able to deal with things
better. In any case, I'm not exactly the innocent party.
You suggested that perhaps I was too young to get married early on. Maybe you were right…not because I didn't
genuinely love you or want to be with you, but because I
too was looking for the love and the sense of belonging
that I didn't have in my childhood and I projected all that
need onto you. It was probably a heavy burden.

'It wasn't your job to make me happy or to give me a
sense of worth, but when you worked late night after night,
weekend after weekend, I told myself it was because I
wasn't enough of a woman for you…that I must be lacking
in some of the qualities a man needed in a wife because
if I had them then you would be home more. The trouble
was I had no real sense of myself as a worthwhile person
at all, and you working all the time didn't help lessen that.
I thought marriage was the answer for me because I was
afraid to be alone. Yet I'd spent most of my life until I met
you on my own! I've realised I'm perhaps more resilient
than I believed. Starting the craft business and taking care
of Saskia has shown me that.' Her lips formed a shy smile.
'I don't regret the time I spent with you Jake…even the

sad and difficult days. I don't regret it one bit. I want you to know that.'

The statement didn't seem to reassure him. His steady gaze was definitely troubled. 'So where does all this leave us?' he asked.

'Well…at least we're being real with each other at last, don't you think? By the time you leave here at least you'll know that we've been honest with each other…that we're both dedicated to making the future different…to making it *better.*'

With another shaky smile she turned away, her aim to fill the kettle and make tea for her and coffee for Jake— anything to take her mind off the provocative track of get-ting close to him where it seemed disturbingly to want to linger.

What Ailsa wasn't prepared for was for Jake to step up behind her and draw her body firmly back against his. *Had he somehow read her mind?* The sensation of steely male warmth behind her made her insides melt. Lifting her hair off the back of her neck, he pressed his lips against the place he'd exposed, and although they were chilled from his winter stroll, the heat they injected into her blood-stream was near volcanic.

'What are you—?' The rest of her question helplessly died away as he laid his hand over her breast and cupped it.

'It might not fix anything or put everything right… but I can't help how I feel and right now I want you,' he breathed, the volatile words emitted on a throaty rasp as he slid his other hand inside the waistband of her leggings and then down—right down inside her cotton panties. 'I want you so bad I can hardly think about anything else…'

The answering gasp Ailsa emitted turned into a ragged whimper. Her whole body trembling with mindless need, she turned in his arms and the ravenous collision of mouths, teeth and tongues that followed turned the bones in her legs to running rapids that seriously threatened to unbalance her.

'I think what we need is a nice soft bed...don't you?'

She'd barely uttered, 'Mmm...' before Jake scooped her up in his arms as though she weighed not much more than one of the bundles of fabric she kept in her workroom and headed out into the hallway. She hung on with her arms round his neck, dropping incendiary little kisses onto his face and mouth as they travelled, even onto his indomitable chin with its sexy little cleft.

His intent burning gaze held hers all the way up the stairs to the guest bedroom. By the time he laid her down on the bed, with the ochre and scarlet silk eiderdown that she had crafted over a period of several months during a dry spell in her work, Ailsa was so consumed by longing and desire that her awareness of anything else but Jake simply dissolved...became utterly unimportant.

Staring up at him as he straddled her, she felt her focus intensify. Such deliberate examination at close quarters re-acquainted her intimately with the features she had fallen in love with all those years ago. It didn't matter that time and tragedy had left their mark on them. Nothing could detract from the beauty of the precisely carved face and the blue eyes that were a sunlit lake one minute and a sultry moonlit night the next. Then there was the strongly defined nose that on a less handsome man might not be seen as an attribute but on Jake was simply absolutely right. But it was his mouth that she fixated on, because with a frisson of delicious anticipation she intimately knew the kind of immeasurable delights it could bestow...

In the otherwise silent room, Ailsa was suddenly very much aware of her own heightened breathing. *They didn't talk*... Words could come later, but for now their bodies would do the talking instead.

As her lover sat astride her, he jettisoned his sweater and tee shirt, then leant forward to tug her angora jumper over her head. As soon as he'd got rid of it he lowered his dark blond head to draw an aching rigid nipple into his mouth through the filmy gauze and cotton of her bra. The pleasure was so intense, the force of it far beyond mere words, that tears welled in her eyes. She couldn't begin to express how much she'd missed him. Over the years since they'd separated, when the thought of him caught her un-awares—for instance when she was out shopping or work-ing at her crafts or cleaning the house—it would instigate a deep ache of longing in the pit of her stomach that made her want to weep a veritable ocean of tears. Now, every-thing inside her burned for his possession.

Freeing her tingling breasts completely from her bra, Jake turned his attention to the rest of her clothing, and Ailsa luxuriated in the feeling of his hands moving impa-tiently over her skin. When she was naked beneath him, she eagerly wove her slender arms round his strongly corded neck as their lips hungrily met for another scald-ing kiss.

His senses were consumed with an awareness of every-thing about her that he'd loved and missed...the unique se-ductive scent of her body that was an aphrodisiac above all others, the beautiful long hair that resembled spun silk as it splayed out in chestnut waves on the pillow behind her, the almond-shaped amber eyes that needed no make-up in order for them to be sexy or appealing because they already had those attributes in abundance. Even the sight of the tiny mole behind her earlobe aroused his passion.

Jake had never fantasised about an ideal type when it came to women. He'd never preferred blondes over brunettes or vice versa, or tall and slim over shorter and more diminutive. Ticking boxes had never come into it. But if the idea of the perfect woman *had* ever unconsciously entered his daydreams, then surely Ailsa was it?

The fire in his loins reaching a near inferno of longing, he started to ease himself inside her. Unable to hold back the need to be closer, he pressed deep, then deeper still. It was as if his entire body became the living beating heart that throbbed so passionately in his chest. Ailsa's softly arousing moans filled the air and Jake filled his hands with her small pert breasts, before drawing them into his mouth and then running his tongue over the firm satin buds at their tip. Outside it might be the dead of winter, but here in this soft warm bed it was a sultry Indian summer.

The lithe shapely body beneath him stilled suddenly. The incandescent amber gaze darkened. The hot silken purse that enveloped him clenched him tight again and again. 'Jake…' She whispered his name as though caught up in a spell, then drew him down to her again, buried her face in the hollow between his neck and shoulder.

The stunning thought that he must have done something good he wasn't aware of to be rewarded with the pleasure of loving this incredible woman again crept up on him. The fresh realisation that she was the mother of his precious child hit him squarely in his gut, awakening almost primal feelings of possession and pride. This was Ailsa… the woman who'd stirred a wealth of passionate emotion in him he'd hardly known he possessed almost on sight… the woman who might have borne him a son if only—

He wasn't quick enough to cut off the tide of pain and fury that accompanied the agonising memory. The power of it caught him on the raw and he thrust inside her so deep that his volatile feelings spilled over into his passion, his body jolting helplessly, as though swept away by a furious current. In that drowning moment he surrendered all desire for control, simply let the force that carried him take him straight to the dizzying heart of its power. The feral cry that poured straight from his lungs when he got there was like a savage shout of pain. What shocked Jake even more was that as he cried out boiling tears submerged his eyes.

Breathing hard, he lowered his head, desperately trying to recover some composure, turning his face away from Ailsa so she wouldn't see the evidence of his distress. But the consoling gentle hand on his forearm and the deep sigh that made the tiny hairs covering his skin immediately stand to attention told him that she *did* see.

'What's wrong? Jake, tell me *please.*'

He didn't answer straight away. Still breathing hard, he lifted his body from hers. Moving to the side of the bed, he leaned over to reach for his discarded jeans. Delving into a back pocket, he removed his calf leather wallet. Hesitating for only a moment, he extricated the grainy black and white print he kept in one of the sections and handed it to her.

'I just got to thinking about our son…*Thomas*. It was an early summer's afternoon in Copenhagen when we— when we made him…remember? Not long after that we discovered you were pregnant. I kept the ultrasound photo you gave me after we'd been to the clinic. You see? I didn't forget him. How could I? He was—he was my boy…the boy I didn't get to see grow up…'

'Oh, Jake…Jake…'

'Remember how ecstatic we were when we found out the sex of the baby? We couldn't believe how lucky we were to have a boy and a girl…the perfect little family.'

'I know you didn't forget him.' Her hair falling round her face as she moved up onto her knees, Ailsa sounded seriously shaken and Jake saw that her eyes were bathed in tears. 'I never knew you kept this. I'm sorry if I ever gave you the impression that I thought you didn't care about our baby as much as I do.'

'Maybe it was my fault because I never talked about it? It's the way I was taught. Not by my mother, but by my father. He had the belief that it showed strength of character if a man kept his feelings to himself. My mother was the only one he ever let his guard down with, and even then probably not very often. Anyway, he's gone too now and it's all water under the bridge. He's not coming back and neither is our son. And I can't keep going back there…to that cold, dark time when we lost Thomas. It's too hard. Can I have that?' Swallowing across the pain inside his throat, Jake leaned forward to take the picture. Then he carefully returned it to his wallet. Shoving it back down into his jeans pocket, he lifted his head, his gaze squarely meeting Ailsa's. 'The other thing I can't forget is how hurt you were. The sound of you crying out still haunts me.'

'You were hurt too.'

Almost afraid to see the compassion in her eyes, he was all but ready to dismiss it. *How could he possibly be deserving of care or compassion after what he'd done?* he wondered. During the last six months, since he had become CEO of the company, due to his hard work and dedication their profits had gone through the roof—but he didn't feel as proud of the fact as he once might have done. He'd just made one sacrifice too many to take any pleasure in it. And the burden of guilt at not protecting Ailsa and the baby seemed to grow heavier year by year, instead of lessening. Somehow he had to start to ease that burden. He didn't exactly know *how*, but at least he was open to entertaining the idea at last.

'It was a tough time for both of us,' he remarked quietly. 'But, like you said earlier when we spoke about the legacy we might be leaving Saskia, we have to find a way of moving on…agreed?'

'Agreed.'

Ailsa's smile was tinged with sadness, but hope also lingered in the softened amber glance Jake saw. Climbing back onto the bed, he gently took her into his arms. 'We'll stay here for a while, hmm?' he suggested, dropping a warm kiss on the top of her head. 'And when we're ready we'll talk some more.'

The promised continued conversation didn't ever manifest itself. Just a few minutes after Jake had folded Ailsa against his chest the sound of someone hammering on the front door made them guiltily spring apart.

'Who can that be?'

'I'm sorry, baby, but I'm not psychic. Why don't you go and see? And when you find out, tell them you're busy.'

Ailsa's heart pounded—not just with shock at the unexpected sound of the door knocker shattering the peace that had enveloped them, but because of the possessive inflection she clearly heard in Jake's tone.

'Were the roads any clearer when you went out this morning?' she asked him urgently, even as she reached for her discarded clothes and hastily pulled them on—not the easiest thing to accomplish when his blue eyes were observing her bare form with a hotly lascivious glint. 'I mean…were there any signs that there might be vehicles getting through?'

'The ice was melting a little, but I didn't see any car tracks. If it does thaw tonight then I can probably get to the airport tomorrow and catch a flight home. Who do you think is at the door? Not that ever so helpful neighbour of yours again, I hope?'

Silently reeling at the idea of Jake leaving the next day,

Ailsa took a second to get her bearings. 'If it is Linus then I don't want you to be rude to him. Why don't you just wait here? I'll be—I'll be back in a minute.'

As she self-consciously tucked her hair behind her ear, due to the disconcerting interest Jake was still displaying in her body, Ailsa prayed that it wasn't Linus calling. If it *was* she hoped she could quickly get rid of him—particularly if Jake decided to come downstairs…

His thick dark hair looking as though a comb had subdued the naturally curling locks especially for his visit, Linus surveyed Ailsa warmly as she opened the door. She had no control over the guilty blush that heated her cheeks. How could she when she'd just got out of bed with Jake?

'Linus…is everything all right?'

'I was going to ask you the same question,' he came back, jerking his head briefly behind him. 'I see the Range Rover's still here. Your ex hasn't gone back to Copenhagen yet, then?'

She frowned, then folded her arms across her black angora sweater, conscious of the fact she was braless underneath it because of her hurried dash to get dressed and answer the door. 'No. He hasn't. There wasn't a chance with the snow still lying so thick on the ground. Was there—was there a particular reason you dropped by?'

'There was, as a matter of fact. Mind if I come in for a minute?'

'I'm—I'm rather busy at the moment, as it happens.'

'Oh…' Clearly taken aback at having his plans thwarted, the farmer's son took a few seconds to reassemble his thoughts. 'I suppose I'll just have to say what I want to say out here, then.'

Stealing a furtive glance down the hall, Ailsa half expected to see Jake descending the staircase at the end of it. Thankfully, no such disturbing vision appeared. She returned her full attention to the man in front of her, noticing just then that his breath made little clouds of steam whenever it hit the frosted air. Feeling suddenly guilty at making him stand outside in such bitter weather, she opened the door wide, adding a cheery smile for good measure.

'On second thoughts, why don't you come into the warm for a minute? Go into the kitchen, I've just got to pop upstairs for something.'

As soon as a pleased Linus passed her in the hallway, Ailsa shut the door behind him and fled up the stairs. In the bedroom, now fully dressed, Jake was fastening his leather belt round his jeans. When he glanced up to acknowledge her return his accusing glare made her insides turn over.

'Why did you ask him in? I thought you were going to tell whoever it was that you were busy...*especially* him.'

'He came round to ask me something. I couldn't leave him shivering on the doorstep, for goodness' sake!'

'Does he always make such a nuisance of himself?' Jake scowled.

Hating the idea that he was disappointed in her because she hadn't put Linus off and returned to bed, Ailsa was also resentful that he seemed to be assuming some kind of right to say who she could or couldn't invite into her own home. 'He's not being a nuisance. I told you—he's a good neighbour and friend. The sooner I go downstairs and talk to him, the sooner he'll leave. I'm sure it won't take long. You can wait up here, if you like.'

Not waiting to hear his answer, she grabbed her bra off the silk eiderdown and, with her back to Jake, lifted her sweater over her head so that she could put it on. Before she had the chance to secure the front fastening he stepped up behind her and—*shockingly*—pushed the thin straps aside, cupping her breasts. Molten heat, want and need suffused her.

'Jake…*don't*!' But even as she instructed him in the negative her body and senses were silently pleading for more of the same. It took *Herculean* strength of mind to divert him. 'You mustn't… We mustn't… For goodness' sake, Linus is waiting downstairs!'

'Let him wait' His low-pitched growl was sexy and commanding as he caught an aching nipple between thumb and forefinger and pinched it.

Suppressing a groan, she grabbed onto her swiftly diminishing will with all her might, turning in his arms to chastise him. As soon as she did, her mouth was crushed relentlessly and passionately beneath his, his silken tongue hotly invading her so that they shared the same devastating breath. With a supreme effort Ailsa tore her lips away, holding onto his iron-hard shoulders because if she didn't her knees would crumple and she might well fall over. The warmly delicious scent of his body and teasing blue-eyed smile fired another devastating aside into senses that were already overwhelmed by him.

'You don't play fair.'

'Did I ever claim to? Sometimes a man has to use whatever advantage he can lay his hands on.'

'You've got to let me dress. The sooner I go downstairs and talk to him, the sooner he'll go. Then we can carry on talking. We were going to do that…remember?'

Sighing ruefully, Jake gently stroked back some drifting strands of her hair with his fingers. 'How can I deny you anything when you stand there looking at me with those big doe eyes—and half naked to boot?'

'It's not just the male sex that knows how to use the advantages in their armoury.' She smiled. Standing on tiptoe, Ailsa planted a brief affectionate kiss on his mouth, then

firmly pushed him away. 'I won't be long,' she promised, finally able to fasten her bra and slip her sweater back on.
    'You'd better not be.'

CHAPTER NINE

'SORRY to keep you waiting, Linus. Can I get you a cup of tea or coffee?'

'No, thanks. I can't stay very long, I'm afraid.'

Her neighbour's assertion was music to Ailsa's ears right then. But even as she sighed inwardly with relief, she didn't escape feeling guilty. He was standing in the middle of the kitchen, his shoulders hunched defensively, like a schoolboy about to confess some errant misdemeanour. She'd never seen him appear so ill at ease.

'All right, then. Would you like to sit down while we talk?'

Moving across to the kitchen table, she pulled out two chairs—one for her guest and one for herself. After that, apart from the hum of the radiator and the steady tick of the wall clock behind her, silence stretched out between them for what felt like a disconcertingly long time. Just when Ailsa wondered if he was ever going to sit down or speak at all, Linus dropped down into his chair and leant earnestly across the table.

'I was wondering what your plans were for Christmas Day?' His dark eyes anxiously roved her face. 'Only, if you're free, I was going to ask if you and Saskia would like to have lunch with me... That is...it won't be just me... unfortunately.' He grimaced. 'My father and uncle will be there as well. To tell you the truth, we'd really appreciate some female company. An all-male household can get a bit much sometimes.' A red flush tinged his weathered cheeks for a moment.

Sheer surprise stunned Ailsa into silence. Of all the things he might have been going to ask her, she definitely hadn't expected an invitation to lunch on Christmas Day. Staring at him blankly for a moment, she knew it was her turn to swiftly reassemble her thoughts. 'It's very kind of you to invite us, Linus, it really is... But I was actually planning on just staying at home with Saskia. We've come to regard the day as a special mother-and-daughter time. We've been looking forward to it for months now.'

'Oh...'

'Linus...hello.'

The familiar smoky voice that sounded behind them startled her. Her visitor seemed taken aback too—as if Jake's sudden appearance had put him on edge.

'Hello,' he answered reluctantly.

Wishing that Jake had simply waited until Linus had gone, Ailsa felt her gaze magnetised by him as he moved to stand by her side, her heart racing as with a lazy little smile he reached for her hand and raised it to his lips. The provocative kiss he bestowed didn't just graze her knuckles, as she'd expected it to, but was deliberately planted in the centre of her palm instead. Even though she knew the gesture was probably designed to stake his claim in front of the other man, it still made Ailsa tingle as if she'd received a mild electric shock.

'Am I interrupting something?' Jake asked smoothly.

Linus shook his head, his air that of a man who had just been well and truly *crushed*. A wave of guilt rolled over her.

'I was inviting Ailsa and her daughter to spend Christmas Day with us, but she's told me they usually spend it on their own.' The farmer pushed to his feet, the scarlet flush beneath his skin that had appeared earlier returning with a vengeance. His dark eyes moved from Ailsa to Jake, then back to Ailsa again. 'I didn't realise that you and—'

'Jake.'

She registered the controlled politeness of her ex-husband's voice, but knew instinctively that his tone might change to a far less agreeable one should Linus be foolish enough to challenge it. Thankfully…he *didn't*.

'You didn't realise what?' Jake pressed mildly.

'It doesn't matter.' The other man was already moving towards the door. 'You're a very lucky man, if you don't mind my saying so? Ailsa is one of the nicest people you could wish to have for a neighbour, and her—your daughter—is charming.'

'I definitely have to agree with you on both counts.'

'You must be relieved that the snow is thawing at last, so you can get to the airport and fly back to Copenhagen in time for Christmas. It must be especially beautiful at this time of year.'

'It is.'

'Well…I hope you enjoy the holiday when you get there.'

'Thanks.' Jake's glance settled thoughtfully on Ailsa for a moment, before moving back to Linus.

'I'll—I'll see you out.' Slipping into the hallway ahead of her visitor, Ailsa almost held her breath all the way to the front door. She couldn't help feeling as if she'd been caught in the middle of a threatening storm. When the rumbles died away, as they had now started to, her whole body would be limp with relief. Her hand fumbled a little with the heavy brass doorknob. As she exposed Linus and herself to the raw wind blowing outside, she said, smiling, 'I really do appreciate your invitation, you know?'

Stopping thoughtfully beneath the peg-tiled porch, Linus turned round to survey her, 'Do you? I hope you don't think I was being a bit too presumptuous? I didn't realise that you and your ex were getting back together or I would never have asked.'

She supposed it was only natural, after Jake kissing her hand in front of him, that Linus would assume they were getting back together... She glanced awkwardly down at the ground. It wasn't as though she'd ever encouraged Linus in any way, yet she still felt uncomfortably as though she was deceiving him.

'I'm really sorry that I couldn't accept, but I hope you can still have a nice Christmas with your family.'

A drop of melting ice from the roof above him splashed down onto the dark curls that were slowly springing back into life after being so tidily combed down. Almost absent-mindedly, he patted it away. 'I expect it will be very much the same routine as other years. I'll still have to get up early to feed the animals and clean out the pens. My uncle will cook the dinner as he usually does—we're having a goose—and my father will drink a bit more malt whisky than is good for him. After that we'll watch some daft re-run on the television. Anyway, however you spend it, I hope that you will also enjoy the day. I expect we'll see each other at some point after the holiday?'

'Take care, Linus and—and thanks for all you've done for me and Saskia throughout the year.'

'It was my pleasure. Bye, now.'

Her chest tightened in sympathy as she watched him negotiate the now less than pristine snow on the path that led out from the stone-walled confines of the house. Waiting until he'd climbed into his tractor, she gave him a brief wave, then shut the door and returned inside.

'I told you he had more than just being a friendly neighbour on his mind.'

Turning round to face her from his stance in front of the window, Jake was unsmiling...*irritated*, Ailsa would have said.

'That's neither here nor there, and you know it!' Irritated or not, she wasn't going to put up with it. 'Why didn't you wait upstairs until he was gone, like I suggested?'

Raising a dark gold eyebrow, he scowled. 'Are you telling me that you would have accepted his invitation to lunch?'

'You heard him tell you I'd already declined as I'm spending Christmas Day on my own with Saskia.'

He exhaled a heavy sigh. 'Is that really what you want to do... Spend Christmas on your own with our daughter?'

'It's what I usually do...why?'

'I know I haven't got round to asking you yet, but the idea of you coming back and spending Christmas with me and Saskia in Copenhagen has been on my mind since I woke up this morning. That's why I got up early and went for a walk. I needed to think about plans. Plus I wanted to check out the state of the roads—see if we could make it to the airport either today or tomorrow. Preferably *today*... It's a good idea, when you come to think about it. That way you get to see our daughter much sooner, and you don't have to spend the season alone.'

'So you're feeling sorry for me now, are you?' she snapped, feeling inexplicably emotional.

'Sorry for you? If you think that's what's motivated me to ask you—*especially* after last night—then I'm honestly stunned.'

It had seriously upset Ailsa when Jake had shown up a

couple of days ago to tell her that Saskia would be extending her stay in Copenhagen. How could she have known that the situation would change so dramatically in so brief a time? That their enforced togetherness would stir up feelings that wouldn't easily be subdued and that she'd be deluged by taunting reminders of how good they had once been together? Now, because he had made that remark about leaving soon, she was privately climbing the walls at the reality of him not being around. That was why the idea of going to Denmark was more than tempting.

But, as much as her heart ached to be with him, and to see her precious child much sooner than she'd expected, how could she do it? How could she return there as if everything between them had been put right and there were no more problems? There was so much still to discuss, and she had no idea where any of it would lead when they did talk about it. She might have even made the situation *worse*, because now that she and Jake had been intimate again her heart was wide open to even more hurt.

He'd denied there was anyone else, but she couldn't be absolutely certain that he didn't have some woman waiting for him when he returned to the luxurious town house that was his home. If he did, no doubt she would be a much more glamorous and *worldly* woman than Ailsa. Perhaps she was one of those women he had mentioned who was of the opinion that his cruel scar gave him a certain 'piratical' appeal?

'Whatever you might think,' Jake said now, 'my intentions are good. To learn that Linus had invited you and Saskia to Christmas lunch made everything even clearer to me. I'm sure he's a decent guy, Ailsa, but I'm not going to give up the chance of you spending Christmas with me just because he's around. I *want* you to come back with me. I know that Saskia will be delighted if you do, and so will my mother. She often asks after you. Unfortunately, up until now, I haven't been able to tell her how you're doing. I really regret that we haven't talked since—since what happened.'

He was standing by the granite worktop and Ailsa saw his fingers visibly tighten round the rolled edge. They flexed so hard that they turned corpse-white. A cold chill ran down her spine. Then she was moving towards him, as if her body's volition had overridden her mind's, and she trembled with the force of the feelings that gripped her.

'We've become so good at not saying the right words, haven't we? At not calling a thing what it is? I know we talked about some important stuff at last, but we've skirted around the issues that really matter like they're unexploded bombs that might go off in our faces. Well, I've got news for you, Jake... The bombs have already exploded and we've caught the fall-out good and proper. When you say "what happened" you should say "when our baby was killed and the love we had for each other died too." Isn't that what you really mean to say?'

The blue eyes that lifted towards her were as desolate as the bleakest of winter nights. 'And that makes everything better, does it? Calling a thing what it is?'

She threw up her hands in near-despair. 'At least it's being real... At least it's the truth. I'm not saying I want to hang on to these feelings for ever—they've already cut my heart to shreds, so why would I? I don't want to add to my suffering, and I really do want to move on. For the past four years I've been stuck...*welded* in the mire of that terrible event. Trapped so deep in it that at times I've felt almost paralysed. I dread to think what that might have done to Saskia. She's so vibrant and alive, and I haven't been the mother I want to be for so long that I know that things have to change. They've *got* to change. What I'm telling you now, Jake, is that I want to speak my truth and then I want you to speak yours…to really tell me how you felt then and how you feel now. After that… Well, we'll see.'

'Then tell me, Ailsa. Tell me your truth and I'll listen. Then I'll tell you mine.'

Catching her by the hand, Jake stared hard at her slender, ringless fingers. As if disappointed by what he saw, he let it drop back down to her side again. She wondered if the pounding of her heart was as audible to him as it was to her just then.

'Very well, then… When I came to after the operation and they told me I'd lost the baby I thought I was in the middle of the most terrifying nightmare. I thought, *Any minute now I'll wake up and see that I'm at home in bed with Jake.* I thought…I thought I'd tell you about my horrific dream and you'd comfort me…lay your hand over my tummy, where our baby was still growing…still thriving… and say, *"See? It was only a dream, Ailsa. Everything is fine."'*

Her throat tightening unbearably, she threaded restless fingers through the long dark skeins of her hair. She hardly dared glance at Jake for fear she would come undone completely. 'But it wasn't a dream,' she continued huskily. 'And although they gave me morphine to dull the pain I still hurt. I hurt *beyond* any pain I'd ever experienced before. I'm not just talking about physical discomfort. I felt empty…empty and useless now that my baby was gone. Like a mere husk of the woman I used to be. They say that sometimes the bereaved are numb with grief, but I felt everything—as though my very skin was being flayed with knives. I mourned my child and then I mourned *us*, Jake. I mourned us because I knew it was the end even then. I thought things had been hard enough, but how could we ever get over that? How could we carry on and behave like normal civilised people?

'It wasn't long before we both realised that we couldn't. Our lives would never be "normal" again, and because of that we took all our rage and pain out on each other. I was glad when you asked me for a divorce. I mean it. I was glad that you would have the chance to rebuild your life with someone else—to father a baby with someone else. But when you left…' Lifting her head to face him squarely for the first time since she'd started speaking, Ailsa found it almost impossible to continue, because her throat swelled and ached so much. 'When you left…' With a little shake of her head she indicated she couldn't go on.

Jake's natural instinct was to haul her into his arms and hold her for the longest time. She looked ridiculously young and vulnerable with her chestnut hair framing the perfect pale oval of her face…like a child. But her raw admission of how she had felt at the time of their baby's death and then afterwards, when she'd believed that their love had died too, was like a small but devastating tsunami crashing inside him.

When the dust began to clear a little he had the peculiar sense of having missed something important…something *vital*. The realisation hit that he'd perhaps not been as aware of his good fortune as he should have been when they were married. Instead he had blithely greeted each day imagining that the comfortable existence they'd enjoyed could go on for ever, without anything too serious ever endangering it. Even the fact that he'd become a workaholic like his father. Foolishly, perhaps even *arrogantly*, he had cocooned himself from the remote and terrible possibility that everything he loved could be ripped from his arms in less than a blink of an eye… *He'd never even considered it.*

But then why should he have? His friends and colleagues had always told him that he had the Midas touch—that everything remotely associated with him effortlessly turned to gold. Jake had it all, they said—supportive parents, a fabulous career, wealth beyond most people's wildest dreams and then, if that wasn't enough, he had a beautiful wife and daughter as well. Up until that horrific day when that drunken driver had ploughed into his car he had seen no reason to dispute that gilt-edged belief. The very notion of such a cataclysmic event had truly been the stuff of nightmares…

His agitated gaze came to rest on the moist bronze-gold of Ailsa's bewitching eyes. 'I was like a sleepwalker,' he began. 'Not just after the accident, when life became a living nightmare, but before it too. I didn't notice enough of the things that were important to me. I was so fixated on the business that I missed the fact that I was lucky to have you in my life at all. It's a terrible thing to admit, but maybe I even took you for granted. My focus was all on my work—on wanting to prove to my father that I could be everything he wanted me to be and more. My great desire was to show him that when the time came for me to take over the business I could make it even more successful. I became so fixated on that goal that I didn't pay proper attention to my life…to *our* lives together. In the split second before that car hit us I didn't see my life flash before me, as people sometimes say they do. What I saw instead was that I was about to lose everything I loved *more* than life itself.'

Pausing to inhale a steadying breath, Jake absently touched his fingertips to the ridged contours of his scar. Noticing with a jolt that the tears in Ailsa's eyes were spilling over and sliding in an unchecked stream down her face, he pulled his hand away and, still agitated, tunnelled his fingers through his hair. It was perhaps the hardest thing he had ever done—to talk candidly like this. While the instinct to stop—to hide behind his defences as he had so often done in the past—surfaced again and again, he forced himself to stay strong and, as Ailsa had asked, to speak his truth.

'It brought me to my knees, losing our son. I could hardly believe that such a thing could happen to me…to *us*. And because I was hurting so bad I took it out on you, Ailsa. I meant to be a support to you, a comfort, but instead I effected an even greater distance between us than the one we'd been struggling with already. It was probably far crueller than the bitter words I sometimes threw at you. You were bitter with me too. The truth is it was our emotional *neglect* of each other that finally drove us apart, wasn't it? And, because *finally* I couldn't bear what was happening to our relationship, I knew I had to be the one to bring the misery to an end. The act was a double-edged sword. Yes, it freed us a little from our pain as a couple, but individually…it simply left us to endure it alone. Was that any better?' He stared hard at Ailsa. 'It certainly didn't feel like it to me. You asked me to tell you how I feel now? Well…to be honest, I'm still trying to figure that out. In the meantime, I'm simply grateful that we're talking again.'

'Thank you.'

Her words were so soft—softer than the delicate brush of a summer breeze against a voile curtain. Jake wondered if he'd imagined hearing them at all. But when he studied her face, she was scrubbing her tears away and smiling. Not comprehending, he stared at her. 'What for?'

'For telling me your truth.'

The doubt and fear inside him eased a little. 'You're welcome.' Closing his fist, he glanced it lightly against the smooth granite worktop beside him. 'Are we done now?'

'If you mean am I going to raise the topic again while we're together, then, no. I'm not. I've realised that to keep going over the pain of the past can make for a very sad existence. Well, I don't just want to *exist*, Jake. I want to live…properly and fully. Today is a new day…a clean page that has yet to be written on. From now on I want to treat every day like that. I want to believe in the possibility of being happy again.'

'So…will this new affirmation have any bearing on your decision to come to Copenhagen with me?' he asked, his lips wrestling with the surprising desire to smile too.

'I think it will…yes.' She hugged her arms over the black sweater that Jake was suddenly jealous of, because of its intimate proximity to her lovely body.

'And your decision is…?'

'I think I *will* take the opportunity to go back with you—to see Saskia and to meet up with your mother again. I'd like to tell her personally how sorry I was to hear about your dad's passing, and that I'll always remember him. But, Jake…?'

'Yes?'

'Just because we've been honest with each other at last it doesn't mean that we're making any promises about the future, does it?'

Feeling his heart miss a beat, like a hurdler who had miscalculated the distance to the next hurdle, knowing his mistake had cost him the race, he forced another smile to his lips. 'No. It doesn't. Like you, all I want to do now is to take one day at a time.'

'Okay. I suppose I'd better cook us some breakfast and then tidy up the house a bit, in case we have to leave soon.'

'It might be a good idea if you packed too.'

'I was just coming round to that, but— Oh! I've just thought of another thing.'

Watching her tap her fingers against her adorable chin, Jake smiled benevolently. 'What's that?'

'Saskia's Christmas presents. I mean, I still have some to get, but I've got quite a few that are already wrapped. Can I bring them with us?'

'Maybe a couple of small things—but you're going to have ample opportunity to visit the Christmas markets and get some more. At any rate, she won't lack for gifts on Christmas Eve…not if her grandmother has anything to do with it!'

Ailsa's animated face told Jake she'd just remembered something else. 'Didn't you say that she'd given you a letter to bring with you that had a list of things she might like in it?'

With a stab of guilt, he remembered the envelope he'd hastily thrown into his overnight bag when he'd left Copenhagen. 'She did. Why don't we read it when we get home? We're not going to be able to shop here if we want to leave today.'

'You're right. Well, I suppose before I do anything else I'd better go and pack…just in case. Do you think we *can* get a flight today?'

'If the planes are flying out of Heathrow I don't doubt it. I'll make some calls in a minute.'

'What about the roads? Do you think they'll be clear enough for us to get to the airport?'

'I'd forgotten how much you worry. Trust me, sweetheart… If I say we'll get there and everything will be all right, then it will.'

Colouring, she tucked a long strand of silky chestnut hair behind her ear and shrugged. 'Okay, I believe you. One more thing… Where will I be staying? At your mother's with Saskia? Or—or…?' She coloured again, this time a deep shade of russet-pink.

'I thought that you could stay with me.' Unable to help it, Jake inserted a hint of steel into his tone. 'I'll probably have to work up until Christmas Eve, but I'll make sure that Alain is at your disposal for whenever you want to visit Saskia at my mother's or go shopping. I imagine we'll all spend Christmas Day with my mother. How do you feel about that?' His gut felt as if it was clamped in a steel vice as he waited apprehensively for her answer.

'That sounds fine. Will you ring Saskia and let her know that we're coming?'

'I'll ring as soon as I've booked our flight.'

'Good.'

Ailsa left him alone then. For a long time Jake just stood staring out of the window at the melting snow, the lingering scent of her perfume tying his insides into knots as he fought to get his churning emotions under control….

CHAPTER TEN

WITH the usual commanding ease with which he was able to make most things happen, Jake got them an afternoon flight out of Heathrow that day. By the time Alain had picked them up from Kastrup Copenhagen airport at the other end and driven them to Jake's five-storey house at one of the wealthiest addresses in the city it was getting on towards eleven in the evening.

Having spoken to her daughter a couple of times before and after the first-class flight from Heathrow, Ailsa could hardly wait to see her again. Even though their reunion would have to wait until tomorrow, because they had arrived so late, she didn't forget that it was thanks to her ex-husband that they would be meeting up much sooner than she'd expected. It was a precious gift she wouldn't take for granted.

Throughout the seamless journey, Jake had been unusually quiet. Ailsa was hardly surprised when she recalled the depth and frankness of his reflections about the tragedy that had driven them apart. That would be apt to leave the strongest person emotionally drained. And, because she was mindful of the deeply emotional places they had both visited over the past few days, she'd chosen not to disturb his reverie by talking. In fact, apart from eating lunch, she had slept for most of the flight. When she'd woken, she hadn't told him that she'd been dreaming about him… dreaming about the exotic honeymoon they'd shared in the Caribbean island of St. Kitts after their wedding.

Although they'd been in one of the most beautiful locations for a honeymoon in the world, surrounded by tropical forest and a sapphire-blue sea, they had hardly ventured out from their luxurious villa. Apart from a welcome dip or two in the jewel-like warm sea, and enjoying first-class cuisine prepared by their chef out on the patio, their long hot days had mostly been languorously viewed from their opulent bed through the open French doors. The erotic memory of that time still had the power to flood her body with heat and make her tingle.

'Home sweet home,' Jake drawled now, bringing Ailsa sharply back to the present.

Just as her ex-husband had only set eyes on her traditional English country cottage for the first time a short while ago, it was now Ailsa's turn to reciprocate and experience for the first time the opulent modernity of his own elite abode. For a girl who had been raised in a very basically furnished children's home with minimal creature comforts the sense of wealth and exclusivity that reached out to embrace her as she stepped into the white marble hallway quickly reminded her of the stark differences in her and Jake's backgrounds. Even though she was well acquainted with the rich trappings of the Larsen family's wealth, it still took her aback to experience it first-hand. Her gaze sweeping the 'winter palace' furnishings, and the very contemporary modern art that Jake had always had a strong preference for on the walls, she suddenly had the sense of being ridiculously shy and ill-prepared here on his home turf.

'It's very beautiful,' she murmured quietly, slipping off her leather gloves.

'I say home, but you understand that I use the term loosely?' With a wry smile, he stepped towards her. 'Are you hungry?'

'I had a meal on the plane, remember?'

'That was hours ago.'

'Are *you* hungry, Jake?' Unthinkingly, Ailsa batted the question back at him. It was only when she saw his arresting eyes darken to a sultry navy blue that she realised how it had affected him.

'For food? No. But if you're asking if I'm hungry for you, Ailsa, then the answer will always be yes.'

Lightly touching her hair, he gave her a smile that was tender rather than passionate, but it still had the effect of quickening her pulse and warming her heart as if she'd just imbibed the most intoxicating brandy.

'Would you mind if I freshened up? You know what it's like after making a journey…even a first-class one… you can feel quite washed out.' Awkwardly, hardly even knowing if the words that spilled out of her mouth made any sense at all because of Jake's disturbing proximity, she smoothed her hand down over the lapels of her long camel-coloured coat and moved towards the familiar tote Alain had left standing alongside her suitcase on the marble floor.

'I asked my housekeeper Magdalena to prepare a room for you,' he declared, stopping her in her tracks. 'I'll show you where it is.'

Why did he appear to be deliberately avoiding her gaze as he made this statement? Ailsa wondered. A pang of disquiet coiled in the pit of her stomach.

As if intuiting her confusion, he exhaled a deep sigh. 'I didn't want to presume that you'd want to share my room…plus, I thought you'd like a little privacy to gather your thoughts. Anyway, let me take that for you.'

Carrying her tote as well as her suitcase, Jake led her up the gracefully curving staircase, and as she followed him, silently admiring the impressive width of his shoulders beneath his coat and the straight dark gold hair that grazed his collar, she hoped he was being honest about the reason he was giving her a room of her own. Her insides boomeranged at the idea it might be because some other woman had recently shared his bed and perhaps had left some of her belongings there. *After the intimacy they had shared at the cottage, just the thought of such a possibility made her feel ill.*

As she'd anticipated, the room he showed her into was furnished in a very clean, 'no frills' elegant Scandinavian style. The furnishings were all painted in antique white and had a very appealing faded charm—*shabby chic*, as some designers called it. The ambience was restful and inviting, and definitely peaceful. Ailsa loved it straight away. Although, when her glance came to rest on the double bed, with its curved headboard inlaid with delicate floral marquetry, her heart skipped a regretful beat. Yes, it looked inviting and restful, but without Jake beside her she knew it would be a lonely experience sleeping there on her own.

'The bathroom is just through here.' He opened another door to reveal a dazzling *en-suite*, giving Ailsa a glimpse of graceful pine and polished stainless steel.

She smiled, wishing she didn't feel so deeply disappointed at not being invited to share *his* room. If he was always hungry for her, as he'd asserted, then why hadn't he asked her?

Moving to the doorway that led back onto the hall landing, he glanced down at his watch. 'It's very late. I think I'll turn in too. In the morning, over breakfast, we can discuss when we're visiting Saskia.'

'I'd like to go as early as possible, if that's okay?'

'That's fine with me.'

'Jake?'

'What is it?'

'We didn't look at the letter she gave you—the one with her Christmas list in. I'd like us to glance over it together before we leave for your mother's house.'

'No problem.'

The smile he returned in answer to this request was brief and disappeared far too quickly—like a glimpse of sunlight that she wished would stay on a day that was grey and unpromising. One minute it gave her hope for better times to come, then in the next the clouds reappeared to cover it, leaving the day *and* the spirits gloomy again.

'Goodnight, Ailsa. Sleep well, huh?'

The door clicked shut even as she murmured, 'Goodnight. I hope you sleep well too.'

Going downstairs to find her way to the kitchen the next morning, Ailsa was greeted by Jake's housekeeper, Magdalena. The woman was probably in her mid to late forties, had a crisply cut white-blond bob, and was tall and slim. Her eyes were as grey as an icy lake, but somehow managed to reflect genuine warmth despite their glacial hue. She was definitely a far cry from the plump and grandmotherly Rose, who had been their part-time housekeeper when Ailsa and Jake had lived in London.

'*God morgen.* You must be Ailsa. I am so pleased to meet you at last.'

The woman greeted her as if she truly *was* pleased, and Ailsa's small hand was soon engulfed by the blonde's slender larger one. 'And you must be Magdalena. I'm very pleased to meet you too.' She smiled back.

'I can now see where your lovely daughter gets her

beauty from. What amazing hair you have, if you don't mind my saying so.'

Alisa had sat in front of the dressing table mirror that morning and brushed out all the snags and tangles that had accumulated on her travels yesterday, as if psychologically she needed a bit of a boost to face the day. If she also wanted to look her best for the man who had once been her husband, then Ailsa kept that disturbing realisation to herself. Even though she'd slept surprisingly well, she was still smarting a little at Jake giving her a room of her own rather than inviting her to share his.

'Thank you,' she murmured in reply to the housekeeper's compliment.

'Why don't you sit down at the breakfast table and I will get you a hot drink?' Magdalena suggested.

'A cup of tea would be great...thanks.' Ailsa moved across to the rectangular pine table that was positioned opposite French windows overlooking a narrow but long garden. She shook her head with wry humour when she saw the light snowflakes that were tumbling from the skies. Already they were rendering the immaculate lawn lacy white.

Seeing the interested direction of her glance, the Danish housekeeper shrugged and smiled. 'Most of the snow we have had over the last few days melted away yesterday. Today, when you and Mr Larsen are home, it returns! Little Saskia will be so pleased, yes?'

'She'll be overjoyed. I think she's been praying for a white Christmas all year. By the way, do you know if Jake—if Mr Larsen is up yet?'

'Goodness me, he got up hours ago! I made him a good breakfast and afterwards he went straight to his study to work. Your husband is a very early riser and he works so hard... He puts us all to shame.'

'He's not my hus—'

Ailsa's pained admission that she and Jake weren't married any more was prevented by Magdalena's cheery, 'My own husband Kaleb admires him greatly. Even though Kaleb is not as experienced as some of Larsen's staff, he would work day and night for your husband—I know it.' The cheery smile suddenly vanished, to be replaced by a soft, thoughtful frown. 'He gave him a chance when no one else would even think of it. Kaleb was an alcoholic, you see,' she explained. 'He lost his brother after he'd helped take care of him through a long and crippling illness and it went downhill from there. He just lost the belief that anything mattered any more and started to drink. We—we had parted, and he was sleeping rough, living on the streets. Mr Larsen stopped to talk to him one evening, outside a conference centre where the company had been holding a meeting, and spoke to him for a long time. Yes... Mr Larsen helped him believe in himself again. When Kaleb and I got back together, he offered me this job as his housekeeper. I was working for a hotel chain before this, but I wasn't happy there. Forgive me—I am talking far too much and you are probably longing for your cup of tea and some breakfast, yes?'

'Please don't apologise.' Moved that this woman had shared her personal story of hardship and sadness with her, Ailsa felt her spirits lift at hearing of Jake's great kindness to her and her husband. 'I'm very glad that you shared this with me, Magdalena. Thank you.'

'And I am glad that you do not mind me telling you about Kaleb and me. Now I will get you that cup of tea!'

'Thank you.'

'And, after I make the tea, what would you like for breakfast?'

The woman was already at the streamlined stainless

steel cooker, placing a copper kettle onto a burner to boil. For a few uncertain moments Ailsa stared at the back of her precision-cut bob and neatly dressed figure, in an unfussy ecru sweater and slim black skirt, and wondered how someone so obviously efficient and in such clear admiration of her boss's work ethic and personal kindness would receive a request for just a slice of toast. She definitely got the feeling that 'a good breakfast' round here meant something a bit more substantial than that.

A much more appealing if *risky* idea slid into her mind. Already having located the state-of-the-art coffee machine, she moved towards it, reaching up to the pine shelving above, where the pristine white crockery was uniformly displayed, for a single cup and saucer. 'I'd like to take a cup of coffee to Mr Larsen. Can you show me how this machine works, Magdalena?'

'Of course.' The older woman smiled approvingly. 'It will be my pleasure.'

Finishing his umpteenth call to the office that morning, Jake threw his mobile phone down onto the satinwood desk, then leaned wearily back in his chair. Several thoughts jockeyed for precedence in his brain all at once. One fact was indisputable. He desperately needed some air to clear his head.

Glancing through the panoramic window in front of him, to see the flurry of snowflakes that were drifting down, he hoped the snow wouldn't settle too deep—at least not until they had driven safely to his mother's house in the country. Was Ailsa up yet? Had she slept at all last night? *God knows, he hadn't!* He'd swear he'd barely shut his eyes for even a minute. How was he supposed to sleep when his body was gripped with a fever of need to hold her, to make love to her, to hear her whimper and moan his name out loud when she came?

He loosed a heartfelt curse under his breath. Had he imagined that her beautiful amber eyes had reflected disappointment when he'd shown her into her room last night? A room that she would sleep in *alone*? Still privately stunned that she'd agreed to come back to Denmark with him, Jake hadn't wanted to push his luck by assuming she would continue to want to sleep with him. Common sense told him to tread carefully, even when his heart ached for him to risk everything. If he was too eager, too desperate, he reasoned it might just as likely drive Ailsa away. The last thing he wanted was to make her feel trapped.

Head in his hands, he let another groan escape him. It was a double-edged sword, he knew, but he could really use some more coffee to clear his thumping head and help him think straight!

Right on cue, there was a knock at the door. 'Magdalena, you must be a mind-reader.' He sat up straight, then swivelled round in the leather office chair that was on casters. At the unexpected sight of his svelte ex-wife in slim black cords and a pink V-necked sweater, her glorious chestnut hair flowing down over her shoulders to her hips, Jake stared in mute surprise. She was bearing a small tray with a single cup of coffee on it.

'It's me…not Magdalena.'

She threw him a smile that was naturally sweetly self-conscious—the sight of which made the blood thicken and slow in his veins. 'So I see,' he drawled.

'I thought you might like some coffee?'

'Coffee is always welcome…thanks.'

Moving towards the desk, Ailsa set down the tray beside Jake's blotter. As she did so, his senses were held in thrall by the hypnotic scent of perfume and warmly beguiling woman. 'There you are,' she murmured, straightening to glance down at him.

'And here *you* are,' Jake answered, low-voiced, anchoring his palms either side of her slimly curvaceous hips and pulling her down onto his lap.

Even as her amber eyes rounded with shock his lips hungrily sought hers, and all thought of needing something to clear his head so that he could think straight went out of the window. When he was with this woman—this beguiling, intoxicating woman—he didn't *need* to think. Not when all he wanted to do was to *feel*, to experience every glorious sensation, every touch of her arresting body right down to the very depths of his innermost being—just as though it was the purest, sweetest oxygen he could ever breathe.

As he curved his hand round the back of her neck to deepen the searching, ravenous kiss he intended on continuing for a long, long time, her freshly shampooed hair glanced warmly against his jaw, curtaining them both from the rest of the world. Gliding his tongue into the hot satin interior of Ailsa's mouth was akin to submerging himself in the sweetest wild honey. When he felt her shapely bottom wriggle against his groin as she attempted to break off the feverish coupling of their lips, erotic near-*scalding* heat mercilessly hardened him.

Cupping her face, he made a sound that was half aroused groan, half dismayed protest at her calling a halt to the mindless pleasure he ached to prolong. 'Have you any idea what you do to me?' he husked.

'I—if I have such an effect on you—an effect we both don't seem able to fight—why didn't you invite me to stay with you last night instead of giving me a room on my own?'

A faint bloom of dusky pink seeped into her cheeks as

she posed the question, as if her own need embarrassed her. With his heartbeat thundering in his chest, Jake reached up to press the pad of his thumb almost fiercely across the exquisitely shaped mouth he could never seem to get enough of.

'Did you want me to invite you to share my bed, Ailsa?' he asked, gravel-voiced.

'How do you expect me to know anything when you look at me like that?' Clearly flustered, she sprang off of his lap to create a distance of several feet between them.

Jake got to his feet with a sigh that was part satisfaction and a whole lot frustration. 'Like what? How am I looking at you? Why don't you tell me, hmm?'

'Like—like…' She was coiling her hair round her ear, and even from a distance he could see that she trembled. 'Like you want to eat me!' she burst out, then spun away as if it was almost too much a test of endurance to stay facing him.

Chuckling, he dropped his hands to his jeans-clad hips. 'What if I do? What if I want to touch you—to kiss you everywhere—to make your heart pound and your blood turn to fire? Would you let me, Ailsa?'

Slowly, as if helplessly fascinated, she turned back. 'This is ridiculous. I only—I only came in here to bring you a cup of coffee.'

'Why didn't you just let Magdalena bring it?'

'Because I…' Her straight white teeth visited some unfair punishment on her plump lower lip. 'Because I wanted to know if the reason you didn't invite me to share your bed last night was because another woman had recently shared it with you!'

Jake walked slowly across the carpeted pine floor to plant himself in front of her. 'Do you really believe that? The only reason I didn't ask you to sleep with me last night was consideration for how you might be feeling. We'd had a long day's travelling and you looked tired. I thought you'd have more rest in a bed of your own. It was simply that, Ailsa.'

'Even so…you said—that is you told me that you don't live like a monk, or words to that effect. You're perfectly entitled, of course—to sleep with another woman, I mean. I haven't forgotten we've been divorced for quite some time. But still I…I hoped… Oh, never mind. I hardly even know what I'm saying. The whole situation is just too crazy for words.' She dropped her head to stare down at the floor.

With firm fingers, Jake raised her chin. Her beautiful amber eyes were a little moist, he saw. 'Just so that you know…I've never brought a woman back home with me here to share my bed. When I've been with someone— and it's only ever been purely for sex—I've taken her to a discreetly located hotel somewhere. The last time I was with a woman like that was about six months ago… okay?'

No, it's not okay! Ailsa wanted to yell at him and then thump his chest. Her reaction was crazy, possessive and jealous, and she hardly knew what to do with the pain her feelings wrought inside her. She loved him. He had equally endured the devastating hurt of losing their baby, even if they hadn't been able to stay together at the time, and she would *always* love him. For her, there was simply no other man nor ever would be. Jake was the father of their precious daughter and that counted for more than she could say. But even in the midst of her distress she knew it was hardly fair of her to expect him to have remained celibate for four long years.

She drew in a steadying breath and, stepping away from the touch that did indeed set her blood on fire, she made herself nod. 'Okay. When you've finished working, do you think we can discuss when we're going to see Saskia? Only the snow seems to be getting heavier, and we don't want to leave it too late to travel.'

He smiled at her then, and his haunting eyes had never seemed more heavenly blue. 'We'll go just as soon as I've finished my coffee…happy now?'

'Yes.' Crossing her arms over her dusky pink sweater, Ailsa moved across to the door. 'I'm happy. I'll just go to my room and get myself ready.'

'Ailsa?'

'Yes?'

'When we get back later on this evening, perhaps you'd like to move your things into my room?'

Swallowing down the egg-sized lump in her throat, she shrugged and murmured softly, 'Okay…'

It was unfortunate, Jake told her, but he had to look over some documents as they travelled out of the city into the Danish countryside. Ailsa smiled at him, knowing that because of the past it made him feel uncomfortable to tell her that, and saw he clearly regretted having to work instead of relaxing with her. The quiet, silver-haired Alain was driving them, and they both made themselves comfortable in the luxurious heated seats in the back—Jake to work and Ailsa to enjoy the sights and scenery as they travelled, and also to anticipate the joy of being reunited with their little girl.

Thinking about Saskia jogged her memory about something important. She turned to the preoccupied, darkly attired man sitting next to her, knowing she wouldn't think of disturbing him at all but for this one vital thing. His gaze was clearly absorbed in what he was reading, and there was a small but distinct frown between his dark gold brows as if what he read perturbed him in some way. Every now and then his pen scratched out several lines from the printed document resting on his lap.

'Jake?'

'Hmm?' He didn't even glance round.

'Did you bring Saskia's letter? I'd like to have a look at it if you did.'

'Saskia's letter?' As if snapping out of a trance, he refocused his compelling blue eyes to study Ailsa. 'Of course...it's right here.' Opening the tan leather attaché case that was positioned across his thighs, so he could rest his document on it as he wrote, he extracted a slim, slightly crumpled white envelope. He handed it to her with a grimace. 'I should have looked at it earlier with you, I know. I'm afraid that work got in the way this morning.'

'Never mind.' She gave him what she hoped was a reassuring smile. 'I'll look over the list and tell you what she wants, okay?'

'Good idea.' About to return to his paperwork, Jake paused. 'I'm giving my attention to this now so that I can take a few more days off than I'd anticipated taking. I'll probably finish up tomorrow...just so that you know.'

A flood of warmth poured into her belly. 'Thanks for telling me.'

Sitting back in her seat, Ailsa started to tear open the envelope. To her surprise, there were *two* neatly folded sheets of cream vellum. Grinning at the idea that Saskia's Christmas list was longer than her parents had anticipated, she carefully studied the first sheet of paper. The sight of the familiar childish handwriting in blue coloured pencil stung her eyes. Discreetly wiping them, so that Jake wouldn't see, she read the short, succinct request for presents that her daughter had written. As she'd expected, the requests were endearingly modest. In her mind, Ailsa added a few

ideas of her own. When she turned to the next sheet of
paper, what was written on it made her catch her breath.

Dear Mama and Papa
I don't mind if Father Christmas doesn't bring me
anything on my other list. The present I would like
most of all is for you two to get back together. It's
very sad that my baby brother died and I never got to
meet him, but I really want us to be a proper family
again, with you both living at home with me.
All my love, Saskia
XXX

Biting her lip, Ailsa returned the first sheet of paper
to the crumpled envelope and surreptitiously slipped its
companion into the pocket of her wool jacket.
'Can I see?'
Jake's request jolted her.
'Of course.' Trying her best to stay calm, not to betray
the stormy feelings that were crashing through her, Ailsa
handed him the envelope. Turning her head, she stared out
of the window. Scenery flashed by in a blur of trees and
tarmac.
*Now wasn't the right time to share with him what was
so poignantly written on that second sheet of paper, she
decided, Even if her heart leapt with hope at the very idea
of fulfilling their daughter's wish.* It would be a grave mistake to presume anything about the future, to pressure him
in any way.
Helplessly glancing at his preoccupied chiselled profile
as he smilingly read his little girl's list, she let her gaze fall
upon his scar. Not for the first time her stomach clenched
with remembered sorrow at how he had come by it. She
made herself breathe out slowly. He needed time to get

to know her again, she thought. She wouldn't show him
Saskia's request until he was ready. Jake needed to see that
Ailsa had sincerely let go of any grudges from the past—
that she forgave him for any of his own transgressions. She
had meant it when she'd declared she wanted to move forward in life with a lot more optimism and faith. She kept
it to herself that she hoped ultimately that it would be with
him.

Serious doubt washed over her as she silently came to
such a momentous conclusion. She might be willing to try
again to make their relationship work, but could Jake tie
himself to a woman who had no prospect of ever bearing
the son he craved? Shutting her eyes for a long moment,
she prayed that he wouldn't see it as the most awful negative. Most of all she wanted him to know that her love for
him was strong and true, and that if he agreed to be with
her again she would never again allow him to doubt it....

CHAPTER ELEVEN

THE stunning white house appeared in a wooded clearing at the end of a winding and narrow country road. Its impact was picturesque and magical. Bathed as it was in the familiar blue light common to this part of Europe, its enchanting impression was emphasised even more by the flurry of frozen white drifting steadily down from the sky.

But, however beautiful it was, Ailsa's attention wasn't absorbed by the house for long. For standing on the wooden steps that swept down to the curving gravel drive was a small girl dressed in jeans, a long hand-knitted pink cardigan, and a pair of light brown sheepskin-lined fur boots. She was out of the car and running towards the child before the ever-dutiful Alain could get to the passenger door to do the usual honours his job as chauffeur entailed.

'Mama!' Calling out to her in delight, Saskia hurried down the steps with her arms held wide.

Raining kisses down on the small blond head the minute they were reunited, Ailsa hugged her daughter tight, her heart pounding with joy and her senses breathing in her longed-for scent even as she sent up a fervent prayer of thanks. 'My goodness, I think you've grown! What on earth has Grandma been feeding you to help you get so tall?'

'I've been eating lots of home-made soup and potatoes.

It's so lovely to see you, Mama.' The big china-blue eyes so reminiscent of her handsome father's sparkled with happiness.

'It's lovely to see you too, baby. I've missed you so much.'

'And it's snowing too! I prayed and prayed for a white Christmas and my prayers have been answered.' The little girl glanced up at the sky in wonder.

'We've had lots of snow back home too.'

'Did you and Papa build a snowman?'

Ailsa flushed almost guiltily. 'No, darling, we didn't. I'm afraid it was so cold we were too busy just keeping warm.'

'Hello scamp.'

Jake reached them just as she finished speaking. Now it was his turn to bestow upon Saskia a loving embrace and to smother his child in warmly affectionate kisses. Still keeping hold of his daughter's small hand, over her head his smiling gaze fell into Ailsa's. A lock of tarnished gold hair had tumbled onto his still unlined brow, and it made her hand itch to sweep it back for him. She almost didn't breathe at the unrestrained look of pleasure and satisfaction so evident in his eyes. It struck her forcibly how different he appeared when he was truly happy and not weighed down with grief and regret. *How she had missed seeing him like that.*

'Let's go inside, shall we?' He started to walk up the steps with Saskia, then stopped to glance round at Ailsa. 'Come on, slowcoach… No doubt my mother's busy in the kitchen. She's been looking forward to seeing you again, Ailsa.'

'Has she?' It was hard to keep the doubt from her voice. What must Tilda Larsen think of her, making herself so distant from her son these past few years? Was she perhaps angry that her ex-daughter-in-law had all but cut him out of her life so thoroughly that she'd scarcely even had a conversation with him, even on the telephone? Ailsa could easily see that Jake's mother might feel aggrieved about that.

'Of course she has. Come on. It's cold out here.'

'What about Alain?' She swung round at the same time as the luxurious car started to reverse and pull out of the drive.

'He's going into the city on an errand for me. Don't worry—he'll be back later to take us home.'

'Grandma, they're here! Mama and Papa are here!'

Their daughter let go of Jake's hand and bounded ahead into the house in search of her grandmother. As soon as they stepped over the threshold Ailsa's senses were submerged in comforting warmth and good smells. She'd visited the Larsen family house many times during her marriage to Jake, and was no less enchanted now by the bright open spaces of the interior, with its blond wood floors, high ceilings and panoramic windows that let in every bit of light available—essential when the days were as short as they were in the wintertime.

After they'd both removed their shoes and hung up their jackets, with his hand placed lightly at her back Jake led Ailsa into the large bespoke kitchen—handmade by a local cabinet-maker when he was a teenager, he'd once told her. The petite, fair-haired woman holding out her arms to them both while Saskia hovered eagerly by her side hardly looked a day older than when Ailsa had last set eyes on her over four years ago. Yes, there were a few more threads of elegant silver weaving through her shoulder-length hair, but her lovely face was as warm and full of life as ever.

Waiting for the couple to reach her, she embraced Jake first of all, murmuring softly, 'My beautiful, beautiful son…' Her still stunning blue eyes lovingly drank him in, as though she would never be able to get enough of the sight of him.

Her throat tight, Ailsa forced a wobbly smile to her lips as Tilda turned her attention to her.

'Welcome home, Ailsa…my beloved *daughter.*'

It was that one simple word that broke the dam that was already pressing so impossibly behind her lids. Unable to curtail her emotion, she hugged the older woman as affectionately hard as she was being hugged, her fingers pressing into the soft black jersey of her dress with perhaps the greatest need for love and acceptance that she had ever experienced before. As if intuiting this, Tilda held her fast, her hand tenderly patting her back. Then, moving her hands to Ailsa's shoulders, she gently manouvered her to stand in front of her. The infinitely kind blue glance gently examined her face.

'Your heart has been darkened by sorrow for too long, my angel. It must be the worst pain of all for a mother to lose a child. I feel for you *and* for my dear son. I too have known sorrow since losing my Jacob. But our dear ones will not rest peacefully if we spend the rest of our lives in grief. They would want us to live, Ailsa…to live and to love and enjoy the time we have left, no?'

'You're right.' She sniffed, wiping her tears away with the tips of her fingers. 'Of course you're right. I was *so* sorry to hear about Jacob. I know how devoted you were to each other.'

'It has been hard without him, but every day gets a little easier if I can learn to be at peace—to accept rather than fight what has happened. Having my darling Saskia with me has helped me more than I can say, Ailsa. I thank you for agreeing to let her stay a bit longer with me. Now, Jake, why don't you take Ailsa into the living room and warm yourselves by the fire? Saskia and I will make you both a hot drink. Later we will have a late lunch of *steggt flaesk*.'

In the fading light of the afternoon and with the red and orange glow from the fire crackling in the grate, the elegant Christmas tree positioned just to the side of the wide picture windows wore a gentle cloak of illumination even without the benefit of the small white lights coiling through its branches. At the tip of the topmost branch resided a large gold star, and the rest of the tall spruce was dressed with a charming mix of traditional and home-made decorations.

The sight of it warmed every corner of Ailsa's heart. When she'd been in the children's home she'd used to dream of a home like this—a home where every important tradition was lovingly and joyfully celebrated. She glanced up. Hanging from the ceiling rose was a traditional Advent wreath, with its four red and white candles—one lit on each of the four Sundays leading up to Christmas Eve. She remembered being completely charmed by it when she'd first heard of the ritual.

Jake lightly caught her hand and led her to the invitingly comfortable sofa nearest to the fire. 'Are you okay?' he asked, concerned.

'I'm fine. It was quite emotional for me to have your mother greet me as warmly as that.'

'Why? Did you expect her not to?'

Discomfited, Ailsa lightly shrugged her shoulders. 'She hasn't seen me for over four years…I've barely spoken to her. I thought she might be angry that I haven't communicated very much with you either.'

'If you expected her to be angry then you don't know her very well at all.'

Ailsa stayed silent. What could she say when all Jake had done was speak the truth? It made her realise that she'd become very good at keeping the people who had been the closest to her at arm's length. She prayed she'd never employed that tactic with her little girl and never *would*.

'Hey...' His fingertips grazed the side of her face and the edges of his sculpted lips lifted to form a smile. 'It's good to have you here, Ailsa...really good. It's been a long time.'

In his mind, Jake added, *It's good to have you back where you belong...back with the people who really care about you.* He'd often observed over the years they'd been together that sometimes she looked like a lost little girl. A far-away unhappy look would creep into her amber gaze, telling him that she was lost in the past—in the insecure, uncertain world of her childhood. His mother—his father too, in his own gruff way—had given him unstinting care and support throughout his life, and he couldn't begin to imagine how it must have been for Ailsa to have no one there for her except the staff at the children's home where she'd been raised.

When he'd fallen in love with her, vowing to marry her just as soon as it could be arranged—*yesterday* hadn't been nearly soon enough—he had promised himself that she would never again have to doubt that she was loved and cared for. *But when she'd lost their son, Jake had seemingly forgotten that promise.* He'd been so wrapped up in his own misery and grief that he'd somehow neglected to convey that one day everything would be all right again... that he would love her until the end of his days come what may. That the fact she could never again have children would not mar their happiness. He should have reassured her that he was totally happy with the precious little family he was already blessed with, and needed nothing else to complete his quota of joy. *But he hadn't reassured her.*

Instead he had walked away from their marriage to try and escape his own unbearable hurt.

'Papa, Grandma has helped me make some coffee for you and some tea for Mama, and we made these biscuits together too. But Grandma said to tell you that you mustn't eat too many or else you won't eat your lunch.'

'How am I supposed to resist them when you've made them look so tempting?' Jake grinned, helping himself to a slim piece of shortbread along with his cup of coffee.

Saskia held the tray towards her mother. 'Shall I take that for you, sweetheart?' Ailsa offered, smiling. 'It looks heavy.'

'I can manage. I'm getting very good at helping round the home—aren't I, Grandma?' The child saw that Tilda had entered the room and come to stand beside her.

'You are a constant surprise and wonder to me, *min skat.*'

'And now that you've served us our drinks, my angel, let me put that down for you.' Leaving his coffee on the small table beside the sofa, Jake relieved his daughter of the tray and set it down on the floor by his feet.

'Jake? Saskia has made some more shortbread that has yet to come out of the oven. Would you mind going into the kitchen with her and taking it out? While you do that, I will stay here and talk to Ailsa.'

Jake knew a moment's anxiety that his mother wanted to talk privately with Ailsa, but because he didn't have a chance to quiz her about it he had to trust that it wasn't going to be anything upsetting.

'No problem. Come on, sweetheart, we'll go and rescue your cookies from the oven before they burn to a crisp!'

Saskia pouted indignantly. 'They won't burn, Papa, because Grandma and I put them in at exactly the right temperature. And besides, I'm a very good cook who never burns things. Aren't I, Grandma?'

'You certainly learn fast, little one.'

'Come on, then.' Fondly ruffling her long fair hair, Jake collected his coffee and followed his happily skipping daughter back into the kitchen.

In the living room, Tilda Larsen sat down beside Ailsa in the seat her son had vacated. Sighing, she proceeded to take the younger woman's slim hand and hold it firmly in hers. 'My son looks happy,' she started. 'At peace with life for once instead of being in a battle with it. My intuition tells me that's because of you, Ailsa.'

Could she *dare* to believe that what she was hearing was true? Once again hope lit within her, and, having learned that Tilda was anything *but* disappointed or angry with her, Ailsa allowed herself to relax and let down her guard. 'It's been—it's been nice spending the past few days together,' she admitted softly. 'And we've talked...*really* talked... for the first time since the divorce. I think that it's helped both of us.'

'That is good...very good. But now, my dear, I am going to speak my mind.' Still holding onto her hand, Tilda gazed steadily into her eyes. 'You should never have divorced. I can see that it shocks you to hear me say that, but please do me the honour of just listening for a moment, will you?'

With her stomach plummeting to her boots, Ailsa grew tense again. 'All right...'

'It was nobody's fault—neither yours nor my son's. You were both so heartbroken that it was a wonder you could make a decision about anything. It was certainly not the time to make a decision to divorce. I knew you were both struggling with your relationship...how could I not when I saw my son so busy with work and not his family? It was the same behaviour that my own husband exhibited throughout our married life. It makes it very hard for a woman to cope. I knew that Jacob loved me, but it didn't come easily to him to demonstrate it. I know that Jake found the way his father was very difficult to deal with. Do you know even on his deathbed my Jacob was worrying about the business—about how our son would handle things? They had clashed many times about the innovations Jake wanted to make. My husband was old school… he believed in learning to do a thing and sticking to that method for the rest of his life.'

Tilda sighed softly, shaking her head. 'After the accident you both needed much more support than you believed. But again—because of your great grief—neither of you was open to receiving it. It grieves me to say it, but in the years since you have separated my son has become a changed man…a man I can't seem to reach no matter how hard I try. It isn't just the tragic death of the baby or the harsh wound on his face that has altered him. Without you in his life, Ailsa, he is like a ship without a rudder. He's become more and more isolated and alone. The only thing that makes life worth living, he told me once, is Saskia. It's only when he's with her that he becomes animated… alive. Now…I am going to ask you something and I want you to tell me the absolute truth. Don't say what you think I want to hear…do you understand?'

Biting her lip, Ailsa nodded. Tears were already swimming into her eyes.

'Do you still care for Jake?'

Retrieving her hand from the older woman's warm clasp, she drew it back onto her lap. 'Yes, I do…very much.'

'Then I am going to make a suggestion.' Tilda's smile was tender as well as infinitely understanding. 'I want you to leave Saskia here with me until Christmas Eve and go and spend some proper time alone with Jake. You tell me you have talked, but I sense there is more to say…I am guessing the most important things of all. Then, on Christmas Eve, you must both come and spend the day here with us. I will make up one of the guestrooms and you can stay as long as you like.'

'What about taking Saskia to the market? I know she has some presents she wants to buy, and I've yet to get her the things she wrote down on her list.'

'Let *me* take her to the Christmas market. It makes sense when she probably wants to buy gifts for her mama and papa. You mentioned the list she wrote?'

'What of it?'

'There were *two* letters in the envelope she gave to Jake, yes?'

Remembering the sheet of paper she'd slipped into her pocket in the car, Ailsa felt her heart start to race. 'Yes… there were.'

'Did he read them?'

'No. He gave the envelope to me.'

'So he has no idea what Saskia wrote on those two pages?'

'I let him read her Christmas list…but that's all.'

'Ahh…'

There was a wealth of knowing in the other woman's softly-voiced response, and Ailsa squirmed uncomfortably. 'I *will* show him the other letter—I really will. But—but the time has got to be right.'

'That is true. Take this chance to be together—just the two of you—and you will find the right time, my dear. That is my advice. Have lunch with me and Saskia, then go home—back to the city with Jake. If Jacob was still here I have no doubt he would give you the same advice. He loved our son with all his heart, Ailsa, even if he often didn't display it. He was so proud of him.'

It wasn't up to Ailsa to tell Jake's mother that he had always doubted his father's love. That was a conversation they would have to have between themselves. But right now, much as she yearned to spend time with her daughter, she knew that the opportunity to be with Jake and finally express her true feelings was not one she should let pass by. No more would she turn and run away from the things that scared her in case they wounded her, or didn't turn out as she had hoped. *In truth, she'd been running away all her life.* Instead, she would face *everything.* If nothing else, she would teach her child by example to be brave in all things.

'Okay. I'll take your advice…providing, of course, that Jake agrees.'

Tilda got to her feet, lightly brushing down the soft folds of the elegant black dress she wore. 'Trust me, my daughter…he will *definitely* agree. To take the chance to spend some important time with you, to talk and rekindle the wonderful closeness you used to enjoy, to try to ease the hurts of the past and hopefully look to make a happier future…why would he refuse? Now, I must go and prepare our lunch or else it will be nearly dinnertime before we eat!'

Jake was strangely subdued as Alain drove them home through the night, back to the town house. They had enjoyed a delicious lunch prepared by Tilda and, afterwards he had gone out into the garden to make a snowman with Saskia. The flakes of white frosting had ceased falling soon after they'd arrived, but it had left a generously thick blanket on the ground. Their little girl had been thrilled that her papa had joined in her play, chasing her and pelting her with lightly fashioned snowballs as she screamed in delight.

It had been a real joy for Ailsa to see them both looking so pink-cheeked and exhilarated by their fun, but now that they had left the magical house in the woods behind Ailsa wondered if Jake was perhaps regretting agreeing to his mother's suggestion that they spend some time together alone over the next few days. The fear she'd been nurturing about him maybe feeling pressurised to rekindle their relationship when he privately didn't want to had worryingly returned. The last thing she wanted was for him to consider them reconciling out of guilt.

To counteract her deep concern, she sought for a safer subject to discuss. 'It was lovely seeing Saskia again, wasn't it? She's clearly very happy staying with your mother.'

'I think it means a lot to them both to be together.' He rubbed his hand round his jaw and gave her a smile...*just*. It was hardly reassuring.

'Are you sure you don't mind us returning home alone, Jake? I somehow get the feeling that you're not altogether happy about it.'

'Let's wait until we get inside to talk about it, hmm?'

Lapsing into an unhappy silence, Ailsa went back to gazing out of the passenger seat window. Staring at the tall shadows of trees and bushes and the snowy landscape that swept past, she clasped her hands tightly together in her lap and wished she could return to feeling more hopeful. Now the journey home felt interminable.

When at last Alain drove the car into the generous-sized private parking space in front of the impressive town house, this time she waited quietly for the polite Frenchman to open the door for her.

'Goodnight, *madame*. I hope you enjoy the rest of your evening,' he said with a smile.

Already at the front door, inserting his key into the

lock, Jake waited for her to join him before going inside, holding the door wide for her to precede him.

'Would you like a nightcap, or a maybe a coffee?'

He took her wool jacket from her to hang it up on the elegant coat stand by the door—but not before Ailsa had quickly retrieved the crumpled piece of paper she'd jammed into one of the pockets. Closing her palm tightly around it, she felt it all but *burn* her soft skin. 'I'll have a coffee, please.'

'Coffee for two it is, then.' Shrugging off the black cashmere coat he wore, Jake left it on the stand and headed across the marble reception area to the kitchen.

She silently followed his tall, dark-clothed figure, trepidation tightening her chest.

Beneath the bright kitchen lighting Jake deftly and silently went about sorting their drinks—carefully measuring out coffee grounds, turning on the gleaming machine that would make it, and setting out the cups and saucers as if he was deliberately taking as much time as possible to gather his thoughts.

As she sat quietly but restlessly at the table, Ailsa remembered that he had suggested only that morning that when they returned from their visit she should move her things into his room. Had he since changed his mind?

'Jake?' Unable to remain silent, or stay still any longer, she rose to her feet, her grip on the crumpled note in her hand lessening just a little, knowing that whatever happened now she would definitely show it to him.

He turned towards her, the bright glare of the lights above his head making his straight dark gold hair gleam as fiercely as she had ever seen it. His deep blue gaze grew wary. 'What's up?'

'About—about Saskia's Christmas present list.'

'You were right. She asked for very little.'

'Yes, she did. But, Jake, there was—there was another request that she made.'

'I know.' His blue eyes glittered, and amid the hurt Ailsa saw conveyed there she was certain she glimpsed anger too.

'You do? How do you know?'

'How do you think? I was with her all afternoon and she mentioned it to me—wanted to know if we'd read her note while we were in England together. Before I could admit that we hadn't, because we were saving it until we arrived here, she asked me whether we were seriously considering what she'd asked and if we agreed—whether we were going to make it happen in time for Christmas? I guessed then that it had something to do with us getting back together.'

'Oh, God…'

The note curled inside her fist seemed to be on fire now and, feeling almost faint with anxiety, Ailsa unfurled it and held it out to Jake.

He took it, briefly read the contents written in bright blue pencil, sighed, and then left it on the steel counter behind him. 'That's quite some request,' he drawled.

'I know,' Ailsa agreed, her breathing feeling tight and constricted in her chest.

She'd promised herself she would face *everything*—but now, when it came down to it, she was terrified that Jake might say it simply wasn't going to happen…that it was an altogether impossible notion and the sooner they told Saskia that her heartfelt wish wasn't going to come true— not in time for Christmas nor in fact at any other time in the future—the better it would be for all of them.

'Why didn't you show me this straight away, when we were in the car travelling to my mother's? You gave me the other note.'

'Maybe I should have done. But I was worried that you might…' Running her hand over her long hair, she made herself return Jake's steady examining gaze with a firmly fixed one of her own, even if inside she was feeling anything *but* steady. 'I thought that it might make you feel pressurised in some way—trapped, even.'

'Couldn't you let me be the judge of that?'

Alisa flinched guiltily. 'I'm sorry. But, although Saskia means the world to us, I didn't want you to feel that you should agree to her request simply to make her happy. *You* deserve to be happy too, Jake… I want you to do the thing that's best for *you*. And if that means you prefer to have the freedom of being a single man, or ultimately that you want to be with someone else, there'll never be any blame or bitterness in my heart towards you. I promise you that.'

'You mean you'd just let me walk out on you like I did before?'

As the words he uttered in his rich, low voice registered in her brain, Ailsa stared at the striking-looking man in front of her in shock. Moving her head from side to side, she barely managed to swallow down the anguished sob that was so close to breaking free. 'I let you walk out because I believed I had nothing more to offer you. And it was near killing me to see you so unhappy.'

'It was a dark time. I don't think either of us was in our right mind.'

'You're right—we weren't. Who would be after such a shattering thing? But if you—if by some miracle you *did* decide you want to stay with me…to try and rekindle what we once had before things became difficult…you do know I can't bear you any more children? I can't give you the son you always wanted?'

The silence that followed this declaration crackled with

the most unbearable tension. But then Jake spoke, and the cramping in the pit of her stomach started to ease a little.

'You gave me a daughter, Ailsa…a beautiful, bright girl with sunshine in her hair and laughter in her eyes…*and* you gave me a son. Thomas might not have survived, but he's still my son and I'll never forget him. Do you honestly believe that the only reason I wanted to be with you was so that you could give me children and not simply because I—?'

He was suddenly in front of her, his hands urging Ailsa's trembling body hard against his. She thought she would melt from the sheer wonderful contact alone but it was what he was trying to say to her that ensured she was utterly rapt.

'Because…what, Jake?' she whispered.

CHAPTER TWELVE

'CAN'T you guess? Don't you know?'

If his heart pounded any harder Jake was sure it would leap right out of his chest. It wasn't exactly easy to think straight about anything when those bewitching amber eyes were all but making him quake with the need to hold her and kiss her, to quench the thirst for her taste that he never seemed to be free of.

'I love you, Ailsa. I've never stopped loving you and I never will. When you kept Saskia's note from me I was afraid you were totally against the possibility of us reconciling—else why not show it to me? That's why I was so morose on the journey home.'

'Jake, I've never stopped loving you either...even when I agreed to the divorce. I've since learned that real love isn't something that dies—even when tragedy hits like it hit us. It endures even in the face of tragedy.'

She settled her exquisitely soft palms either side of his face as she spoke, and he was suffused with joy at hearing the words he'd never thought to hear her say again.

'I didn't want us to part,' she continued tenderly, her amber gaze glistening. 'How could I when the very idea was like being threatened with a living death? I lost our baby, then I lost *you*, my love.'

'I was confused and desperate to ease the heartache for

us both when I asked you for a divorce. But if I thought it would make things easier then I must have been crazy. I don't know about you, but I was even more tormented when we couldn't be together.'

Covering one of the gentle hands that cupped his face with his own, he turned his mouth towards her palm and pressed his lips there. The rush of not only pleasure but soaring hope that washed over him at the touch of her velvet-smooth skin beneath his lips almost made him lose his bearings for a moment.

'When I saw you again I knew straight away that my feelings hadn't diminished in any way since we'd parted. They'd grown stronger, in fact. When your farmer friend showed up I wanted to hit him for daring to presume he could have what was mine. If that makes me sound jealous and possessive then I make no apology for it. Not now— not ever! Sometimes I think I might die from wanting you, Ailsa. I certainly don't need a miracle to make me decide to come back to you. Marry me. Marry me as soon as we can arrange it. I don't just want to live with you. I don't just want you to be my companion and lover. I want you to be my *wife*.'

'Do you think—? Do you think I could—?'

'What?' Impatience and a frisson of old fear unsteadied his voice. 'Do you have doubts? If so, tell me what they are so I can reassure you.'

For answer her arms came around his waist and, standing on tiptoe, she planted a firm, arousing, near-*incendiary* kiss on Jake's mouth that was clearly designed not just to stop him talking, but to prevent him from thinking altogether. Now it wasn't fear that unsteadied him but desire hotter than the coals in a blacksmith's fire. He just about suppressed a groan. To add to his torment, Ailsa levelled a mischievous grin up into his eyes. It illuminated a face that in his opinion was already *beyond* merely beautiful. He felt as if he was looking straight at the most wondrous view he could ever hope to see.

'I was only going to ask if I could move my things into your room tonight. Would that be all right?'

'What things do you think you're going to need, baby?' Burying his hands in her hair, he stole a long, leisurely hot kiss. When he lifted his head again, he saw with primal male satisfaction the immediate effect of his passionate caress. Her lips were tantalisingly damp, and a little swollen too, and her golden eyes shone brighter than stars. 'You're certainly not going to need any clothes. At least not until tomorrow's lunchtime.'

'Does that mean we're going to stay in bed until then?'

'Damn right, we are.'

'In that case, do you think we might bypass the coffee and simply go straight there now?'

He would have happily demonstrated his intense delight at such an enticing request if the little minx hadn't laid her finger across his lips so that she could continue talking without interruption.

'Oh, and in answer to your proposal...I would *love* to marry you. You and me...we were meant to be together, Jake. I see that now. You asked me about doubts. I can honestly tell you I don't have any at all. Instead I have hopes... *lots* and lots of hopes for us, my love.'

The full moon shone through the uncurtained window, illuminating the fascinating planes and hollows and sculpted firmness of the masculine face that still had such extraordinary power to enthral her—in spite of what some might judge a cruelly disfiguring scar. To Ailsa that scar would always be heroic, and it didn't mar the man she was going to remarry in any way. Only those with eyes that couldn't really see beyond the surface would call his face anything less than beautiful.

She pushed back the lock of tarnished gold hair that so often flopped onto his indomitable brow...just because she could. She had the immediate satisfaction of seeing Jake's arresting blue eyes darken hungrily. Sitting astride his muscular lean body in the bedroom's plush king-sized bed, with its sensuous silk sheets, she thought she might die from the sheer happiness that welled inside her heart. To be this close to him again—to be intimate without keeping her guard up because she knew she could trust him beyond any other person in her life—was *beyond* happiness to her. Her mouth already tingled and throbbed from his devouring kisses, and her body ached in so many delicious places from his tirelessly passionate attentions. In his arms, she'd had the great good fortune to visit another dizzying galaxy *twice* now, and still Jake clearly had no intention of making that enough. Now she ached to deliver some pleasure exclusively for him.

His hand snapped round her wrist as she moved to disengage her body from his. 'What are you trying to do to me?' he growled in protest. 'Can't you see I'm on fire for you?'

'I'm not going far, I promise. I just want to... I just want to...'

Sliding down his body—a body that was well made and fit enough to make any woman crave touching it, whether experienced in the arts of love or not—she started kissing him...beginning with the pink-tipped flat male nipples that were outlined by fine curling tiny gold hairs. The heady mix of musky flavours was like nectar on her tongue. Following her own specially constructed path across his chest and ribcage down over his taut stomach—a path designed to give her lover maximum pleasure and to build the already great tension in him higher and higher—Ailsa used her velvet tongue to the most provocative effect her imagination could devise. She kissed his hard, honed flesh all the way down to his belly button and beyond—to the fine column of dark gold hair that trailed to the place where she had joined her body so ecstatically with his, so that they could be as one…just as she knew their hearts and souls had always been a part of each other.

'Ailsa… For God's sake, have mercy.'

She called a halt to her provocative kissing to gaze up at him. 'You hardly showed *me* any mercy when you drove me half wild just now.'

'You'll pay for this… I'll drive you even wilder when you—'

The full-bodied groan Jake emitted made Ailsa smile even as she cupped him in her hand and, with a feminine satisfaction borne of intimately knowing her man, felt the power and strength of his manhood.

'Is that a promise?' she asked.

Feeling his hand snake round her wrist once more—this time hard enough to impel her body straight back up to his— She let Jake drop both hands to her softly rounded hips and, as her long hair spilled forward over her bared breasts, fill her yet again. And this time he showed not the slightest restraint at driving her just about as wild as a woman hungry for her man could get…

Christmas Eve, Tilda Larsen's house…

Saskia was eagerly helping her mother lay the long polished dining table for dinner. Several of the Larsen family's relatives and friends were expected to sit down with them that evening and the house looked more beautiful than Ailsa had ever seen it. Candles glowed on every windowsill, exquisite crystal vases and pretty ceramic bowls full of flowers sat on every available surface, and everything in sight was bright, gleaming and festive. The silver-grey skies that day had even obliged with another light smattering of snow—not enough to stall their visitors travelling by road, but adequate enough to make the scenery surrounding the lovely woodland house appear utterly magical.

The mouth-watering scent of roast duck that wafted out from the kitchen stimulated Ailsa's tastebuds into realising just how hungry she was. Her body heated when she recalled that over the past few days she'd spent with Jake not a lot of cooking or eating had gone on. It was just as well he had given Magdalena a few extra days off, insisting to the concerned housekeeper that he and Ailsa would manage well enough by themselves. They would eat out as much as possible, he'd told her, so there wouldn't be much need for cooking anyway.

He had been true to his word. They *had* visited some of the city's most exclusive restaurants. But each time they had, more time had been spent simply gazing hungrily at each other across the table than eating the delicious food they'd ordered. And when they had finished dining they'd hurried home to make love…

The sense of wellbeing that had taken over Ailsa's body had the frequent ability to make her sigh contentedly and smile to herself every time she remembered just *why* she was feeling so good. And now the sense of something wonderful about to happen was definitely in the air—and it wasn't simply because it was the most magical season of the year. Every time she glanced over at Jake and caught his eye as he stoked the coals in the dining room fireplace, she saw that he felt it too. They both had surprises up their sleeves, but they wouldn't be revealing them until later.

'Do you think that Father Christmas will bring me a

surprise, Mama? I mean something that I really didn't expect?'

Her little girl's entrancing blue eyes were studying Ailsa intently.

'You mean like another poster of that young movie idol you're so crazy about?' Moving to stand behind his daughter, Jake dropped his hands onto the small slender shoulders, then affectionately kissed the top of her head.

Saskia's cheeks turned crimson. 'I'm not crazy about him, Papa—I just like the movies he's in!'

'Your father's only teasing you, sweetheart.' Finishing her folding of the last pristine napkin, Ailsa grinned at the man and child she loved more than life itself. 'I'm sure you're going to get lots of lovely surprises.'

'Well, I really want to look my best for dinner, so I'm going up to my room to change. Grandma bought me the prettiest red dress *ever* and I want to wear it.'

'Do you need any help, angel?'

'It's all right, Mama, I'm a big girl now. I don't need any help. I'll be back in just a few minutes.' With a furtive little smile at both her parents, Saskia left Jake and Ailsa alone again.

Giving the festively laid table a final scan, to make sure that everything was as perfect as she could make it, Ailsa smoothed her hands down over the dark skirt that she had teamed with the delicate mulberry-coloured silk blouse she was wearing. Just as she briefly lifted the heavy fall of chestnut hair off the back of her neck Jake stepped up behind her and kissed her nape. Then his arms circled her waist. He smelled wonderful. He was wearing her favourite cologne and, coupled with the masculine warmth that enveloped her, it made her heart miss a beat.

'You look ravishing,' he told her, moving round to urge her against him.

'You look pretty edible yourself,' she teased, loving the way the classic maroon sweater and black jeans made him appear so effortlessly sexy and virile just by virtue of being on his hard, honed body.

'Is that a fact?' His electric-blue eyes helplessly turned dark, as they so often seemed to do whenever he was close to her these days. 'Maybe I'll get you to prove that to me later?'

'Don't keep saying such provocative things to me, or I won't be in any fit state to help your mother in the kitchen.'

Jake flashed an incorrigible grin. 'She'll understand. Right now she's over the moon because we're back together. She'll keep the news to herself, of course, until we tell Saskia—but did you hear her singing earlier? Surely you must realise now where I get my supreme vocal talent from?'

Her fingers already affectionately pushing back the rogue lock of shining gold hair that glanced against his brow, Ailsa studied him in earnest. 'I love your voice—I really do. It's just like… Well, it's a combination of fine cognac heated over a flame and rich, dark velvet…at least when you're speaking. But unfortunately it definitely loses its power to mesmerize when you're singing!'

'I didn't realise you had such a cruel streak in you.'

'Baby, I'll never knowingly be cruel to you again… that's a promise.' Her laughter dying away as she examined the haunting male features before her, she tenderly touched her lips to Jake's.

When she drew back he dropped his hands lightly to her hips, his expression serious. 'I don't expect you never to get mad or frustrated with me again—you know that?' he said. 'There's bound to be days when old hurt or resentment might kick in, and days when grief about our son over-whelms you. But when that happens I want to know that you'll talk to me about it and not just keep it to yourself. Is that a deal?'

'It's a deal—but you've got to agree to do the same.'

'Absolutely—I promise. There's something else I wanted to talk to you about. Let's go sit down for a few minutes before the visitors get here, hmm?'

'It's not that I don't want to talk, Jake, but I'm worried about leaving Tilda for too long on her own in the kitchen without any help.'

'Why? Don't you know the greatest help that both of us can give her is for us to be happy again?'

'Okay, then. But just for a few minutes. We'll have all the time in the world to talk later tonight, when we go to bed.'

'Trust me,' Jake replied with a knowing lift of an eye-brow, '*talking* is not exactly what I have planned when we go to bed tonight.'

Heat surging into her cheeks, Ailsa didn't protest. Why would she when she was still thrilled to know that the man she loved found her so irresistible? Their passionate re-union really was a dream come true.

They moved across the elegant dining room to a sump-tuous sofa laden with several luxurious silk cushions. 'I've been thinking about where we're going to live when we remarry. I mean our main home,' Jake said.

'Oh, yes?'

'I know you love the cottage, but I've been mulling over the idea of basing myself in London full-time again. The Copenhagen branch of the company is flourishing, and there are at least two people there who could easily oversee things by themselves for me. But the cottage is too far a commute, and I don't want us to be apart—not even for a day. Anyway, I was wondering how you would feel about moving to the Westminster penthouse for a while? It will only be until we can find something more suitable—something with a good-sized garden for Saskia to play in and nice views—a riverside place by the Thames, maybe? I've asked my business manager to start looking for me. What do you think?'

'Yes, all right. That sounds fine.'

'I know you've got your business established now, but you can always trade online. I could find you some premises near where we live in London, or when we find a suitable house with plenty of spare room you can work from home if you'd prefer that.'

'I said yes, Jake…I agree.'

He stopped talking then, and Ailsa exhaled a long breath—as if she did so for the both of them.

'Just *yes*? You mean you don't have any reservations about making such a move?' His smooth brow creased in puzzlement.

Lifting his hand, she thoughtfully examined the long fingers, with their blunt-cut nails and the still evident scarring that criss-crossed the otherwise unblemished flesh. Her heart squeezed. 'Right now, I'd go to the ends of the earth if it meant I could be with you, Jake—and that's the truth. As much as I love what I do, my craft business isn't my top priority. My family is…you and Saskia. As long as the three of us can be together then everything else has to fall in with that. Like I said to you before…I don't have doubts any more—just *hopes*.'

'If I drank wine I'd raise a glass to that.' Her husband-to-be smiled.

'What's wrong with orange juice?' Ailsa asked softly.

* * *

It wasn't until dinner was at an end that Jake—seated at the head of the long festively decorated table, with Ailsa on his right and his enchanting daughter in her poppy-red dress on his left—finally lifted his glass to make the toast he'd been aching to make all day.

Knowingly catching his eye, Saskia clanged her dessert spoon against her drinking glass to get the full attention of the assembled friends and family who had shared the delicious food that Tilda had prepared. Seated at the opposite end of the table from her beloved son, Tilda Larsen gave her granddaughter an approving wink as the child got confidently to her feet.

'Everybody…my papa would like to say something.'

She sat down again with flaming cheeks and, leaning forward, Jake lifted her slender little hand to his lips and kissed it. Then he got to his feet, glancing down the table at the sea of faces now waiting expectantly for him to speak.

'Christmas is traditionally a very special time for us all,' he began. 'And although six months ago I very sadly lost my father, and my mother her devoted husband, I am certain that Jacob senior would not begrudge me calling this day extra-special this year.' During the charged silence that fell, one could have heard the proverbial pin drop. 'It is extra-special because my darling Ailsa has agreed to marry me again,' Jake finished.

'You've given me my surprise! Oh, thank you—thank you! It's the best present ever…better than anything Father Christmas could bring!' Jumping to her feet, Saskia enthusiastically flung her arms round her father, then moved round to where her mother was sitting, rushing to do the same to her.

Everyone cheered and got to their feet, clapping hands

and turning to the people either side of them to exclaim their surprise and delight.

Emotion almost overwhelming him, Jake reached for Ailsa as she somewhat shakily stood up too. Echoing the powerful sensations of joy and happiness that flooded his heart, her lovely eyes glistened with tears. Raising his glass, he made the toast he'd been longing to make. 'To the love of my life—Ailsa. You've given me back my life and made me happier than I perhaps have a right to be. I hope you never have cause to regret coming back to me. I'll work hard every day to make sure you always believe your decision was the right one.'

'You don't have to do anything but be the wonderful man you are, Jake. You've given me back my life too.' His wife-to-be deliberately kept her voice low, for his ears only, and there, in front of his assembled family and friends, he kissed her openly and passionately on the mouth...

In the middle of her careful packing of the photographs she would take with her to Westminster, when she and Saskia moved in with Jake, Ailsa lifted one of the latest framed pictures that stood on the living room mantelpiece and sighed. It was a lovely portrait of herself and Jake, taken on their wedding day two weeks ago. The occasion itself had been a quiet affair in the county town's local register office—nothing like the big wedding they'd had when they'd first got married, nearly ten years ago—but it had truly been the best day of her life. Tilda had flown over from Copenhagen to join them, and Jake's loyal chauffeur Alain and a lovely young woman from the florists who had created Ailsa's bouquet for her stood as witnesses. Saskia had been the most exquisite flower-girl. After the ceremony they had gone to a very charming country house hotel to have dinner.

Smiling, she touched her fingertips to the portrait. Then, carefully wrapping it, she laid it on the very top of the packing case she'd been filling. Straightening, she glanced down with quiet satisfaction at the familiar circle of ravishing diamonds on her finger. *She was Mrs Larsen again.* Even now she could still hardly believe it.

As long as the commute to London was, Jake had temporarily returned to the cottage with his wife and daughter, until they could all move to Westminster together. But they wouldn't even be staying there for long, because his company manager had found them the most wonderful house by the river in Windsor.

Now, noticing the time, Ailsa went to the foot of the stairs and called out to Saskia, who was undertaking some packing of her own in her bedroom. 'I'm just going to start making dinner, darling. Papa will be home soon.'

It sounded like the most normal statement in the world, but it still gave her a thrill to say it. In the kitchen she checked the ingredients for the meal she was making, put the kettle on for a cup of tea, then stood gazing out of the window at the darkening winter sky, her hand absently rubbing her belly. The snow had all but melted now, but the ice in the air still cut like a knife. She grimaced as the sensation of nausea in the pit of her stomach grew a little more intense. Without realising she'd intended to, she depressed the swtich on the kettle to turn it off. All she was aware of was that suddenly the thought of tea made her feel quite sick.

Moving across to the table, she pulled out a kitchen chair and sat down. Still rubbing her belly, she stilled suddenly, calculating in her mind. She'd been suffering from this disagreeable nausea for several days now. At first she'd thought she'd picked up some kind of tummy bug—or perhaps it was just a combination of nerves and excitement because so many changes in her life were happening so fast? *Now it dawned on her that she'd missed her last period.*

She shot up from the chair and started to pace the floor. 'Oh, my God…' she whispered under her breath. 'This can't be happening…it's impossible. I know it's impossible!'

But, despite her impassioned declaration, Ailsa found herself climbing the stairs to her bedroom. From the lowest dressing table drawer—safely put away beneath a colourful woollen shawl that she no longer wore—she withdrew a slim brown envelope stamped with the name of the hospital she'd been taken to after the accident. Dropping down onto the end of the bed, she took out the medical report that she'd only ever read once. The contents were too shattering for her ever to want to look at them again. But now, with her heart thumping heavily beneath her ribs, Ailsa made herself read the report extra carefully.

With shock and disbelief she saw one statement that screamed out at her above all the others: *It is unlikely that Mrs Larsen will ever be able to become pregnant again and carry a child to full term.* It was the word 'unlikely' that jumped out at her most of all. 'Unlikely' was not exactly definitive, was it? That meant that there was a possibility—in her own case a *distinct* possibility—that she might indeed have become pregnant and *could* carry her baby to full term.

Why had she never noticed the word 'unlikely' in the report before? Why had she believed for all these years that she was some kind of hopeless case? When Jake had suggested they'd both been out of their minds after she'd lost Thomas in the accident it had been truer than they'd realised!

She ran across the hall into Saskia's room. Her daughter

was perched on the end of the bed, which was strewn with all manner of colourful clothing. The pink suitcase that lay open in front of her already had several items folded neatly inside it.

'I've got to drive into town and I want you to come with me, sweetheart. There's something I need to buy from the chemist's.'

'But won't Papa be home soon?'

'We can be there and back before he gets home. Come on, scamp…get your coat and boots on and we'll go.'

'Okay—but as long as I can keep packing when I get back.'

'Of course you can. I'll even come and help you.'

At the old-fashioned look her daughter gave her, Ailsa held up her hands. 'Okay…I know you're a big girl now— but sometimes even big grown-up girls need a little help. I know *I* do from time to time.'

An hour or so later Ailsa was in the bathroom, retouching her lipstick, when she heard Jake's key in the door. She'd exchanged the serviceable jeans and sweatshirt she'd been working around the house in for smart black trousers and a cream blouse with broderie anglaise on the bodice and cuffs. She'd brushed her waist-length hair so many times that it positively crackled. Now she was seized with butterflies as she slowly descended the staircase, to find her handsome husband waiting for her with the most stunning bouquet of flowers in his hand. The look in his arresting diamond-chipped blue eyes commanded her attention far more avidly than the glorious bouquet did.

'Well, well, well—what have we here? You're looking particularly ravishing today, Mrs Larsen… Did you dress in that outfit especially for me?' he drawled.

'Yes, I did. They're beautiful…are they for me?' She gazed appreciatively at the flowers.

'They certainly are. Put them on the sideboard there for a minute, will you? I want to kiss you hello.'

Seconds later she found herself enfolded in Jake's arms, luxuriating in the sense of warmth and security and strong male protectiveness she always experienced whenever she leant her head against his chest and he embraced her. 'Mmm…' she murmured. 'You smell nice.'

'A man's got to do his best to keep his woman satisfied—and that includes wearing her favourite cologne.'

Lifting her face up to his at that provocative comment, Ailsa happily received the urgent, hot, hard kiss he gave her. She made a little sound of pleasure as the tips of her breasts tingled fiercely, then drew her lips away so that she could talk. 'The flowers are a lovely surprise. Coincidentally, today I have a surprise for you as well.'

'You do?' He gave her one of his charming crooked grins.

'I do.'

'Well? Are you going to tell me what it is? Or do you intend to keep me standing here in suspense all evening?'

She took a deep breath in, wanting to savour every moment of this time when she would share her momentous news with her beloved husband, knowing that the memory would be written on her heart for ever. 'I'm pregnant.'

'What did you say?'

'I'm pregnant. As unbelievable as it sounds, I really am. I've done a test and everything.'

'But…but how?'

Ailsa smiled. 'Now is hardly the time for me to tell you about the birds and the bees, Jake.'

He held her away from him for a long moment, his

hands curled round the tops of her arms, his expression stunned, as if he hardly dared believe that what she told him might be true.

'I reread the doctor's report I was given when I left the hospital after the accident and it said that I was "unlikely" to be able to get pregnant and carry a child to full term. It didn't say it was *impossible*. I missed that crucial part, Jake. All these years I've believed that I could never have another child and it wasn't true…it wasn't true!'

'What about the part that says you might not be able to carry the child full term? As wonderful—as *beyond* wonderful—as this news is, I don't want you risking your life to have another baby, Ailsa. Just the thought I could lose you makes me go cold.'

'I'm not going to risk my life, I promise. I'll see a doctor as soon as possible. I'll have all the checks, I'll do everything I can to maximise my chances of having a healthy baby and a safe delivery. What do you say to that?'

She anxiously held her breath when Jake didn't immediately reply.

'Do you think it's too soon?' she asked. 'Do you think we should wait until we've been together for a while again…before we have another baby, I mean?'

Just when she thought he might believe just that, his sculpted lips formed the most dazzling, heartrending smile. 'Okay. Okay, this is really happening, isn't it? Tomorrow I'll take the day off and we'll make an appointment with the best damn obstetrician I can find. You'll have the best care—the best treatment that money can buy. And I *don't* think we should wait to have another baby until we've been together for a while…are you crazy? Dear God, Ailsa…what did I ever do to deserve a miracle such as this?'

Pulling her into his arms again, this time Jake held her

as if he never wanted to let her go, and in her mind she told herself that, whatever happened, everything would be all right. It would be all right because she was with the man she loved—this time for good. Whatever fate had in store for them they would face it bravely, hopefully and together—*united* as one…

* * * * *

THE BROODING
STRANGER

To the wonderful Conar and Sandy,
and the equally wonderful Luke and Mia,
with my everlasting love.

CHAPTER ONE

TO KAREN, the thumping tread thundering in her direction sounded like a herd of wildebeest on the rampage, and for a few vivid seconds she imagined she had somehow stumbled into some other dimension. Lord knew it couldn't be beyond the bounds of possibility in these deep, labyrinthine scented woods she'd recently taken to wandering in. A lively imagination was bound to go haywire. And right now Karen's imagination was doing just that. She regretted taking the sleeping pills she'd swallowed last night to help her drop off—especially when her head felt as though every percussion instrument in the world was being played inside it. Her wits needed to be razor-sharp—not dulled by medication of any kind.

As the thumping tread drew nearer, she glanced through the tangle of trees and foliage, fear coating her mouth as surely as if her dentist had numbed her in preparation for a filling. She couldn't run. The bones in her legs had turned to water and it was impossible to think straight. Her gaze swept down desperately to the sensible walking boots she wore that were liberally caked in mud. She told herself she could sprint if she had to—but from what? She had yet to find out. *Oh, Lord! Don't let me faint...anything but that. Please don't let me lose consciousness.* Her desperate silent plea was bordering on a mantra as she waited for whatever was coming towards her, ice-cold terror jack-knifing through her heart.

Seconds later, a fawn-coloured monster hurtled out of the trees into the clearing where Karen had turned to stone—heading with a great lolloping gait towards her. A strangled gasp left her lips as she came face to face with the unseen terror that had halted her morning walk with such spine-tingling fear, her heartbeat mimicking an increasingly loud drumroll in her ears. He was a beast and no mistake! What idiot would let such a creature loose? Left alone to roam and terrify and possibly attack at will? At the thought of the latter possibility, she made her gaze home in anxiously on the huge fawn head and wide mouth, saw the creature's long tongue, lolling and wet as he panted heavily, and felt physically sick.

A commanding shout rang out that took them both by surprise. The beast pricked up his ears as though he were a transmitter receiving a signal, and came to an abrupt stop only bare inches from her, his ears cocked, his intimidating energy streaking between them like lightning.

'Oh, God!' Karen covered her mouth with her hands and cursed the foolish tears that hazed her wide blue eyes. It was going to be all right, she told herself. The creature had an owner. Irresponsible clod he must be, but he hadn't let the beast out on its own. Thank God for small mercies.

When he appeared from out of the trees, the man appeared as shocked to see her as Karen had been at the sight of his animal—*shocked but apparently unrepentant...* That much was evident even in the space of just a few seconds. Pausing briefly to assess the situation, he immediately gave her the impression that he was the one who held the upper hand, and something told Karen that apologies or concern for another didn't come easily to him. Remorse was probably just as alien. There was something innately proud and overbearing in his lean rugged stance that immediately raised her hackles and put her senses on high alert.

Tall and unquestioningly commanding, with black hair that

edged untamed and untrimmed onto his shoulders in arrogant defiance of trend or convention, he had a hard, unforgiving face that even at a distance looked forbiddingly incapable of any notion of kindness whatsoever. Perhaps it would have been better if she *had* fainted, Karen thought wildly. Here she was, at not much past seven o'clock in the morning—despite her sleeping pills—alone in the woods with an intimidating dog and his equally intimidating owner. If only she had listened to the instincts of her tired, aching body and succumbed to an extra hour or so in bed. But, no… As usual she'd had to push herself to the limit. Past events might have taken their toll, but no one would accuse her of being lazy or idle. Maybe she'd have cause to revise that opinion later, she fretted now, her gaze fixed on the dominating individual striding towards her. She'd have to wait and see.

As he walked there was a kind of reined-in anger in his tread, and his boots were crunching through the carpet of twigs and mulch as if tolling a death knell on Karen's peace of mind. When he came to a stop just behind the animal, he reached out and roughly stroked the oversized head.

'Good boy.' He stopped petting the dog, then pushed his hand deep into the pocket of the battered leather jacket he wore, which might have been a high fashion item for the mouth-watering effect it had on that hard rangy body. Nonetheless, Karen all but shook with the effort of trying to contain her rage.

'Good boy?' she echoed in a disbelieving rasp, 'Your damn dog—if that's what he is, and I have my doubts—scared the living daylights out of me! What do you think you're doing, letting him run loose like that?'

'This is a free country. You can walk for miles in these woods without meeting a soul. Besides, Chase wouldn't hurt you…not unless I told him to.'

A glint crept into eyes that were the winter-grey of an

icy lake. Strangely light. Teamed with that rich, cultured voice, they were potent enough to cause a ripple of unease in anyone.

'Chase? That's his name? How apt. What is he, exactly?' Karen plumped for bravado to waylay the pulsing thud of fear that was rolling through her in increasingly disturbing waves.

'Great Dane.' He spat the words out as if only a fool would have to ask him that.

'Well, he still shouldn't be off the lead.' Ignoring his obvious contempt, she folded her arms defensively across her thick navy fleece, silently cursing his innately masculine ability to intimidate and belittle—and amazed by her temerity in pursuing a conversation with such a man for even a second longer than necessary. His accent was rather more clipped than the softer lilt she had became used to from the locals.

Just in front of her, Chase breathed heavily in a cloud of steam, his ears still pricked, as if waiting for the next instruction from his master. Karen kept a wary eye on him in case he should suddenly make a lunge, despite what his owner had said. Right now she trusted neither one of them.

'The problem seems to me to be strangers in the woods making a fuss over nothing.' An innate arrogance angled his jaw, highlighting the high, sculpted cheekbones and the disdainful slash of his mouth. 'Come on, Chase. It's high time we headed home.'

The dog leapt away at his master's words and Karen knew she had been dismissed—dismissed and discarded as nothing more than a trifling annoyance, a gnat on the end of his battered leather sleeve. He hadn't even offered her the most grudging apology for frightening her half out of her wits.

Okay, perhaps she'd overreacted a little at the idea of his dog being off his leash, when these woods weren't exactly overpopulated with folk out for a stroll…but even so. Her body tight with indignation, she was even more unsettled when the stranger turned back to regard her with a glance that could easily have matched the temperature in a deep freeze.

'By the way, if you're planning on coming this way tomorrow I can assure you we won't be taking this route again. We value our privacy, Chase and I.'

'Do you seriously imagine I'd want to come this way again after the fright I've just had?' Karen's chin jutted forward, her blue eyes challenging the cutting arrogance in the stranger's hostile glance, despite her desire to escape as soon as possible.

The corners of his lips curled upwards in an almost wicked caricature of a smile. Karen blanched.

'Nothing surprises me about the female species, little girl. Now, run along—and if anyone asks why you look so pale, you can tell them that you just bumped into the big bad wolf in the woods. Be thankful he didn't eat you for breakfast.' And, smiling his cold unnerving smile, he turned away.

'Very funny,' Karen murmured under her breath, but silently acknowledged it was anything *but*.

A nearby branch whinnied and creaked in the wind, almost making her jump out of her skin. Alarmed, and shaken by the anger that still lodged like a red-hot stone in her chest, she stomped off in the opposite direction from the dark, hostile stranger, furious with herself because she was crying again. Only this morning she'd promised herself that today was the day she would finally turn off the waterworks for good. Fat chance of that after that highly unpleasant little encounter!

That reference of his about the 'big bad wolf' had chilled her to the bone. Had he been referring to that beast of a dog, or himself? *Most definitely himself*, she decided, shivering, and walked on.

Back at the old stone cottage where she had hidden herself away for the past three months, she saw with satisfaction that the fire she'd started in the ancient iron grate was well underway, the peat and twigs hissing and crackling nicely. It was amazing how small, everyday things like that gave her such a sense of achievement these days. She supposed it was because she'd had to learn how to do them all by herself. The heat that started to permeate from the blaze lent some much needed warmth to the chill damp air that clung like frosted mist round the old place—that seeped into its very walls.

Sometimes it even made her clothes feel damp when she put them on in the morning. And at night it was so cold that Karen had taken to wearing both pyjamas and a dressing gown in bed. Her mother would absolutely hate such an abode. She'd probably ask just what she was trying to prove by living in such primitive conditions. Just as well, then, that she wasn't around to comment.

Shivering, Karen stripped off her rain-dampened fleece and hurriedly laid it over the back of a chair. Lighting the gas burner on the stove, she filled the slightly dented copper kettle and plunked it down with a sense of something vitally important being accomplished... *tea*. She couldn't really think until she'd imbibed at least two or three cups. This morning she was even more in need of it than usual, since that horribly frightening incident with the man in black and his beast of a dog.

Great Dane, indeed—he was more like a slavering cave troll! Just who was that hostile stranger, and where was he from? She'd been living in the area for three months now, and hadn't heard mention of him from anyone. Mrs Kennedy in the local shop was the font of all wisdom, and even she hadn't mentioned the strange well-spoken Irishman and his huge dog—at least not in Karen's hearing. Sighing, she registered the sound of the kettle whistling, and hurriedly put the makings of her tea together with a determined purpose that had definitely been absent when she'd forlornly left the house to venture into the woods.

Her fellow walker might have been unpleasant, antisocial and taciturn, but, recalling his image now, Karen wondered if his unsettling demeanour wasn't some kind of shield that cloaked some deep, personal unhappiness. Even though he'd probably not cared that both he and his dog had frightened her, the morose expression in those unusual compelling grey eyes of his had somehow haunted her. What had put it there? she wondered. Was he recovering from some terrible shock or sorrow? *Karen could relate to that.* Not least because in the past eighteen months she'd been to hell and back herself.

In fact, she was far from certain whether she'd returned yet. There were days when she was so dark in spirit that she almost couldn't face waking up in the morning. But slowly, inch by inch, she'd begun to see that the possibility of healing her wounded spirit in this beautiful place in the west of Ireland was real and not just wishful thinking. With its wild mountain backdrop, mysterious woods and the vast Atlantic Ocean only a short walk from her door, its beauty had started to penetrate the gloom that had overshadowed her since the tragedy. The wildness and isolation of her surroundings had provided a welcome sanctuary to help ease the fear and heartache that so often deluged her, and she'd learned there was a good reason why people referred to the healing powers of nature.

One day when she was whole again, she told herself, she might find the courage to go home… One day…but just not yet.

Gray O'Connell couldn't seem to get the image of the pretty blonde stranger who had lost her temper with him out of his head…*feisty little thing.* He grimaced. With every step he took on the route back to the house, her exquisite features—particularly her lovely blue eyes—became clearer and more compelling. *Who in blazes was she?* There were a few Brits in these parts who had holiday homes, but in the midst of October the homes usually stood empty and forlorn.

Then he remembered something that made him stop and shake his head with a groan. He should have kept on top of things better. Instead he'd been progressively letting things slide, he realised. *It certainly wasn't the sharp, incisive mindset that had helped him make his fortune in London.*

Suddenly aware of who the girl might be, he wondered what made her stay here when in another month winter would bite hard, quickly replacing the mellow autumnal air and making even the local inhabitants long for summer again. Perhaps she was a loner, like him? he reflected. What if personal circumstances had driven her to take refuge here? Gray of all people could understand the need for solitude and quiet—though a fat lot of good it seemed to be doing him lately.

Not wanting to explore that particular line of thought, and irritably snapping out of his reverie, he lengthened his stride and determinedly headed for home....

'And I'll take some of that lovely soda bread, if I may, Mrs Kennedy?'

Standing on the other side of the counter from the ebullient Eileen Kennedy, Karen was in silent admiration of how such a plump, elderly woman could still be so robust and also graceful on her feet. Bustling here and there, reaching up to sturdy home-made shelves that had probably been there for ever, rooting amongst tins of fruit and packets of jelly and instant sauce mixes to supply Karen's grocery list, she kept up a steady stream of chat that was strangely comforting. The trouble was Karen had grown so used to being on her own here that there weren't many people whose company she could tolerate for long. The grandmotherly Irish woman was a definite exception.

'Now then, me darlin', is that all you'll be wanting today?' The groceries piled up on the counter between them, Eileen smiled warmly at the young woman who for once didn't seem in a particular hurry to rush away.

Holding out her money, Karen felt a faint flush stain her cheeks at being the recipient of such unstinting warmth. 'That's all, thank you. If I've forgotten anything I can always come back tomorrow, can't I?'

'Indeed you can. You'll be as welcome as the flowers in May, and that's the truth—though I can't help thinking it must be awful lonely, living up there in Paddy O'Connell's old cottage all on your own. You've been here for quite a while now, haven't you? What about your family? Sure, your poor mother must be missing you something awful.'

Smiling uneasily, Karen said nothing. Who was she to disenchant this lovely old lady of the idea that her mother must be missing her? The truth was that Elizabeth Morton was probably glad that her tragic daughter had moved to Ireland for the foreseeable future. That way, she wouldn't have to deal with all the messy, 'inconvenient' emotions she so clearly detested and that Karen's presence would inevitably bring up. With Karen settled in Ireland for a while, Elizabeth could fool herself that all was still well in the world. A world where she'd become a master at keeping up appearances and disguising her feelings—a realm where she could continue socialising and lunching with her friends as though tragedy had not hit her only child like a tidal wave and all but dragged her under.

Eileen Kennedy was too astute a woman not to see that the reference to her mother had unsettled Karen. Her reluctance in commenting easily conveyed that something had gone on there. Not that Karen blamed the shopkeeper for being curious. She'd often sensed that the locals she bumped into in the small but buzzing Irish town were curious about the 'aloof' English girl who had rented 'Paddy O'Connell's old place', as it was regularly referred to—not least of all the local lads who whistled and tried to engage her whenever she passed by. All Karen wanted was some peace and quiet, but people wouldn't know why unless she told them. And she wasn't ready to do that. Not by a long chalk.

'Now, love…' Carefully arranging the groceries in Karen's large wicker basket, Mrs Kennedy rang up the amount on the old-fashioned till—another charming relic from long ago. The cosy corner shop set-up was much more appealing to Karen than a soulless supermarket. As the elderly lady counted out her change, her watery blue eyes seemed to consider her un-smiling expression sympathetically. 'Please forgive me if you think I'm being too forward, but I get the distinct feeling that you could use some cheering up—and I have a suggestion. There's music and dancing down at Malloy's Bar just off the high street on Saturday night, and you'd be made as welcome as if you were one of our own. Why don't you come and join us? I'll be there about eight or so, with my husband, Jack, and we'd love you to come and sit with us. Sure, a bit of music and dancing would do you the world of good. Put the bloom back into those lovely cheeks of yours.'

Music… Inwardly, Karen sighed with longing. How she had missed it. But how could she return to it with any enjoy-ment after what had happened to Ryan? It had been eighteen months—eighteen long months since she'd even picked up her guitar. What if she couldn't sing again? What if the tragedy had robbed her of her voice for good? What was the point anyway? Karen's singing career had been her and Ryan's joint dream. Now that her husband was no longer living, she didn't have the heart to pursue it on her own. 'Tragic Princess of Pop' the local papers had dubbed her. Maybe that would always be the case. That was one of the reasons why she had eventually fled to Ireland—Ryan's homeland—selecting the most westerly and rural location she could find, where no one would have heard of the singer who had been starting to make a name for herself back home in Britain.

Now she sighed out loud, wishing with all her heart that she didn't feel so emotionally ambushed by a simple kind invitation to an evening out. If only she could be normal again—if only she could reply easily and with pleasure at the thought of being amongst people having a good time again. Her gaze focusing on the neat row of canned baked beans and tinned tomatoes behind Eileen Kennedy, she willed herself to say something. Anything. Before the kindly shopkeeper concluded she had lost her manners. But the lady behind the counter didn't seem in a hurry for a reply. All the shopkeepers Karen had met here had easily transmitted to her that there was nothing they liked better than passing the time of day with a customer.

Finally, sighing again deeply, she found the words she was searching for. 'I don't think so, Mrs Kennedy. It's very nice of you to ask me, but I'm—I'm not very good around people just now.'

'And sure, no one will expect anything different, sweetheart. They understand you've come here for your own private reasons. My guess is to get over something…or someone, maybe? No one expects you to be the life and soul of the party. If there's any nonsense from anyone my Jack will give them short shrift and no mistake! Come on, now—what could it hurt?'

That was the six-million-dollar question as far as Karen was concerned, and one she still hadn't figured out the answer to. What *was* certain was that she definitely wasn't ready to socialise yet—the way she was feeling she'd sooner jump out of a plane without a parachute. 'I can't. I appreciate you asking me, I really do, but right now I…I just couldn't.'

'Fair enough, dear. You come and join us when you're ready. We're always at Malloy's on a Saturday night, me and Jack, so we are.' Eileen rubbed her hands down her wraparound apron, its worn cotton fabric quaintly adorned with sprigs of red berries on a faded pink background, and smiled.

'Mrs Kennedy?'

'Yes, my dear?' The old lady leaned across the counter at the unexpected lowering of the younger woman's voice, resting her well-covered forearm on the scratched wooden surface.

Karen cleared her throat to give her courage. She respected everybody's right to privacy, she really did—she hated hers being invaded—but she suddenly had an imperative need to know about the man in the woods. The 'big bad wolf', as he'd sardonically dubbed himself.

'Is there a man in the area who owns a huge fawn-coloured dog? A Great Dane, he said it was.'

'Gray O'Connell,' Eileen replied without hesitation. 'His father lived in the very cottage you're staying in.'

'His father? You mean his father is Paddy O'Connell?' Karen frowned as a wave of shock shuddered through her.

'*Was*, you mean… Yes, Paddy was a fine man until the drink did for him—God rest his soul.' The old lady crossed herself, then leaned conspiratorially towards Karen. 'His son owns practically everything of any worth around here—including your cottage, of course. Not much pleasure it brings him, either. 'Tis a wonder he hasn't gone the way of his father himself, with all that's happened. But there, I expect he finds solace in his own way, with his painting and such.'

'He's an artist?'

'Yes, dear…a good one, too, by all accounts. My friend Bridie Hanrahan works up at the big house, cleaning and cooking for him. If it wasn't for Bridie we wouldn't hear anything about the man at all. Turning into a real recluse, he is. 'Tis true that money doesn't buy happiness. More than true in Gray O'Connell's case, I would say.'

Karen said nothing. It wasn't her business to pry, or to try and tease more information out of the effusive Mrs Kennedy. She'd heard enough to know that the man had good reason to keep himself to himself, and she of all people could respect that.

'Well, I'd better be going now. Thanks for everything, Mrs Kennedy.'

'Do you mind if I ask why you wanted to know about Gray O'Connell?'

Colouring hotly at the question, Karen let her glance settle momentarily on the fat barrel of rosy-red apples by the door, their overripe scent filling the shop.

'I take an early-morning walk in the woods sometimes. I bumped into him and his dog, that's all.' She wouldn't tell the other woman that she had been scared out of her wits at the sight of the pair of them.

'He's an early riser, too, so I hear.' Eileen shrugged one plump shoulder. 'I daresay he managed to keep a civil tongue in his head?'

'Just about.' Karen's expression was pained for a moment. 'I don't think he was feeling very sociable, either.'

'That sounds like your man. Don't pay any mind to his dark ways, will you? Once upon a time he was an entirely different kettle of fish, I can tell you, but tragedy has a way of knocking the stuffing out of folks, and that's the truth. Some are never the same again.'

I can vouch for that, Karen acquiesced silently. 'Well… thanks again, Mrs Kennedy. I'll be seeing you.'

'Take care of yourself, love. See you soon.'

And with the clanging of the bell behind her, Karen stepped out of the snug little shop, climbed into her car, and hurriedly headed home….

She didn't venture into the woods over the next few days. Instead she walked along the deserted beach, wrapped up warmly in sweater and jeans, waterproof jacket and gloves. It rained most mornings—a fine, drizzly affair that the locals lyrically referred to as a 'soft' rain—and the truth was Karen didn't let the weather bother her. It suited her sometimes melancholy frame of mind, and if she waited for the day to be fine she'd never get past the front door.

She'd taken to collecting shells here and there. Her gaze naturally gravitated to the delicate pretty ones, but lately she'd added a couple of bigger specimens to her collection. Taking them back to the cottage, she'd arranged them on the windowsills, and she swore the scent of the sea still clung to each one. But mostly she just walked along the fine white sand until her legs ached, with nothing but the infinitely wise music of the ocean and the gulls screeching above to keep her company.

Often, her thoughts turned to Ryan. Most days she thought sadly how much he would have loved sharing her morning walks. How he would have been keen to share his knowledge of local plants and wildlife with her and fuel her hungry imagination with tales of old Ireland, of kings and storytellers, of myths and magic. She learnt afresh that she'd lost her best friend as well as her husband and manager.

One morning on the beach she discovered she wasn't alone. Transfixed by the huge paw-prints dug deep into the sand, Karen felt her heart start to gallop. Shielding her eyes with her gloved hand against the diamond-bright glare of the sun, she glanced up ahead. There they were, just on the horizon, the 'big bad wolf' and his sidekick, Lurch. Karen grinned. She hadn't found much to laugh at during the past interminable few months, and it was strangely exhilarating feeling this sudden desire to dissolve into mirth.

Grinning again, she kicked at some seaweed, then strolled slowly across the wide expanse of sand to the edge of the beach. As the foamy sea lapped at her booted toes, she determinedly resisted the urge to glance up ahead again and see if the man and his beast had gone. Instead, she fixed her sights on the horizon, on the pair of little boats that bobbed up and down on the waves—fishermen, most likely. Men who regularly braved the vagaries of the sea to make their living. There was definitely something heroic about them, she decided. After idly watching them for a while, she silently wished them a good day's catch and turned to go.

She sucked in a surprised breath when she saw Chase pounding across the sand towards her. Behind him strode his master, and even with the distance between them Karen could see he was not best pleased. *Tough*, she thought, bracing herself for another terse encounter. But she was completely amazed and almost bowled over when Chase came to an abrupt halt just inches away from her. He sat back on his haunches with a look of such expectancy in his great dark eyes that Karen actually found herself smiling at the beast.

'You silly hound,' she murmured, reaching out to pat his head. To her relief, he didn't try and bite her hand off, but instead made a sort of contented gurgling sound in his throat almost like a cat purring. It made her laugh out loud.

'So…Little Red Riding Hood tames the beast.' Gray O'Connell stopped about a foot away from them to regard Karen with a half-amused, enigmatic glance.

Immediately wary, she stopped fussing over the huge dog and dug her hands deep into her waterproof. All of a sudden the urge to laugh at anything suddenly deserted her.

'Which beast are you referring to?' she asked boldly.

A dark eyebrow lifted mockingly. 'It would take more than a slip of a girl with pretty blue eyes to tame me, Miss Ford.'

'You know who I am, then?' Ignoring what she thought of as a distinctly backhanded compliment, Karen frowned.

'I should do. You're staying in my father's old cottage. I'm your landlord.'

If he'd thought to shock her, Karen had the advantage—

thanks to Eileen Kennedy. 'So I learned the other day, Mr O'Connell. And, by the way, I wish you'd stop referring to me as a girl. I'm twenty-six and very definitely a woman.'

She'd never meant for the latter part of her statement to sound petulant and annoyed, but somehow it did. All that was missing was the stamping of her foot. To her complete and utter embarrassment, Gray O'Connell threw back his dark head and laughed out loud. Whether that laugh had genuine humour in it was another matter. To Karen's mind, as she studied the handsome, sardonic profile, it sounded mockingly cruel.

'I'll take your word about you being a woman and not a girl, Miss Ford. Who can tell what's underneath that shapeless garment you're wearing?'

Karen's cheeks burned with indignation. 'There's no need to be so rude. It's just a waterproof. You'd hardly expect me to walk on the beach in this weather in something wispy and diaphanous, would you?'

The unsettling mercurial grey eyes insolently swept her figure. His jaw rose fractionally with undeniable challenge.

'It would take more than that to tame the beast in me, Miss Ford—but I feel myself warming to the idea by the second...'

'You're completely impossible!' This time, to her complete dismay, Karen did resort to stamping her foot. As soon as she'd done it she felt immensely foolish, and frustratingly too close to tears to say anything else. In front of her, Chase cocked his head, as if he understood and sympathised. It was funny how she was quickly warming to the dog and not the man.

'I'm afraid you're not the first woman to make that accusation,' Gray muttered darkly, 'and I'm damn sure you won't be the last. By the way, it's rather fortunate that we've seen each other today. There's something I wanted to tell you.'

'Oh?' Karen's brows knit worriedly beneath her honey-blonde fringe. 'And what would that be, Mr O'Connell?'

'I'm giving you notice to quit the cottage. Two weeks as of today. It's no longer available to rent.'

Thunder roared in her ears as she stared at Gray O'Connell's darkly implacable face in disbelief. He wanted her to leave the cottage? In just two weeks? Her plans had not been carved in stone, but she'd counted on staying where she was for at least another couple of months or so. To uproot now, when she was just starting to feel a part of this place… It was upsetting and unthinkable—and all because her devilish landlord had apparently taken an instant dislike to her!

'Why?' When the word came out she sounded winded, as if she'd been running. Disappointment and hurt tugged at the corners of her mouth, pulling it downwards.

Gray O'Connell shrugged one broad shoulder encased in battered black leather. 'As far as I'm aware I'm not legally bound to explain my reasons.'

'No, but it's common courtesy, surely?'

Those strange fey eyes of his glittered with chilling frostiness, openly scorning her indignation. 'Go back to your nice, safe little world in British suburbia, Miss Ford. Don't be fooled by the scenery or the supposed peace of this place. There is no peace to be had around here. Only heartache and tragedy and that's a fact. A place like this—a life like mine—has no time for such petty considerations as common courtesy!'

His words were released with such savagery that for a moment Karen didn't know what to do. There was one part of her that wanted to run away—to hasten back to the cottage and pack—yet there was also something perverse in her that willed her to stay and face him out, make him see that he wasn't the only one who was hurting. *Not that he'd listen to her, of course.* Not when he'd already clearly dismissed her as a silly little girl.

'Then I feel very sorry for you, Mr O'Connell.'

Her gaze lingered dangerously on the cold, unfeeling glance that was bereft of anything remotely akin to human warmth, then moved curiously down to the strongly patrician nose. It was a work of art, that was for sure… A fraction lower and her glance finally came to rest on the perfectly sculpted brooding mouth, whose upper lip was an uncompromising line of bitterness and hostility. With jolting awareness she saw that in spite of its currently bleak outlook he had a face that could be quite devastating in its beauty.

'I feel sorry for you…yes, sorry. It seems that you've forgotten what it is to be entirely human. My guess is that you're angry about something…hurt, too. But rage only creates more rage, you know. It hurts *you* more than it hurts anyone else. I don't know what's tormenting you, but I like your father's cottage… I'd really like to stay there for a little while longer. If it's more rent you want, then—'

'Keep your damn money, woman! Do you think I need it?'

He glanced bleakly out to sea for several long seconds, his jaw hard and angled with rage, his eyes glittering—a prisoner in his own morose, walled-off world. A man who had deliberately isolated himself from the rest of humanity and the comfort he might get from it. Karen was chilled right down to the bone. He was like an iceberg—remote, glacial and impervious. If she'd hoped to appeal to his better nature it was becoming glaringly obvious that he didn't have one.

That established, she started to turn away, surprised when Chase followed her for a few steps, whimpering as if he didn't want her to go.

'You've put a damn hex on my dog, you little witch.'

Gray's next words stopped her in her tracks. Karen sucked in an astonished breath.

'The sooner you go, the better, Miss Ford. Two weeks…
then I want you gone!'

He pivoted and strode off up the beach. The long legs that
were encased in fitted black denim jeans hinted at the powerful muscle in his thighs, and Chase, after one more sorrowful
glance at Karen, turned and raced after him…

CHAPTER TWO

THE day after Karen's second unfortunate encounter with
Gray O'Connell, the cold that had been brewing for days arrived with a vengeance. Having had very little in the way of
sleep the night before, she decided to be sensible for once
and stay indoors. After a tiring struggle to get the ultimately
feeble fire going, she flopped down wearily into the one worn,
tapestry-covered armchair with its lacy antimacassar, nursing
her mug of hot water and lemon, trying not to succumb to a
strong wave of self-pity—a challenge when her eyes were
droopy and red from lack of sleep and her nose was stinging
and sore from blowing it.

Outside, the rain increased with sudden force, the branches
of the trees creaking eerily beneath the weight of it. It was a
desolate, lonely sound, but surprisingly it didn't bother her.
Not when she was despondent because of something much
more disturbing to her peace of mind. *She didn't relish the
thought of leaving this old stone cottage.* It was so unfair when
Gray O'Connell had only demanded she leave because he'd
taken a personal dislike to her. What other reason could there
be, when he hadn't even thought it necessary to explain?

Well, perhaps it would end up being for the best in the
long run—his ill-mannered ways certainly didn't bode well
for future encounters if she stayed. Even so, Karen would
now have to search for another property to rent in the area.

Whatever happened, she wasn't ready to return home yet. Not when the inevitable questions and perhaps criticisms from family and friends would be waiting for her. She wasn't nearly ready to explain her feelings or her actions to anyone. The truth was she didn't know if she'd ever be ready for that. She'd struggled for over a year, pretending she was handling things, and in the end had realised she just had to get away.

Sometimes it had been hard to breathe, staying surrounded by the same old people and the same old scenery. She'd longed to escape.

Putting aside her drink, she sniffed gingerly into her handkerchief, doing her utmost not to irritate her already sore nose. The next instant the sniffing somehow manifested as a muffled sob, and before she knew it her heart was breaking once more. *She missed Ryan so much.* He'd been her constant companion, her rock. Her heart was submerged in a drowning wave she didn't have the strength to kick against. He'd been taken from her so suddenly and cruelly that they hadn't even had the chance to say goodbye. Her mind and body had been incarcerated in ice ever since. No one could comfort her. Not her mother, any of her family, or even well-meaning friends. *No one but Ryan.*

She held her arms across her middle, as if to comfort herself, but knew it was an ultimately useless exercise. Nothing could heal her heartache. Only the passing of time might blunt the edges of sorrow, and eventually when she was ready, the letting in of people who genuinely cared. The crumpled square of linen in her hands quickly became soggy with more tears.

When the knocker hammered in a staccato echo on the front door she froze in her seat, silently willing whoever it was calling on her in this foul weather to go away. The truth was, the way she was feeling, even stirring out of her seat required a colossal effort she didn't feel up to making right now.

When she didn't rise to see who it was the knocker hammered again. The sound cut like a scythe through Karen's already thumping head, making her wince. Hastily wiping her face with the damp, crumpled handkerchief, knowing miserably that she must look a wreck, she reluctantly roused herself to answer it.

Outside in the rain, droplets of water coursing down his coldly handsome face, his arms folded across his chest, Gray O'Connell leaned impatiently against the doorjamb. As Karen stared up at him in surprise, he straightened and jerked his head. 'Can I come in?'

Frankly amazed that he hadn't just barged in anyway, Karen nodded dumbly. Inside, the sitting room's crackling fire blazed a cosy welcome, despite the definite lack of sociability on the part of the house's tenant. Resignedly making her way back to the armchair, Karen resumed her seat. If only she wasn't feeling so pathetic she'd tell him to go away—even if he *did* own the house. She still had some rights as a tenant. Slowly Gray approached the fire. His jacket dripped onto the stone flagged floor. It was partially covered with a hand-woven rug that must have been beautiful and vibrant once, but was now a dull shadow of its former self.

Reluctantly Karen made herself speak. 'You'd better take off that jacket. You're soaked.' Heaving herself back onto her feet again, she forced herself to wait patiently as he reluctantly took it off. He handed it to her without a word, and she took it and hung it on the peg at the back of the door. It smelled of the wind, the rain and the sea, and for a wildly unsettling moment Karen fancied she could detect the arresting male scent of its owner, too. Surreptitiously she allowed her fingers to linger a little longer than necessary on the soft worn leather.

Turning back into the room, she was immediately struck by the intensely solitary picture that her visitor made. He was holding out his long-fingered hands to the fire and his handsome profile was marred by a look of such unremitting desolation that Karen's heart turned over in her chest. Why had he come here? she wondered. A feeling of desperation clutched her chest. What did he want from her? He'd already told her that he didn't want her as a tenant. There was no need to tell her again. She'd received the message loud and clear.

'I couldn't paint.' Turning briefly to regard her, almost instantly he returned his gaze to the fire, as though locked deep inside the prison of his own morose thoughts. 'Not today. And for once I didn't want to be alone.'

'I heard that you were an artist.'

'And I'm sure that's not *all* you heard. Am I right?' He shook his head disparagingly.

In spite of her innate caution, Karen moved hesitantly towards him, surprise and compassion making her brave. Suddenly the inexplicable need to offer this man comfort overshadowed everything—even her personal feelings of misery and pain.

'Is there anything I can do to help?'

'Help what? Free me from this incessant gloom that follows me everywhere? No. There's nothing you can do to help.'

His voice harsh, Gray pivoted away from the fire and started to pace the room. He was an imposing broad-shouldered man, with hair as black as tar—a dramatic hue that gleamed fiercely as though moonlight was on it—and his very stature made the already small room appear as though it had shrunk. The two of them might have been occupying a dolls' house.

'There's nothing you can do except maybe refrain from asking questions and be silent,' he uttered less irritably. 'I appreciate a woman who knows how to be silent.'

Intuitively Karen understood his need for quiet. She'd already registered the turmoil reflected painfully in his eyes and in the grim set of his mouth. This time she wasn't offended by his sharp words. On soft feet encased only in the thick white socks she wore beneath her jeans, she made her way back to the armchair and sat down. Gathering up the book that earlier on she'd been attempting to lose herself in, she laid it on the coffee table beside the chair and offered him a weak and watery smile.

'Okay…no questions, and I'll just sit here quietly.'

She might have meant it when she'd told him, that but it didn't stop Karen's mind from teeming with questions and speculations about her taciturn landlord. And heaven knew it was nigh on impossible to concentrate on anything else, with his brooding figure moving restlessly round, up and down in front of her.

'Why were you crying?'

The question pierced the silence that by mutual agreement had enveloped them. The sound of it reverberated through Karen like the shattering of glass.

'I wasn't crying,' she quickly denied, picking up her book again and staring unseeingly at the cover. 'I've got a cold.' She sniffed into her handkerchief as if to emphasise the point.

'You were crying,' Gray reiterated, his gaze steely. 'Don't you think I'm capable of knowing when a woman's been crying?'

'I don't know. I don't know anything about you.' She blinked sorrowfully down at the pale cold hands that covered the book in her lap and a shudder of distress rippled through her. Why did he have to call on her today of all days? It was said that misery loved company, but if only he would just go and leave her to her own misery in peace.

'I don't want you to know me, either.' He shook his head, as if warding off further unsettling thoughts, then glared at her.

Karen retreated even more inside herself. Wrenching her glance away, she stared back down at her book. She hadn't a hope in hell of reading any more of it today—at least not while her brooding landlord was taking up space in the house.

Gray exhaled deeply. 'You're probably thinking that's hardly fair, when I've invaded your own peace and quiet and you're clearly upset.'

'If you need to talk…just to have someone listen without judging or commenting…then I can do that,' she answered softly, her heart racing a little because she didn't know how he'd react.

'All right,' he said aloud, almost to himself. 'All right, then. I'll talk.' He breathed deeply, gathering his thoughts. 'My father lived in this house for five years before he died.' He stopped pacing to address her, his distant storm-tossed gaze restless and preoccupied. 'He'd never let me put things right. Liked it just as it was, he said…didn't want my money. He was mad at me because I didn't stay and work the farm that he used to own—until it got too much for him. The farm that his father and grandfather had owned before him. He didn't understand that those days were gone. Working the land wasn't in my blood like it was in his. I had other dreams. Dreams I wanted a chance at. Besides, a man can barely scratch a living out of farming these days—not when the supermarkets can undercut him at every turn and fly in cheap vegetables from Peru rather than buy them from local farms.'

His expression was scornful for a moment, and pressing his fingers hard into his forehead, he twisted his lips angrily. 'What had my fancy university education and my cleverness done for me? my father asked once. As far as he could see all it had accomplished was to send me away from this place— away from home.' He paused, as if weighing up the wisdom or indeed lack of it in proceeding with his story. In the end it seemed he'd decided to throw any caution he might be feeling to the wind. 'He wasn't interested that I'd made a fortune on the stockmarket. He asked me, "How much money does a man need to live a useful life?" I've been pondering that question ever since. I'm not sure how useful it is, but eventually I did find something to do with my life that gave me even more pleasure than making money. I discovered that I loved to paint, and lo and behold it turned out I had some skill at it! My desire to pursue it in the place I grew up finally brought me home, but it was too late for Paddy and me to be reconciled. He was too bitter and too full of regret at what he had lost, and the man was dead from drink three months after I returned. I found him dead down on the beach one morning, a half-bottle of whiskey in his pocket. He'd fallen against a rock and smashed his head.'

A lone tear splashed onto the cover of Karen's book. Gray's raw desolation merged with hers, welling up inside her like a dam strained to bursting. Missed opportunities, families torn apart, lost loves—it was all too much to bear.

'I'm sorry.'

'There's no need to be sorry for me. What I did…everything that happened…was down to my own selfish actions. Oh, hell!' Raking his fingers through the thick black mane that was still sodden from the rain, he shook his head. 'I don't know why I'm even telling you all this. I never did believe the adage that confession is good for the soul. Put it down to a momentary descent into madness and despair, if you like.'

'Sometimes it helps to talk.'

'Does it? I'm not so sure about that. But I can see how tempting it might be for a man to confide in *you*. That soft voice and quiet way you seem to possess suggests you might be capable of easing pain…for a while at least. Not that *I'm* looking for that.' He regarded her suspiciously for a moment, his voice scathing.

'Believe me…I'm no expert at healing anybody's pain, and I wouldn't pretend that I was.' Stung, Karen dipped her head.

'Then we're even, aren't we? Because I'm not looking to be healed. So don't make the mistake of thinking that's what I came for.' Throwing her a brief warning glance, Gray O'Connell stalked to the door and grabbed his still wet jacket almost violently off the peg.

Ignoring the insult, Karen immediately got to her feet, her book tumbling unheeded to the floor. 'Perhaps—perhaps you'd like to stay and have a cup of tea with me?' she offered uncertainly, her smile unknowingly engaging.

The stark expression of raw need in those startling grey eyes impaled her to the floor. A red lick of heat kindled and grew inside her—heat that transcended her cold and the feeble state her body was currently in and put twin flags of searing scarlet into her cheeks.

'Tea's not what I need, Miss Ford. And something tells me you're not the kind of woman who'd be willing to offer me exactly what it is I do need right now...'

He didn't need to explain. The force of his desire was as palpable as a storm about to break.

He pulled on his dripping jacket, then yanked open the door with unnecessary force. 'And, by the way, you can stay here as long as you like. Stay or go—it's up to you. I don't really care one way or the other.'

Catching the edge of the door, Karen unhappily watched him go, head down, striding off into the rain, like a man whose broad shoulders were weighted down with the cares of the world. Shockingly, she wished she knew a way to make him stay. The thought made her heart thump hard inside her chest. *If her landlord had descended into temporary madness then apparently so had she.* It was jolting to realise that craving bold glance he'd shot her just now had had the power to make her feel aroused. Or was it just that it had been so long since a man had regarded her with desire in his eyes?

After Ryan had died she'd told herself she'd never want or need a man again. And it was hard to believe Gray O'Connell of all men wanted *her*...especially in her current unappealing state. Her usually glossy fair hair had lost its lustre, whilst her cold made her resemble some half-starved waif who needed to be tucked up in bed with a hot water bottle and a steaming bowl of broth—never mind a man with winter-grey eyes and a look fierce enough to quell even the indomitable Queen Boudicca.

Her body grew warm at his assessment that she wasn't the kind of woman who could offer him exactly what he'd needed right then. *How did he know that she couldn't?* Spending night after night cold and lonely and hurting in her bed was apt to make a grieving woman slightly crazy.

Karen sucked in a startled breath as she realised she could even contemplate such a thing with a man who was practically a stranger—especially when only minutes before she'd been breaking her heart over Ryan. Reluctantly closing the door, she leant back against the wooden panelling and shut her eyes. Any port in a storm—that was all Gray O'Connell was looking for. And maybe at the end of the day so was she. The man she'd loved and married was long gone. Maybe any port in a storm was all she could hope for now?

But at least her brooding landlord had said she could stay—even if he *had* thrown his decision at her like a scrap of meat from his plate. There was really no need for her to feel so stupidly grateful but the fact remained that she was…she *was*.

On Saturday, Karen made a more prolonged visit to the thriving local town. Elated by her landlord's grudging permission to let her stay on at the cottage, she vowed she'd celebrate by buying some new bits and pieces to cheer the place up. When she left she'd leave them for whoever came after her, but while she was there they would help make the house feel more like home.

With that thought in mind, she browsed contentedly around the quaint narrow streets and thoroughfares, dipping in and out of enticing little craft shops and bookshops, sampling textures, scents and colours, sometimes buying—sometimes not.

Much of the time her exploration was accompanied by the uplifting Irish tunes that drifted out from many of the pubs she passed. The music stirred her soul, as it had always done. It made her happy and sad simultaneously. Happy for the fierce joy it brought her, and sad because she'd probably left that way of life behind for good. But still the fingers that curled round the strap of her shoulder bag itched to pick up a guitar and play, and she had a brief vision of the instrument tucked away beneath her bed.

Squashing the thought, Karen drifted into a coffee shop for a latte and a Danish pastry, content to sit amongst strangers with lilting Irish voices and enjoy her refreshment in peace.

When she came out again the light was slowly fading, and people were starting to head home. On a last-minute impulse she dived into the bookshop she'd spied on the way across the street to the coffee shop and purchased a little book that had given her some much needed consolation in the months directly after Ryan's death. Unfortunately she'd left her copy back in the UK. Tucking the book carefully into her bag, she made her way tiredly but contentedly back to where she'd parked the car.

Lifting the lid on the simmering pot of stew, with its delicious and mouthwatering aroma of braised lamb and fragrant herbs, Karen took a deeply appreciative sniff, hearing her stomach growl in response. Her day out had given her the appetite of a Titan, and she was so glad that she'd thought to make dinner the night before, because now all she had to do was let it properly heat through and enjoy it.

In the tiny sitting room scented candles flickered on almost every surface, the mingled scents of sandalwood, musk and

vanilla creating a soothing ambience of warmth and relaxation, which was exactly what Karen had hoped for. Now that
she'd got over her cold she was fully committed to taking
much better care of herself—not just eating sensibly and
taking regular exercise, but learning how to relax properly.
Something she had never really done up until now.

Her life with Ryan had been wonderful, but the last couple
of years before he'd died it had been pretty much commitment
after commitment, with barely a blank space in the diary to
call their own. Touring up and down the country had taken its
toll, and Karen had for ever been promising herself that one
day she would definitely make more time for herself. Well,
now she had the opportunity.

The atmosphere in the cottage was strangely evocative.
It brought to mind images of past times—of an older, more
simple way of life, when people had worked the land and,
even though they'd struggled to make ends meet, there had
been a real sense of community and pulling together to help
each other. A sense of sadness lingered in the rooms, too—a
melancholy air that was like the wisp of smoke after a candle
had been blown out. Karen yearned to do everything in her
power to dispel that sadness if she could.

The story of Gray O'Connell's father Paddy had been on
her mind ever since he'd related it, and she had an ache in her
heart that hadn't left since she'd heard it. It was all too easy to
imagine the man living here alone, with nothing but his memories and his whiskey to keep him company. No doubt Paddy
had sorely missed his son when he'd left to make his fortune.
In his case, accomplishing exactly that. In all probability the
older O'Connell had been proud of his son's achievements,
but maybe he just hadn't had the words or the courage to tell
him? It was a shame that Gray was torturing himself over
what had happened.

At the end of the day everyone had a choice in how they

responded to life's challenges, Karen reflected, and if his father had sought solace in whiskey then that had been his decision and was nothing to do with his son. That said, Gray O'Connell was clearly a troubled man himself.

He was so different in every way from her gentle loving Ryan. She tenderly recalled how her husband had had a real talent for communicating with people, and had always been able to find an encouraging word for anyone downhearted or in despair. In the music business, a temperament like his had been rare. She was so lucky to have had him in her life, if only for all too brief a time.

Exhaling a long, slow breath, she was gratified to see that her efforts at building the fire that evening were impressive, to say the least. Right now the flames were licking high and fierce into a really good blaze, rendering the room snugly warm as a result. In the background Karen's portable radio added muted sounds of conversation and laughter, and for the first time in a long time she was genuinely at ease. By that she meant she wasn't yearning for anything—not even company.

Her gaze roamed the room with satisfaction. The three small prints she'd purchased, of three different but equally beautiful traditional stone cottages, all set in the emerald-green landscape of the country, had been carefully arranged side by side above the fireplace. Sitting gracefully in a simple but elegant glass vase she'd found in a junk shop were a mixed bunch of cream and red roses, their evocative, fragrant scent mingling gently with the aromatic candles. They were just small, perhaps insignificant things in themselves, but the pleasure they gave Karen was immense.

Combing her fingers through her newly washed honey-gold hair, she glanced ruefully down at the faded blue jeans and red sweater she was wearing. Both items had definitely lost a little of their shape after several washes. The clothing had taken on the comfortable qualities of a dear old friend. Not that she had many 'dear old friends' to call upon since Ryan had gone. She grimaced. It was strange how bereavement either brought people closer or pushed them away.

Shaking off the thought, she wondered if she shouldn't make more than a passing concession to her new mood of optimism and change into something a little more feminine. There were two very nice Indian cotton dresses in her wardrobe—one dark green with a red velvet inlay on the bodice, and the other a rich luxurious purple that she'd bought in Camden Market back home. It might be nice to wear one of them to highlight all the good things she'd done for herself that day.

Contemplating a quick visit to the bedroom to change, she nearly jumped out of her skin when someone rapped on the door. Lifting the latch, she was greeted by the night, the bitter cold air and a handsome if austere Gray O'Connell.

'I came by to tell you that I've bought some things for the cottage. Is it okay if I drop them round in the morning?'

He addressed her without preamble, not even saying hello. Karen stared, feeling an answering jolt in her stomach when her glance collided with his. She'd never seen such heartfelt loneliness in a person's eyes. It didn't help that she knew some of the reasons for that achingly distant look.

'Sure—of course. Tomorrow morning's fine.' What he'd bought and why she couldn't guess, but somehow that seemed irrelevant right now.

'Good.' He turned away, not even bothering with goodbye, and for reasons she couldn't begin to analyse Karen found herself reluctant to let him go.

'I've made some stew for supper.' She faltered over the words as hectic colour suffused her face, fully aware that she had his attention more completely than a hunter fixing his sights on his prey before aiming his gun. Inwardly, she gulped. 'There's more than enough for two—that is if you haven't already eaten?'

'Is this a habit of yours?'

'What?'

'I mean do you normally extend spontaneous invitations to people you hardly know?' Gray demanded irritably, booted feet firmly set on her doorstep like a captain at the helm of his ship.

'You showed up the other day and came in without me inviting you. Is that any different?'

'I asked you if I could come in and you said yes.'

'Of course I did...you're my landlord. So I do know you, don't I?'

'Damn it, woman, you're on your own out here!'

He spoke as though she was far too relaxed about her personal safety for his liking. Karen was taken aback by the vehemence in his tone. Anyone who didn't know them would think that he *cared* whether she was safe or not—which was utterly ridiculous when one considered the facts.

'I know I'm perfectly safe here.' She kept her voice deliberately soft. 'I've only felt anxious once, and that was when I inadvertently crossed paths with the "big bad wolf" in the woods one day.'

For a moment a muscle tensed, then relaxed again in the side of Gray's high sculpted cheekbone. One corner of his mouth quirked upwards in the beginnings of a smile. The gesture made him sinfully, dangerously attractive, and Karen had cause to question her wisdom at so recklessly inviting him to join her. Just then she remembered an adage she'd once read that the most dangerous wolves were the ones who were hairy on the inside. Maybe she'd be wise to remember that?

'And he let you go?' Gray parried dangerously.

Karen caught her breath. 'Yes...he let me go.'

'One day those big blue eyes are going to get you into a barrel full of trouble, little girl.'

'I'm not a little girl, so stop calling me one. I'm a woman... a woman who's been married, for goodness' sake!'

'Have you? Are you telling me you're divorced now, then?' With an impenetrable glint in his eye he shouldered past her into the sitting room.

Mentally counting to five, Karen slowly closed the door on the cold, rainy night outside. She shivered hard, but it was nothing to do with the weather. Glancing across at her visitor, she saw that he'd taken off his jacket and thrown it casually across the threadbare arm of the couch. Once again he moved across to the fire and held out his hands to its warmth—though Karen privately thought it would take a lot more than even a hundred blazing fires to warm the icy river that must pass for blood in Gray O'Connell's veins.

'I'm a widow.' Finally commanding his full attention, she lightly shrugged a shoulder as he turned to survey her.

'How long since you lost your man?' It sounded almost poetic, the way he phrased it.

'Eighteen—nearly nineteen months ago.' She unfolded her arms to thread her fingers nervously through her hair, mentally bracing herself to receive some sort of barbed reply from this enigmatic man who clearly had so many defences that it was a wonder anything could pierce even a chink of his heavy armour. Not that she was looking for sympathy or anything.

'Is that why you came here?' His eyes raked her figure from head to foot, then returned to her face, where they reflected a provocatively unsettling interest in her mouth.

Karen grimaced uncomfortably. 'Now, about that stew...I hope you're hungry—'

'How did he die?' Though he stood-stock still, Gray's relentless gaze ate up the distance between them as though channelling electricity—probing her reluctance to give him the information he sought with all the steely-eyed determination of a professional interrogator.

'I don't—I don't really want to talk about it.' She dipped her head, twisting her fingers into a long burnished strand of hair, then impatiently pushing it away again. Her troubled gaze studied the once colourful swirls woven into the homespun rug at her feet with exaggerated concentration.

'I seem to remember you advising me that it sometimes helps to talk?'

Glancing up at him, Karen was inexplicably annoyed that he should throw what had, after all, been genuine compassion and concern back in her face.

'You didn't buy that idea when I offered it to you—why should you expect me to be any different in return?'

'In my own case I knew it wouldn't be of any use. You, however, are an entirely different case, Miss Ford. By the way, what *is* your first name?'

'You obviously know that it's Karen. You're my landlord. The letting agents must have informed you.'

'Perhaps I wanted to hear it from your own lips.' Curling his fingers round the thick black leather belt he wore round his jeans, Gray seriously considered her. 'You barely look old enough to have been married—let alone widowed.'

'You know how old I am. I've already told you. And Ryan and I were married for five years. His death came as a terrible shock. There was no warning, so I wasn't prepared. He hadn't even been ill. He worked hard…too hard. Long hours, with not enough rest—but that's the culture nowadays, isn't it?'

Her eyes glazed over with distress. 'The culture we're all taught to so admire. As if there's such virtue in working hard and dying young! My husband suffered a massive heart attack at the age of thirty-five. Can you imagine that? When he went, I wanted to die, too. So don't stand there and tell me I don't look old enough to be married, because in the space of those five short years with my husband I lived more life than most people do in ten times as long!'

She was shaking, emotion slamming into her like a train, appalled at giving in to such a passionate display in front of a man who probably regarded such outbursts as a certain sign of weakness…or at least a serious character flaw. If only she could take the words back, keep them private and unsaid, but it was clearly too late for that.

His handsome visage a cool, impenetrable mask of enforced self-control, Gray retrieved his jacket from the couch and wordlessly shrugged it on. As Karen struggled to regain even a shred of her former equilibrium, he came towards her, his expression grim. With her heart in her mouth she automatically stepped back. She saw the glimmer of disquiet in his gaze when she did, as if it took him aback that she might be afraid of him.

'I'm sorry for your trouble, Miss Ford, and sorry that I clearly intruded where I had no right. I didn't come here to make you revisit painful memories and upset you. I'll see you in the morning as arranged—if that's still all right? If not, we can leave it for another time that's more convenient.'

Nodding miserably, Karen plucked the material of her soft wool sweater between trembling fingers, twisting it into a knot. 'Tomorrow morning will be fine.'

'Good. I'll wish you goodnight, then.' Gray's glance greedily swept her pale solemn face, the distressed China-blue eyes with their long dark blonde lashes that reminded him of a fawn, and the full, almost pouting, trembling lips devoid of so much as a trace of lipstick. *A man would have to go a long way to find such innocent unaffected beauty in a woman*, he thought.

Karen heard him go to the door, lift the latch and step outside. As he went, her body seemed suddenly to move of its own volition, and she found herself hurrying after him. Out into the rainy night she ran, her eyes squinting up at the water that splashed onto her face, ignoring the cold, ignoring the wind that tore into her hair, sweeping the long sun-kissed strands into a dishevelled cloud.

'Gray!'

The voice that called out his name was full of anguish and something else—something that Gray registered in his mind with tight-lipped control. Heat seared him like a brand at the realisation, making him rock-hard with need. He turned to survey her. Even in the dark he knew his light-coloured eyes burned as brazenly as a cat's.

'What is it?'

'I just—I just want you to—'

'Don't ask me to stay, Karen. I'll only end up hurting you. Trust me.'

Her lip wobbled as she struggled for the words to tell him what she felt. 'I want— I need— Dear God! Do I have to spell it out for you?'

She was crying even as she spoke, her tears mingling with the rain. Why was it so hard to just say what she wanted? She missed the physical side of married life. She missed having someone to hold her and touch her and make her feel like a woman again. She didn't want a relationship with Gray O'Connell. He was the last man on earth she could ever want that with. He was too angry—too wounded to be kind. But they'd both been hurt by life. Why shouldn't they find comfort in each other's arms for a little while? It didn't have to mean any more than that, did it?

'It would only be sex, sweetheart,' Gray asserted coldly, as if intuiting her thoughts. 'Nothing else. Not "making love", not hearts and flowers and violins… Just sex. *Screwing*, plain and simple. Would you really settle for that?'

Shock slammed into Karen at his words. The strength

seemed to drain out of her legs completely. Yet she stood her ground, blinking back tears, blinking back the rain that had already left a fine damp sheen on her sweater, soaking its way onto her skin.

'Were you always this cruel?' she asked boldly into the night. 'I'll bet you pulled the wings off dragonflies when you were a boy. I'll bet you laid traps for poor defenceless animals... I bet you broke your poor mother's heart!'

In two strides Gray was in front of her, his dark face just inches away from hers, his warm breath fanning her face, making little clouds of steam in the rain. 'My mother took her own life when I was three. Maybe having me was to blame? Who knows? But whether it was me or my father I'll never know, and I have to live with that every day. So my advice to you, Karen, would be to think twice before you make such a throwaway comment again, damn you!'

The impact of the bitter words made Karen go rigid. Then, hardly realising what she was doing, she slowly raised her hand tentatively to touch his lips with her fingertips. They were infinitely soft to the touch—soft, but inherently stubborn. *Velvet clad in iron.* But right then she saw past the anger of the man, past the torment of the grown-up who didn't know where to go with his pain, and instead saw the small three-year-old boy who had been abandoned by his mother and ultimately abandoned by his father, too. Grief twisted her heart.

Gray grabbed her wrist to wrench her hand roughly away. Before she could react he wove his hands through the damp tresses of her hair to crush her lips beneath his mouth in a bruising, destroying kiss that made her body go limp with dazed reaction and turned her blood into a river of seething, molten desire so hot she thought she would be consumed by the sheer, staggering ferocity of it.

His tongue mercilessly swept the soft warm recesses of her mouth, taking brutal hostage of her flesh and her senses with all the insatiable relentless hunger of a man who'd gone without meat or drink for days—tearing into her with passion, demanding everything, sparing her nothing, until her heart pounded in her chest as if she was riding in a speeding car bent on crashing. When his hands left her hair and moved downwards to drag her hips hard against his, his manhood surged like steel against the giving flatness of her belly, leaving Karen in no doubt of the heat and the hardness in him. A kind of drugging sensuality rolled over her like a wave, robbing her of the power to think, to rationalise, to remain sane.

'Was it like this with your husband, Karen?' As he tore his mouth from hers Gray's eyes burned down at her as though in the grip of a fever. He ignored the rain that was soaking them both as though it didn't even exist. His midnight lashes blinked the moisture away temporarily.

It took several moments for Karen even to register the question. Her lips were aching and bruisingly tender from his passion, her body crushed against his hard, lean length as his arms held her captive, and it was hard to even remember who she was... *Tragic Karen Ford from suburban England—a woman who wrote lyrics about passion, who sang songs all about the kind of love that consumed body and soul but had never personally experienced herself.*

The shocking realisation was both a revelation and a trauma. It was as though she was utterly betraying Ryan's memory by even contemplating it. A sudden vision of her husband's tender smile imposed itself on her mind, cutting through the sensual fog that enveloped her. It made her twist urgently out of Gray's embrace to call a halt to the madness. Disgusted with herself for almost succumbing to nothing more than base lust, Karen wiped the back of her hand across her still throbbing lips.

Moving several steps away from the man who had only

moments ago taken her body hostage, she anxiously straightened her sweater, pushed back her hair to tidy herself, and tried desperately to summon back the woman who always strove to do the right thing, who didn't give way to wild, uncharacteristic impulses that threatened to land her in a cauldron of hot water that would scar her for ever and play havoc with her soul.

'My husband was a good, kind man.'

'But it's plainly not kindness you want from me, Karen—is it?'

Gray's lips twisted mockingly, and Karen felt a shaft of pain pierce her heart like a hot red spike.

'Don't.'

'Don't what?' he demanded derisively, hands either side of his hips, an imposing dark figure dressed in black, his sombre face a pale, startling contrast in the eerily atmospheric light of the moon. 'You've got to decide, Karen. Either you're just a girl or you *are* a woman. When you know the answer perhaps we can come to some mutually satisfying arrangement?'

'I don't want—I mean I'm not interested in—'

'Liar.' He spat the word out like a poisoned dart headed straight for her heart, making Karen feel deeply, unforgivably ashamed of her own wanton nature. A nature she'd had no trouble keeping under strict control when she was married to gentle, undemanding Ryan, with his beguiling smile and soft voice. Yet in a few short minutes with this hard unyielding stranger that unknown trait had burst free like some wild wind, sweeping everything aside in its path—including her dignity and common sense…

'I think you should leave.' Her words made a liar of her, too, because even now her body was craving Gray's touch as powerfully as any drug a person could be addicted to in spite of her shame and remorse.

'Yes, I think perhaps I should.'

With a distant look in his eyes that told her he wasn't even seeing her any more, Gray pivoted abruptly and disappeared into the rainy night as if he had been nothing but a disturbing figment of Karen's fevered imagination, conjured up by her longing and her loneliness.

Biting back a sob as she turned unhappily back towards the house, she knew with certainty that in her rational everyday mind there was no way on this good green earth that she would ever have conjured up a man like Gray O'Connell. Only a fool could expect anything more than hurt from such an angry, embittered soul as him....

CHAPTER THREE

GRAY splashed whiskey into a tumbler about a quarter of the way up the glass, then raised it to his lips. Despising himself for succumbing to a device that really was a last resort in his book, he took one long draught, emptied the glass and set it carelessly back down on the old oak sideboard. An answering fire burned in his gut, but even that wasn't hot enough to scorch out what ailed him. Just what did he think he'd been doing, treating a grieving young widow as if she was his for the taking? Just because she'd done him the courtesy of listening to his litany of regrets when he'd turned up unannounced at the cottage that first time, it didn't mean that he should presume she would now give him anything he asked for!

He groaned out loud, shaking his head. Chase looked up curiously from his place by the fire, then dropped his head mournfully down onto his front paws again as if to say *What's the point?*

Precisely... What *was* the point? Gray agonised. There were plenty of likely women in the town and thereabouts—women who would be only too willing to warm his bed. Some of them had done just that—if only briefly—in the past. After Maura had left him he hadn't cared about who they were, just that they were willing.

He almost reached for the whiskey bottle again at the thought of such recklessness. He'd protected himself, of

MAGGIE COX   49

course—he didn't want anyone jumping up and down accusing him of making them pregnant—but just the same it wasn't the kind of behaviour he was proud of.

But now, after two years of being unattached and heart-free—he scowled at that—he couldn't believe he could be so affected by a little witch with honey-gold hair and an angelic smile, and a body that he ached to have wrapped round him naked. Neither the faded jeans nor the baggy shapeless sweater she'd been wearing had been able to totally disguise the long-legged, shapely body beneath the clothes. It had taken every ounce of willpower Gray had in him to refrain from taking her out there in the rain—up against the wall of the cottage, most likely. Desire had been running high in both of them, like sizzling sparks along a fuse wire. He'd felt it in every exquisite tremble of that taut and sexy little body of hers. Gray imagined her big blue eyes widening in shock, then capitulating in passion as she opened to receive him.

The vivid picture he conjured up had heat slamming into him with such ferocity that there wasn't a single cell in his body that didn't want her right there and then—that wouldn't have pushed aside every single scruple he had left just to lose himself in the heat and softness of that alluring young body even as her sweetly musky scent drove him slowly crazy.

He was a passionate man—a man who put his heart and soul into everything he did, whether it was pushing his body hard in a workout, making money, painting pictures or making love. But he could honestly not recall another time in the whole of his thirty-six years when he had wanted a woman as badly as he wanted the chaste little widow. And the damnedest thing about it was that he had no business wanting her at all. Not when she was clearly still nursing her hurt over the death of her husband. Only a heartless bastard would take advantage of such a situation, and that was one title he'd tagged himself with for long enough.

'She's nothing but trouble with a capital T,' he said out loud, his rich, resonant tone ringing out in the big, sombre drawing room with its dark oak panelling and ruby-red carpeting. For such an impressive room, its furnishings were sparse, to say the least. A more kindly observer might suggest minimalist. One large antique couch sat a few feet back from the huge brick fireplace with its open hearth, its once deep red cushions now sadly flattened and faded to a more sedate and dusky plum.

There was nothing comfortable about it, if the truth be known, but then Gray had become so careless of his own comfort of late that he scarcely gave the matter much thought. A few once beautiful but now faded Turkish rugs were laid indifferently here and there across the rich carpet, and one large oak sideboard and a heavily embossed armchair—renovated for Maura's benefit, not *his*—was the only other furniture. On the walls were various old portraits that he'd got as a kind of 'job lot' when he'd purchased the grand old house, but none of them was of any relation of his as far as he knew. He'd been meaning to put them into storage, but lately he hadn't had the heart to even *think* about the task, let alone do it.

The house was beautiful, right enough. It had the kind of faded grandeur that many old Irish houses descended from the landed gentry often possessed. But now many of the owners of such houses couldn't afford the soaring upkeep they entailed, and despite the fact that Gray could afford it easily it was still soulless when all was said and done—even with his housekeeper Bridie's loving administrations. What else could it be with just one singularly unhappy man and his bear of a dog living in it? It occurred to him just then that his father's cottage was far more homely and welcoming. But then that was down to his beautiful shapely tenant and nothing to do with him.

As a picture of Karen filled his mind, scented candles and

blazing fire an alluring backdrop, he shook his head with a fresh spurt of anger, desperately trying to dismiss it. He couldn't understand it. The woman set him on fire with just one innocent glance from those incandescent blue eyes of hers. Doubly so because there was no falsity to be detected anywhere in their crystal silky depths—just a warmth he wanted to gravitate towards and a hurt that he found himself desperate to ease. That wasn't like him. *It wasn't like him at all.*

Besides, it was as plain as day that she didn't need a hard, embittered man like Gray. The woman's trusting soul and generous heart needed a man more in the mould of the way he guessed her husband must have been. Someone gentle and loving, no doubt—someone with infinite patience, someone selfless who worshipped the ground her perfect little feet walked on.

A rueful grin split his lips. The thick white socks she'd been wearing on a previous occasion hadn't gone unnoticed. She had feet like a ballerina, perfectly poised, with a delicate but distinct little arch that was positively sexy. He wondered what she'd look like wearing nothing else but those chaste white socks and that beguilingly angelic little smile of hers? The thought caused him serious agony. *For God's sake! Just give her a wide berth from now on, man!*

The instruction careened through his brain, wiping the grin clean off his handsome face. Scowling, Gray turned and stalked across the sea of ruby-red carpet, heading determinedly for the large scullery-type kitchen to chop up some steak for Chase's dinner….

Karen sat in the window seat sipping her tea, straining for the sound of the ocean, which on a calm, still day could just be detected by those of a soulful enough disposition wanting to hear it. Her whole body was tense with waiting. Waiting for Gray O'Connell to show up with whatever bits and pieces of furniture he wanted to install in the cottage. Perhaps after last night he'd changed his mind?

Her heart took a dive as she remembered how vulnerable she'd made herself to the man, how incapable she'd been of holding back the tide of feeling so strong that it had threatened to knock her off her feet. *Was that what passion did to a person?* Made them lose their reason and dignity?

If Gray hadn't strode away when he had, like some compelling black shadow melting into the darkness, Karen had serious doubts as to whether she would have restrained herself from practically *begging* him to share her bed. No wonder she was so keyed-up at the idea of seeing him again. How on earth was she even going to be able to look him in the eye? As if the man didn't have enough advantages, without his sexually frustrated tenant throwing herself at his feet!

With a little groan she shook her head, then scrubbed at the condensation from her breath that clouded the windowpane. Everything could do with a coat of paint, she thought suddenly, her glance assessing. The white emulsion on the small square frames was grey and flaking, and the same washed-out tone on the walls was equally ready for some kind of springlike makeover. Would it be presumptuous of her to ask her taciturn landlord if she could apply a fresh coat of paint here and there? she wondered. After all, it could only be to his advantage. She was quite prepared to buy the paint and undertake the task herself.

The sound of a vehicle approaching had her leaping off the seat and hurrying to the kitchen sink to empty her half-consumed mug of tea. Pulling out a drawer, she let her fingers busily scramble through the jumbled contents that consisted of matchbooks, packets of incense and the odd battery and paperclip, to reach for her hairbrush. She pulled the cushioned comb through her hair, wincing at the occasional tangle it wouldn't easily unravel.

Squinting into the small make-up mirror she'd left propped up against a line of cookery books on a shelf above the fridge, she grimaced at her flushed cheeks and over-bright eyes. It was hardly the composed visage she so desperately needed to present to her intimidating landlord, with his rangy good-looks and stinging glance that was currently the major stumbling block and disruption to her peace of mind.

A loud rapping on the door had Karen dropping the hair-brush haphazardly back into the drawer and slamming it shut with a bit too much gusto, causing the ill-fitting container to get jammed halfway and then refuse to budge. Cursing her own impatience, she left it as it was, then flew out into the sitting room to get the door.

'Hello!' Breathless, she stared up at Gray, winded by her sudden exertion as well as an unsettling feeling of intense anticipation at seeing him again.

Those mysterious grey eyes of his considered her for several tension-filled seconds without him uttering a word. *Was he even going to say hello back?* Karen's stomach lurched, then lurched again. Dry-mouthed, she let her gaze move downwards to the deliberately provocative curl of those ruthless brooding lips. The same mocking lips that only just last night had all but burned her, highlighting an aspect of her nature that she now knew without a doubt she'd long suppressed.

'My, my… What big eyes you have, Miss Ford.' His voice, low and laced with a deliberate taunt, turned the blood in her veins to the consistency of sluggish warm treacle.

'Barring the name—isn't that supposed to be my line?' she quipped back, astounded that she'd managed to even get the words past her throat. Trouble was, she was remembering the provocative, compelling taste of that taunting mouth and wondering how she was going to pretend that nothing disturbing had happened when they both knew it had. That destroying, passionate kiss from Gray had turned everything

Karen believed about herself on its head, and there didn't seem to be a single thing she could do to restore that belief to where it had been before.

After assessing her for a couple more seconds, Gray bestowed upon her a disturbing lingering smile. 'A man could quite forget his own name, standing here looking at you,' he ruefully told her. 'And that wouldn't do. It wouldn't do at all. Regarding the furniture that I've brought—if you don't like it, or it's not to your taste, then I'll change it for something that suits better. Not that I'm enamoured of the idea of a shopping trip any time soon, but maybe for you, Miss Ford, I'll make an exception.'

'I'm sure whatever style you've chosen will be just fine,' she murmured, the mere *idea* of going on a shopping trip with Gray O'Connell churning her insides like butter.

'Good.' He grinned. 'What a refreshing change to meet a woman that's so amenable.' Turning abruptly, he stepped back outside.

When she finally remembered to breathe again, Karen's breath was distinctly shaky. There was no doubt that the man was good-looking—if in a kind of arrogant, couldn't-careless, everybody-else-be-damned kind of way—but when he smiled… His smile was like the sun lighting up the greyest of gloomy days, or a full moon brightly showcasing the myriad stars that it shared the night sky with. His fathomless long-lashed eyes were stop-you-in-your-tracks amazing, and his mouth—his mouth had a deliciously enigmatic curve that was without a doubt provoking and made her toes curl. It also transformed his face from darkly handsome to hauntingly, irresistibly beautiful. *How could a woman ever forget it?* All Karen could do was blink up at him, saying nothing. It was as if she had suddenly lost the power to *think*, let alone speak, when he looked at her like that.

Striding across the grassy area round the house onto the

narrow unmade road that led to the dwelling, Gray opened the rear doors of a large white transit van. Karen saw a tall, slim young man with a thatch of unruly fair hair, dressed in paint-splattered jeans and a scruffy black tee shirt, clamber out of the front seat and amble up beside him—presumably to assist with whatever he'd brought in the van.

The first item to emerge was a beautiful Victorian two-seater sofa with cabriole legs, upholstered in natural linen. Its condition was immaculate, and between the two of them the men brought it into the house and deposited it beside the older worn version that it would replace. Lifting the three small green velvet cushions that adorned the old couch, Gray threw them down onto its smarter replacement, then glanced directly over at Karen where she stood awkwardly and bemused by the door.

'That's a lot better, don't you think?'

There was something almost endearing about the glance Gray gave her—almost as if he was unsure of her reaction and sought her approval. The thought was so surprising that an answering sensation of warmth curled in Karen's belly, bringing with it a surge of affection towards the aloof, complex man who acted as if he didn't need anything from anyone—let alone affection.

'It's great.' She lifted her shoulders with a shrug of plea-sure.

'By the way, this is Sean Regan. Sean—meet Miss Ford.'

'Call me Karen.' She stepped forward to shake the younger man's hand, already warming to the unrestrained friendliness she saw on his eager, attractive face, and noting the two little silver earrings he wore in one earlobe with a feeling almost akin to maternal indulgence. Which was ridiculous, because he could only be a couple of years her junior—if that.

Her shy gaze slid furtively across to Gray. Perhaps it was just that she preferred her men to be a little more mature and

rugged? Gray certainly fitted into that criteria as far as life
experience went. She frowned at the preoccupied expression
on his face, aching for that glorious smile of his to revisit the
sternly handsome features even though she'd intuited that such
smiles were probably incredibly rare.

'Pleased to meet you, Karen.' Sean stepped back with a
grin as Gray indicated he wanted his help in taking the old
sofa outside. 'I've seen you round the town and sometimes
walking the hills or down by the sea. How do you like it out
here? Not too lonely for you?'

'I like it just fine, Sean. The peace and quiet is just what I
need.'

'Are you going to stand round all day chatting to Miss
Ford, or are you going to give me a hand like I asked you to?'
Scowling at the younger man, Gray picked up one end of the
old sofa and waited with barely concealed impatience for him
to lift the other.

'I suppose I'm going to help you, boss—that's why I'm here,
isn't it? But it's a sad day when a man can't take the time to
share a few words with a new neighbour, don't you think?'

This gently amused remark elicited another dark scowl
from Gray, and as the two men passed Karen with the sofa
Sean gave her a conspiratorial wink.

Biting her lip to keep from grinning, Karen followed them
outside again. 'Shall I make some tea?'

'Got any coffee?' Gray came back.

Tucking her hair behind her ears, Karen felt her cheeks
burn at the sudden intense inspection he subjected her to. She
personally thought such interested scrutiny was ill-deserved
when she was wearing her second oldest pair of jeans and a
plain, too-big lilac shirt that had lost a couple of its buttons.

'Sure. How do you take it?'

'Black and strong, no sugar,' came the clipped reply.

Karen nodded. She should have guessed. It probably

summed up the way Gray lived his life, she thought. No frills, just the basic essentials. Milk and sugar would have been far too much of an indulgence for such a man.

'And you, Sean?'

'Tea for me, darlin'…plenty of milk and three sugars.'

'Okay—and how about a slice of home-made fruitcake to go with it?'

'I'm a sucker for home-made cake any time, so I'll say yes, please!' Sean winked at her.

'And you, Mr O'Connell?'

She'd deliberately kept her address formal, so he wouldn't think she was being forward, but there was a maddening twinkle in his eyes as he replied, 'You clearly know how to tempt a man, Miss Ford.'

'Refreshments coming right up, then.' Blushing and smiling shyly, Karen turned back into the house to put the kettle on.

Altogether Gray had brought her a sofa, two matching armchairs in the same tasteful natural linen, and a couple of Victorian brass table-lamps that complemented the traditional interior of the cottage so well that Karen could have hugged him with delight. The new furniture transformed the place. Now all she needed to do was apply a couple of coats of paint to the walls and window frames and it would resemble a home again, rather than a place haunted by the twin ghosts of sadness and neglect.

Taking a sip of tea from a pink mug labelled 'Primadonna'—a long-ago gift from Ryan—she surveyed the two men currently gracing the new armchairs.

Sean had the ease and careless body language of his youth, and was oblivious to anything but the enjoyment of his sweet milky tea, while Gray… Well, Gray was another matter entirely, Karen thought. The long legs clad in close-fitting black jeans seemed almost too long for the chair he sat in. He'd rolled the sleeves of his rust-coloured shirt halfway up his forearms, revealing strong limbs with a distinct smattering of fine dark hair. The fingers that curved round his blue china mug were long and slender, and definitely hinted at artistic leanings. But, unlike Seán, he *wasn't* at ease. His handsome face seemed singularly distant and preoccupied, barely concealing the fact that he was scarcely comfortable with the situation at all and would probably much rather be anywhere else but there.

Was it her? Karen couldn't help wondering if he was regretting that explosive hungry kiss they'd shared last night. Maybe she should bring the matter up? Tell him that it meant nothing and suggest they start again on a more businesslike footing? *Yeah, right.* She could just imagine how that little suggestion would be received. He'd probably laugh mockingly and tell her to grow up.

With a sudden ache in her heart, she smoothed down an imaginary crease in her shirt, then almost choked on her tea when she caught Gray studying her with indisputable heat in his eyes—heat that scorched her even when there was a distance of a good three or four feet between them.

'It was good of you to replace the old furniture,' she said quickly. 'It's nice and cosy now.'

'I should have done it a long time ago,' Gray replied, unsmiling. 'Anything else you can think of that you'd like?'

Karen's fingers tightened round her mug of tea. Unable to meet his gaze just then, because his question had elicited a rather *risqué* response in her brain, she jerked her head vaguely towards the windows. 'I was going to ask if I could give the walls and window frames a fresh coat of paint. I'll buy it myself. I'm a dab hand with a paintbrush.'

'Sure, I'd be happy to come up and do the job for you myself, darlin',' Seán piped up, blue eyes wide as he contemplated the unknowingly stirring picture Karen made with her long slender legs encased in tight faded denim and her waist-length honey-gold hair tumbling freely over her shoulders in the plain lilac blouse that she managed to elevate to 'classy' just because she was wearing it. 'Sure, I could even get you the paint. What do you say, boss?' The younger man glanced at Gray, whose unsmiling countenance appeared immediately forbidding.

'If anyone's going to paint this house it will be me,' he said tersely, his aloof glance clearly berating Sean for imagining anything else.

'I don't want to put you to any trouble.' Fielding the surge of embarrassment that flooded her, Karen folded her arms uncomfortably. Of course she hadn't expected her landlord to offer to come and do the job himself. She suddenly wished she had just gone ahead and done it and suffered the consequences afterwards if he really didn't like it.

She watched Gray get up and stalk to the small galley kitchen to rinse out his mug. When he came out again he walked straight to the front door and wrenched it wide. 'I'll be back around ten tomorrow to make a start,' he said and disappeared outside.

Karen exhaled a long slow breath.

Amused, Sean got to his feet, leaving his mug and plate on the coffee table.

'Don't let him get to you, darlin'. Sure, his bark is worse than his bite. And, by the way, that cake was out of this world. The best I've ever tasted and I'm not joking. I couldn't trouble you for a slice to take home, could I? My sister Liz runs a café with all kinds of home-made fare, and I'd like her to try it.'

'Of course. Just give me a minute and I'll wrap some up for you.'

She was back almost straight away with the promised cake, and after thanking her, then winking at her for a second time, the young man left the cottage with a cheerful whistle.

* * *

As a waft of fresh paint floated through the air and assailed her nostrils, Karen stepped out of the kitchen to watch Gray as he crouched low to tackle the skirting. This morning he was again dressed from head to foot in black, his longish hair gleaming even more darkly than his clothing, and as her covetous glance surveyed him Karen knew the most compelling urge to touch him…to make him turn around…to make him notice her. She was beginning to feel frustrated beyond belief that his aloofness seemed to be growing rather than diminishing, and something inside her wanted to try and coax him back to the land of the living—which was quite ironic when she contemplated her own desire for isolation. Still, one step at a time…

'Why don't I give you a hand?' she asked, her voice faltering despite her need to sound confident.

The paintbrush stilled in Gray's hand. Carefully wiping the drips on the inside of the paint can, then laying the brush across it, he looked up to meet her gaze. Karen's heart took a slow elevator ride to her stomach.

'I prefer to get along on my own,' was the slow but succinct answer she received.

She wasn't surprised, but when curiosity and downright foolhardiness got the better part of common sense, she folded her arms across the orange tie-dyed tee shirt she wore, willing herself not to flinch beneath that cool-as-a-cucumber gaze of his that would surely freeze out even the most dogged admirer?

'Why is it that you prefer to do everything on your own?'

'Does that bother you?' He looked directly into her eyes.

Every cell in Karen's body seemed to vibrate with heat. Flustered, she shook her head, wishing she'd never started this. Why couldn't she just have stayed put in the kitchen, making her scones?

'No. I mean yes. If I'm honest, it *does* bother me. No man is an island. We all need a bit of help and support from time to time.'

'That why you hide yourself out here on your own?' Gray probed, getting to his feet.

Nervously moistening her lips with her tongue, Karen swallowed hard. His immediately interested glance caught the movement and turned from ice to fire in less than a second. Her knees buckled.

'I wasn't talking about me.'

'What if I told you I *wanted* to talk about you?'

Somehow his voice had acquired a hypnotic resonance that sent goosebumps scudding across Karen's skin like out-of-control wildfire. It was all she could do to keep herself from crossing her legs, because the sensation at her innermost core was suddenly hotly, sweetly, demandingly sexual.

'What do you want to know about me?' The question left her lips in a hoarse whisper.

'I want to know if you have a sense of adventure, Karen… or are you the type of woman who likes to play safe?'

'I don't know what you mean.' Her gaze lowered, because the expression in his eyes was too hot for her to handle just then. It was having the same effect as a branding iron held too close to her skin.

'You know damn well exactly what I mean.' A dark eyebrow quirked upwards towards his brow.

All the blood seemed to rush to Karen's head. Inside her chest, her heart throbbed like some heavy tribal drumbeat that she couldn't make stop, even as her nipples grew almost unbearably achy and hard. If he could do this to her body— make her ache and want and need just with words—what effect would his touch have? Recalling his fierce, bruising kiss the other night, she already knew the answer. There was no question he would set her on fire.

'I don't think you should be asking me such personal questions.' Completely out of her depth, Karen went to turn away, her wary blue eyes widening in shock when Gray gripped her upper arm in a vice and spun her back towards him.

'Don't you? Then stop coming on to me with those coy little-girl looks of yours. You have no idea what you're getting yourself into...*none*.'

Wrenching her arm free, Karen rubbed it with resentment and hurt. 'I'm not coming on to you! You really flatter yourself, don't you?'

He gave her a maddeningly knowing little smile. 'Go back to your baking, sweetheart. If you're good...or maybe I should say *bad*...I'll come and tell you later about a particular erotic fantasy of mine about women in the kitchen.'

'No, thanks.' Humiliated and indignant, Karen tossed her head and beat a hasty retreat.

'I never had you down as a coward!' Gray called after her, chuckling out loud.

Karen put her head round the door and glared back at him, blue eyes sparking like a firecracker. 'And I *definitely* had you down as a sadist,' she retorted angrily, her jaw aching with the effort of restraining her fury. 'Sadly, I haven't been proved wrong yet!'

'Now you've really hurt my feelings.' Affecting an expression of pained disappointment, then grinning like a schoolboy, triumphant at getting the last word, he dropped down onto his haunches to resume his painting...

CHAPTER FOUR

IT HAD started raining again, and Karen's restlessness grew. Gray was striding in and out from the van, oblivious to the downpour, clearing away dustsheets and decorating implements, evidently not the least bit inclined to attempt conversation of any kind. What was wrong with the man, for goodness' sake? Apart from his humiliating accusation earlier, about her trying to come on to him, he hadn't said another word. Every time she'd dared put her head round the door to see how he was doing, he'd been diligently painting, moving the thick paintbrush up and down the wall with sure smooth strokes that were fascinating to observe. It had made Karen wonder what he looked like when he was creating *real* works of art.

Sighing, she filled the kettle and put it on to boil. When in doubt, make tea—or in Gray's case strong black *coffee*. But whether he intended to stay or go Karen would have to wait and see.

Bending down to the oven, she withdrew the tray of newly baked scones, her mouth watering at the tantalising smell they exuded. Picking them gingerly off the tray one by one, she laid them on the wire rack on the worktop to cool, gratified at the way they had turned out—faintly golden on the outside and hopefully moist and soft inside. Just the way she liked them. Unable to resist, she broke one in half and, blowing on it briefly, popped a small wedge into her mouth.

'Mmm—delicious! Even if I do say so myself.'

As the cake melted on her tongue, Karen genuinely savoured it. She had always loved her food, and wasn't ashamed to admit it. It was one of life's greatest pleasures. Akin to reading a good book, listening to a beautiful piece of music or making love...

'They look good.'

She nearly jumped out of her skin as she glanced guiltily round to find Gray leaning against the door jamb, his face and hair glistening from the rain, a teasing smile on his lips that made her feel like a child caught with her hand in the cookie jar.

'Would you like one? I was just going to make some tea... or coffee if you prefer?' Wiping her hand across her lips, she prayed there weren't any betraying crumbs in evidence.

'Coffee would be good.'

'I'll get you a towel first. You're wet through.' Flustered, Karen moved to slide past him. The doorway was narrow, to say the least, and Gray, with his tall broad-shouldered physique all but filled it.

He didn't move. All of a sudden she found herself wedged between his chest and the door jamb. The damp warmth of his sweater pressed provocatively against her breasts in the thin tee shirt, and she knew with a little zing of panic that he had no intention of letting her pass.

'I...I...'

Her senses were overwhelmed. Assaulted by the fresh, clean outdoorsy smell of his clothes, the faint woody tang of his cologne and the provocative testosterone-laden scent of the man himself, she felt an answering tremor wing its way through her body, bringing an aroused flush to her cheeks and a soft, discernible tremble to her lips.

Raising her eyes, Karen gazed up into a deep silvery-grey ocean—a wild, storm-tossed sea on a cloudy day—and knew that she was irrevocably captured…a willing prisoner with no desire or even the remotest urge to escape. At that moment she was right where she wanted to be. Just then she could pretend she was once again a woman with no troubled past or uncertain future, because only the arousing present existed, with its tangible heat thrumming like a silent steady current between herself and Gray. And suddenly the little old-fashioned kitchen, with its warm, homely smell of freshly baked scones and a faint, musky dampness from old stone walls seemed like the most romantic, intoxicating place on earth.

With one long lean finger Gray traced the delicate line of her jaw, his touch electrifying her, making her pupils dilate, causing her breath to still for a second while her heartbeat raced hard, like an athlete towards the finishing line. She'd never known it was possible to desire anyone so much until even the mere thought of them could make her want to give him body and soul without a care. *Why hadn't she felt that way about Ryan?* Guilt consumed her at the thought. He'd given her everything, yet she had definitely kept something back from him…a vital, important, passionate part of herself that needed expression—and not just through her writing or performing.

'Gray, I—'

'Don't talk,' he ordered, eyes widening as if suddenly coming out of a trance. 'Just let me look at you.'

And he did. Gray's artist's eye scrutinised her face, noting the exquisitely aligned features with silent but fierce appreciation. Her beautiful blue eyes were her most beguiling asset, he thought, deep and sensual and almost almond-shaped, with fine curling lashes—the kind of eyes that surely most men would willingly drown in. His gaze moved up a little to the smooth dark blonde wing of her brows, then back down to the small elegant slope of her nose and the prettily contoured mouth, with its sultry full lower lip, pink and plump, bereft of lipstick and just begging to be kissed.

In less than an instant blood rushed to the core of Gray's manhood, and he wanted her as he wanted his next breath. But he didn't give in to the almost overwhelming urge to plunder and ravish because he knew a sudden, much greater desire to tease and provoke and sensually savour. He'd make the pretty widow want him so badly that every thought of her husband and any other man she had been romantically involved with would be wiped clean out of her head. Only then would he allow himself to take what they both so desperately wanted. And when they did succumb to the desire that was shimmering between them, like an oasis in one-hundred-and-twenty-degree heat, it would need more than a whole fire brigade to put out the conflagration.

For Karen, it took a few seconds longer for reality to sink in. When she realised Gray had no intention of doing anything more than just looking at her, instead of winding his arms around her waist as she needed him to—as she *ached* for him to—she let her hands drop redundantly down by her sides and dipped her head. It hurt to know that he desired her but wasn't prepared to do anything about it. What was it about her that put him off? Did he think she came with too much baggage? Was that it? Did he imagine that she would want much more than just an intense physical fling?

She suddenly wished that Ryan was around, so that she could ask him what was the best thing to do, then realised how preposterous the notion was. This was one situation that she was going to have to sort out for herself. Wherever he was, Ryan would only want what was best for Karen—the outcome that would cause her the least pain. Somehow she knew that, as far as Gray O'Connell was concerned, on some level she'd already signed up for a truckload of that particular commodity.

'Hey...' His fingers sliding beneath her jaw, he tilted her chin to align her glance with his.

It was amazing how many shades of silver-grey there were in his pupils, Karen mused with wonder. She hadn't realised how varied the colour could be.

'I think I'd like to paint you,' he said.

Karen felt a little throb of panic at the idea. 'A portrait, you mean?'

'A life study.'

'You mean without—without clothes?' She couldn't prevent the tremor in her voice.

Gray smiled as if her flustered confusion amused him. 'Most life studies are nude,' he told her evenly. 'Does that bother you?'

'Not generally, no. But me posing for one definitely does.'

'Live a little, Karen. Isn't that what you'd really like to do?'

How many times had she promised herself that very thing? She was only twenty-six, for goodness' sake! Was she going to spend the rest of her life in recrimination and regret? *Ryan would turn in his grave.* But, just the same, she had to live a little by degrees. Becoming an artist's model for this aloof, enigmatic man—posing without clothes on to boot—was too much to expect in too short a time. Even if she *was* craving his attention a little too much for her peace of mind.

'I'm not the kind of person who can easily throw caution to the wind,' she started to explain, going alternately hot and cold beneath Gray's laserlike glance, because she had nowhere to hide when he looked at her like that. 'I'm—'

She tried to summon up words that would adequately describe how she felt about exposing her body without sounding like a complete prude. She'd performed on stage to audiences varying from small to large, yet she was innately shy. Apart from her jeans, her clothes were generally soft and free-flowing, rarely tight or figure-hugging. Even Ryan had teased her about her reticence to show off her figure.

'Repressed?' Gray suggested softly, his gaze lingering with deliberate provocation on her mouth.

'No. I wouldn't say I was repressed.' Her face aflame, Karen tried again to pass the man who was holding her prisoner with just a look, and gasped out loud when he caught hold of her arm and pressed her back up against the door jamb.

The kettle whistled to indicate it had boiled. Outside the rain beat a steady tattoo against the windows. The sharp intoxicating scent of fresh paint wafted in from the sitting room, and Karen began to wish that Gray had just got straight in the van and gone after he'd packed up his things.

His intimate interrogation was beginning to make her squirm with unease. It was one thing longing for him to kiss her—quite another allowing him to put her under the microscope as if she was some interesting dissection. But then, what was she supposed to do, when her body was so over-stimulated and yet languorous with need at the same time? What those mystifying eyes were doing to her body would tempt the most devout celibate to give up their vows.

She was helpless to disguise the intensely intimate reaction of her body. Inside her white lace bra her nipples surged and hardened into prickling distended buds, making her squirm in embarrassment as she realised Gray had seen immediately what had happened. His pupils darkened to fierce midnight. Whatever Karen was feeling he was feeling it too…maybe even more so.

'You'd better go get me that towel, Miss Ford, before I succumb to a temptation that it's becoming increasingly painful to resist.' He let go of her arm with a scowl as her brows knit in confusion.

'Why? Does that worry you?'

'You're not like any of the other women I've known.' His face contorted in a flash of anger. 'You're basically a very decent, loving woman, Karen. You need a man who's the same. Not some dark-souled outsider like me. I'm afraid if I touch you I might never want to stop—and then where would we be?'

His lips twisted in a mocking little smile that caused Karen untold agony, and because she couldn't think of a single thing to say that would persuade him differently, she scooted past him and fled into the bathroom. As she selected a fluffy white towel from the airing cupboard, she pressed it close to her cheek for a moment. Staring into the square wooden-framed mirror above the sink, she saw with a shock the physical effect Gray O'Connell was having on her.

Her blue eyes were dilated and sparkling, and there was a hectic flush to her skin that made it appear as if she'd just stumbled out of bed after a night of pure, unrestrained passion. Had she ever looked like that after a night with Ryan? Of course she must have! She'd just never noticed it, that was all. Skimming her hand along the side of her cheek, Karen discovered her skin was as hot to the touch as it appeared. She was all but burning up. Even her pulse was still racing. And all because of her shocking attraction to her infuriating landlord.

Frustration and anger throbbed simultaneously through her, and she wished again that she possessed some of the necessary sophistication that would help her be more appealing to the man she desired. If only she didn't look younger than her age. If only she could beguile him with wit and warmth and irresistible charm. *If only she didn't have her heart in her eyes every time she so much as glanced at him.*

Clutching the towel to her chest, she opened the door of the tiny narrow bathroom, with its old-fashioned claw-footed bath, and returned to the kitchen.

Gray was leaning against the door jamb where she had left him, his handsome face preoccupied. Handing him the towel, Karen slid past him without a backwards glance. She saw straight away that he'd turned off the kettle and moved it to a back burner on the cooker, and she tried not to mind that he wouldn't stay for coffee if she asked. It was obvious that he was eager to get out of there as soon as possible, and she bit her lip to stifle the tears that kept threatening. She was determined to keep them at bay at least until he'd gone. To distract herself, she selected half a dozen scones from the wire rack where they'd been left to cool and popped them into a plastic sandwich bag. She held them out to Gray with an uncertain little smile and prayed she looked more composed than she felt. Yes, she desired Gray O'Connell, but she didn't want to make herself totally vulnerable to him. Only a fool would do that.

He stopped drying his hair with the towel and stared at her.

'I thought you might like to take some of my baking home,' she said softly.

When he made no move to take the scones, but continued to examine her with an expression she was beyond explaining right then, Karen shrugged her shoulders and put the bag on the worktop.

'Even if you don't want them, maybe Chase might like them? I've made too many and they don't keep.'

'One kiss,' he said hoarsely, and threw the towel on the worktop.

Startled, Karen was still gathering her wits as he stepped towards her and hauled her roughly up against his chest. The sensation of heat and damp from his sweater enveloped her, even as the wild fresh scent of the sea and the Atlantic air invaded her senses so profoundly that she suddenly felt dizzy as well as exhilarated. As Gray bent his head to kiss her she didn't have even the remotest inclination to protest. Instead, her lips parted easily as his mouth lowered with unstoppable urgency and took hungry, greedy possession of hers.

She tasted heat, heartache and desire, all wrapped up in one intense compelling package, as he plundered and took what she so willingly gave, his tongue dipping in and out of her velvet softness like a man possessed, the faint stubble on his angled jaw scraping her chin as his hands slid down to her bottom and impelled her hips hard into his own. Shaking with need, Karen kissed him back with soft little moans that seemed to leave her throat without her realisation. She was near mindless with wanting, and she no longer wished for sophistication—simply ached in every muscle and limb for the fire they had stoked between them to be sated.

Then, as suddenly and abruptly as he had pulled her into his arms, Gray released her, his hands gripping her by her shoulders to hold her away from him. The next instant he abruptly let her go and, dazed, Karen stumbled, hitting her lower back against the worktop. She stared at him as pain and humiliation hazed her eyes, her lips still throbbing from his hungry kisses, her body languid with the desire he'd stoked, and at an utter loss to know what to do or say.

'Are you okay?' He voiced his concern almost grudgingly, as if he couldn't wait to be gone.

Karen suddenly wanted him gone, too. Now she understood why hate and love were so closely intertwined.

'Why should you care?' she tried, but was unable to prevent the sob that accompanied her words.

'I *do* care, damn you!'

Shaking her head, Karen blinked up at him through eyes that were helplessly brimming with tears. 'No, you don't. Just go. Please…just go.'

His lips pressed grimly together, Gray turned and did just as she asked…

* * *

Wiping his palette knife clean of the worst excesses of paint, Gray laid it carefully down beside the black metal box of paints. The sun filtered in through the huge uncurtained window, pouring light onto the picture fastened to his easel. The rough sketch was of a woman with long rippling gold hair and almond-shaped blue eyes that gazed back at him with hurt as well as temptation in their depths. *Karen.*

He hadn't been able to think about anything else since he'd left her crying in the kitchen of his father's old cottage. That had been two weeks ago. He'd made no attempt to get in touch in all that time. He wondered what she'd been doing. He hadn't seen her on the beach or in the woods—not that she would have welcomed bumping into him. She'd probably chalked him up to bitter experience by now. It was nothing less than he deserved, but still a pain twisted through his guts, making him scowl.

Cursing out loud, he raked his fingers through his already mussed black hair, then reached out to tear the rough portrait from the easel. In spite of himself his fingertips lingered on the likeness he had created, smoothing down the soft curve of the feminine cheekbone he had captured only too well, despite having to work from memory only. But there it was. Karen's face was indelibly printed on Gray's mind like a photograph he couldn't erase.

The door of his studio creaked open just then, and Chase padded hopefully across the bare wooden floor and nudged his head into Gray's side. His master glanced down distractedly at the huge dog, absent-mindedly stroking the impressive fawn head.

'Give me half an hour, hmm? Then I'll take you for your walk.'

As if understanding perfectly, Chase turned round, loped back across the floor and went out through the door.

Replacing the unfinished sketch of Karen on the easel,

Gray exited the large sunlit room that was bereft of heating or adornment of any kind, except for the haphazard stacks of paintings propped up against two of the walls. Without realising why, he found himself hurrying downstairs to the first-floor landing.

In the middle of the largest bedroom in the house was a beautiful handcrafted bed, with a plain navy blue throw flung across the duvet. Apart from the sensually coloured Moroccan rug on the floor next to the bed, there was one large chest of drawers in reclaimed pine, and two cherrywood bedside cabinets, but that was it as far as furnishings and fittings went. No curtains or blinds hung at the windows, and right now, as the sunlight hit the bare wooden boards of the floor, highlighting the dust-motes dancing in its beam, the room appeared almost stark in its emptiness. But Gray paid no mind to that. Stalking across the floor, he pulled open one of the drawers in the pine chest and took out a faded brown envelope.

Dropping down onto the huge bed, he shook out the contents onto the navy blue throw. Three photographs lay face upwards on the bed. He picked up the first one that caught his eye and held it up to examine it more closely. It was Maura, with her pale blonde hair and laughing green eyes. They'd started an affair when Gray was working in London, and she'd stubbornly followed him back to Ireland—even though he'd tried to end it between them—and somehow moved in. He'd been glad of her company then. She'd been with him when Paddy had died and things had been pretty bleak. Just knowing someone else was in the house had helped, because he'd ultimately been terrified of facing himself. Now he wondered how she'd stuck it. If Gray had been morose before, he'd been worse after the tragedy of his father's death.

For six months after it had happened he'd become a virtual recluse. He'd never meant for that to happen. Somehow he'd withdrawn so far into himself that he'd known he wasn't fit

company for anyone—let alone a bright, vivacious woman
with a bold laugh and a love of life he couldn't possibly begin
to emulate. So he'd lock himself in his studio, where he would
paint into the early hours until he was grey-faced and frozen,
only leaving the room to use the bathroom or grab a bite to
eat. He hadn't cared what—it might as well have been cardboard for all he'd been able to taste of it. He had grown numb
to everything. His heart, his mind, his senses had all been
frozen.

Maura had been more or less left to her own devices—
but she was a resourceful woman, who'd forged a successful
career in the still mainly male-dominated world of investment banking, so she wasn't exactly short of determination
or grit.

Surprisingly, she had made herself a life of sorts in Gray's
once fashionable, still beautiful old house, and had started to
interest herself in restoring it to its former glory. In the process she had involved herself in the life of the community—
making friends with shopkeepers, publicans and neighbours
alike—and had generally been well thought of. *Until her less
than discreet dalliances with some of the local lads had come
under scrutiny, that was.* Gray had eventually got wind of the
gossip that was circulating like wildfire in the small close-
knit community, but he hadn't actually cared very much. Not
then. He'd reacted by immersing himself even further in his
painting, and when on occasion he'd found himself in need of
some intimate companionship Maura had still been a willing
and enthusiastic lover.

He shook his head now at how crazy things had got. How
low, how dark, how plain bloody miserable…

When Mike Hogan, his best friend from university, had
shown up out of the blue, begging a bed for a week or so
before he jetted off to Canada and a new job, Maura had immediately set her sights on him. And who could have blamed

her? Mike was pleasant-looking, witty, intelligent—and, more to the point, a far more sociable creature than Gray could ever hope to be. Within a couple of days of setting eyes on each other the pair had been making plans to leave together.

'You're welcome to each other,' Gray muttered darkly, then tore the photograph cleanly straight down the middle and dropped the two glossy halves carelessly on the bed—something he should have done a long time ago.

The second photograph was an old black-and-white print of his mother, and his heart lurched as he studied it.

A pretty woman, she was smiling tenderly down at the dark-haired baby she held in her arms as if he were her sun, her moon, her stars. It was himself as a baby. Only Gray thought if she had really loved him that much, why had she chosen to end her life and leave him when he was only three? He'd never found out the truth about why she'd committed suicide. Paddy had kept stubbornly silent about Niamh O'Connell's reasons for doing such a shocking thing, and in his heart Gray had started to blame him for her death. It had tainted their already poor relationship.

Swallowing down the painful swell inside his throat, Gray put the photograph carefully back into the envelope.

The last print was a colour photograph of Paddy himself. It had been taken on a jaunt with some locals by none other than Eileen Kennedy, the shopkeeper-cum-postmistress. He was standing on a hillock, a bottle of Guinness held aloft, and a devilish grin splitting his mouth wide. It had been taken just three months before he'd died. Probably around the same time that Gray had found out that his last investment had helped his portfolio run into millions... *Poor comfort the knowledge had brought him.*

It finally dawned on him that it was the journey he'd loved—the wheeling, dealing and speculating that had lit his fire—*not* the actual destination. Money hadn't impressed his father and why should it have when the pursuit of it had taken his only son too far away from him?

'Wherever you are, I hope you're happy, you old devil.' He addressed the picture with a painfully rueful smile, then relegated the photograph—along with the bittersweet memory of his father—back to the confines of the brown envelope.

Downstairs again, Gray pulled on his battered leather jacket, speared a hand through his already ruffled black hair and whistled up Chase to go for a walk. He deliberately headed for the beach, thinking that the sea air would do him good, blow away the proverbial cobwebs, and help him think more clearly. Looking at the photographs, delving into his past, hadn't helped. He'd known it wouldn't before he'd even undertaken the exercise. Sometimes sheer bloody-mindedness just got the better of him.

Anyhow, now there was a tight band of tension round his head and it served him right. He was too bloody destructive for his own good sometimes.

Relaxation—if he'd ever really given house-room to such a concept—was a thing of the past. Now all he seemed to do was spend every day regretting more and more the bad decisions he'd made and punishing himself with the memories.

Not exactly the best way to live a life, he thought. Still, as he climbed the hillock that led down to the vast strand of white sandy beach it was his beautiful fair-haired tenant that predominantly occupied his mind—not the perpetual inner turmoil that seemed to accompany his every waking moment. Just what the hell was he going to do about this persistent dangerous fascination he had for her? A fascination that had crept up on him and taken too strong a hold before he had time to avert it?

She didn't deserve a man as inwardly craggy as him. She deserved better…much better. But even so Gray's heart suddenly seemed to beat more strongly in his chest just at the mere possibility that he might see Karen again sometime soon, and there was a rare spring in his step as he increased his stride to catch up with Chase…

CHAPTER FIVE

KAREN answered the door with a crazy leap of hope in her heart—only to have it recede with bitter disappointment and surprise when she found Sean, Gray's young assistant from a couple of weeks ago, standing on the step. Blinking up at him in the strong morning sunlight, she shivered at the cold gust of air that also greeted her, wondering why he had come and if Gray had sent him. She knew she was probably clutching at straws but, having not seen the man for a fortnight, she was beginning to feel a little frayed around the edges.

Sean grinned and Karen waited for him to speak first, still nursing the vain hope that he was bringing news of Gray.

'Hello, there.'

He was wearing a short denim jacket faded to the palest blue over a once black tee shirt now almost grey. With his long legs encased in similar light blue denims, he had the lazily optimistic grace of youth and his fair share of beauty, too—making Karen feel a sudden deep pang for the lost innocence of her own youth. For a moment she gazed up at his boyishly handsome face, with its unruly halo of uncombed fair hair and clear blue eyes, and wished somehow that she could be more like him. She knew it might be an unfair assumption, but he really did look as if he didn't have a care in the world on that bright blustery morning. She couldn't help but envy that.

Yet his appearance still engendered a heaviness of heart, because he wasn't the man she'd been hoping to find standing there. Instinctively she knew that Gray was deliberately keeping his distance. If he'd wanted her to get the message that this craziness between them wasn't going to progress any further then she'd received it loud and clear. For two weeks now she'd hardly been able to sleep nights for thoughts of him. It was crazy and futile, but she seemed powerless to put a stop to it. And Karen would bet her last penny that he hadn't suffered similarly sleepless nights over *her*.

If only she'd been able to deal with their attraction a little better. If only she had some knowledge of the rules of this game maybe she could have handled things with a bit more finesse instead of feeling so painfully lost. Maybe then she wouldn't have scared him off the way she'd done. But she couldn't turn back the clock and be something she wasn't. All she could do was deal with what was right in front of her— and right now life had brought Sean, with his twinkling blue eyes and ready smile. The least she could do was greet him in a civil manner.

'Hello.' She smiled back, genuinely taken aback to see the flicker of pleasure in his face that her greeting had provoked.

'Karen,' he replied in a rush, reddening slightly, 'I was wondering if you wouldn't mind taking a walk with me?'

'A walk, Sean?' She resisted the wild impulse to giggle. His request seemed so incongruous that Karen's interest was snagged in spite of herself.

'Yes. You like walking, don't you?' He looped his fingers behind the black leather belt fastened round his worn blue denims and managed to look sheepish and endearing all at once.

Wiping her hands carefully on the checked tea towel she'd been drying the dishes with, Karen frowned. As endearing as the young Irishman appeared, she really didn't feel like going anywhere just now. Her mood was a little too blue, for one thing. It was the result of another sleepless night over Gray O'Connell, along with sadness and guilt because suddenly she couldn't seem to remember her husband's face any more.

'Of course I like walking. But I'm—I'm rather busy just now, Sean.'

'I thought you might say that.' Running a hand around the back of his neck, he glanced down at the grass verge just to the side of him. Then, to Karen's surprise, he seemed to regroup himself. He lifted his chin, then gazed directly into her eyes once more, as if reaching a decision.

'I've seen you walking on the beach from time to time. You're always alone. I thought that if you were going that way today you might like some company.'

'That's very sweet of you, Sean, but I—'

'Don't think I'm coming on to you or anything like that—not that I wouldn't mind, if you see what I mean…' He shifted awkwardly from one foot to the other, momentarily ill at ease. 'But I've got something to ask you about. Will you come for a walk so that we can discuss it?'

'You mean now?' Karen glanced over her shoulder at the spick and span sitting room, with its new coat of paint and the smart new furniture that had immediately revived the cottage's previously careworn appearance. She'd just spent the morning cleaning the place to within an inch of its life. The comforting smell of polish floated up from the furniture surfaces she had vigorously shined, and the black iron grate round the fire positively gleamed from her enthusiastic administrations. The stack of washing up from her baking had been done, and her latest batch of bread and buns lay cooling on wire racks on the worktop.

Baking…

She did it because it was an outlet for the creativity she

wasn't expressing through her music and it helped to pass the time. But because she didn't have a freezer on the premises nearly half of her baking ended up in the bin. It was a shame, but she wasn't exactly on friendly enough terms with anyone in town or thereabouts to give it away. Something she would have done willingly. Even Gray hadn't taken the scones she'd offered him that day. But then the atmosphere between them had been so tense that it was understandable he'd left without taking them.

Unconsciously her teeth worried at her lip. *Why shouldn't she go for a walk with the amiable Sean?* She would have gone anyway at some point this afternoon. Staying in the house for a whole day without venturing outside would hardly help her melancholy mood, whereas a walk just might.

'It's a fine day. All you have to do is put some shoes on and get your coat.' Glancing down at Karen's feet, Sean saw with amusement that they were bare. Pink coral-painted toenails and all.

'All right, then.' Caving in to his undoubtedly natural charm, Karen stepped back from the door with her cheeks suddenly as pink as her toenails.

Acting spontaneously was not something she was used to, and it caused her more anguish than it ought to. It made her aware that she still had a lot to learn as far as loosening up a little went. Still, today she would make the effort to be different. Sean was likeable, and seemed trustworthy. And Gray had employed him, so he must be okay.

Throwing down the tea towel onto the nearest chair, she stooped down to the shoe stand behind the door to get her walking boots. Rescuing the thick yellow socks that were stuffed inside, she took them over to the armchair to put them on.

'Don't stand outside, Sean. Come in. I won't be a minute.'

Stepping inside, Sean glanced interestedly round, his nostrils twitching. 'Something smells good—and I don't mean the polish.'

'I've been baking.' Karen grinned up at him through her mane of silky honey hair as she bent to do up her laces.

'Sure, you're a dangerous woman, Miss Ford. What is it this time? Another delicious fruitcake?' Sean volleyed her grin with one of his own, momentarily transfixed by the sight of her loveliness and all that glorious long hair.

'I've been baking bread and making buns,' she answered.

'Well, it's good to know that you like cooking.'

'Why?' Laughter bubbling up inside her, Karen pushed to her feet, tugging the hem of the blue chambray shirt she was wearing tidily down over the waistband of her jeans.

'My mother's always said it's a useful skill to have—for a woman or a man. Are you ready?'

For answer, she lifted her thick sheepskin coat off the peg and slipped her arms into it. It was amazing how a little human contact and humour could change one's mood for the better, she thought, feeling herself warm towards the boyish Sean even more.

'Ready as I'll ever be. Lead the way.' She stood back as he passed her, catching the scent of a spicy cologne that was a little too overpowering, and wondered briefly if he was wearing it for her benefit. Then, dismissing the thought as too silly for words, she followed him outside.

Despite her previously downbeat mood, her spirits lifted almost instantly as she breathed in the brisk fresh air that blew her hair into a wild burnished gold cloud behind her head. The wild and stormy weather never failed to make her fiercely glad that she'd come to this place. A place she now almost regarded as home.

* * *

'So you've lived round here all your life?' Karen dug her hands into the deep pockets of her sheepskin as she walked beside Sean, vainly trying to keep up with his long-legged stride across the beach.

'I have. I like it well enough.'

He flashed a smile that Karen was certain must make the local girls light up like neon when it was trained on them.

'How about yourself, Karen? Where are you from?'

'A suburb of London. It has its advantages, living there, but often I yearned for some peace and quiet. If I was from here I couldn't ever envisage wanting to live anywhere else.'

Her announcement was passionate because it came from the heart. Glancing up at the cloudless azure sky, at the gulls circling above them with their coarse shrieking cries, she felt a definite sense of rightness roll over her. There wasn't anywhere else on earth she'd rather be right now. Her gaze moved down along the vast stretch of empty beach that lay before them, with the sea lapping relatively calmly at its edge today, and she wondered how she could bear going home to England again. Wondered, too, if the day would come when she would even *want* to. This place was her idea of heaven.

If only she had someone to share it with. She didn't mean right now, because Sean was amiable enough company for sure. She meant someone to share it with permanently. *Someone like Gray O'Connell.* The dangerous thought slammed into her hard, making her throat ache and her heart race. Not seeing him for two whole weeks had begun to feel like an eternity. What was he doing? Was he seeing someone else? Was that why he'd been so angry and so eager to leave that day when he'd finished the decorating? Did he feel torn because he was attracted to her when there was already another person in his life? Her stomach cramped with jealousy at the idea. Why did just the thought of him with someone else hurt so much? It didn't make sense. None of this crazy obsession she was developing for him made sense. *Surely she couldn't be in her right mind?*

'Karen?'

'Sean?' She came to a standstill beside the tall young Irishman, blinking up at him as the hauntingly handsome dark face in her mind, with its sculpted cheekbones and glacial eyes, reluctantly receded. Strands of silky blond hair blew across her face in the wind, temporarily shielding her embarrassment at being caught out not paying attention.

'I asked you a question, but you're away in your own little world.'

'I'm sorry.' She screwed up her face in sheepish apology. 'I do that sometimes…space out, I mean. I didn't mean to be rude.'

'No offence taken.' Digging his hands into the pockets of his jeans, Sean looked thoughtful for a moment. 'I was asking if you'd be interested in a bit of a part-time job? I briefly mentioned it to you before. My sister Liz has just opened up a café in town, and she's looking to recruit some help. As soon as she tasted your fruitcake she wanted to meet you.'

Karen frowned in bemusement. Of all the things he might have asked her, offering her a part-time job wasn't the first thing that had naturally sprung to mind. 'A café, you say?'

'Oh, it's not just an ordinary breakfasts and sandwiches sort of place. It's more upmarket than that. Liz has travelled all over the world, you know. It's a themed café…Mexican. She's called it Liz's Cantina. And she doesn't just serve Mexican food… There's cake and all kinds of great desserts, too'

'Your sister has started up a themed café here in town?' Karen grinned from ear to ear. 'What a crazy, wonderful idea!' She'd noticed some building work going on at one of the previously boarded-up buildings just off the main street a while ago, but she'd had no idea what it was being renovated for. She didn't like the idea that she'd been walking round so preoccupied with her own troubled thoughts that she hadn't even noticed what was going on around her.

'You really think so?' Sean stuck the toe of his boot into the sand and gouged a hole.

'Of course I do!' Clasping her hands momentarily to her chest, all of a sudden Karen was inspired by Sean's enter-prising sister, whom she hadn't even met yet. She'd never considered the possibility of a part-time job before, but right now it held an almost irresistible appeal. It would get her out of the house more, for one thing, and she would get to meet other people.

'Liz wants to hire someone a bit more worldly than some of the local girls. A bit more "clued up", as she puts it. Will you come and see her? At least have a chat with her about a possible job?'

'When was she thinking of?'

'Later this afternoon? She closes at five, and I usually go round to give her a bit of a hand tidying up. I'll pick you up at about a quarter to, if you like?'

'I suppose I ought to at least go and meet her...thank her for thinking of me. But I have my own car. I can drive myself rather than have you go out of your way to pick me up.'

Karen shrugged a little nervously. It seemed such an ordi-nary simple thing to do, to go and see someone about a job, but it was actually something she'd never done before. When she'd finished college she'd met Ryan almost straight away, married him, and then started to pursue her singing career. As far as promoting her career, arranging gigs and doing all the accompanying paper and telephone work that had been involved—all of that had been Ryan's domain. He'd taken care of everything. He'd worked in record management for ten years before they'd met, and there wasn't much he hadn't known about the music industry.

She'd depended on him for so much. Had she given enough

back in return? She really hoped so. She was desolate at the idea that maybe she hadn't.

'I'd prefer to pick you up, if you don't mind? Liz has already instructed me, and she'll have my guts for garters if I don't. So...shall we finish our walk, then?' Sean interrupted her wayward thoughts.

Staring out at the shimmering white strand ahead of them, Karen smiled. Tasting the briny tang of the sea spray on her tongue, she vowed not to spoil this unexpected opportunity to enjoy the fresh air and exercise. All in all, today was turning out to be a much better day than she'd anticipated. This morning all she'd had to look forward to was cleaning, baking, and her own solitary company. And for once she'd actually felt scared that it might not be enough. Clearly she wasn't as hardy or as resolved to the isolation of living alone as she'd thought. Certainly nowhere near as hardy and resolved as Gray O'Connell seemed to be...

Shielding his gaze from the fierce glare of the noonday sun, Gray blinked at the two solitary figures some distance away from him on the beach. A gust of wind lifted a lock of black hair from his forehead, and in profile his brows were knit together in stern contemplation. When he realised that one of the figures was Karen his jaw hardened instantly, jealousy jack-knifing through his guts so sharply that he actually took a step back to steady himself. Beside him, Chase chafed at the bit, longing to be allowed to bound up the beach unrestrained like he usually did, but right now his master was holding on to his collar a little too tightly for that wish to become a reality.

'Be still!' Gray's huskily angry voice brooked no argument. Chase hung his great fawn head and looked duly chastised.

But it wasn't the dog that had fuelled his temper. It was the sight of the woman down on the beach that had kindled the

flames of his ire. The woman who had the ability to tempt him
like no other woman had ever done before. Tempt him with
her blue eyes with whites so white that it looked as though
milk had been poured into them, and her serene, lovely smile
that hinted of peace in a cruel and crazy world should he
dare relinquish his guard and succumb to it. His desire for
her was constantly on simmer every time he was in her company. Every time she so much as came into his mind! He
was captivated by the graceful yet sexy way she moved, her
soft velvet voice made him shiver, and her unerring ability
to reduce every vow he made to keep his hands off her to a
bare-faced *lie* went without saying.

Gray loved the way she smelled, too—just like a warm
summer breeze, even on a cold day when winter bit hard.
Just what the *hell* did she think she was doing? Out with Sean
Regan, of all people! He swore softly under his breath. He'd
known he missed her. But he hadn't realised just how much
until he'd seen her there in the flesh with another man. He had
a temper, God knew, but he wasn't generally given to violence.
For the first time since he had got into scraps at school with
the other boys he was genuinely tempted to demonstrate his
superior strength to the younger man.

His eyes narrowed as he saw that the two figures on the
beach had started walking again. Just what had they been
discussing so intently? He'd seen Karen smile—or was it
laugh? He resented it like hell that Sean had the ability to
make her enjoy herself. He had to clamp down on the almost
overwhelming urge to call out—to let her know he was there
and demand to know what she was doing out with Sean. And
when he got her attention he'd insist that she come home with
him to his house, to his bed… Yes, to his bed. Where he'd
soon make her forget the younger man's ready smile and easy
charm and make her ache and moan and cry out with wanting

him instead. *He'd lose himself in her.* He'd drown them both in the scalding heat of their urgent coupling.

An almost painful surge of desire ricocheted through Gray, so that for a moment he forgot to breathe as the world seemed to sway around him.

'What the hell have you done to me, Karen Ford?' He furiously cursed her name out loud, as if to exorcise the effect she was having on him, and Chase pricked up his ears, as if hearing something he longed to hear.

'I know, boy.' Loosening his hold on the thick collar, Gray ruffled the great fawn head. 'You miss her, too, don't you? I'm afraid there's not much I can do about that right now. Not when she's with someone else. Maybe later, though?' An idea stole into his brain. 'Come on. Let's go home.'

Surveying the various outfits she'd laid across the patchwork bedspread, the myriad colours, styles and textures making her bed closely resemble a stall in a Turkish bazaar, Karen sighed. She frowned deeply as she mentally mixed and matched and came up with…nothing too inspiring, to be frank. She'd never been a slave to fashion, nor was it her forte, but she wanted to feel good when she went to see Liz Regan at the newly opened Liz's Cantina.

Should she go for her usual bohemian look? Or would the well-travelled Liz be expecting some trendy upmarket look? She couldn't imagine that that would be the case. The town— although thriving—was situated in a mostly rural area, for goodness' sake. Not in the centre of some busy urban sprawl. It wasn't as if her customers would be young hotshots from the city. Even so, it was still immensely difficult to make up her mind what to wear.

Sighing, she picked out a coral-pink scooped-neck top with narrow pink ribbons threaded through the wrists, and found a long multi-coloured flared skirt that looked vaguely Mexican to match.

Having divested herself of her plain white tee shirt, Karen had the top halfway over her head when there was a knock at the door. She froze. Who in blazes was that? Surely it couldn't be Sean, arriving already? Struggling to tug her top down into place, she angled her wrist to read the time on her watch. Four-fifteen… He was way too early. Oh, well, he'd just have to amuse himself for half an hour while she sorted herself out.

She was still in two minds as to whether she really wanted this job or not. One minute she did—the next she didn't. What did she know about working in a café, for goodness' sake? Not much. But at least she knew how to clean and cook. The little cottage was testimony to that.

Feeling flustered and nervous, she checked her jeans were properly zipped up, then shot out of the bedroom to answer the door, her cheeks burning and her hair tumbling wildly about her shoulders as she went.

'Gray.'

Her heart almost stopped when she saw who her visitor was. Even though she hungrily absorbed his image—like someone nearly drowning who'd just been thrown a lifeline—he transmitted no such similar appreciation or pleasure at seeing her in return.

His grey eyes, naturally cool and aloof at the best of times, looked as if they had frosting on them from the Arctic. The broad shoulders filling her doorway in the customary black leather jacket had fury rolling off them in waves, while his jaw was clenched with barely contained restraint. Restraint that made the arresting planes of his cheekbones seem as though they were carved out of granite. The impression he gave was an austere one, with not so much as a hint of warmth to soften

those prickly rough edges. Karen's stomach flipped. What
had she done to deserve such a look?

'I've obviously called at a bad time,' he finally said, in a
clipped icy tone that warned her his patience was at the end
of a very short rope.

'A bad time? Why would you think that? I was just—I was
just—'

There was something in the way those disturbing eyes of
his dipped suddenly to the region of her chest that made her
glance downwards. She saw instantly that her scoop-necked
top had not been properly adjusted and totally bared one silky
shoulder, where her bra strap had slipped down in her haste
to dress. The top of a softly rounded breast was more exposed than it should have been, and that was coupled with her
flushed cheeks and disarrayed hair. Karen suddenly realised
with devastating horror that her visitor had immediately and
wrongly put two and two together and made five.

Making a grab for her wayward sleeve, she hiked it up
again over her shoulder, and embarrassed heat hotly assailed
her as Gray followed every move like the proverbial hawk.

'It's Sean, isn't it?' he ground out.

Because he was so furious Karen automatically stepped
back. A violent tremble seized her even as her throat dried up
like a desert.

'Wh-what makes you think that?' she stammered.

'Where is he? Is he still here?' Striding angrily into the
room, Gray slammed the door shut behind him. He slammed
it so hard he almost rocked it right off its hinges.

Sensing herself pale as the discordant sound echoed threat-
eningly round the room, Karen eyed him nervously. 'Gray...'
She put out her hand to explain, and found it grabbed and
hauled towards him, so that she lost her balance and fell hard
against his powerful chest. It was like hitting granite, and for

a dangerous moment she was winded and almost overcome by the disturbing scent of fury and heat.

'Was it to get back at me?' he growled into her face, eyes burning hotter than a furnace as they blazed down at her. He was so angry he was scaring her.

'Sean isn't here, Gray.' Her voice rose in protest, and her hands pressed against the warm worn leather of his jacket as she realised his fingers were biting into the soft flesh of her upper arms with scant consideration or care.

'I saw you together on the beach.'

'And you drew your own conclusions?'

Something snapped inside her—because he'd managed to turn a perfectly innocent event into something almost sordid. Who the hell did he think he was, coming into her home and treating her as if she belonged to him in some way? She didn't need his or anybody's permission to do *anything*. She was a totally free agent.

'I can take a walk with whomever I damn well please! You're my landlord, not my keeper.'

Scowling fiercely, Gray abruptly let her go. Then he walked over to the window to stare out at the grassy bank outside, where his mud-splattered Range Rover was parked on the verge. His gaze barely even registered it was there. He was staring beyond it into the distance, where the purple shaded mountains loomed darkly to the right and the sea to the left. Inside, his heart was beating way too fast. He'd never experienced jealousy like this. *Never!* Maura would attest to that. Hell, any number of women in his past could attest to that. That had been one of their most persistent gripes. Gray hadn't cared enough for any of them to be jealous. *Until now...*

Turning slowly back into the room, he boldly regarded the reason for his painful introspection. In the revealing pink top, her creamy breasts pressed unknowingly provocatively against the flimsy fabric. Her long golden hair was sexily mussed, and her blue eyes clear as polished crystal. Karen was surely the epitome of male fantasy. Raw aching need slammed into him like a train hurtling at full speed into a wall as he drank in the vision of her. He told himself that it didn't matter that Sean Regan had bedded her first. It hurt like hell, but he'd get over it. Gray still wanted her.

'If you're suggesting that something went on between Sean and me,' Karen began, her hands nervously clasped together in front of her waist, 'absolutely nothing did. We went for a walk—that's all.'

'Why?' There was a sudden lessening of the tight band of tension round his chest. He wanted to believe her. Right now Gray wanted it more than anything else in the whole wide world. Wanted it more than he wanted to paint—and that was the supreme accolade as far as he was concerned, because painting was his *life*.

'Why?' That endearing little way she had of frowning lightly crumpled her brow, and Gray's mouth went dry. Even the way she frowned was sexy. 'Because he asked me to.' She shrugged, as if it should be obvious.

'What did he want?'

'Look…I don't understand why all these questions. I've done nothing wrong. I don't see that I have to answer to you anyway. Up until a few weeks ago I didn't even know you existed.'

'Well, you know now.' Pushing himself away from the window where he'd been leaning, Gray started to move slowly towards her. He emitted the same raw energy as an athlete at the peak of his fitness, and the air all but crackled round him. Karen's focus involuntarily slid from his enigmatic laserlike gaze to the long, muscular legs encased in fitted black jeans. It didn't take a professor of human biology to deduce that he was more than a little aroused, and she forced herself to inhale a shaky, steadying breath, because suddenly she knew she was way out of her depth—*drowning* in fact.

'So you weren't in bed with Sean when I knocked?' The sexy timbre of his voice all but pinned her to the floor.

'As if I— Search the bedroom if you want!' She bit her lip to stop herself from crying. This was absurd. Did he really believe she was so desperate for physical contact that she'd jump into bed with the next man who asked her? *As if her desire for Gray could be so easily transferred*—as if it was a mere whim instead of a soul-destroying, earth-shattering experience that kept her awake at nights, aching and longing for just the mere sight of him? Nothing made sense any more because of him. She should be grieving for her husband, not pining after some cold, cynical stranger who was too angry and wounded to be kind.

'I don't need to do that. I'll take your word for it.' Sighing heavily, he drew his hand round the back of his neck, as if he'd been under strain. But then, incredibly, the corners of his mouth curved in a near dazzling smile that came totally out of the blue, and Karen's insides were submerged in the sensual warmth of heated honey.

She caught her breath, inwardly struggling to appear calm. Why should he have things all his own way? Just because he hit her where it hurt with that unfair killer smile, it didn't mean that she had to turn to putty in his hands. Even though she knew she easily could. His presence alone had the power to make her feel exhilarated and alive. More exhilarated and alive than she'd ever felt before. But she knew that he could also make her plunge to the depths of misery, and she wouldn't forgive him for his Neanderthal behaviour that quickly. Yet again he'd hurt her with his thoughtless innuendoes and she had every right to be furious.

'Am I supposed to be grateful?'

'Never mind that—are you planning on taking more walks with Sean any time soon?'

'That's none of your business.'

'I'm making it my business.'

The smile went as quickly as it had appeared, leaving in its place a dark, brooding intensity that made Karen regret her tart reply. Should she tell him that Sean was expected at any time now? That his sister wanted to see her about a potential job? Why put herself in the firing line again? she thought. It would keep. She'd done nothing wrong, and refused to be made to feel as though she had.

'I can't accept that when it's totally unreasonable. Anyway...' She glanced meaningfully down at her watch. Four-thirty... Sean would be here in fifteen minutes. She had to get her skates on if she was going to be ready, and regrettably she had to get Gray to leave—or she'd be a nervous wreck by the time the younger man arrived. 'I'm going out very shortly. Thanks for dropping by.' She lowered her gaze because his brooding hot glance was scorching her. 'Even if it was only to tear me off a strip.'

'Where are you off to?'

She'd been praying he wouldn't ask her that, and now all the blood rushed dizzyingly to her head. Telling him that she was off out with Sean—albeit on a perfectly innocent expedition—would surely be tantamount to rubbing salt into an already open wound. But all the same she was going to have to tell him the truth, because she couldn't lie. Not outright.

'I'm going to see someone about a job.' She crossed her arms in front of her, still conscious of the fact that the pink top wasn't perhaps the most suitable item of clothing she could have chosen to wear. Gray had hardly taken his eyes off her figure since he'd come in—a fact that was making her more than a little hot under the collar.

'I didn't know you were looking for work.' He frowned, as if the thought disturbed him.

'I wasn't.' Karen shrugged. 'But someone thought I might be interested in this particular job.'

'So what is it?'

She moistened her lips with her tongue. The interest this innocent action evoked in the tall, rugged man standing just bare inches away from her was instant and tangible. It emanated from him like an electrical current that hit her squarely, deeply in the solar plexus. Swallowing hard, she felt her nipples suddenly surge against the thin barricade of her top, her stomach muscles tighten uncomfortably. Shifting onto her opposite hip, she lifted her chin to help bolster her confidence. 'I don't know, exactly. That's what I'm hopefully going to find out.'

'Are you telling me you need the work?'

'I wasn't aware that I was telling you anything very much at all. And stop quizzing me…I don't like it.' Exasperated by his questioning, which somehow managed to make her feel ridiculously guilty even though she hadn't done anything to warrant it, Karen moved across to the bedroom door, anxious that she wouldn't be ready by the time Sean appeared. Somehow she had to get Gray to leave before that.

'Karen? Are you short of money? I can help you out if you are.' His statement was so surprising that it stopped her in her tracks, and she turned to study him, blue eyes widening in bemusement.

'No…I'm not. I wasn't considering the job for that reason. I don't mean that as it sounds—I'm not a millionaire by any stretch—but I'm okay financially for now. Thanks all the same.'

She was very fortunate that Ryan had left her comfortable in that department, and her own earnings had made a sizeable contribution. Still, she was somewhat taken aback by the idea that Gray would willingly help her out, as he'd so succinctly put it. Again he'd surprised her. Like turning up with the new furniture and giving the sitting room a fresh coat of paint himself, when surely a man of his purported wealth could easily afford to pay someone to take care of such mundane tasks for him? It was difficult to equate his willingness to offer help with the often abrasive arrogance of the man.

'I really have to get ready now.'

'I can give you a lift if you're going into town? I can even wait and bring you back…'

The leather sleeve of his jacket squeaked a little roughly as he raised his hand to wipe perspiration from his brow. The movement dislodged the wayward black lock of hair that usually dropped back onto his forehead, and Karen saw the double row of faint yet distinct lines indented in his slightly weather-beaten skin. There was something that touched her deeply about the sight—as if those lines had been put there by too much suffering—and she knew a sorely intense need to offer him some kind of comfort. But now wasn't exactly the right moment. Not when time and commitment were constraining her.

'Sean's coming to collect me. He's taking me and bringing me back as far as I know.' She let her hand drop helplessly to her side instead of pushing wide the door to the bedroom, where she'd been about to go and change, witnessing the sudden flash of angry emotion in Gray's clenched jaw and narrowed glare with trepidation.

'I see.'

'No, you *don't* see!' Karen burst out, exasperated. 'It's his sister Liz who wants to see me about the job. She's opened up a café and is looking for help. Sean told her about my baking and gave her some of my fruitcake to try. She thought I might be interested in working for her.'

When this explanation failed to elicit any response from

Gray, verbal or otherwise—nothing but a darkly smouldering glare, in fact—she threw up her hands and groaned.

'She sent Sean to ask me about it. He's only collecting me as a favour to his sister. It's hardly a big deal, is it?'

'That rather depends on whether Sean thinks it is or not.'

CHAPTER SIX

'WHAT do you mean?' Karen's expression was as guileless as a newborn babe's, and Gray was torn between the need either to shake her or pull her into his arms and stop her talking altogether with a long, drugging kiss. The woman had been married for five years, for God's sake, yet she acted like a total innocent when it came to men. He shook his head slowly from side to side, trying to figure it out.

'Do I really have to spell it out for you? You're a beautiful girl. Sean's a young, unattached, *reasonably* good-looking male. Am I making it any clearer?'

The penny dropped. Anxiously, Karen drove her fingers through her hair. 'He doesn't see me that way.' She willed away the faint, nagging thought that perhaps he did, and like Scarlet O'Hara resolved to deal with it tomorrow. 'Besides, I'm not in the market for any kind of romantic liaison.'

'That a fact?'

'You don't have to act like you know everything. Especially when you clearly don't.'

The sound of a vehicle pulling up outside had them both turning their heads towards the window. 'I've got to finish getting ready,' Karen muttered, deliberately avoiding Gray's disturbing glance.

'He makes so much as one move on you and I'll knock his

block off,' he asserted irritably, fists bunching down by his sides.

'How charming… And that's how you treat a friend, is it?'

Gray scowled. 'He's not a friend, just someone who occasionally works for me. I don't have any friends. Nor do I need any.'

Shaking her head in dismay, Karen started to head through the open bedroom door. 'I don't have time for this.'

'Just so you know—I'll be back later this evening.'

'Why? What on earth for?' She glanced back at him over her shoulder.

'Now, there's a leading question if ever I heard one.' Grinning like the devil himself, he opened the front door and strode outside.

Sean was just getting out of his van when Gray reached him. 'Hello, Gray.' The younger man gave him an uneasy smile. As he straightened, his occasional employer frowned warningly.

'If you're thinking of asking her out on a date…*don't*,' he growled. 'She's come here to heal—to get over the death of her husband.'

'She's a widow?'

'Be respectful, and don't—*don't*—go looking for anything you shouldn't.' The frown that was already etched on Gray's handsome face intensified.

'Sure, I'm only taking her to see my sister about a job,' Sean replied defensively.

'That's all well and good. Just make sure you bring her straight home afterwards.'

'I really don't think that—'

'It's any of my business?' Gray interrupted with a wolfish glare. 'Well, that's where you're wrong. As far as— Never mind!'

Clearly deciding he'd said enough, the older man strode away with his usual impatient stride, and Sean heard the Range Rover's engine fire up behind him.

Liz Regan, Sean's sister, was pretty as a pixie, with cropped red hair, merry green eyes and a slender, tiny frame, and Karen liked her on sight. She also liked what she'd done in turning a once dilapidated old building into a trendy but friendly Mexican café, with terracotta-tiled floors, pumpkin-yellow and blue walls, and sturdy wooden furniture. The tables had yellow vinyl cloths with pictures of fruit depicted on them. As the last two customers of the day paid their bills and left, Liz whipped off the sunny yellow apron she'd been wearing over her tee shirt and jeans, grabbed Karen's hand and led her into the back room she clearly used as an office.

'You look like just the kind of shot in the arm this place could benefit from,' she declared, grinning, furnishing her brother Sean, who was lounging in the doorway, with a wink at the same time. 'And you smell as good as you look, too. I won't be able to keep those frisky lads away if you come to work for me, Karen.'

'Sean said that you needed some help… What kind of thing were you thinking of, exactly?'

'I've heard you're great at baking the cakes. Being the proprietor and all, I don't always have time to do much my-self—even though I love it. There's a local woman that works part-time doing a good bit of the baking right now, but I could really use another hand. Think you'd be interested?'

'Well, I—'

'It wouldn't be just the baking,' the other woman said hur-riedly. 'Having seen you, I think I'd really like you somewhere visible—front of house, so to speak. You're so pretty you'd bring in the male population in their droves!'

Bemused, Karen shrugged. 'I've never been a waitress before…but I suppose I could learn.'

Glancing at Sean, Liz grinned. 'What else can you do? What are your strengths?' Liz drew out the well-worn chair with a curved backrest that sat in front of her desk, then with a nod of her head indicated that Karen sit down.

Linking her hands as she made herself comfortable, in her mind her nervous visitor scanned the meagre list of things she considered she was good at.

'My strengths are that I'm a quick learner, and I'll do a good job whatever I have to do. But I suppose more than anything I can confidently say that I can clean and cook… I've never tried cooking Mexican before, but I'm willing to be your assistant if that would be of use?'

'A general assistant with paperwork and managing the place, maybe, but I've already got someone who does the Mexican cooking. So is there anything else you can do?'

'Like what, for instance?'

Under her ribs, Karen's heart had started to knock. She was slightly deflated that cleaning and cooking and being an assistant might not be good enough for this diminutive, colourful woman to employ her—not that she'd exactly pinned her hopes on getting a job here in the first place—and old feelings of insecurity couldn't help but surface.

'Do you have great ideas? Are you good with people? Can you sing? That kind of thing.'

Now Karen's heart started to thump even louder. Across the room, as if sensing her discomfort, Sean threw her a reassuring smile.

'Can I sing?'

'Sure—everybody likes a tune here. I was thinking some kind of entertainment in the lunch hour a couple of times a week while folks eat their meal would be a great selling point.'

Did this place get enough customers to warrant entertainment in the lunch hour? Karen wondered in further bemusement. Meeting Liz Regan's dancing emerald eyes, she
suddenly knew that if anyone could make such a maverick
venture a success it was *her*. Clearing her throat, she smoothed
some drifting strands of hair away from the side of her face
and sat up straighter.

'Yes, I can sing.'

'You can? I don't suppose you play an instrument as
well?'

Karen smiled. Inside her chest, her heartbeat resumed
its normal beat at last. Now she was confident that this was
something she *did* excel at. 'Guitar,' she replied. 'I play the
acoustic guitar.'

'Eureka!'

To Karen's surprise, Liz hauled her out of the chair and
danced round the room with her.

'Liz...for God's sake, what are you doing?' Sean grabbed
his sister's arm to curb her enthusiasm, but she still whirled
round and round with a helplessly laughing Karen.

When she came to a sudden standstill, Karen pushed the
hair from her eyes breathing hard. 'You don't even know if I
can really sing a note!' she exclaimed.

'Can you?' The grin plastered across the other girl's wide
mouth froze, as though the possibility had never even crossed
her mind.

'I sang professionally,' Karen admitted, her heartbeat
racing slightly again. It was perhaps only at that moment
that she realised how terribly she'd missed the pleasure of
performing—'singing for her supper', as Ryan had used to
teasingly call it—and how much she longed to do it again.

'You did?' Now it was Sean's turn to look surprised.

'I did. My late husband was my manager.'

'You're a widow?' Liz's expression turned serious.

'I am. But moving here has been really good for me…
helping me come to terms, if you know what I mean?'

'I knew you were special the moment I first clapped eyes
on you. There's a light round you that draws the gaze. And
it's not just because you're the prettiest thing this town has
seen in years, Karen Ford!'

Spearing icy fingers through his rain-dampened black hair
as he stood outside Karen's door that evening, all thought
of discomfort and cold left Gray as the music drifting out
from the house made him still. She must be playing the radio.
Whatever the song was that accompanied the gently strumming guitar he heard, it was riveting…*haunting*. The singer
had a rare talent.

Before he knew it the backs of his eyes were pricking with
tears. He rarely ever listened to music these days, but his father
Paddy had loved it with a passion. He'd often been found at
Malloy's Bar on a Saturday night, tapping his feet to whatever
tunes were on offer, for a while forgetting his troubles and
helping to numb them with a pint of Guinness, or three…

Grimacing, Gray raised his fist and pounded on the door.
Instantly the music inside stopped. The urgency which submerged his senses every time he thought of Karen gripped him
with a vengeance as he silently asserted that her enjoyment of
the music on the radio would have to be postponed until he'd
had his fill of her company this evening. He'd spent a miserable afternoon imagining her with Sean, and the antique clock
on the mantelpiece had barely chimed seven o'clock before
he was striding from the house and climbing into his car to
make his way here. *To make his way to her…*

Gray's heart thudded hard when she opened the door.

'Oh…it's you.'

He hated it that she seemed disappointed to see him. Was it
Sean she'd been hoping would knock on her door this evening?

Jealousy stabbed through his insides with all the stinging hurt of a hot dagger. Wearing black leggings, a black silk top and a red fringed cotton scarf draped round her shoulders, with her pretty hair left long and loose and her blue eyes shooting irritated sparks at him, right then Karen was the answer to any prayer for good fortune to visit him that Gray had ever prayed.

'Yes, it's me. I said I'd drop by, remember?'

'You'd better come in, then, I suppose.'

She held the door wide, albeit reluctantly. Swallowing down his regret that she wasn't happier to see him, he went inside. The first thing that he registered on entering the small sitting room, after the soporific perfume of scented candles, was the acoustic guitar propped up against the couch. His brow puckered, then his stomach clenched.

'I heard music just now, while I was waiting outside the door…I thought it was the radio.' Gray hadn't meant for the remark to sound accusing, but somehow it did, and he found himself silently cursing the lack of sensitivity that seemed to be ever growing the more time he spent on his own.

'I suppose you're going to tell me now that it's not allowed for a tenant to play the guitar?'

'Don't be foolish.' He jammed his cold hands into the pockets of his leather jacket. He was tempted to cross to the fire crackling in the grate to warm them, but he wouldn't concede to any such comfort until he'd reassured the woman in front of him that he hadn't come to visit her merely to be difficult. His glance cleaved to her as though magnetised, and he knew it didn't hide the hunger building inside him. 'Was that you singing?'

Folding her arms across her chest, Karen sucked in a breath. 'Yes…it was me.'

Gray dropped his voice in awe. 'The sound almost stopped my heart.'

She flushed, then stared down at the ground.

Seeing how the compliment undid her, he closed the gap between them. Without giving himself time to change his mind, he impelled her urgently into his arms. 'You're a surprise and a delight, *a mhuirnín...*'

'Your hands are freezing.'

'That may be so, but inside I'm burning up...burning up from wanting you so bad that I can't think of anything else.' His voice a husky grate, Gray cupped her face, stroking her soft satin cheeks with the sides of his thumbs.

She trembled, her warm breath drifting over him like a scented summer breeze. 'We wouldn't be good for each other Gray.'

Her voice had a catch in it, but even before she'd finished speaking he was kissing her, plundering her mouth as if she was supplying life-giving oxygen. He hardly knew his own name any more. He'd yearned to hold her...to *love* her if she'd let him...

'How do you know until we try?' he whispered.

Flattening her palms against his chest, Karen tried vainly to push him away.

'I may have gone a little crazy lately, but I'm not some witless lemming about to hurl myself over the edge of a cliff—because that's what I'd be doing if I let you—if I let you—' She broke off to bite her lip, and Gray saw that her beautiful sky-blue eyes had grown moist.

'If you let me what? Keep the cold away for a little while?'

As if surrendering the urge to somehow try and stem the powerful attraction that flowed between them Karen laid her head against him. Holding her to him with a sigh, Gray stroked his palm over her hair, murmuring soft words in Irish as he marvelled at its silken fall as well as silently registering the warm quivering curves of her compact slender body. 'Hush,

hush, *a chailín álainn*.' He'd never felt as protective or possessive of a woman before. Briefly closing his eyes, he kissed
the top of her head.

Lifting her gaze, Karen stared up at him. 'If I let you keep
out the cold for a little while? That's all it will be?'

'If that's all that you want.'

'You won't expect anything more from what we share?'

Fielding the jolt of dismay that hurt his heart, Gray stoically
bit back his disappointment. 'No.'

'Then neither will I.' Curling her palm inside his, Karen
glanced wistfully back into his eyes as she led him into her
bedroom in silence.

When she saw he was going to reach for her first, to help her
undress, Karen gripped the front of Gray's still damp leather
jacket as though indicating no, and then slowly, carefully,
slipped it from his shoulders. His quixotic grey eyes were
full of longing, and she sensed the powerful self-restraint
he had to employ to keep from hauling her roughly to him.
A dizzying, almost *painful* excitement gathered force inside
her, making her shiver. Gray O'Connell was a man hardened
and embittered by his past, but with his wind-tossed raven
hair and feral, hungry gaze he was heartbreakingly beautiful
as well as wounded, and right then he was everything she
needed…even if ultimately the fire he stoked in her would
burn her to cinders.

'For pity's sake, Karen!' He was all but shaking as she continued to methodically remove his sweater, then the maroon
tee shirt he wore underneath. Both were cast heedlessly onto
the floor.

The faint, musky warmth of his body sent a wave of aching
desire bolting through her blood that threatened to buckle
her already shaking knees. Gazing in nervous wonder at the
display of strongly toned muscle beneath the fine little coils

of ebony hair on his chest, she couldn't resist laying her open palm there, softly stroking it across the flat male nipples and feeling him tense with longing beneath her touch. Lifting her glance, Karen silently registered the near desperation she saw in his gaze and slid her hand over his sculpted high cheekbone to push her fingers curiously through his unruly mane of dark hair. *It was far softer than it looked.* Just like raw silk.

'Do you want to drive me insane? Do you?' With a growl, Gray grabbed hold of her hand and pressed a hot kiss deep into the centre of her palm.

'You're beautiful,' she said softly. 'I just wanted to see you.'

'And I want to see you in all your glory, too. But more than that I need you in my arms, before I die from the sheer agony of wanting you.'

After hastily removing his jeans, Karen was at last hauled against him and lifted high against his chest as Gray eagerly carried her to the bed. She had already turned down the sheets in preparation for her night's rest, and the smooth cotton was cool against her heated skin, even through her clothes. But Gray soon removed the last flimsy barriers between them to sit astride her, his strong thigh muscles trapping her between them before lowering his dark head to steal a deeply voracious kiss.

It was a kiss such as she had never experienced before— a kiss that flooded her with such intoxicating heat that she barely registered the soft moans that filled the air as her own. The wild ocean-swept taste of his mouth and tongue stoked her longing to a level almost beyond bearing. When his lips closed over one burgeoning tight nipple, his teeth grazing the tender flesh there, Karen gasped her shock and desire. *When Ryan had been intimate with her it had never been like this… had never created this wild storm of need that ripped her from her moorings and threatened to cast her out to sea for ever...*

She wanted to weep at what felt like the worst betrayal of the love she had shared with her husband. But she remembered, too, that he'd often been uncomfortable with the desire she'd sometimes expressed for more uninhibited intimacy, telling her that it was a fact of life that some men had a lower sex drive than others and he was sorry but that was just the way it was for him. He might not be able to love her in the way she needed, but he promised he would put every ounce of his effort into helping her forge a wonderful career and being the best, most devoted friend she could ever have...

Karen shut out the unwanted recollection as she lost herself in Gray's ardent drugging kiss. Her hands slid down his long muscled back to cup his taut firm buttocks, and his expression of pleasure was instant and vocal. That unrestrained, almost *feral* sound made her feel more desirable and womanly than she'd ever felt before. Silently she acknowledged she *wanted* to be ripped from the moorings that anchored her too painfully to the past—she *wanted* to be somehow set free. Free to fall or fly—she didn't care which right then...

'I want...'

'What do you want, my beautiful little songbird, hmm?'

Her lover kissed the side of her neck just behind her ear, making Karen quiver. Her hips grew soft and pliant as volcanic heat flooded into her centre.

'More of this?' Gray teased as he palmed her breasts and then pinched her nipples until she almost came up off the bed.

'Yes!' she rasped, almost delirious with need.

Raising his head, then sitting up, Gray reached for the jeans he had thrown onto the bed before taking Karen into his arms and hurriedly sheathing his hardened sex with the protection he'd brought.

Transfixed by the honed male beauty of his strongly corded arms and chest, shyly observing how well endowed he was, Karen didn't waste time speculating on the fact that he'd been so sure of her capitulation he'd come prepared. *What would be the point?* They were both adults—both knew that the near *violent* chemistry they shared would sooner or later have to have an outlet.

But she was shivering so hard that it was almost impossible to relax. Clearly some fear and tension had inadvertently crept into her reckless bid for sensual freedom. Might it even be *guilt?* In any case it was a long time since she had been with a man, so when Gray started to penetrate her, even as her mouth hungrily melded with his and their tongues hotly entwined, she couldn't help the little gasp of pain that left her.

'What's wrong? Am I hurting you?' He stared down at her in the dusk-filled room, surprising her with the genuine concern that she saw blazing from his long-lashed eyes.

'No. I'm fine. There's nothing wrong.' *She didn't want his kindness.* If he was kind to her then that might make her care for him too much. That was a risk she didn't want to entertain for long. Wanting Gray O'Connell to stay in her life would be like trying to hold on to a sea breeze, or to the morning birdsong that died away when winter came. 'Just hold me,' she murmured.

'I'll do more than that, *a stór...* I'm going to take you to a place where we can both be free for a time...free from grief and pain...that's a promise.'

Another gasp left her as he penetrated her fully and then, like a big cat, watched her register her pleasure and surprise, a small knowing smile playing about his roguish lips. Gray's loving of her body was hard, strong and demanding, and Karen revelled in it with every fibre of her being as she had never revelled in this most intimate act before, meeting every thrust with a lift of her hips to take him even deeper inside her.

So lost was she in the sensual ride that she couldn't say when it changed to an unstoppable rocket, taking her to the stars, but she heard Gray's deeply gravelled tone urging her onwards. Tears washed into her eyes as she flew apart in his arms.

As revelations went, it was pretty damned wonderful. That was why she cried. And it had happened so quickly and so easily. She hadn't even had to try. It grieved her to admit it, but with Ryan that part of their lovemaking had always been a cause of great frustration for Karen. Knowing that her husband could more or less live without sex had seemed to inhibit her ability to just let go and enjoy the act when they *did* spend time in bed together.

But now, even as the warm salty trail of tears slid into her mouth, a savage cry from Gray near shook the rafters as he held himself still inside her for long seconds and then shuddered hard. Catching his stunned glance as the waves of sensual fulfilment washing through her began slowly to ebb, Karen reached up and drew his head down between her breasts. His warm breath, unshaven jaw and the heavy weight of his strong, fit body pressing her down into the mattress felt like the nearest thing to heaven she could imagine…

CHAPTER SEVEN

THE intoxicating scent of Karen's body aroused an inexplicable longing in Gray for something he couldn't or wouldn't name as she tenderly cradled his head between her breasts. The realisation unsettled him, made him quickly bring his attention back to the physical aspect of their union…something he definitely *could* handle. His climax had sent his pleasure thermometer shooting right off the scale into another stratosphere, but it hadn't quelled his insurmountable need for her. Again he sensed himself harden.

Reaching out for the tissue box beside the bed, he disposed of the latex protection he'd sheathed himself with and, keeping his passionate gaze locked with Karen's, fitted a fresh one. Desire was swift as a flaming arrow, shooting through him as he began once again to move inside her. Rising up so that he could observe her, he smiled, enjoying the expression of surprise and languorous pleasure on her face. In the fading dusk her blue eyes were dark sapphire, with the emphasis on *fire*, and her beautiful mouth was a lush, sensual paradise he could easily explore for the rest of his life…

Silently, she lifted her hands to cup his face and pull him down to her, gifting him with a hot, sexy kiss. Near on fire with lust, Gray altered his position, urging Karen on top of him. Even before she settled her delicious peachlike rear across his arrow-straight hips he was pushing inside her, desperate to maintain the seismic contact that he knew awaited him. He groaned as she started to rock her hips, not just taking delight in the time-honoured motion of passionate lovers everywhere but in the sight of her gorgeous face, her tumbling honey-gold hair and ravishing pert breasts. He promised himself he would paint her, vowing the study would be his best work yet…

'You're a goddess—but even that description doesn't do your loveliness justice.'

When Karen opened her mouth to reply, Gray's hands enfolded her hips to pull her down even more firmly onto his silken rigid shaft and hold her there. Her dazzling blue eyes widened and ragged breath punched from her lungs. For long seconds he was deluged with the most incredible sensations of unbelievable connection, as well as a fierce longing for a way to make this breathless pleasure last for ever.

But in amongst that longing doubt reared its head. *He didn't deserve her*, he reflected painfully. *But, by God, now that he had her he wouldn't let her go in a hurry!* Making love with Karen was everything Gray had dreamt it would be, and no stain or recrimination from his past or guilt about her husband dying would keep him from hoping for more…

Karen woke in the early hours of the morning to the rapid tattoo of rain against the window. But as she adjusted the eiderdown more snugly across a chilly bare shoulder she examined the still sleeping man lying by her side. In the depths of slumber the two faint furrows crossing his brow were relaxed, barely discernible, and the sensual mouth was free of cynicism and hurt, innocent as a child's.

Gray's regret over his father not accepting his decision to forge his own way in life and his sad, ignominious death on a lonely beach clearly tormented Gray—tormented and *punished* him—as did the terrible fact of his mother's suicide.

Empathising with his sadness, Karen sighed, gently touching his bristly beard-shadowed jawline with her fingertips.

After returning home from her interview with Liz, she'd tried hard not to keep anticipating his promised visit that evening. After all, he could so easily change his mind. He was still an unknown entity to her…an unpredictable maverick. But even as she'd sat singing and strumming her guitar, trying to recall songs that had at one time been second nature to her—songs that she might perhaps perform at the café—her insides had swooped and dived every time the image of Gray's hauntingly handsome face had stolen into her mind.

Now his muscular arm was anchored possessively round her waist. Whenever she moved even slightly it immediately tightened again, as if he was determined not to let her go—even in sleep.

Reflecting on the passion they'd shared over and over again, before succumbing to an exhausted slumber, Karen felt her heart leap with hope that something good might ensue from their liaison, and prayed that it wouldn't end badly as she secretly feared it might. Gray had unlocked something deep inside her that her loving husband had never been able to release. For the first time in twenty-six years she felt womanly, desired and confident of her femininity, and as she lay there beside him she sensed a new resolve building inside her. A resolve that she wouldn't be frightened to try new things any more—that she would embrace life. She would allow herself to experience enjoyment whether she believed she deserved it or not. Most of all she would stop searching for approval all the time—and that included her mother's…

Burrowing her head between Gray's arm and hard-muscled shoulder, she spread her palm out across the dark swirl of soft hair on his chest—and drifted back off to sleep.

When she woke again, sounds emanated from the kitchen that definitely suggested tea being made. Sniffing the air, she also scented toast. Briefly stretching her lips in a smile, she plumped up the pillows behind her, then sat up. Grabbing the edge of the pretty patchwork eiderdown to cover her naked breasts, she was just in time to ensure her modesty—because, seconds later, the bedroom door was flung wide to admit the arresting reason for the sounds in the kitchen. His dark hair uncombed and tousled from sleep, his jeans riding low across his hips and his chest and feet tantalisingly bare, Gray was bearing a tray with two mugs—one tea, one coffee—and a plate of hot buttered toast. In all her days Karen had never seen a sexier or more welcome sight.

'Good morning.' Her insides clenched tight as she strove to subdue the intense carnal ache that automatically throbbed through her.

'Morning,' he replied, his voice a little husky. 'I've made breakfast.'

'So I see.'

'You're not surprised, then, at the extent of my talents?'

Karen blushed at the innuendo in his voice and the lingering sexy glance he gave her. 'I'm not surprised at all,' she murmured, tugging the eiderdown up a little higher over her breasts.

'What are you doing?' Leaving the tray on the small cabinet beside the bed, Gray suddenly gave her his undivided attention.

'What do you mean?'

'Why are you covering yourself up?'

Karen didn't know what to say. The temperature in the room was comfortably warm, despite the hammering rain outside—how could it not be after the heat they'd radiated last night?—so she could hardly use being cold as an excuse for pulling up the eiderdown.

'I—'

She held on to the material with a near death-grip, but her

fingers were prised gently but firmly away as Gray tugged the bedspread free, letting it fold gently round her waist. She shivered as the kiss of air stroked its feathery fingers across her naked skin—but again *not* because she was cold. There was little chance of being cold with her lover's fire-lit glance blazing hungrily back at her.

Dropping down onto the bed beside her, he made no pretence of looking anywhere else but at her bared breasts, the dusky nipples already puckering tightly beneath his bold examination.

'If Shakespeare himself had witnessed you as I do now he would have composed a sonnet to these beautiful breasts.' He smiled. 'And Byron would have surpassed himself with an incandescent poem in your honour.'

Just as she reached forward to grab the eiderdown Gray dipped his head to capture a tingling sensitive nipple between his lips. His even white teeth clamped down a little on the already raised flesh, and the bolt of pleasure-pain that flashed through her made Karen helplessly yelp as he started to suckle hard.

'Oh, my God!'

He glanced up at her, the look in his long-lashed eyes lascivious and unrepentant. 'Is that "Oh, my God, I don't want this?" or "Oh, my God, this is so good I don't want you to stop?"' he challenged huskily.

'What do you think?' Karen answered low-voiced, and she settled her palms either side of his unshaven jaw, then drove her fingers a little desperately through his hair…

Liz had said she wanted to try an entertainment slot two lunchtimes a week to start with, and Karen was relieved that she didn't expect more. Although she'd been practising as much as she could, she somehow felt she was a complete rookie, starting up again like this. Since Ryan's death she had barely sung a note.

There was also another reason for maybe not giving her rehearsals her utmost concentration. Her evenings had become snared by another more compelling distraction…*Gray*. He'd taken to calling in on her around the time of her evening meal. Sometimes he ate with her. Other times, when his mood was dark and he didn't want to engage in even the smallest pleasantries, he took her by the hand and led her straight into the bedroom.

If he was using their passionate lovemaking to help stave off some of the demons that haunted him, Karen told herself she didn't mind—so long as he found some peace for a while. *It shocked her to realise how much she was putting his wellbeing before her own, and how dangerous that was, but somehow she couldn't seem to help herself.* The man had seriously got into her blood. Sometimes he fell asleep in her arms, but often he woke in the early hours and went home. He usually used Chase as his excuse for leaving. The hound missed him when he wasn't around, he told her, and Bridie his housekeeper—capable as she was—couldn't handle him as he could.

Now, standing in a clear space in Liz's Cantina one busy lunchtime, with the seriously appetising smell of Mexican cooking wafting out from the kitchen, Karen watched the ever-obliging Sean plug in the small amplifier he'd found for her to use and attach her guitar lead. Several patrons turned their heads expectantly towards her as they ate their meals or waited for their food to arrive. Liz had informed her earlier that she and Sean had 'put the word out' about Karen singing, and that was why they were busier than usual. Nervously, she began to tune her guitar. The amplified sound was deep and rich, and she mentally revised the small programme of songs she'd chosen.

Last night she'd told Gray she was performing today, and she'd secretly hoped he would show up to support her, even though he'd shrugged and said, 'I don't doubt you'll be great, sweetheart,' then slid his gaze cagily away without commenting further. Scanning the collection of heads again, already guessing he probably wouldn't show, she bit back her disappointment and made herself smile.

Sean had also set up a microphone, and now he stepped up beside her to give her shoulder a reassuring squeeze. 'Best of luck,' he said in her ear. 'Not that you'll need it.'

Karen wanted to tell him that he and his sister had misplaced their trust in her…that she really wasn't very good. *They hadn't even insisted she audition, for goodness' sake!* But then she remembered the resolution she'd made that first time she and Gray had made love. That she would no longer compulsively seek approval—that she would have much more faith in herself.

'Hi,' she said into the microphone with a smile. People smiled back, and a young lad with dyed black hair and ripped jeans sitting at a table by the door with another youth similarly attired wolf-whistled. 'My name's Karen Ford, and I've been asked to do a few numbers for you. This first one is called "From the Heart."'

From the moment she strummed the opening chord it was as though something so familiar and natural in her took over that barely any effort at all was required. Everything just came together perfectly on its own. The audience was almost deathly quiet as she sang, but as soon as the number came to an end they were applauding hard and calling out for more. Standing by the ranch-style doors to the kitchen, Liz Regan, in her swirling Mexican-style skirt and indigo tee shirt, was perhaps clapping the hardest of all. She even gave several piercing whistles. Meeting the other girl's eyes across the room, Karen guessed she had made a friend in the avant-garde Irishwoman—an ally as well, perhaps?

Flushed with pleasure that her music had gone down so well, she got ready to perform the next number with much more confidence.

Then Gray walked in and she froze.

It was raining again, and the broad shoulders of his battered leather jacket gleamed with damp, almost steaming in the heat of the warm café. His mercurial, almost *fevered* gaze fell on her straight away.

There was no doubt his presence had caused a minor shockwave. Even as Karen's own heartbeat registered his appearance with a jolt, she made herself turn to Sean and ask him for a chair. Suddenly her legs felt like damp noodles, and if she didn't sit down soon they might just crumple beneath her. As she announced the next number she saw Liz fly across the room to guide Gray to a nearby empty table, just as if he was some sort of VIP. A chair was pulled out for him, and Liz must have asked him if he'd like anything to drink. Karen saw him mouth the word 'later.' Then he planted his elbows on the cheerful yellow vinyl tablecloth and gave his utmost attention to Karen.

To Gray's surprise, last night Karen had confessed to him that she'd sung professionally and had been about to sign a record deal when her husband had suddenly died. The deal had never been signed. Instead she'd retreated from the world of music, and when that hadn't seemed to help—her words—she'd escaped to Ireland. He'd heard what she was capable of with his own ears that evening outside her door, but now it hit Gray afresh what a sublime talent she was.

Sensing the tangible ripple of excitement circulating the room, he noticed that people were listening to Karen sing rather than eating their meals. But, more than that, the sight of her sitting there alone with her guitar damn near stopped his heart. She was dressed in well-worn but neatly pressed denims, and a multi-coloured knitted cardigan over a plain white tee shirt, her pretty hair unbound and catching the one thin ray of sunlight that broke through the rainclouds to high-light the honey-gold strands. His stomach knotted with tension and need. He'd spent hours last night with her body pressed up close to his, but it hadn't subdued the powerful desire in him to have her close all the time, to keep her to himself... Yet the moment she started to sing and strum her guitar Gray knew it would be wrong to try and monopolise her attention exclusively.

A talent and a loving personality like Karen's should be shared equally, he realised with a painful stab in the region of his heart. Maybe he should leave her alone?

Even as the thought came to him Gray irritably snuffed it out like a guttering candle. He wished he was stronger, but he couldn't deny himself the one thing that made him feel halfway human again...

After waiting until Karen's song came to an end he beck-oned to the ever watchful and attentive Liz Regan to order a double shot of whiskey...

Going into the kitchen to fill the kettle, Karen sensed Gray follow her. His brooding presence was making the tight knot of anxiety beneath her ribs tighten even more. Sean had in-sisted on delivering her to the café for her performance, and arranged to take her home again, but Gray had coolly usurped him, announcing that *he* would give her a lift home and that there was no point in arguing. Karen had stood mutely by, torn between the possessive need she saw written on his face—and silently echoing it—and Sean's clear disappointment. But he had barely said a word to her on the journey back to the cottage.

She hadn't a clue what he thought of her performance, and was too nervous to ask. He'd stood silently and impatiently at the back of the room while everybody else enthused about her singing and asked when she'd be back to sing again, and she'd been so flustered that she couldn't even recall what she'd said to anyone.

Unable to contain her emotion a second longer, she slammed down the pottery mugs she'd retrieved from the cupboard and spun round to face him. 'What's wrong? Didn't you like my singing? I didn't force you to come and hear me, you know.'

'No... You didn't.'

'Then why are you so—so...?'

'Reticent to pour praise in your ear and tell you how wonderful you were?' His perfectly sculpted lips shaped a sardonic, slightly bitter smile. 'Didn't you have most of the customers in the café falling over themselves to brush up against you just in case you became famous one day? Wasn't that enough adulation to be going on with?'

'I wasn't looking for adulation. Is that what you think?' Her heart bumping in indignation and hurt, Karen sensed her face flood with heat. 'I was surprised you came to hear me at all, if you want to know the truth. I never know what you're going to do—when you're going to show up. When you do I feel like I'm walking on eggshells in case I say the wrong thing. If you had any idea how hard it was for me to play again this afternoon, after all that's happened, then you might have a bit more sensitivity and tact. I certainly wasn't expecting praise. And I don't give a fig about becoming famous! I only got into the music business because of my love of singing. If I can use my talent to earn my living then what could be better? But you know what, Gray? Frankly, I'm not going to waste my time trying to convince you of anything. I've got far better things to do than go down that futile route.'

She would have crossly flounced past him if it weren't for the fact that his hand shot out and held her fast.

'I don't want you to walk on eggshells around me. I'm a morose bastard—I know that. And I don't remotely deserve you even though I want you so badly.'

He sounded so bleak that Karen barely registered the warm grip of his fingers round her wrist. She sighed as she lifted her concerned gaze to examine the misty grey depths of his fascinating eyes, 'You're not a bad person, Gray... A troubled one, maybe... But that doesn't mean you don't deserve happiness or respect. Why do I sense that's what you believe?'

His hold on her slackening, he retrieved his hand and shoved it into the pocket of his jacket. A flicker of some deeply corrosive pain flashed across his handsome face, making his mercurial eyes glitter. 'Why do you think? All the evidence in my life points to the fact that people don't think I'm worth the trouble. Haven't you considered they may be right?'

Before she realised his intention, he'd turned and swept back into the sitting room.

'No,' she said softly, following behind him. 'I've never considered that.'

'Well, then, perhaps you should.'

'I make up my own mind about people.'

'You do, do you?'

'Yes, of course.'

'And I suppose you're never wrong?'

She swallowed across the sudden ache inside her throat— evidence of her sympathy for a man who had built such high walls round himself that even a trained mountaineer would be severely challenged to successfully scale them.

'I'm not wrong about you, Gray.'

'How do you know?'

'I like to think I have good instincts.'

'I'll bet your husband loved that about you.'

'What?'

The man in front of her grimaced. 'Your ability to see the best in people...to forgive.'

Karen shrugged. 'It's just the way I am—but I'm certainly no saint. I have made and still do make lots of mistakes. Ryan was quite aware of my faults, too.'

'And I'll bet he overlooked every single one.'

'Do you want to talk about Ryan, Gray?'

The shake of his head was vehement. 'No. I most definitely *don't* want to talk about him. Do you think I'm some kind of masochist? Just the mere thought that he knew you before I did, held you in his arms before I did, causes me untold agony. He's your past. What I'm interested in is right now.'

Visibly relaxing his shoulders, despite the passion in his voice, he removed his jacket and threw it onto the linen-covered couch. Then he crossed the room to stand in front of her. His warm breath and earthy, masculine scent made Karen tingle right down to the tips of her toes. His long fingers pushed back her hair from her face, then cupped her jaw. *Did she imagine that they shook a little?*

'I really *don't* deserve you. Your singing was outstanding, and your bravery in standing there performing your songs in front of a bunch of strangers even more so. But I'm afraid that if you become too popular your gift will take you away from me, Karen...' He lowered his voice. 'And I'm not ready for that...not yet.'

'I don't want to become popular,' she breathed, losing herself in his intense heated glance, deliberately closing her mind to the words *not yet.* 'I only want to stay here with you.'

His lips descended to bestow the sweetest, most tender kiss he'd ever given her. *It was in that blissful shattering moment that Karen knew she'd lost her heart to Gray O'Connell.* But even amidst her joy in the realisation she recognised the ever-present shadow of potential heartbreak...

'I want to paint you,' he declared, smiling when he lifted his head to study her, repeating his earlier desire and hoping this time her answer would be different. 'Will you come to my house tomorrow and sit for me?'

'Do you mean just a portrait?'

His lips curved in amusement. 'Are you still afraid to take off your clothes for a nude study?'

Blast her unerring ability to blush at the drop of a hat! It was ridiculous, when nearly every night she lay bare in his arms in bed. 'You probably think I'm a dreadful prude.'

'I don't think that at all. I love it that your nature is basically shy. I certainly wouldn't change it, or want you to be any different.'

'In that case, if I agree to sit for you, could we start with a portrait? Just head and shoulders, maybe?'

'A portrait it is, then.' Gray dropped a kiss on the top of Karen's head and grinned.

Bridie Hanrahan heard the frequent thumps and curses emanating from her employer's studio and smiled indulgently. *Something had rattled him.* Rattled him or inspired him, she thought. He'd practically mown her down this morning as he'd torn through the house and up the stairs, yelling out as he went to, 'Make me some strong black coffee would you, Bridie? After that I don't want to be disturbed. I'll be working in my studio all day!'

In that brief encounter the housekeeper had noticed there'd been a light in his eyes that she hadn't ever seen before. If she hadn't bumped into Liz Regan this morning in Eileen's shop then she wouldn't have a clue as to what had put that light there. But after a few minutes' conversation with the young redhead who owned the café she'd learned that Gray O'Connell had turned up yesterday afternoon to hear Karen Ford—the pretty tenant of his father's old cottage—sing.

Bridie was intrigued. The news was akin to hearing that the Pope had dropped into Malloy's Bar and had a couple of pints of Guinness. It was a known fact that Gray didn't socialise…at least not locally, at any rate. He was a regular 'Howard Hughes', and rich as Croesus so the rumour went. But little good his money seemed to have done him so far. He could probably furnish this big old house like Buckingham Palace, but the thought had obviously never even crossed his mind. The man was no doubt still grieving for his father.

Thinking of poor Paddy, and the sad end he had met down there on the beach, Bridie tut-tutted softly, shook her head, then continued along the wide black-and-white tiled hallway to the kitchen to make Gray his coffee.

Sketches of Karen fairly flew off the point of his pencil. Again he worked from pure imagination and memory, which for an artist wasn't entirely satisfactory, but soon, he told himself, he would be working with the real thing. Sheets of smooth cartridge paper were scattered everywhere, and on his easel Gray had stretched and prepared a canvas, ready to start painting when she arrived. At last she had agreed to pose for him. He'd almost held his breath when he'd asked her, fearing that she might say no. Again he found himself moved by her bravery in forging ahead with a new life embracing new experiences and not staying stuck in a grief that anchored her to the past and prevented her from really living.

He could learn a lot from Karen. The woman totally inspired him—and not only with her courage to sing again after the tragedy of her husband's sudden death. One mere glance into her incandescent sky-blue eyes seemed to fill him with an unstoppable flow of energy and excitement. When Gray was lost in her bewitching gaze it helped him forget that he'd been such a terrible disappointment to his father, and that his mother had been too wrapped up in her own misery to hang around and see what he made of his life…

'You've a visitor, Mr O'Connell.'

He was so wrapped up in his thoughts that he didn't even register the fact that his housekeeper stood in the doorway, her florid, kind face somewhat bemused.

'A visitor?' he echoed. He *never* had visitors. The locals knew better than to risk disturbing him. But in the next instant he realised exactly who that visitor was and leapt up off his seat. 'Is it Karen Ford?' he demanded.

'Yes, Mr O'Connell. Shall I bring her up to your studio?'

'Seeing as Miss Ford is sitting for a portrait, then I'd say yes—bring her up to me straight away, Bridie!'

CHAPTER EIGHT

GRAY was seated on a stool, staring out through one of the huge ornate windows that overlooked the sea of rolling green surrounding the house. He cut a lonely, if compelling figure, with his slim but muscular physique, black sweater and familiar tousled black hair. She'd seen him only a few hours ago, yet Karen's heart still bumped against her ribs as if she was seeing him for the very first time.

'The drive up to the house is so long I thought I'd never get here,' she announced nervously, slightly out of breath at the interminable ascent up the staircase with Bridie to the top of the house where Gray's studio was situated.

The open door in sight, she had told his kind-faced housekeeper to go back down. She'd heard the older woman trying to catch her breath behind her, and wondered that she wasn't as skinny as a rake with all the stairs she must regularly have to climb in such a mansion. Even though he'd told her himself that he'd made a fortune, Karen was still overwhelmed at the beauty and size of the great house Gray lived in. He was certainly no starving artist living in a garret! No. Instead, he lived in self-imposed isolated splendour.

The thought made Karen's brows pucker as she glanced round the lofty attic, with its stack of paintings propped up against the walls. His output certainly looked to be prolific. Was his relentless painting the only thing that gave him refuge from pain these days? Even though she ached to examine every canvas, her heart constricted at the thought of him living here alone with just his dog, and seeing only his housekeeper for company.

'The map I drew for you worked out all right, then?'

Her handsome host left his seat to come and greet her, catching her by the elbows to draw her to him. Again she was struck by the chiselled perfection of his extraordinary face. If she were an artist she would beg, borrow or steal for the chance to paint him.

'It was perfect,' she answered.

'No problems understanding it?'

'I presume you're referring to the tired old chestnut that women can't read maps? I actually find it dead easy!'

Gray's generous black brows creased mockingly. 'Is that true?'

'Well…' She couldn't help grinning. 'Not all the time. But you're an expert at drawing, and that's why it was so clear.'

'Carry on in that flattering vein, madam, and you'll go right to the top of my Christmas card list. You might even win yourself a prize.'

Karen loved it when he joked with her like this. When the cloak of brooding darkness that he sometimes wore was laid aside he was a different man entirely. Right now, with Gray in a much lighter frame of mind, it didn't seem as daunting as it had done at first to sit for him and have her portrait painted. At least it would mean time together, she thought wistfully. Time when the words *not yet* could be forgotten for a while and not haunt her…

'Could my prize be permission to look at some of your paintings?' she asked, careful to maintain her light-hearted tone.

It was as though a cloud had streaked across the sun and blotted out the light. 'What for?' Wiping the back of his hand across his mouth, Gray gave her a glance that was guarded, even a little angry. 'So that you can ascertain whether I'm any good or not?'

'It's only natural that I'd be interested in your work, don't you think? Please don't take it the wrong way.'

The light returned—if a little self-consciously. 'Sorry... Old habits die hard, so they say. Do you want to take a look now, or later—after I've made a start on your portrait?'

'Later is fine...thanks.'

'Then in that case we'll crack on, shall we? Here, give me your coat.'

Handing him the duffle coat she'd donned that morning, because there was a distinct wintry snap in the air, Karen watched him stalk across the room to the door, close it, then hang her coat on the single hook behind it—all the while her gaze hypnotised by his taut, firm behind and the long, muscular legs snugly contained in faded worn black denim. He was an artist, but in truth Gray O'Connell was a work of art himself, she thought in silent appreciation.

Releasing a sigh, for the first time she noticed the little puff of steam her warm breath made on the cold air. 'It's chilly in here.' She crossed her arms over the cornflower-blue sweater she wore with her jeans and shivered. 'Don't you feel the cold?'

'Not when I'm lost in my work.'

Returning to her, Gray surprised her by enfolding her in a tight bear hug. In an instant all thought of cold was banished, to be replaced by the most delicious spine-tingling warmth— warmth that made Karen feel like butter melting over hot toast.

'Better?' he teased, lifting his head to smile down at her, two perfectly edible dimples creasing his cheeks.

The man had a smile that could lift a heart so high you never wanted to come down to earth again.

'Much better… Can we stay like this for the rest of the day?' The words were out before she could check them. The thing was, it didn't matter how many nights she spent in Gray's arms—it just never seemed to be enough. *She always craved more.*

The dark pupils engulfed by haunting shades of silvery-grey grew darker still, and his hands dropped to her hips to drag her closer. With his lips just bare inches from hers, Gray intimately lowered his voice. 'Perhaps I was wrong about you being shy? I seem to be uncovering a whole other side to you that leads me to believe you're quite the little seductress.'

'If I am,' Karen breathed softly, 'it's only because you keep putting irresistible temptation in my way.'

'So it's irresistible I am, is it?'

His lips brushed Karen's in a flirtatious, sexy little kiss that made her insides clench and her eyelids drift closed. But right at that moment there was a firm knock at the studio door and they automatically sprang apart. Bridie, pink-cheeked and puffed from her climb up the stairs, opened the door wide to beam at them.

'Sorry to disturb you, Mr O'Connell, but I was wondering if the young lady might like a cup of tea?' she asked brightly.

Karen reddened as Gray's amused glance locked with hers. 'What a perfectly timed entrance, Bridie.' He smiled. 'Not to mention a great idea. Would you like a cup of tea, Karen?' he asked politely, but she saw the corners of his mouth wrestling with the urge to grin, and found herself struggling to keep her expression serious as she turned towards the housekeeper.

'A cup of tea would be lovely, Mrs Hanrahan…thank you.'

'Call me Bridie…everybody else does. Now, what about yourself, Mr O'Connell? Is it coffee you'll be wanting?'

'Coffee would be grand, Bridie,' he agreed, but then he frowned, glanced over at his easel and said, 'But not right

now, if you don't mind. Could you bring our drinks up later?
Say in about an hour?'

'Of course, Mr O'Connell. That's no trouble at all.'

The door closed and once again Karen found herself alone
with Gray.

'No more distractions,' he announced firmly with a glint in
his eye. And then suddenly he was all business as he instructed
her to sit in the solitary high-backed Victorian armchair by
the window. 'I'll put the heater on to keep you warm,' he
added.

'Lift your chin a little.' He made a swift practised sketch of
her onto the silver-grey backwash he'd painted onto the paper
earlier.

As soon as Gray had seen Karen ensconced in the rather
grand Victorian armchair it had come to him what a naturally regal air she exuded. Perhaps it was her exquisite bone-
structure or her flawless skin, or a combination of both, but
she definitely had an intriguing 'touch me not' shimmer that
would surely make any man studying the portrait ache to
break down that naturally English reserve and make her smile.
Unknowingly, he found his own lips twitching.

'What are you grinning at?'

'That's for me to know and you to wonder.'

'So you're going to be cryptic now, are you?'

'Fold your hands in your lap...pretend you're royalty visiting an impoverished but brilliant artist in his lonely garret.'

'What?'

She chuckled, and Gray's insides were suddenly submerged
in near volcanic heat. *Did she have any idea how sexy and
endearing her laugh was?* How it brought to mind hot but-
terscotch poured over the creamiest vanilla ice cream?

'That's a stretch! I'm not remotely royal, and neither are you
impoverished as far as I can see.' She swept her hand round

the lofty proportions of the once grand attic. 'I'm about as un-regal and ordinary as you can get, I assure you. I'm at my happiest baking cakes, singing and playing my guitar.'

'It's true that I'm not impoverished, and you may not be royal, sweetheart, but you have no idea what you've got—and trust me...it's *not* ordinary'

'You're biased.'

'I don't deny it. Sit up! Don't slump in the chair. And if you insist on smiling try for more of a "Mona Lisa" smile rather than a cheeky schoolgirl grin.'

Karen's blue eyes sparkled impishly. 'Are you usually this bossy when you paint someone's portrait?'

Emphasising the clean flowing line of her jaw with his pencil, Gray pursed his lips. 'A man has to lay down the law with a difficult character like you.'

'I'm not difficult.' She gave him a theatrical glare.

Reluctantly, he knew it was time to end the charming banter and get a little more serious. Studying the sketch he'd made for a moment, he drew the small table with his palette on it nearer to the easel and began to block in the figure and background with his brush. Before he'd got very far he glanced over at Karen, noting that her expression had grown pensive.

'I didn't say you had to stop talking,' he remarked gently. 'In fact the bond between the sitter and the artist is a very important factor in creating a good picture. Tell me when you first realised you could sing and what you loved about it.'

'You really want to know about that?'

Gray nodded, but it grieved him that she'd thought he wouldn't be interested. 'Of course.'

'Well...there was always music in the house when I was growing up—mainly because of my dad. He was always playing his records. He loved female vocals best of all, funnily enough.' Her gaze drifted far away for a moment, and Gray elected to stay silent rather than comment. 'I used to sing along.' Her slim shoulders lifted in a shrug. 'He told me my voice was pretty. So I suppose that's when I knew I could sing—when I realised I loved it.'

'And is he still around? Your father, I mean?'

'No. He's not. He died when I was fourteen.' Her hand brushed back her hair.

'Keep still, can you? Let your hair fall back the way it was. That's it.'

Gray stopped painting to study her for a few moments. Her expression wasn't sad, he noted, just resolute. As if she'd *had* to be. But he guessed she'd loved her father very much and clearly still missed him. *Who would be fourteen again, sailing in an untried vessel across the storm-tossed sea that was the experience of most teenagers? Especially when it involved losing a parent,* he reflected sombrely. Although he had grown up with his father, it hadn't made it any easier for Gray to lose him as an adult…especially when his mother was already off the scene. Touching upon the subject even momentarily made his gut twist with pain. It also prompted him to ask Karen about her own mother.

Her expression seemed a little pained as she replied, 'She's still here. Still determined to pretend everything in the garden's lovely, no matter what's going on. She would have made a first-class actress.'

Letting out a long, slow breath, with the tip of a slim sable brush Gray coloured in the dark golden lashes on the beautiful face clearly emerging on the easel in front of him.

'She wasn't supportive when your husband died?'

'Being supportive isn't her forte. She likes to be the Queen Bee—the pivot that the rest of the world revolves around. She also holds the firm belief that families should close ranks when disaster strikes and put on a brave face. They certainly shouldn't let on by word or deed that they're devastated, or act like they need help. That would really let the side down.'

'And you're her only child?'

'Yes.' The blue eyes appeared downcast for a moment. 'Personally, I would have loved to have had a brother or sister, but my mother told me early on that having me had been far too exhausting for her to consider having any more children.'

'So you're not close, then?'

'Not remotely. I mean, I love her—and I think she loves me—but…'

She fell silent for what seemed like a long time. Gray was working on her hair now, trying to capture the little flecks of golden light that the watery sun beaming in through the window brought into arresting focus. *From where was the masochistic impulse coming then to get her to talk about her husband?* He hardly knew. But he saw the surprise and shock in Karen's eyes when he voiced it. 'Tell me about Ryan,' he said.

'What do you want to know?' The lovely blue eyes were distinctly wary.

'Where did you meet him?'

The tip of his paintbrush shaped colour and texture on the canvas as if steered by some unseen force of its own. In her lap, Karen's slim hands unfolded restlessly, then quickly folded again.

'It was at a friend's housewarming. Ryan was an acquaintance of my friend's husband. At the end of the evening someone—probably after too much wine—suggested we all do a turn. I didn't have my guitar with me, so when it came to my turn I sang a very simple unaccompanied folk song. Later, when we were having coffee, Ryan came over to talk to me and complimented me on my voice. Before I left that night he'd asked me out.'

'And what did he do for a living?'

'He worked in music management.'

'So that's when your career in music took off?'

'Obviously not straight away... But I'd been writing my own songs for quite a while, and along with my voice he thought they had potential.'

Her quizzical glance examined Gray for a moment, as if she were trying to work out where he was coming from. Gray had to privately own to feeling a little discomfited by it.

'Why are you asking me about all this?' she asked. 'I got the distinct impression that under no circumstances did you want to talk about Ryan.'

'I don't...not really. But I am interested in *you*. The fact that you were married to someone else before you met me and that he died isn't something I can easily sweep under the carpet, no matter how much I might secretly want to. I want to know what's shaped you, Karen, what's made you the woman you are. If I can't ask questions about your past, how am I supposed to find these things out?'

'I could turn that question around and ask you the same thing.'

Now Gray *was* uncomfortable. He'd voluntarily led himself down a blind alley from which he couldn't easily escape. 'You know who I am,' he muttered, irritably shoving back the stray lock of black hair that fell against his brow.

'How can you say that? Apart from that rainy night when you turned up at the cottage for the first time you've hardly spoken about yourself at all. I get the distinct impression that your own past is strictly off-limits.'

'Well...you should know by now that I'm not the kind of man that feels the need to spill his guts to all and sundry.'

'Am I "all and sundry", then?' It was with faint alarm that Gray saw the film of moisture hazing Karen's beautiful eyes. He laid down his brush with a sigh.

'You must know you mean more to me than that.'

'I don't know any such thing at all. So tell me...what *do* I

mean to you, Gray? Am I just someone you turn to occasionally to keep the demons away?'

He winced. 'I thought you said that all you wanted was for
me to keep out the cold for a little while? Are you telling me
now that you want something more than that?'

She swallowed hard, shaking her head. 'I don't know… I'm
confused *and* a little scared about it all, if you want to know
the truth.'

Karen had given him an in—an opportunity to really open
up for once and share his doubts and fears and maybe his
hopes, too—but Gray didn't take it.

'Then perhaps we'd better drop the subject and just get on
with what we're doing.'

'Fine… That suits me.'

His lovely model sucked in a breath and a strained little
smile touched her lips. He could tell it didn't suit her at all to
drop the subject, and again Gray deplored his lack of courage
and sensitivity in not having a proper discussion about the
matter. But realistically he already knew that Karen deserved
far better than him. Why not just be grateful for her being in
his life right now and stop muddying the waters by fantasising
about a future that would never, *could* never be his?

He resumed his painting in silence, and shortly after that
tense little episode Bridie arrived with their refreshments.
As Gray invited Karen to bring her tea and come and survey
the stunningly impressive view from the huge pre–Palladian
windows, he found himself longing to make things right between them again.

'Is there anything else you need back at the cottage?'

'I've got everything I need, so no. But thanks for asking'

'Are you sure?'

'Yes, I'm sure.'

'You can have anything you want, you know? Hell, I'd even
pull the place down and build a new house for you right on

the spot if you wanted.' His long fingers tightened in agitation round his coffee mug.

Her gaze perturbed, Karen turned to look at him. 'Why would you do that, Gray? Pull down your father's cottage, I mean?'

He felt a little desperate for a moment. 'Until you came it held too many unhappy memories for me… I don't even know why I decided to rent it out in the first place. I wouldn't be sorry to see it pulled down.'

'I understand how you would feel that way, but I'm personally very glad that you did decide to rent it out. I like it there very much. As for suggesting you build a new house—I don't even know how long I'll be staying. Right now the cottage suits me fine just as it is.'

'I want—I *need* to give you something…don't you understand?' Plucking the mug out of her hand, Gray placed it on the windowsill next to his own. Inside his chest his heart was racing as he gripped her hands to stare long and hard into her beautiful upturned face. 'And don't even *think* about leaving… not for a long, long time.'

'There *is* something you can give me.' Withdrawing one of her hands from his clasp, Karen gently touched the side of his beard-shadowed jaw. 'You can give me a promise that you'll start to think better of yourself and allow a little happiness into your life from time to time. Can you do that, Gray?'

As he met that mesmerising warm gaze, emotion ambushed Gray and he wanted to hold on to her for the longest time. But, true to form, such a strong sensation of need scared him, too. It wasn't his style to need anybody…at least not in a way that made them essential to his life and happiness…

'I'll try,' he answered, his smile awkward, almost as if it didn't fit his face.

'Good.' Karen's smile was much more natural. 'Will you show me some of your paintings now?'

'Sure…why not?'

Dropping down onto her haunches to examine a breath-taking landscape of verdant emerald hills rolling down to a stormy sea at sunset, Karen surveyed the stunning skill of the artist in amazement. She'd hardly known what to expect when it came to Gray's work, but she knew she'd anticipated nothing half as good or tremendous as this.

'This is incredible. It's got so much presence you can almost breathe the wind-blown air and hear the waves crashing,' she commented. 'And that fiery red and gold sunset…it stirs the heart, Gray.' She could almost *sense* him moving awkwardly behind her, as if the compliment unsettled him—unsettled him and probably made him inwardly deny it, she guessed.

'I did that one about a year ago,' he murmured. 'Chase and I came upon the scene one evening during one of our long walks. Luckily I had my sketchpad with me at the time.'

'It's clear you enjoy painting landscapes,' Karen murmured, rising to her feet and carefully going through the stack of work behind the painting she'd been examining.

'I do.'

'You don't do many portraits, then?' She halted her study of the paintings to give her full attention to the man waiting beside her.

'Not very often.'

'Is there a particular reason why?'

'I don't care to have people coming to the house.' Lifting a shoulder, he glanced away.

'Then I'm honoured that you asked me.'

'Are you fishing for a compliment?'

'Do I need to fish?' she teased.

'No.'

The grey eyes that had the haunting quality of the sea in them were so intense for a moment that Karen felt as though she was melting in the heat they emitted.

'No, you do not.'

Heart clonking against her ribs, she blurted, 'How come your pictures aren't framed and displayed all over the house? It seems a shame to keep them up here, just gathering dust. People would love to see them, I'm sure.'

'You mean the same people that don't come to the house?'

'Even so, you should display them out of respect for yourself. I'd certainly enjoy seeing them, and so I'm sure would Bridie. Why not get them framed and put up? I'll help you if you like.'

'I'll think about it.'

Karen got the distinct impression that he wouldn't. But now she was a woman on a mission—a mission to get this talented and wounded man to wake up to his own potential, to leave his traumatic past behind and enjoy the one thing he was clearly passionate about, the thing that could open doors to a new and more fulfilling future...even if that future didn't include *her*.

'You'd better finish your tea. I need to get back to work on the portrait. The light will be fading in another couple of hours, and I'd like to get as much done as possible.'

Already moving back towards his easel, Gray didn't glance round to see if Karen followed him. It seemed as though he was retreating behind that protective wall again—the wall that made Karen feel as if he would only invite her so far into his private enclave before putting her safely at a distance again.

Folding her arms across her chest, she sighed. Now she *did* have his attention.

'What's wrong?'

'Don't you think we should get some air? Take Chase for a walk, perhaps?'

'We will after I've finished working on the portrait for the day... Are you getting bored already, sitting for me?'

'No. I suppose I'm just a little restless.'

She found herself on the disturbingly arousing end of one of his rare melting smiles.

'Restless and beautiful... It's a good title for your portrait.'

'If you say so.' She made a face at him.

'I do. Now, get your pretty little butt over here and sit for me—before I find a strap and tie you to the chair!'

Her skin burning at the very idea, Karen couldn't even find words in her scrambled brain to reply...

CHAPTER NINE

'MY CHEF Jorge made the coffee. He trained as a barista in Italy, and I kid you not—it's to die for!' Liz Regan beamed at Karen across a table at the back of the closed café as the two women sat together for a coffee and 'a cosy little chat', as she had put it to Karen.

Happy to count the enthusiastic redhead as a new friend, Karen took a sip of the fragrant cappuccino in front of her and briefly squeezed her eyes shut in pleasure. 'You're right…it's divine. Where on earth did you find this Jorge?'

The sparkly green eyes of the other woman effervesced even more. 'I met him on holiday in Majorca last year. He's Spanish. To tell you the truth he was planning on working in the UK, but I very cheekily enticed him away from that idea and persuaded him to come to Ireland and work for me instead.'

Karen grinned, sensing there was more. 'And?'

'Winters here can be grim. A woman needs a fit and active male to help keep her warm at nights. Call it clever strategic planning on my part, as well as unashamed self-interest.'

It didn't escape Karen that Liz had used a similar phrase to Gray's, when he had promised to 'keep out the cold' for her for a while. She fell silent, thinking about last night and the heat they had generated again in bed after they'd agreed

he'd follow her home to the cottage. Once again, Gray had left
her in the early hours of the morning to return home...

'And what about you, Karen?' The redhead leaned across
the cheerful yellow tablecloth with a knowing glint. 'It can't
have escaped your notice that everybody was very much
surprised when our local Heathcliff himself turned up the
other afternoon to hear you sing...feeling up to spilling the
beans?'

It was inevitable, Karen supposed, that sooner or later
someone was going to quiz her about Gray. But it didn't mean
she was ready or even *wanted* to discuss it with anyone...
even Liz.

'No, not really.' She shrugged, shielding both her gaze and
her feelings briefly behind her mug of coffee.

Running her fingers through her cropped red hair, Liz grimaced. 'I know you probably don't want to say anything in
deference to him, and I'm sure you think we're all a bunch
of dreadful nosy parkers, but the people here are still very
sympathetic towards Gray O'Connell, and at the end of the
day we look after our own. His father Paddy was well-liked,
and everyone was shocked and saddened when he died. Not
only had Gray to deal with the trauma of that, but then his
flighty girlfriend Maura left him for his best friend and ran
away with him to Canada—we could all see how he turned
in on himself and became a virtual recluse. It's not natural
for a fit, handsome man like him... To be alone, I mean...'

Her insides churning, Karen was trying hard to process the
startling revelation that Gray had had a girlfriend who'd left
him to run off with his best friend. *Was that the reason he
seemed so wary about committing to a proper relationship or
discussing anything personal?* Who could blame him, when it
seemed that anyone he'd ever cared about had abandoned him?
Under the circumstances it was hardly a surprise that he kept
everyone at arm's length and chose to isolate himself. If only

he'd told her about what had happened with this Maura—even though it would be excruciating for her to hear about another woman and even harder to imagine Gray suffering because he'd lost her.

'We're just…good friends,' she explained—without conviction, it had to be said. But how could she tell Liz anything else when she was too scared to trust that her passionate and volatile relationship with Gray might last?

'Good friends, is it?' The other girl's eyes easily transmitted her doubt.

Distressed, Karen moved her head from side to side. 'To tell you the truth,' she admitted, heart pounding because Liz looked to be hanging on her every word, 'I'm mad about him. I'm mad about him even though I have this terrible fear that he'll tell me goodbye almost every time we meet. There…' She blinked back the moisture that surged into her eyes and shuddered. 'The thing is I never expected to fall so hard for someone so soon after losing Ryan…my husband. I think I'm still in shock about what's happened between me and Gray.'

'What was your marriage like?' the other girl asked thoughtfully. 'Did you fall for Ryan as hard as you've fallen for Gray?'

Feeling guilty and wretched, Karen sighed softly. 'No,' she whispered, 'I didn't. He was my best friend—the one I could turn to when I was unhappy or hurt—the person who was always there for me.'

'But the sparks didn't exactly fly in bed?' Liz smiled gently.

Blue eyes enormous, Karen stared. 'How did you guess?'

'It's not uncommon…a girl thinking that she should marry her best male friend and then finding out when the deed is done that she's made a mistake.'

'Ryan was never a mistake!'

'I'm sure he wasn't, Karen—but the fact that you've fallen

so hard for Gray suggests that you weren't really in love with Ryan. Don't look so shocked… He was still your best friend and you loved him—just not in the same way that you love Gray O'Connell. Passion is never neat and tidy, you know. It rarely ticks all the right boxes and behaves itself as people think it should. And when it descends your whole world is turned on its head and won't ever be the same again.'

Reflecting on the other woman's unexpectedly revelatory words, Karen touched her hand to her forehead, imagining her heartbeat sounded like crashing waves slamming against rocks in her ears. 'How do you know all this? Did it happen to you?'

'Yes…when I was working in London for a hotel chain in the west end. He was a visiting CEO from Australia, and he came to the hotel for a meeting. I served him his coffee, our eyes met, and that was it… *Wham!* I felt like I'd been hit by a cyclone.'

'But it didn't work out between the two of you?'

'No.' The redhead winced. 'It didn't. But right now we're talking about you, not me.'

'I expect you think I'm an awful fool, falling for someone as emotionally unavailable and damaged as Gray.'

Reaching across the table, Liz gave Karen's hand a sympathetic squeeze. 'You're not a fool, sweetheart. Far from it. But it sounds to me like you didn't have much choice in the matter of the fascinating Mr O'Connell. Sure, hasn't he got it all? He's tall, dark, handsome—and has a tragic past. We women seem hard-wired to fall for the wounded ones, don't we? Plus he has an air of mystery about him that would tempt any woman with an ounce of curiosity in her blood to try and unravel what makes him tick. But, passion aside, I won't pretend I'm not concerned about how you'll cope if what you have together should suddenly come to an end.'

'I'll manage…I'll have to. It's not as though I've never had to deal with the sudden end of a relationship before, is it? It's a risk every woman takes when she falls for a man…that he'll end up hurting her, I mean.'

'True. But losing your heart to a man who can't or won't give you his love in return because he's built a fortress round his own heart to protect himself… Well, that's no easy path, for sure. Be good to yourself, Karen. That's my advice. Take one step at a time and keep something back just in case it doesn't work out as you might hope.'

Karen didn't reply, because a numbing wave of dread was washing through her at the realisation that she didn't have a hope of 'keeping something back'—because she'd already given everything she had in her to Gray.

'In the meantime—' her companion smiled warmly '—I want you to know that I'm your friend as well as your some-times employer, and I won't be blabbing any of what you've told me to a soul. Not even my brother Sean…who, by the way, has quite a thing for you.'

'He has?' Dismayed, Karen crumpled her smooth brow.

'Yes, he has—even more so since he heard you sing. He swears you've the voice of an angel, and I'm inclined to agree. You won't be singing for me for long before some bigwig music executive gets to hear about you via the local tom-tom drums and tempts you away with a record deal, I'm sure! We may be situated in the back of beyond, but news of a talent like yours travels fast. But, that aside, Sean's seen the way it is between you and Gray O'Connell, and he won't make a nuisance of himself.'

Thinking of the afternoon she'd spent with Gray yesterday, having her portrait painted and looking through his sublime landscape paintings, Karen realised how much she'd been hoping for some sign from him that he considered them to be in a proper relationship—a relationship that truly meant something to him. His passionate admission that he wanted to do something for her...that he *needed* to do something for her...had honestly taken her aback. But she knew it didn't mean he was any closer to wanting some kind of real commitment, and she couldn't prevent the sense of desolation that arose inside her at that.

Her astute companion picked up on her despondency straight away. 'You need a night out, my girl,' she announced enthusiastically. 'You need to have yourself some fun and forget about Gray O'Connell for a while. It's Sean's birthday tomorrow, and I'm throwing him a party here at the Cantina. I was going to ask if you wouldn't mind playing some music, as well as joining us with a few friends in some dancing and a few laughs...how about it?'

A party... Since when had the concept become so alien to her? Karen wondered. When had it become something to fear instead of an event she could enjoy?

'Hey!' Her emerald eyes twinkling mischievously, Liz reached forward to playfully slap her on the arm. 'Don't you dare tell me you can't remember how to have fun. If you do, then I'll just have to help refresh your memory in any way that I can—and I'm warning you...I don't take any prisoners!'

Gray swept into Karen's sitting room that evening with a preoccupied glance that didn't bode well, and as she shut the door on the seemingly perpetual icy rain that filled the night behind him she deliberately gave him one of her most welcoming smiles.

'Hi. I see you've brought the rain with you again...must be a knack.'

Crossing to the hearty blaze in the fireplace, as was his habit, Gray held out his hands to its warmth for a few moments before turning to reply, 'Yeah, it's a knack, all right. Bad weather seems to follow me around, right enough.'

'What's wrong?'

'Nothing.' The smile he tried hard for made Karen want to weep. 'Would you make me some coffee?'

'Of course… I've been baking. I've made a Victoria sponge. Shall I cut you a slice?'

'No cake. Just coffee…thanks'

Moving to the door again, he shucked off his wet jacket and hung it on the hook there. About to turn away to the kitchen, Karen felt her heart skip a beat when he caught her and pulled her gently but firmly against his hard lean body. His hands were cold as winter, as were his sweater and jeans, and his handsome sculpted visage glistened with droplets of icy rain and his arresting silvery eyes crinkled at the corners.

'No matter what the weather's like outside, you always remind me of sunshine.'

His voice was the sensual equivalent of smooth Irish whiskey and a crackling log fire. The disturbingly arousing combination made Karen melt. A muscle contracted in the side of his cheek just before he lowered his face to hers and kissed her. His lips were cool as a sheet of cold glass, but almost immediately heat and hunger broke through to warm them and his silken tongue swept the soft contours of her mouth as if she was fresh clean air he desperately needed to breathe.

Karen's knees all but crumpled. But, while she ached to lose herself in the magic of Gray's kisses and the unfailing seductive touch of his hands, she sensed that beneath his raw and hungry need for her something had upset him. *She wanted to know the reason.* Slowing the kiss, gradually moving her lips away, she cupped his unshaven jaw between her hands, staring concernedly up into the long-lashed, depthless grey eyes.

'Something's bothering you. Won't you tell me what it is?' she urged softly.

Sometimes it was hard for Gray to think straight when his gaze tumbled into Karen's. It was so easy to just get lost in that flawless sea of blue for the longest time. But his heart constricted for a different reason at her question. Dropping his hands from around her slender shapely hips, he restlessly moved away. His chilled fingers tunnelled through his mane of damp black hair.

'It's the anniversary of my father's death,' he explained dully. 'I visited his grave today.'

'Oh, Gray. I would have come with you if you'd said.'

'It wouldn't have helped. No matter how hard I try, I just can't forget what happened to him…the way he died out there alone on the beach. I revisit the scene over and over again in my mind, trying to make right how it ended, trying to come to terms and accept it—but how can it ever be right? It was a mess…a bloody mess! Living with the legacy of it just seems to get harder as time goes by…the pain doesn't lessen. Maybe it's because the old devil never forgave me for leaving? For not helping him keep the farm?'

'That's just a story, Gray…a fantasy. You don't know that it's true. Nobody can know what was in your father's mind when he died. You'd returned, hadn't you? You returned because you wanted to make amends…he must have known that.'

It was true that Paddy had been glad to see him, Gray remembered. But it had only taken a few minutes before he'd glimpsed the defeat and disappointment in his eyes, too. How was he supposed to reconcile that?

'I offered to set him up with a new farm,' he said out loud to Karen. 'Offered to pay for any amount of hired help to make it work. But he told me it was too late for that. He was too old and too tired, he said, and he didn't have the heart for it any more.'

'Even so, I can't believe for a moment that your father would have wanted you to feel as wretched as you still do about his death. You did your best by him, Gray. He may have wanted you to stay and help run the farm, as his father had done before him, but that doesn't mean it was the right thing for you. At the end of the day your father made his own choices and so did you. We all do. That's not a crime.'

Suddenly Karen was in front of him, her gaze spilling over with tenderness and concern. For the life of him Gray couldn't think what he'd done to attract such heartfelt regard.

'And I'm certain that whatever happened between you he'd want you to forget it and leave the past behind,' she insisted. 'Yes, leave it behind—so that you can live the present to the full. You have every means of doing that. You've got the resources and you've got your talent for painting. So why not concentrate on all the things you've got in your favour, make a new start and try to enjoy life again?'

He so wanted to believe that what she said was possible. Part of him was furious with himself for wallowing…for not just counting his blessings and vowing to make the most of his life as Karen suggested. But the ghosts of the past wouldn't easily let him go. Their clammy touch crawled up his spine whenever he was alone in that great mausoleum of a house, mocking him and making him despise the man he'd become. The only light on the horizon was the beautiful blue-eyed angel who stood in front of him. But what right did Gray have to embroil her in his troubles? Hadn't she suffered enough with her own tragic loss?

The great need to do something wonderful for her, to do something purely for her enjoyment and pleasure, arose inside him again.

Catching her hands, he tugged her towards him. 'Come away with me for a few days.'

'What?' Her expression was genuinely stunned.

'Come away with me to Paris. I have an apartment there, in the Rue Saint-Honoré. I haven't been there in quite a while, but there's an agency that takes care of it for me. All I have to do is make a phone call.'

'You have a place in Paris?'

'I do. We'll go tomorrow. What do you say?'

'Tomorrow?' she echoed.

To Gray's immense disquiet, Karen freed her hands, then crossed her arms over the front of her dress. The material was a soft plum-coloured jersey and it fitted her eye-catching figure to perfection, hugging her breasts and hips just as he longed to mould his hands to them himself. But as she studied him her glance was torn.

'I can't go tomorrow.'

'Why?'

'I've had an invitation. An invitation that I've already accepted.'

'And who might that be from?'

'Liz Regan. She's throwing a party at the café tomorrow night.'

Unable to conceal the crushing disappointment that welled up inside him, Gray knew his reply sounded accusing and unreasonable. 'So you'd rather go to this party than come away with me?'

'I didn't say that. But if I make a promise I like to keep it. Liz also asked me to sing. Anyway, I'll go and make your coffee.'

As she turned towards the kitchen Gray followed her. 'What's it in aid of, this party that you're so keen to attend?'

Straight away he saw the scarlet tinge that flooded into her otherwise pale cheeks.

'It's to celebrate her brother Sean's birthday,' she answered, coming to a sudden standstill before him.

Just the sound of the other man's name on her lips cut him to the quick. Inside his chest, his heart rioted. 'What is it about

Sean Regan that you find so irresistible?' he demanded with a snarl.

'I don't find him irresistible. Why do you always have to jump to such ridiculous conclusions?'

'Obviously I wasn't invited as well?'

The slender well-shaped brows on the beautiful face before him lifted in surprise. 'Would you have gone if you had been?'

'Of course I wouldn't. But it still galls me to think that you'll be there, singing and helping to entertain that young pup, when you could have gone to Paris with me instead.'

'You're being completely unreasonable, and I'm sure you know it. Why can't we go to Paris the day after tomorrow?'

Gray shrugged, unable to keep a lid on his temper. 'Because I've already decided I want to go tomorrow. I'm not going to change my mind simply to pander to the whims of a woman!' he answered furiously. 'The sooner you realise that, the better off we'll be.'

'Is that why your previous girlfriend Maura walked out on you?' Karen came back at him, her skin flushed and her blue eyes glinting. 'Because you were so selfish and unreasonable that she finally couldn't tolerate living with you any longer?'

The shock of her words was like iced water being poured down his back. Not because Gray had even *cared* that Maura had left, but because Karen was more or less telling him that she wasn't surprised that a woman would leave him. *Who had told her about Maura?* he wondered. He quickly dismissed it as unimportant. Half the town would know his sorry history. But it still stung that the woman he respected more than any other clearly thought him a poor bargain. That hurt more than a thousand scores across his heart.

'Forget the damn coffee,' he muttered, grabbing his leather

jacket off the coat hook and flinging angrily out through the door into the bitterly cutting chill of the rainy night...

Dressing for the party the following evening, Karen went over and over again in her mind the way Gray had stormed out of the cottage the previous night. At first she'd mentally cursed the rash, angry words she'd thrown at him about Maura, had wanted to chase after him and tell him how sorry she was. She didn't mean it, she'd say, but he had goaded her into retaliating when he'd said he didn't pander to the whims of a woman. Was she so unimportant and inconsequential to him that any suggestions or preferences she might have were instantly to be dismissed?

Calming herself down, she had been struck that maybe Gray needed to mull over the idea that he was selfish and unreasonable. It couldn't hurt to stand her ground and hope he would reflect and take stock, could it? But what if she'd gone too far? What if he decided to end what they had there and then and wouldn't see or speak to her ever again?

In the middle of applying her lipstick in front of the bathroom mirror, Karen suddenly felt quite nauseous.

Blinking back the hot tears that surged into her eyes, she wished she wasn't going to the party—wished she'd declined or, if not that, agreed to go to Paris with Gray and explained later to Liz why she hadn't shown up for Sean's birthday. *Blast!* Now she'd have to do her make-up all over again. She looked like a sad clown, with black mascara streaking down her face. *Yesterday had been the anniversary of his father's death*, she recalled painfully. And she'd heartlessly left him alone with his grief, his guilt, and no doubt his self-loathing, too...

The groan that left her lips might have been that of some wounded animal. The idea that she'd never see him again, or that he might pass her in the street or down on the beach and

ignore her, made her feel physically ill. Karen had broken her
heart over Ryan's sudden unexpected death, but her grief then
was nothing to the agony that gripped her now at the idea of
losing Gray...

He'd spent the night in front of the fire, brooding and drinking
whiskey. Eventually he'd succumbed to a heavy troubled sleep
in the armchair, and woken in the early hours of the morning
with his body aching as if he'd been trampled and kicked by
a mule and to the cold grey ashes of the fire. Making his way
upstairs to bed, he'd yanked the covers over him and cursed
himself soundly for behaving like some ill-mannered oaf last
night. When he'd recalled Karen's angry, crestfallen face when
he'd made that infantile comment about not pandering to a
woman's whims he'd had the blackest moment, feeling certain
he'd screwed up the one chance he had to bring some peace
and happiness back into his life.

   Getting up and moving across the room, he had opened
the windows wide and gulped in some long deep breaths of
the frosted early-morning air. At last he'd managed to wrench
his thoughts away from his tormenting introspection and had
found himself mulling over his painting instead. When the
surprising urge to try and rebuild his life and make a fresh
start had come unexpectedly to him he'd been filled with such
a surge of renewed energy that he had urgently got dressed
and gone straight to his studio...

'Thanks very much.' Gray shook the stout sandy-haired
picture-framer's callused hand at the front door as he prepared to leave. 'You've done a grand job.'

   'Any time, Mr O'Connell. It's been a pleasure doing business with you, so it has. If there's ever any more paintings
you'd like framed, don't hesitate to give me a call.' The man
thoughtfully scratched his head beneath his flat dog-tooth cap

'That's some talented artist who's painted those pictures. Are you acquainted with him or her, by any chance?'

'Why? Do you want to buy one?'

'Sure, I wish I could afford to, Mr O'Connell, but a picture-framer's wages don't stretch to buying great works of art, I'm afraid!'

Suppressing a highly amused guffaw...*great works of art, indeed...!* Gray reflected on the surprisingly fulfilling morning he'd had, selecting the paintings he wanted framed. At times he'd wrestled with displaying them at all, but there'd been other times when Karen's heartfelt encouragement not to hide his work away had spurred him on. Why had it taken him so long to realise that she was right about that? *She'd been right about a lot of things,* he reflected ruefully... He'd had the worst night he'd had in ages after leaving her last night—*deservedly so.* When he saw her next he would tell her why.

It had been midmorning when he'd rung the local picture-framers and told them he wanted to employ them straight away. After being told they had a list of commissions to see to before they could get to him, Gray had cut through the 'Well, now, I don't know...' and ums and ahs and offered them an eye-watering fee they couldn't refuse.

All in all it had been a good day's work, and he couldn't believe the time when he finally glanced at his watch. It was almost time for dinner, and going by the delicious aroma wafting out of the kitchen Bridie was making one of her tantalising and hearty stews. Walking past the line of paintings he'd hung in the long downstairs corridor that led to the kitchen at the end, he glanced at them critically, but with some satisfaction, too, as he passed.

What would Karen think about what he'd done? he mused. She'd been hovering on the edges of his mind all day, and every time he conjured up her beautiful face Gray's gut would painfully clench with longing. He ached to hold and kiss her and tell her how sorry he was for being such an out-and-out swine—so sorry that he was willing to *beg* her forgiveness if she seemed hesitant to give it. At any rate, after eating his meal he fully intended on going down into the town to discreetly set up a watch on Liz's Cantina, wait for Karen to leave the party, and hopefully convince her to come home with him tonight. It hardly bore contemplating that she might reject his plea and tell him to go to hell…

CHAPTER TEN

THE party was still in full swing when Karen realised that she'd had enough and wanted to leave. She'd enjoyed singing the uplifting tunes she'd performed for Sean, his sister and assembled friends, but as for dancing and engaging with the other guests in conversation—well, she'd found that increasingly hard when her heart was weighed down with anxious musings about Gray.

Weaving her way through the hotly perspiring bodies gyrating to the latest hip-hop sounds, she located Liz near the back of the room, with her Spanish boyfriend and chef Jorge, and started to make her apologies.

'You're not leaving?' the redhead exclaimed, clearly disappointed. 'It's not even late yet, and tomorrow's Sunday. You can lie in all day if you want. Come on, my pretty little songbird, have another drink and let your hair down for once.'

She could see that her vivacious employer in her pink satin party dress and flashing green earrings was more than a little intoxicated as she leaned against her well-built Spanish boyfriend, and Karen was quite glad that she'd stuck with fruit juice and hadn't succumbed to alcohol—apart from champagne to wish Sean a happy birthday. Aside from the fact she had to drive herself home to the cottage, she was determined to keep a clear head to think about her future.

Serious misgivings about the wisdom of staying in Ireland
were arising—misgivings she couldn't deny.

She was no longer sure it was the best thing for her, because
if Gray ended their relationship then what was the point?
She honestly didn't believe she could cope with bumping
into him, knowing the passion they'd shared was no more.
Or—worse—maybe seeing him with someone else.

Leaning forward, Karen planted an affectionate peck on
Liz's cheek. 'I don't want another drink, thanks. I've had a
great time, but now I'm going home. I'll see you next week…
enjoy the rest of your weekend, won't you?'

'What about Sean?'

'What *about* Sean?' Karen echoed, bewildered. The last
she'd seen of Liz's handsome young brother he'd been dancing
with a pretty brunette who—going by her entranced expression—was completely enthralled by him. Now, glancing over
the bobbing heads of the dancers on the floor, she failed to
spy his tousled fair head anywhere.

'I'm a bit concerned about him. For someone celebrating
his birthday he's a little too down in the dumps for my liking,'
the redhead asserted. 'Do me a favour before you go, will
you, Karen? See if he's outside, and if he is wish him a happy
birthday again…it would mean a lot, coming from you. See if
you can cheer him up a bit. Thanks, my friend…and thanks
too, for your wonderful singing.'

The sharp cold air that hit her as she opened the door to step
outside had never been more welcome. At last Karen could
breathe freely again, without the impediment of the muggy
heat inside and the inevitable fumes of alcohol. Standing her
guitar up against the brick wall, she tied the wraparound-style
jacket she'd donned over slim black trousers and a matching
sleeveless top, and almost jumped out of her skin when Sean
peeled out of the shadows to greet her. She saw him flick the
cigarette he'd been smoking into the alleyway next to the

building. His green eyes were instantly warm as they alighted
on her.

'It's a bit like a sauna in there, isn't it?' He smiled. 'Much
better out here. You're not going home?'

'I'm afraid I am,' she answered, swiftly checking the urge
to ask him where the pretty brunette had disappeared to, in
case it was the worst thing to say because she'd left him. 'I
know you probably think I'm extremely boring, but I'm actually feeling quite tired.'

It wasn't a lie, Karen thought sadly. Emotion—particularly
negative emotion—was apt to sap her energy, and she'd experienced enough emotion to drain her dry since Gray had
walked out on her last night.

'I'd never think you were boring in a million years, Karen.'
As he stepped a little closer to her, Sean's expression changed
subtly to become more serious. 'If you want to know the truth,
I think you're pretty incredible.'

Embarrassed, Karen shrugged. 'That's sweet of you...even
if I can't agree.'

'It made my birthday, you coming to sing for me. I could
listen to you sing every night if I had the choice.'

The next step he took towards her brought his body mere
inches away from hers. He was so close that the almost overpowering scent of his strong cologne made her wince.

Feeling suddenly uneasy, Karen pushed back her hair and
furnished him with an uncertain smile. 'Well...happy birthday
again, Sean—and thanks for setting me up with the amp and
everything. No doubt I'll see you around...probably at Liz's
some time.'

When she would have moved away, Sean reached out to
touch his hand to the back of her waist. In the next instant she
felt herself drawn towards him. The kiss he'd clearly intended
for her lips clumsily dropped against the side of her cheek as

Karen quickly realised his aim and stepped away, her heart drumming hard as she reached for her guitar.

'Don't go,' he implored, expression contrite. 'I didn't mean to offend you—but you just look so beautiful tonight that couldn't resist trying to steal a kiss. Can't we go back inside and at least have a drink together, maybe share a dance?'

'I don't think that would be a good idea, Sean.'

'Karen!'

The sound of a heartrendingly familiar voice coming from the shadows of the small car park across the road almost made her knees buckle with relief. But at the same time Karen was confused. *What was Gray doing here? Surely he hadn't been waiting for her?*

As she peered into the night his dark, imposing figure emerged from the gloom to be highlighted by a streetlamp. He was dressed completely in black. The droplets of rain glinting off his leather jacket and ebony hair sparkled like tiny gemstones beneath the lamp's yellow glare, and made him look like the brooding hero of some cinematic thriller. She froze, torn between running across the road and throwing herself into his arms or moving directly towards her car and driving home.

'Is everything okay?' In a few long-legged strides he was in front of her, his hands firmly on her arms, his stormy grey eyes burning down into her upturned face as if she was the home he longed to return to.

'I'm fine.' She heard the slight quiver in her voice. 'What are you doing here?'

He didn't answer straight away, just continued to stare at her as if mesmerised. But then he glanced towards Sean, as if suddenly aware of the younger man resentfully watching them.

'Good party was it, Sean?' he mocked, and Karen sensed the held-back fury in him.

Her stomach flipped. *Had he seen the younger man's clumsy attempt at kissing her?* Did he believe she'd encouraged him?

'It was fine,' Sean mumbled, awkwardly digging his hands into his jeans pockets. 'It's still going on. Do you fancy coming in for a drink?'

'No, thanks.' His mouth tight, Gray reached for Karen's guitar, then slipped his hand possessively into hers. 'Me and the lovely lady here are going home... Oh, and Sean?'

'What is it?'

'Next time you want to try and kiss some unsuspecting and uninterested woman, make sure it's not Karen...okay?'

'Gray!' Shocked, Karen tried to wrench her hand free, but the man by her side was having none of it.

'He needed to be put straight about us,' he muttered darkly as he led her back across the road to the car park.

Stopping in front of the familiar Range Rover, he opened the passenger door at the back to deposit her guitar on the seat without even asking her. By now she, too, was furious. 'What do you think you're doing?'

'I came to pick you up and take you home,' he announced, slamming the door shut, then turning towards her.

'I don't need you to take me home...I brought my own car. And what do you mean, "He needed to be put straight about us"? Last night you slammed out of the cottage in a temper just because I stood up for myself and wouldn't let you bully me into doing something *you* wanted to do because I'd already committed to coming to Sean's birthday party. Now you're talking about us as if we had some kind of meaningful relationship! Have I missed something, Gray?' Breathing hard, Karen couldn't hold back the tide of emotion that engulfed her.

The man in front of her grimaced painfully. 'First of all, I owe you an apology for the way I lost my temper last night.

Secondly, I want you to know that I wasn't angry with you for saying what you did about Maura leaving me. You had a right to get back at me. But I also want you to know that I felt nothing when she went except relief. For a while she was company for me during a difficult time…when I lost my father, to be exact. But we both knew we neither wanted nor expected a future together. I reacted badly because you seemed to find it so easy to believe that she *would* walk out on me…as if you wouldn't dispute that I must have deserved it.'

Roughly combing his fingers through his hair, Gray furrowed his indomitable brow. 'I don't deny that I was probably hell to live with at the time, and now all I feel for the woman is compassion that she put up with me for as long as she did. I wallowed in grief and guilt for too long, and anyone close to me or who had dealings with me took the brunt of it. I honestly regret that.'

Digesting his frank confession with surprise, and something like hope flooding her heart, Karen breathed out a sigh. 'You didn't love her, then? Maura, I mean?'

'Good God, no… For a while we simply found each other… shall we say convenient?'

Knowing immediately that he meant sexually, she felt a jealous jolt shoot through her like a flame-tipped arrow. 'Oh…'

Gray punctuated the cold night air with a throaty chuckle. 'I'm a man with a healthy libido—I don't deny it. And I'm not going to pretend those needs don't disturb me if they're not met even if admitting it makes you blush, sweetheart.'

Catching her by the waist, he brought Karen's body up close into his lean hard middle, and the chill that was making her shiver fled as though a blazing sun had just appeared in the sky and was shining down on her.

'I owe you an apology, too, Gray. I didn't mean to upset you with what I said. I just reacted in the heat of the moment.'

'Like I said, you had every right to retaliate. It's commend-able that you wanted to honour a promise...I had no right to try and tell you what to do. Was the party good?'

Without you, every minute felt like a lifetime... She didn't say the words out loud, but she longed to. 'It was okay. As it turns out I wasn't really in the mood for a party after all. I would have preferred to have stayed at home.'

'Or gone to Paris with me?' Gray suggested ruefully, the beginnings of a surprisingly tender smile touching his lips.

'Maybe.' Karen dipped her head.

'By the way, was Sean bothering you?' he asked. His tone definitely had an underlying thread of jealousy in it.

'No. I expect he just had one Guinness too many—but then it *is* his birthday.'

Dropping a kiss at the side of her mouth, Gray pulled back to examine her face. 'I expect I'll have to get used to that... then looking at you and lusting after you. But woe betide any man who tries to do more than just look,' he warned.

'That sounds a little possessive.'

His silvery eyes flared. 'That's because I *am* possessive where you're concerned.'

'Well, don't be. I'm human, Gray...not some object you can own like that portrait of me you're painting!'

Karen pushed away from him even before she realised she was going to, swamped with disappointment and hurt that he *still* seemed to mean nothing more to him than the 'con-venient' and unlucky Maura. As much as she loved him, she wouldn't settle for anything less than his love in return. She might be unsure about a lot of things, but she wasn't unsure about that.

Delving into her jacket pocket, her fingers curled round her car keys. 'I'm going home now. Can I get my guitar?' she said with a thumping heart.

Gray caught her hand. 'Wait. Please listen to me. You've

got me all wrong, but I guess that's my own stupid fault.
certainly don't want to own you or just think of you as some
pretty object. Look…this isn't coming out the way I wanted
it to. The truth is I'd hoped you would come home with me
tonight…stay the night with me. At least if you come back to
the house I can better explain my feelings to you. What do
you say?'

Another leap of hope rocketed through her, but Karen
couldn't allow herself to trust it…not when she'd been down
that uncertain and painful road with Gray before. 'I don't
know…' She shrugged, feeling cold again, and couldn't prevent her voice sounding a little disconsolate.

'I've got an idea.' He opened the front passenger door and
held it wide with a flourish. 'Get in and we'll drive down to
the beach. We'll stand in the moonlight and watch the waves
lapping onto the shore. What do you say?'

Regarding the vital, handsome man issuing the invitation,
his haunting grey eyes compelling her like nothing else could,
how could she refuse?

Even if things didn't work out she'd always have the memory
of him asking her to go to the beach one night to look at the
ocean together in the moonlight. Only a man with poetry in
his soul could do that.

Shivering again in her inadequately warm jacket, Karen
smiled tentatively. 'Okay,' she agreed simply.

They travelled in silence down to the deserted beach, and a
strange sense of peace came over Gray that he had never felt
before. He could only put it down to the pleasure of Karen's
company and the feeling that somehow, by some miracle, everything in his world was beginning to change for the better.
It was the most exhilarating thought. For the first time in the
longest time hope had found a chink in the fortress he'd built
round his feelings in order to protect himself from further
hurt, and he was glad it had. Locking the car, he swept his

arm firmly round Karen's waist and guided her down to the seashore.

As they walked, their feet sinking a little into the sand, the raw wind whipped at her hair and her warm, musky perfume subtly invaded his senses—not only making his blood slow and heavy in his veins but making him smile, too. As they reached the water's edge Gray's appreciative glance met the stunning vista before him in silent awe. The lapping of the ocean against the moonlit white sand sounded like hushed breath...*the breath of life*, he realised. It was as though life was beckoning to him to live it again as never before. Being here, with this lovely woman who made his heart beat faster every time he saw her, every time he so much as *thought* of her, made him feel intensely alive—almost as if he'd been holed up behind a hundred-foot wall for years but had now been miraculously freed.

'If I were a painter,' Karen said softly beside him, '*this* is the scene I'd most want to paint.'

Turning towards her, Gray curved his mouth in a smile. 'I'll teach you.'

'To paint, you mean?'

As she fastened her big blue eyes on him her eager glance all but made him dissolve. The moonlight bathed her exquisite features in its soft ethereal ray and her incandescent beauty took his breath away. She was utterly ravishing. Gazing into her lovely face, Gray longed to get back to the portrait he'd started and finish it. When it was done it would occupy pride of place in his house...above his bed.

'Would you like to learn?'

'I'd probably be hopeless.'

'Like you're hopeless at singing and playing the guitar, I suppose?' he teased, catching a long strand of her honey-blonde hair and coiling it gently round his fingers.

'I could teach you to play the guitar in return for you teaching me to paint. Can you sing?'

'Not a note. Someone told me once that I had a voice that could shatter a double-glazed window.'

His even white teeth glinted in the moonlight and the mirth in his unreserved grin made Karen yearn to hug him tight and not let him go for a very long time.

'You're cold,' he observed, suddenly serious again. 'Come here.'

Gray pulled her close into his chest and her arms automatically slid round his waist. Resting her cheek over his heart, she briefly closed her eyes to breathe him in. It wasn't just his incredible physicality that she loved, she reflected—though as men went he was pretty compelling—it was the sheer vibrancy and essence of the man, the innate goodness in him that she loved best of all. The goodness he had withheld from the world for too long through grief and guilt.

'I still miss them, you know.'

Realising straight away who he meant, Karen all but held her breath. Behind them the sound of the ocean lapping onto the shore was like mesmerising music.

'I know I never really knew my mother, but somehow there's a lingering impression of her warmth and softness that I can't shake. The memory steals over me sometimes when I'm least expecting it.' The strong arms that surrounded her tightened a little. 'My father never spoke about why she took her own life, so I don't suppose I'll ever know the reason. For a long time I was angry with him for that. I expect he did it to protect me, but at the same time he probably blamed himself. He liked to promote the image that he was as tough as old boots, but underneath he was soft as butter and sentimental too. He must have missed her like crazy when she went.'

He fell silent. A moment later Karen sensed the shudder

that went through him and, alarmed, glanced up to find the glistening sheen of tears in his eyes.

Stricken by his sorrow, she put her arms round his neck and hugged him hard. 'Oh, Gray...' Reaching up on tiptoe, she planted a tender kiss on his mouth and gently wiped the track of moisture that dampened his cheek with the pad of her thumb. 'It's all right, my darling... They're together again now, and at peace. I'm sure of it.'

Gray's silver moonlit gaze locked with hers. 'That's a comforting thought... And what about Ryan? It must have broken his heart to leave you. Is he at peace, too, Karen?'

Her heart swelled, but she didn't cry. Somewhere locked in time was the ocean of tears that she'd cried for the kind, gentle man who had once been her husband. 'I like to believe he is. God knows he deserves to be.'

'Maybe all the ones we've lost look down on us, silently urging us to live the very best lives we can in their memory?'

'That's so beautiful, Gray.' Laying her palm at the side of his face, Karen smiled gently.

'Perhaps you just bring out the best in me?'

'Maybe... But now that your secret's out you can't ever go back to how you were before,' she told him solemnly.

'What secret?' Stroking his palm down over her hair, Gray stiffened for a moment.

'You act like a lion, but underneath you're just as sentimental and tender as your dad. In truth, you're just a pussycat.'

'A pussycat? That's the most outrageous accusation I've ever heard in my life. Take it back—take it back right now, woman, or you'll be sorry!'

He started tickling her with intent, and Karen could scarce catch her breath for laughing. But then he clasped his hands round her waist and whirled her round and round on the sand, making her utterly and completely dizzy and disorientated.

'Gray, please… Stop right now or I'll be dizzy for the rest of my life!' she begged, even as she laughed.

'Only if you agree to come home with me right now.' Kissing her ear, he came to a sudden standstill.

Out of breath and with her heart racing, Karen didn't hesitate to give him her answer. 'Yes!' She smiled as he returned her carefully to her feet again. 'Yes, I'll come home with you, Gray.' His eyes were languorous with need, she saw, and the realisation thrilled her.

Capturing a handful of her wind-blown hair, he planted a hot hard kiss on her mouth that instantly had her senses clamouring for more.

'Race you to the car,' he taunted, and headed off across the sand like a sprinter.

Laughing again, knowing she didn't have a hope of beating him, Karen chased after him…

When Gray opened the door of the grand old house that was his home, Karen definitely didn't feel like laughing. Straight away she noticed the newly framed paintings lining the high walls, and for a moment was speechless with delight.

Turning to the man at her side—a man who had fallen worryingly silent since they'd left the car—she grabbed his hand and squeezed it. 'You hung the paintings… Gray, that's wonderful!

'I never would have done it if it hadn't been for you,' he answered quietly. 'It was your encouragement and belief in me that did it. You made me face up to a lot of my self-inflicted behaviour, too…my bad habits.' He grinned, looping his arm affectionately round her waist and hugging her to him.

'I think you credit me with far too much. Sooner or later you would have woken up to your true nature as well as your talent, Gray.'

'You think so?'

'I do… But I think sometimes we really do have to hit rock-bottom before we reassess our life. I can't pretend to know what your answer is, but even if it's just to be the wonderful man you are…that's enough.'

'Wonderful, is it?' He brought her hand up to his lips and warmly kissed her fingers. 'That doesn't come close to what I think of you, my bright-eyed girl. But I think it's going to take the rest of the night for me to tell you every superlative that springs to mind.'

'Really…? The rest of the night, you say?' The warmth that flooded Karen at his words extended right down to the edges of her toes. The hope that she'd dared to feel earlier when he'd promised to share his feelings with her returned.

'Really. But first I think we need a drink to warm us up, don't you? What's it to be? Hot chocolate or whiskey?'

'Hot chocolate, I think. I already feel light-headed. But before we get our drinks I want to look at your paintings.'

'Okay. Your wish is my command.'

Hand in hand, they started to walk past the art on the walls together, inspecting it. At the end of the corridor, completely taking them by surprise, Bridie appeared. She had her warm woollen coat on, ready to leave for home. It was way past the time she usually stayed, and Gray's frown was a concerned one.

'Bridie…shouldn't you be home by now? Is anything the matter? It's not Chase?' His stomach rolled over at the mere thought.

Clasping her generous-sized maroon handbag in front of her checked coat, the kind-hearted woman who had cooked and cleaned for him since he'd returned to Ireland, who had put up with his surly moods and dark ways and carried on doing what she could for him regardless, met his anxious gaze with a gentle smile.

'The dog is fine, Mr O'Connell. He's asleep in front of the fire as usual.'

'Then what is it?'

'I was looking at the picture you did of you and your mother—the one that you painted from the photograph your father showed me once. This one.'

She moved towards the painting nearest to where she stood and Gray's heart lurched. Wordlessly—with Karen's hand clasped firmly in his—he found himself standing in front of the lovingly painted portrait of mother and child. At his request the picture-framer had given it his best gilt-edged frame—one embossed with beautifully made golden leaves.

'What about it?'

'She would have been so proud if she'd seen it. "My little man is going to do something great one day," she'd say to everyone. Never had a mother loved her baby as devotedly as your mam loved you, Mr O'Connell...Gray...' Bridie sniffed, her top lip quivering a little.

Gray froze.

'It was herself that she couldn't love,' she continued. 'Your father was always telling her how lovely she was, that she meant the world to him...but she was dogged by this terrible depression that no doctor could help cure. It was pitiful to see the way she got sometimes. We knew it had got bad, but nobody expected her to do what she did. It was an awful shock. She used to go down to the sea all the time, staring out at the horizon as if there was some answer in the waves that could help her. One day she didn't come back. Her poor body was washed up on the shore the next day. When it happened your father wanted to die, too. But he knew he had a child to take care of, and so he devoted himself to working hard on the farm and raising you in a way that would have made your mother proud. I know Paddy never talked about your mother's death with you, Mr O'Connell, and I can't say those of us who knew him agreed with that. We all believed he should have told you the truth long ago, but there...' The housekeeper shook her head sadly. 'He did his best, God rest him. When I saw the picture I realised how much you must still think about her, and I just felt it was right to tell you. I hope you won't hold it against me?'

Breaking out of the painful trance that had taken him prisoner, Gray cleared his throat and forced a smile. 'Of course I don't hold it against you, Bridie.' He let go of Karen's hand, stepping forward to embrace the older woman in a fierce hug. 'Thank you—thank you for telling me. But you'd better get yourself off home now. It's late. I'll see you on Monday morning as usual, okay?'

When the front door had closed behind the housekeeper, Gray dropped his hands to his hips and stared blankly down at the floor.

'Gray?' Moving closer, Karen reached for his hand but, distracted, he turned away and headed for the staircase.

'Just give me a few minutes, will you?' In the midst of the fog of pain that engulfed him he prayed she would understand.

'Of course.' Her reply was softly compassionate...

CHAPTER ELEVEN

HALF an hour passed and Gray still hadn't reappeared. Sitting on the sofa, with Chase's great fawn head in her lap, Karen grew increasingly anxious about his state of mind. She was also getting cold in that big lonely room, but too wrapped up in her concern for Gray to stoke the fire.

Unable to sit and wait any longer, she spoke softly to Chase, telling him to stay. Even before she reached the door the Great Dane had made his way back to the dying fire in the grate and with a great sigh lay down in front of it.

Locating the perfectly tidied kitchen, with its gleaming iron range, meticulously swept stone-flagged floor and beautiful Irish dresser lined with rows of delicate white and patterned crockery, Karen hunted down a saucepan, boiled some milk, and made two mugs of hot chocolate. The rain that lashed rhythmically at the windows was a haunting accompaniment as she worked.

Bridie's story about Gray's mother had been heartrending. She wondered how the housekeeper had borne the truth for so long without being tempted to tell him before. All Karen could think was that she must have respected his father very highly to keep it a secret. If Gray hadn't displayed the portrait of his mother would he ever have found out what happened? She could only imagine the legacy of sorrow he'd had to live with, knowing his mother had taken her own life.

Suddenly impatient to be with him again, she gave the hot drinks a final stir and then, with her heart in her mouth, climbed the great winding staircase to the first floor. She was hoping she'd find Gray without having to search behind every door, and silently prayed that he hadn't descended into so deep a despair that she wouldn't be able to reach him. It was obvious that Bridie's words had profoundly affected him, and now she longed for the opportunity to talk and offer solace.

In the end, Karen didn't have to search very far to find him.

At the end of the first-floor corridor a door was ajar. When she reached it she softly called out his name. Receiving no answer, she nudged the door wider with her elbow and went inside. In the impressive high-ceilinged room, with its taste-ful muted decoration and spare antique furniture, Gray was seated on a huge carved bed with his back to her, his dark head bowed, his hands resting on his jean-clad thighs. She felt such a powerful rush of love for him that for a moment she was literally struck dumb.

Leaving the mugs of chocolate on the nearest cherrywood bedside cabinet, Karen moved quietly round to the still silent man. Sucking in a nervous breath, she reached out to lay her hand on his hard-muscled shoulder. 'I'm so sorry, Gray. I'm so sorry about your mother... It must have been so hard for you and your dad to live without her. But maybe now that you know the truth about why she did what she did it might help you to understand that it was out of anyone's hands? No one was to blame.'

Slowly he raised his head and looked at her. The raw, un-fettered glance he gave her was shocking and said so much more than words. For a moment her limbs felt frozen and she couldn't move. Then, as if a switch had been flicked, Karen's blood turned into a wild river of molten need that suspended everything. Only the desire to comfort and help him in any way that she could remained.

'I've been haunted for a long time about why she would do it…why I wasn't enough to make her stay.'

'Oh, Gray. It wasn't that you weren't enough—there was nothing you did wrong. How could you have? You were just a beautiful innocent little boy, and your mother was suffering from depression. It can be the most terrible illness.'

She put her arms round him to give him a warm, sympathetic hug, but suddenly the tenor of that hug turned into something much more compelling. Karen sensed Gray tense, then breathe out on a ragged sigh. Her heart pumping wildly, she suddenly found herself tipped into his lap, and with his hands placed either side of her face his lips ravished her mouth with the kind of primal urgency and demand that made her feel as if she was at the epicentre of a sensual hurricane.

As he groaned into her mouth his teeth clashed against hers, his scalding velvet tongue mimicking the kind of unbridled sex that made her snatch at her breath. His heat burned her all the way down to her soul. Momentarily lifting his head, he stared intensely into her eyes and his gaze transmitted everything—every emotion, every feeling he had ever felt. If Karen hadn't already been sitting on Gray's lap she would have been knocked off her feet by that shockingly frank glance.

But she barely had time to register what lay in those depths before she found herself on her back, her mind spinning and her blood throbbing heavily through her veins as his hands urgently helped her part with her clothes. Removing the leather jacket he was still wearing, he pulled his sweater and tee shirt over his head, jettisoned them carelessly behind him, then unzipped his jeans. Roughly tugging at the sides of Karen's black silk panties, he yanked them down over her slender thighs and plunged himself deep inside her.

Shutting her eyes, she registered the shock of their passionate union with an unrestrained broken cry—a feral sound that was punched from her lungs and didn't hide her pleasure or her need. Driving her fingers hungrily through the silken mass of his ebony hair, she raised her legs up to clasp his hard, lean hips and take him even deeper. His mouth descended on each breast in turn—first to suckle, then to nip—spearing ecstatic arrows of explosive sensation straight to her womb. The volcanic fever that was already close to erupting inside her clung precariously to the heady precipice of her desire. Then, as Gray rocked her hard, it *did* erupt.

As Karen soared dizzyingly into the erotic sensual stratosphere that he took her to she held on to his arms, her fingernails biting helplessly into the iron-hard biceps that surrounded her. The lean, tight hips above her vigorously slammed against hers as he thrust again and again, then went powerfully still, releasing a throaty groan of ecstatic release that echoed in her ears even as she dazedly realised that he'd knowingly spilled his seed inside her.

Now her heart *did* drum hard.

He dropped his head against her breasts, and as well as the slightly roughened scrape of his unshaven jaw she sensed the warm leakage of moisture from his eyes. She knew Gray was shedding silent, soul-deep tears for the family he had so tragically lost. Her fingers tunnelled softly through his silken hair and gently massaged his scalp. Their wild sexual coupling had been a way to help him purge some of his pain, she realised. Now that the storm had passed he must be feeling empty and raw.

Powerful emotion like that had a way of scraping your insides clean, Karen knew. She'd experienced it many times in the days and months following Ryan's death.

Lifting himself away from her, Gray smiled ruefully down, wiping his hand roughly across his face to remove the traces of his distress before moving to her side and firmly enfolding her in his arms.

'I love you,' he said simply.

The huskily voiced declaration stopped her world in its tracks. When the shockwaves started to ebb, she laid her hand over his heart and lifted her gaze to his.

'I love you, too, Gray,' she admitted softly, without reservation. He went still. 'Gray?' she prompted nervously.

'I've never felt like this about anyone before...never felt that I would gladly surrender everything I have, give away everything I owned, just to be with a woman. But that's how I feel when I'm with you, Karen. At first I thought it was some crazy obsession that had taken hold of me, but now I know for sure that it's love. It was love all along, if I'm honest. From the first moment you angrily tore into me in the woods. I couldn't believe it. You were just a slip of a thing, and yet you didn't hesitate to quite rightly put me in my place. Do you know how much it scares me to want and need you so much?'

He caught her hand and kissed the delicate skin across her knuckles. Her gaze tenderly examined his. 'Why does it scare you to love me?'

'I don't want to lose you.'

As he touched his palm to her cheek his expression had never been so starkly vulnerable, and Karen knew he must be mulling over the tragic losses that had made him wary of giving his heart to anyone ever again.

'You won't lose me, Gray. I mean to stay with you for a very long time. I never thought I'd ever want to be with another man after I lost Ryan...but I was wrong. Even though you were gruff and defensive when we first met—yes, and bossy and angry, too—I knew that wasn't the real you. I'm glad I stayed around to find out the truth.'

'I behaved the way I did because I was lost, Karen. Utterly lost... That is until I met you. I'd made my fortune, but my personal life was a train hurtling towards a cliff-edge. I'd lost faith in everything…didn't see the point in aiming for anything ever again. I couldn't even enjoy my wealth because I despised what I'd done to make it, and I wore my rage and disappointment in myself and the world like a shield.'

'I know it must have been agony for you to hear it, but did it help when Bridie told you about your mother? About her illness, I mean?'

The dark-lashed silvery eyes closed briefly. 'I suppose it brought an end to my wild imaginings that my father might have somehow driven her to end her life. It's a relief to find out the truth at last and get some closure, I suppose. And to know that my dad was the solidly loyal man I always secretly believed him to be. But just the mere thought of her standing there on the beach alone, looking out to sea…it still tears me up.'

'I know, my darling, but you're strong…much stronger than you think you are. And whenever you get down about the past in future I'll be there to listen if you want to talk, and to help you in any way that I can. You won't be alone any more.'

'And I'll do the same for you, sweetheart. You've had a hell of a tough journey, too. I haven't forgotten that. It pains me to ask you, but do you still miss him? Ryan, I mean?'

Karen didn't know the precise moment when missing him had turned into poignant acceptance that he was gone and the realisation that she must build a new life for herself, but somehow that was what had happened. Maybe it wouldn't have happened so soon if she hadn't fallen in love with Gray, but she thanked God that she had.

Looking straight into his worried glance now, she had no reservation in speaking to him from the heart. 'I'll never forget him, but I don't miss him any more…no. And he was the kind of man who would want me to find love again…to build a new life with someone who really cared about me and who I cared for. To tell you the truth, music was the main passion we shared… Ryan wasn't able to love me in the way that you do, Gray.' She felt her blood grow hot at the frank admission. 'But what happened to both of us is in the past. We can't live the rest of our lives in fear of bad things happening again, because living in fear means that we can't ever trust that things can get better—and I honestly believe that they can.'

'As long as you know that you're going to have to make an honest man of me now—because I won't live in sin, you know. I do have morals to uphold.'

'Morals, my—'

'Tut-tut… That's not the kind of response I expect from a lady,' he teased.

Karen grinned, feeling a joyous surge of hope and delight pulse through her. 'Are you certain that you want to be with me, Gray?' she asked, momentary doubt making her anxious.

Stroking her hair, Gray sighed deeply. 'I don't think I've ever felt so certain about the rightness of a thing in my life,' he admitted thoughtfully. 'I'd be an absolute fool if I were to let you go, Karen Ford. I'm many things…uptight, morose, and—yes—too prone to giving in to my temper sometimes. But I'm no fool.'

Rising to her knees, her honey-gold hair spilling wildly across her shoulders, Karen stared in wonder down into the darkly handsome face with the haunting silvery eyes she had so come to love, and inside her chest her heart skipped a beat.

'What did you mean by you won't live in sin?'

'What do you think I meant?' His hands were guiding her over him as he talked, bringing the backs of her slender thighs down flat across his more softly hirsute limbs. She quickly discovered that he was heavily aroused again, and her blood began to thrum as he eased his way inside her, his hands possessively enfolding her hips as he did so.

'I mean that I want to marry you, my gorgeous girl... Will you have me as your husband?'

'Yes, Gray...I will!'

Eagerly she bent her head to meet his lips in a passionately tender kiss, and although their loving was no less intense it was also infused with the joy and wonder of finding each other after all the heartache and pain they had endured before they'd met—and gratitude, too, that they'd both been given this second chance.

Later, lying in the cavernous bed beside Karen as she slept, her lovely golden hair spread out on the pillow beneath her, Gray deliberately elected to stay awake. It was extraordinarily peaceful, lying there with the sound of the rain glancing off the windows, and he just wanted to savour these precious moments when he was on the brink of joining the land of the living again. He'd stay awake all night if he had to, just to experience the joy of watching the woman next to him, knowing that she'd agreed to be his wife and wouldn't be saying goodbye as he had once feared she might. No more would he ask himself what he'd done to deserve such good fortune he vowed. Instead he resolved simply to be grateful and count his blessings.

Before his mother had become so ill had she and his father felt this way about each other? Gray wondered. As if nothing could add to their quota of joy because they had each other? Had his father lain in bed beside his mother, as his son was doing now with Karen, and thought how beautiful and perfect she was and what a blessed miracle it would be were they to have a child together?

A jolt went through his heart. He hadn't protected Karen when he'd so passionately made love to her earlier, and she hadn't mentioned it. *Would she mind if she fell pregnant?* he worried. Because suddenly he knew that he desperately longed for children of his own. To have the chance to be a father…a *good* father…and pass on some of the bravery and devotion that his own father had shown him—despite Paddy's ultimate disappointment that Gray hadn't followed in his footsteps with the farm. That would be something he could really be proud of.

He sighed and stretched, turning back to observe what looked to be an intriguing little smile playing on his lover's lips as she slept. She'd lost that air of sadness and vulnerability she'd had when they first met, Gray realised, and for that he was hugely grateful. He almost couldn't bear the thought of her being unhappy—not even for a moment. Now, as he studied her, he didn't think that she would mind carrying his baby. And if she wanted to pursue her singing career then he would make sure that she had the chance to do that, too. His wife-to-be deserved everything her beautiful heart desired. He'd never known a woman who had so much love to give. There would be more than enough for them all—him and their children.

Settling down at last, he wrapped her in his arms and willingly surrendered to sleep…

Karen was pacing the floor again, one hand pressed into the small of her back to try and ease the ache that had started that morning and still hadn't subsided, even though it was now late afternoon. It had obviously crossed her mind that it might be the onset of labour, but as the pain hadn't exactly intensified or grown worse she had her doubts. No. It was simply that she was heavily pregnant, felt as if she was about to pop, and wouldn't sit down and rest.

Much to her friend Liz's concern, she wouldn't heed any of the advice that either her or the full-time maternity nurse/

midwife that Gray had hired to stay with them regularly offered.

Now Margaret—the plump but agile nurse—had gone to make them all tea, and Karen anxiously watched the clock, hoping that her husband would get home soon from his trip to Dublin. If she did go into labour any time soon, she wanted him there.

He'd gone there yesterday, to make a guest appearance at the gallery that was displaying his work, and because of her heavily pregnant state she hadn't been able to accompany him. The gallery was a highly prestigious one, and she'd told him to mind his p's and q's and not get shirty with anybody. She knew when Gray was tense his patience was apt to get a little short. It was quite likely that he would be tense now, as Karen had just discovered that Margaret had phoned him on his mobile around lunchtime, when he'd been on the road driving home, to helpfully inform him that his wife was showing definite signs of going into labour any time now, and that he should get home sooner rather than later.

'Come and sit down, you stubborn woman.'

Suddenly Liz was there beside her again, her expression concerned, but annoyed, too. The women had become the best of friends over the past year, and Karen sensed that she understood her more than any other female she'd ever known. The enterprising café owner had recently become engaged to the lovely Jorge, and frequent visits to Karen and Gray's beautifully refurbished home were becoming quite a feature, so that Liz could eagerly discuss her plans for their wedding in June.

Allowing the other woman to lead her to a sumptuous couch, not far from the crackling fire in the elegantly stunning Adam fireplace, Karen finally gave in and sat down. Even as she accepted a welcome cup of tea from Margaret she heard Gray's key in the door—the door that was near slammed off its hinges as her husband strode anxiously into the drawing room, his coat undone and its shoulders covered in a melting dusting of icy November rain. Her heart quickening—as it always did whenever he was near—Karen smiled up at him, not hiding her relief that he'd returned.

'You always bring the rain,' she joked. 'Lucky for me that rain is one of my favourite things.'

His handsome face serious, Gray ignored the remark and dropped down in front of her as the nurse and Liz helpfully left the room. Removing the cup and saucer she was holding, he left it on a small side table to take her hands in his and hold them.

'Are you all right? You're not in labour yet? I panicked when Margaret phoned me.'

'I wish she hadn't done that, but she was only thinking of me. She knows how much I want you to be there. I hope you didn't drive too fast?'

'I wouldn't take a foolish risk like that, and thankfully the roads were clear all the way home. So, tell me, has anything started yet?'

'No. I'm not in labour yet—and apart from feeling a little like a floundering whale I'm well and happy.'

'That's my girl.'

He kissed her then, and Karen tasted the rain and the wind on the sculpted lips that she so adored. For a moment she wished that she could go down to the ocean with him, so that she could taste the scent of the sea on them too. But right now she would settle for lying down beside him in their bed and having him hold her. *She'd never told him how afraid she was of giving birth…how terrified she was that something might go wrong.* But in truth she was more scared about the effect such an event might have on him, rather than on herself.

'How did it go at the reception? I'll bet the handsome

guest artist had all the well-heeled Dublin ladies swooning over him!'

'If he did,' Gray replied dryly, 'he didn't notice, because his mind was on his beautiful wife back at home, about to go into labour with their first child any time now. Besides, my female admirers are serious connoisseurs of art, I'll have you know. Not the type of women who swoon easily.'

'Unless they've all got white sticks, I don't believe that for a second. Anyway, I don't think it's going to happen today, my love. Me going into labour, I mean.' Lightly tracing his clean-cut jaw, already showing signs of a five o'clock shadow because he was so dark, Karen shrugged. 'Things will probably kick off tomorrow.'

'In that case you'd better just rest and take things easy. No doubt you've been driving poor Margaret and Liz crazy, ignoring their advice to sit down. Right, then.' He got to his feet and slipped his black cashmere coat from his shoulders. 'I'm going to see if one of them will take pity on your poor husband and make me a cup of coffee.'

'They'll probably fight over the chance. By the way—did I tell you how proud I am of you? Now everyone who sees your paintings will know what a great talent you are. Anyway, I— *Ohh...*' A breathtaking, sharp slash of pain reverberated through Karen's insides.

Immediately Gray dropped down in front of her again, touching his palm concernedly to her cheek.

'Karen?'

'I'm okay,' she breathed, starting to smile. A second, even more acute pain froze the expression on her face.

If this was the onset of labour wasn't there supposed to be a longer interval between each contraction? she thought. She sent up a swift prayer that everything would go well, refusing to believe that disaster would strike at the eleventh hour and rob them of their longed-for dream of a healthy child.

'You'd better get Margaret.' She grimaced as the pain started to subside, already in anxious anticipation of the next one.

'Everything's going to be fine, I promise. I don't want you to worry,' Gray soothed her. 'I'm going to be with you every step of the way, remember?'

Planting a loving kiss at the corner of her mouth, he shot up and hurried into the kitchen, calling out for the nurse as he went...

His wife's labour had been intense and fast—too fast to make it to the hospital, even. Instead, Karen had given birth to their beautiful baby son at home.

Gray had thanked God more than once that he'd hired a midwife to stay at the house with them, to be on hand in case of just such an eventuality, despite the teasing he had suffered for going to such measures. Now, as he cradled his son— Padraic William, as he and Karen had named him: Padraic after Gray's father and William after hers—he couldn't stop inspecting the awesome perfection of the infant swaddled in his soft woollen blanket. Right now his baby son had a thatch of silky black hair and dark blue eyes, and if that stunning combination should remain then he would be a heartbreaker for sure.

A tumult of feelings swamped him as Gray sat there in the armchair by the bed, his elated gaze vying between looking at Karen—still breathtakingly lovely, even after the drama of her unexpectedly quick and intense labour—and his precious baby son. And as he sat there, happier and more content than he had ever felt in his life, he could almost be persuaded that he sensed the loving spirits of his parents come around him and smile lovingly down at him and his beautiful new family, as if giving them their blessing.

'What are you smiling about, hmm?' Leaning towards

him from the bed, Karen was stroking her fingers tenderly down Gray's forearm, her bright blue eyes looking tired but happy.

'What do you think I'm smiling about, you clever, beautiful girl? I'm the luckiest man in the world and I can't quite believe it.'

'Then you'd better believe it, Gray O'Connell, because I'm sure I didn't imagine the agony I went through to present you with your son!'

That wiped his next thought clean out of his head, and he remembered his wife's face, contorted with pain, and the angry words flung at him at the height of her agony. 'Was it very bad?' he asked quietly, his voice slightly gruff with emotion.

She pushed back his unruly hair with her fingers and smiled lovingly. 'There was nothing bad about it, my love. I was only teasing. Every ounce of discomfort was more than worth it to produce our lovely little man. He's adorable, isn't he?' She moved her hand to let it rest lovingly on the baby's head.

'He is. Absolutely adorable.'

'And so is his father,' Karen added, her blue eyes now moist with tears.

'Don't cry, sweetheart, or you'll have me bawling my eyes out, too—and that's not a good look for a man with a reputation like mine for being mysterious and forbidding. By the way, I've got a gift for you.'

Clutching the sleeping baby securely to his chest, Gray reached into his trouser pocket for the envelope he'd put there for safekeeping earlier. It was slightly crumpled as he handed it to her, and his accompanying grin was rueful.

'I should have made a better presentation of it than that... tied it up with a big pink bow, or something...but I'm afraid I'm not very good at that sort of thing.'

'You may not be good at tying big pink bows, but there's

a long list of other things that you *are* good at. You shouldn't have bought me another gift. I've already got everything I could possibly want—and I mean you and little Padraic.'

When she carefully tore open the envelope, lifted out the officially printed sheet of paper inside and scanned the written contents, Karen shook her head and stared at Gray in disbelief. 'You're giving me your father's cottage and the fifty acres of land surrounding it? Oh, Gray! It's too much—it's far too generous.'

'No, it's not. Besides, you more than deserve it—and you love that place. It's just a small gesture from me, to thank you for all the joy and happiness you've brought me. You can renovate or rebuild, and I thought you might like to use some of the land to build your own recording studio on. I've already spoken to a specialist architect, and as soon as you're feeling up to it we can drive over there and you can start making plans for what you'd like. I know how important your music is to you, my love.'

'Gray O'Connell?'

'Yes, Mrs O'Connell?'

'I want you to bring our baby and get into bed beside me right now!'

'If I must.' With a theatrical waggle of his eyebrows, Gray got to his feet and did exactly as his wife ordered...